P9-DTX-556

MASHIACH OF BRODSKII STREET

Terror in Berdichev, 1941

by
M.T. Simkovitz

Copyright 2006 by M.T. Simkovitz

All right reserved. The author is solely responsible for the content of this book. No part of this book may be reproduced, stored in a retrieval system or transmitted by any means, electronic, mechanical, photocopying, recording, or otherwise, without written permission from the author. Brief quotations may be used in review prepared for inclusion in a magazine, newspaper or broadcast.

This is a historical fiction book. All historical information is based upon the author's personal research listed in this book. The Levi and Hirsch families, as well as various other characters named in this book, are fictional representations. Their stories bear no resemblance or accuracy of portrayal to anyone living or dead. Public events and dates given are accurate as far as can be determined insofar as it was possible to be true to the storyline and craft of storytelling. Accurate historical information has been presented without bias or intent to influence the reader away from objective understanding of facts.

Distributed by Granite Publishing & Distribution, LLC
868 North 1430 West, Orem Utah 84057 USA
Toll-free 1.800.574.5779, Tel. 801.229.9023, Fax 801.229.1924

Printed in the United States of America
ISBN: 1-56684-636-6
Library of Congress Control Number: 2006921356

For further information, email the author at:
simkovitz@berdichev1941.com

Book design, typography and cover photo-illustration by Kim Cooney dba Byzintek
15843 SE 47th Street, Bellevue, Washington 98006-3264 USA
kim.cooney@comcast.net; www.byzintek.com; 425.643.2330

Pre-restoration cover photo: N.E. Rasmussen

DEDICATION

This book is lovingly dedicated to the more than 20,000 victims of the Berdichev Shoah of August and September 1941 and the 35,000 victims of Babi Yar soon after in Kiev. Many of my parents' family died in those Nazi massacres. These precious millions of dead still cry for their stories to be heard; they still ache for G-d's* justice to vindicate their hope for a world of peace and an end to hatred. We all await the time when our Father in Heaven will bring to pass the promises the Eternal One has made to His Chosen.

I know that day will come.

---

* Use of "G-d": Symbol for the full spelling of the Sacred Name. This substitution of the dash for the "o" in the word complies with orthodox Jewish belief that the fully spelled-out word must be used only in sacred writings.

ACKNOWLEDGEMENTS

The author wishes to thank Nancy Goldberg Hilton, D. Barney, G. Boyd, F.C., C. Moomey, B. Phillips, my editor Michael McIrvin, and especially N. E. Rasmussen, for their insights and editorial assistance with this record.

CONTENTS

PART ONE: THE MOTHERLAND

PART TWO: THE FATHERLAND

PART THREE: THE KINDER

APPENDICES

UKRAINE LIVES ON

(Shche Ne Vmerla Ukrayina)

Ukraine lives on, so too its glory and freedom,
Good fortune will still smile on us, brother Ukrainians.
Our enemies will die, as the dew does in the sunshine,
And we, too brothers, we'll live happily in our land.

We'll not spare either our souls or bodies to get freedom
And we'll prove that we are brothers of Kozak kin.

We'll rise up, brothers, all of us, from the Syan River to the Don,
We won't let anyone govern in our motherland.
The Black Sea will smile, and grandfather Dnipro will rejoice,
In our Ukraine good fortune will yet abound.

Our persistence, our sincere toil will prove its rightness,
Still our freedom's loud song will spread throughout Ukraine.
It'll resound upon the Carpathians, and sound through the Steppes,
While Ukraine's glory will arise among the people.

— Ukrainian National Anthem

Reflect upon three things, and you will never fall into the power of sin: know what is above you — a seeing eye and a hearing ear, and all your deeds are recorded.

— R Judah, Talmud, Aboth II, I.

PROLOGUE

The Lord speaks to His Chosen:

"For a small moment I have forsaken thee; but with great mercies will I gather thee...

"Oh, thou afflicted, tossed with tempest, and not comforted, behold, I will lay thy stones with fair colours, and lay thy foundations with sapphires. And I will make thy windows of agates, and thy gates of carbuncles, and all thy borders of pleasant stones.

"And all thy children shall be taught of the Lord; and great shall be the peace of thy children. In righteousness...

"Behold, I have created the smith that bloweth the coals in the firs, and that bringeth forth an instrument for his work' and I have created the waster to destroy.

"No weapon that is formed against thee shall prosper; and every tongue that shall rise against thee in judgment thou shalt condemn. This is the heritage of the servants of the Lord, and their righteousness is of me, saith the Lord. "

— Isaiah 7, 11-13, 16-17, KJV

During three hours of each day G-d sits on His throne of justice. When He sees the world is worthy of being destroyed, He moves to His throne of mercy.
— Talmud A.Z. 3b

FOREWORD

I cannot say what propelled me along the dusty meandering roads of the Ukrainian Steppes. It may have been a lust for adventure, or a certainty that somehow I would find in the broad meadows and cool streams that give way to dense alder forests, a lingering peacefulness.

At a particular junction I found in a half-buried, sealed metal box two blood-stained Stars of David, a frightening testament to *Nazi* terror. An unreadable name was etched into the lid in Hebrew. As I touched the rusty edges I was overcome with sadness. The artifact's owner had surely been murdered nearby. In the sudden piercing cry of an owl I imagined the scream for mercy, the plea for help against bewildering, sudden death:

"Give me more life! It is too soon!"

How can we help but shudder? Is this not the scream of all mankind if, as partakers on the moving threshold of time we are told there are no more choices to be made?

But the spirit of man cannot be killed. In these gathered remembrances is irrefutable record of the *shoah* (holocaust) in Berdichev and the heroism of the doomed. I add it to the testaments of Ukraine's holocaust victims that have been gathered. Their fate echoes and aches in my soul against the day I, too, must face my final hour. Will I plead, as the wearers of Solomon's Seal must have cried,

"Give me more life. It is too soon!"

I pray the suffering of this unknown Jew was heeded and that he enjoys a peaceful spirit life with all his departed. I have faith as I peer into the eyes of innocent children or those of seasoned age, that there is a grander Plan for all of us: With that sure expectation, life and its possibilities are endless.

On the broad back of history is borne the future of mankind.

PART ONE

THE MOTHERLAND

THE LEVI STORY

HITLER'S PLAN TO CONQUER THE UKRAINE AND RUSSIA

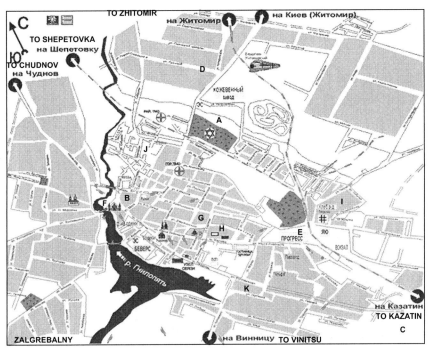

LEGEND

A: Jewish Cemetery
B: Ester's House
C: Airport

D: Former Brodski St. (uncertain)
E: Progress Leather Dyeing factory
F: Babylonian-style synagogue
G: Hotel Friendship

H: Sherentis Theater
I: Bread factory
J: The market area
K: Beit ha'Midrash Chasidic synagogue

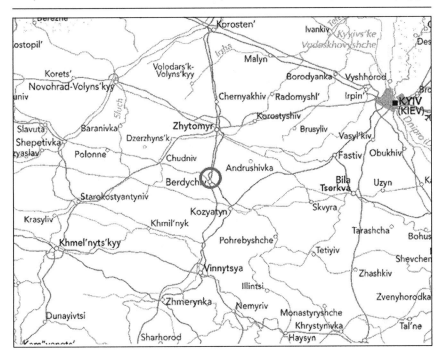

The time of Hitler arrived; a wolfish century. It was a time when people lived like wolves, and wolves lived like people.

— Vasily Grossman

A PERSPECTIVE

German Occupation

Berdichev, also written as Bardichev, Berditchev, Berdithov, Berdyczow, now a part of the Ukrainian Soviet Socialist Republic, is a town of West Russia in the Zhitomir Oblast (district). It is situated at 49° 54' North, 28° 35 East on a world map, sixteen miles SW of Kiev by rail, and about 100 kilometers from the Polish border established in World War II. Berdichev is known to have been in existence since the fourteenth century.

Berdichev is a rail junction. It was the industrial and trade center of an area where sugar beets were raised. Berdichev passed to Lithuania in 1546 and to Poland in 1569; there is no evidence that a Jewish community existed there before 1721 but at that time a community began to form. According to the 1765 census the Jews in Berdichev numbered 1,220. The people of Berdichev were proud of their heritage and there was reason for it. As a small town in 1789, Berdichev was one of many properties of the Polish magnate Count Tyszkiewicz (tisz-ke-vitz) and later was owned by the Radziwill family. Russia acquired it in 1793.

An extensive trade was carried on in the 19th and 20th centuries in peltry, silks, iron and wooden ware, salt fish, grain, cattle and horses. When the Jews settled in Ukraine during the period of Polish rule, they found themselves in a vise. The Jewish lessee, under the *arenda* (group of regions) system, administered estates in the name of their Polish landowner. His customers were the nobility, officials, the Catholic clergy, and the local army garrison. In 1774, Prince Radziwill, the owner of the town, deprived the rabbis of their right to civil jurisdiction. There was a price to be paid for being Jewish in Berdichev. To the enslaved peasants and rebellious Cossacks, Ukrainians, and Greek-Orthodox the Jewish lessee appeared both as an infidel and an alien—an emissary of the Polish Catholic noblemen who sought to dominate them. The Ukrainian towns-man was jealous of his urban rival, the unbelieving Jew, whose success was due to the assistance of the foreign and hated Polish regime. This dichotomy gave rise to severe purges and massacres from the mid-seventeenth century to the recent past.

At that time its Jewish population was a mere 2,000, no different from dozens of other *shtetlakh* (small towns) in Ukraine. But during the following seventy years and despite their despised position among Ukrainians, Berdichev burgeoned into a small city of great commerce, boasting of more than fifty thousand prosperous Jewish souls. Berdichev was renowned for trade in leather and fancy goods. Berdichev was also a center for the development of Yiddish literature. Indeed, that reputation remained unchallenged through the centuries.

By mid-19th century Berdichev had also become the major center of grain trade, money-lending and small manufacturing in Southwestern Russia. It gleamed as a jewel in the Ukrainian crown. The city even claimed fame as the second biggest after Warsaw, in the Russian empire. The development of railroads eventually undermined the unique commercial position of Berdichev and strengthened its competitors, Odessa and Warsaw. Consequently, many people migrated to other areas and prosperity waned. World War I, the October Revolution of 1917 and the Russian Civil War of 1918-1921 again diminished the Jewish population.

But even limited prosperity in Berdichev was not to last. During the "wolfhound" years of 1920 through 1945, purges, famines, *pogroms* [1], the Holocaust, all took their evil toll upon this once peaceful land and people. Lenin's men were always unwelcome; not so at first were Hitler's troops. Most of those who did not run for their lives were torn from their families and quickly murdered in cold blood.

The scarlet stain of their innocent deaths is as spit upon the hallowed name "Mother Russia".

Immediately prior to World War II, Berdichev had a Jewish population of over 30,000, out of a total population of 66,306. When the town was taken by the Germans on July 7, 1941, the Jewish population numbered 20,000. Three days later the military governor imposed a collective fine on the Jews of 100,000 rubles, in cash and valuables. Jews were harassed, some were murdered in groups, and synagogues were set on fire with the congregants inside at prayer.

Establishment of a Ghetto and the First Slaughter

On August 25, 1941 the Jews of Berdichev were ordered to move into a ghetto that had been set up in the poorest part of the town (if they did not live there already), which thus became

20

unbearably congested. On September 4, on orders of the *Hoherer SS – und PolizeiFuhrer*[2] of Ukraine, 1,500 young Jews were seized and taken out of town to be shot to death. A force of German and Ukrainian police surrounded the ghetto on September 15. Four hundred skilled craftsmen and their families, a total of 2,000 people, were set aside, and the rest, 18,600 persons, were taken out of town to pits that had been prepared in advance, to be shot to death.

Liquidation of the Jews of Berdichev

The mass shooting of 10,000 people in one day by the 11th Panzer Division occurred on September 5, 1941. It was reported to be the "largest mass shooting of Jews ever undertaken until that time". They had been "herded" into a makeshift ghetto located in the downtown area of the town several weeks earlier. In the early morning hours of September 15 the remainder of the ghetto's occupants were driven into the street, many undressed, separated into two columns — those who would and would not be spared. They were "thrown" into trucks and carried to the hangars of the military airport. In this way, 20,000 people were murdered in a two-day period. [The Bones of Berdichev, p. 24-5]

Two thousand more Jews were murdered on November 3, leaving only 150 craftsmen alive. The *Nazi* extermination unit was liquidated on October 5, 1941, but the Russians continually caused *pogroms* to be carried out. The following spring, on April 7, 1942, 70 Jewish women, who were married to non-Jews and living outside the ghetto were murdered together with their children. On June 16, the number of craftsmen was reduced to 60 and at the end of October 1943 when Soviet forces approached, those Jews who were still left alive were also murdered. When Berdichev was liberated on January 15, 1944, only fifteen Jews were found in the town.

By the end of World War II, much of Ukraine lay in ruins. Fields were burned, homes and businesses destroyed, millions of citizens were taken from their comfortable family life, quickly shot to death and thrown into hastily dug pits with their fellows or interred by surviving family into silent, neglected cemeteries.

Millions of lives and futures erased in a breath. Think of it: More than a century of continuous invasion, threats, terror and death. It is as though a plague was sent of G-d to ravage beautiful, idyllic Ukraine.

But time replenishes loss. By the 1970 census there were an estimated 15,000 Jews again in Berdichev, as well as a synagogue, a cantor and a ritual poultry slaughterer. Their cemetery was reported neglected, but the Jews had erected a fence around the grave of Levi Isaac of Berdichev, whom they revered. [Gathered from *Beth Hatefutsoth*, Museum of the Jewish Diaspora.]

This birthplace of the Levi family and their kindred is barren now. Berdichev is again a humble, quiet city occupied in the main by Ukrainian peasants. Only a haunted visage of its former prosperity remains. Many residents are aged and blind and barely remember the carnage visited upon them. Berdichev is no longer shown on most maps; it is now a quaint stop along the Gnilopyatka River where few come to mourn their dead. Most travelers prefer to drink kvas at stands along the main roads while they visit or sightsee, pausing only to rest at the Holocaust Memorial recently erected. They move on. As of this "found" journal's publication, fewer than 400 Jews live there but synagogue attendance is active.

---

[1] A Russian word meaning "desolation". Also, an organized persecution and massacre of a religious group.
[2] Higher SS and Police Leader

Author's Note: Journal of The Dead narratives are independent commentary upon the shoah in Berdichev. This "chorus" of victims' voices relate personal experiences independent of any other story.

Journal of the Dead — Martin Brodksii

I was brought up in Berdichev and it was my only home. My father worked in a factory making accessories for many things Russian. I was a grown man when the German *Wehrmacht*[3] arrived back in town on that day in September. I was attending Institute to be a technician and work next to my father and his brother. I was to be married to a woman down my very own street.

On the day in question, I was coming home from school. I was grabbed from behind and forced into an area just outside the school. The Germans at my back jeered and called me a stupid Jew. They stripped me of my class pin and called me insulting names. I held onto the seat in the truck and kept my head down and my mouth shut, contemplating how to get myself out of that jam. I finally gave in and let them take me, as fighting was to no avail. They took me to a holding area where I saw many others, mostly Jews.

"You are going to be killed," one of the Germans told me, with his gun raised to beneath my chin. He was trying to frighten me, but I was already scared. His words scared me and I know I began to cry. He swiped me across my eyes, and his hand stung me greatly. Then he said with a wicked smile,

"I know how to shut you up."

He took me to a tree, stood my against it, back facing outward. Without a word, he fired a shot into my neck and I fell dead.

My fiancée escaped to Kiev, only to face death at the hands of German soldiers at Babi Yar. My father and mother were murdered in their homes, in cold blood. You must tell my story so others will know the murderous wrath of these men. I hate the SS, the army, the German everything.

---

[3] The German word Wehrmacht literally means "defense force". It predates 1930 and originally referred to the entire armed forces of a country. Since World War II, the term has come to refer to the armed forces of Germany during the Third Reich from 1935 to 1945. This included the army (das Heer), navy (die Kriegsmarine), air force (die Luftwaffe), and elite service (die Waffen Schulzstaffel) or "SS".

They that trust in the Lord shall be as mount Zion which cannot be removed, but abideth for ever.

— Psalm 23:1

1 — Nights of Prowling Wolves

The headstones lay at all angles, as if they had fallen from the sky. Ester fell, her legs and arms scraping on vines that scratched and tore at her. Grass grown tall and wild interspersed the gray, grimy monuments of death. Thorns of wild roses ripped her shirt and she let out a yell. The hard gray stone that stopped her progress was broken in three places. As she struggled to rise, a well-fed rodent skittered away into the brush. Whose marker is this? The name was almost obscured, but by the light of early morning she recognized the date of death: 17 July 1941. Quickly she wiped slimy moss from the Hebrew lettering. The first name — Zebulon. Zeb! Her father's dear friend, the furrier! Zeb the Levite, of the ancient family of priests; a faithful Jew in the *Chasidic*[4] community of Berdichev. He regularly accompanied Ester's Papa, Reb Levi, to synagogue to stand in the traditional *minyan* circle of ten Jewish men at the opening of services. Ester rubbed clean the remaining inscription: Zeb was not alone in the ground. Here also was Mordechai, his only son. Their deaths should not have shocked onlookers. Thousands had already died and many thousands more would perish before the winter's frost.

It was spring of the year 1985, but reading the ornate, Hebrew lettered old tombstones Ester recalled those terrible days of summer, 1941. A German *Aktion* was taking place. A contingent of the Red Army fought but was unable to reclaim the town. The SS squads had flushed all the dissidents into the Bazaar that day, meaning to make public examples of them. Some of the older men were rounded up in Taras Shevchenko park at the corner of Lenin and Liebknecht Streets. They were paying respects at the grave of Jewish *tsaddicks*.[5]

German soldiers had help in hunting the Jews from certain non-Jewish citizens who were jealous of the Jews of Berdichev. These informants wanted control of the money and power that came from the trades. Zeb was in his store discussing with a client the type and color of native fox to adorn an expensive dress. Mordechai, at a desk in the corner of his father's haberdashery, had been copying a *Torah* portion he was asked to read in synagogue the following week. Suddenly, German soldiers turned a corner into the main shopping area, and it was as if the Angel of Death had pointed his finger at two of them. One of the soldiers motioned to his companions, his eye on the sign "Brodskii and Son, Furriers".

"Here is the place."

They threw open the door. Zeb was grabbed from behind the counter of his store, yanked away from his client with the fur in his hands. Mordechai rushed to his aid but he was pushed aside by one of the soldiers.

"Papa, papa", he screamed in terror.

But Zeb was virtually lifted up by the back of his collar and marshaled out the door to the street, the German soldiers shouting curses at his back the whole time. Almost as an afterthought they grabbed Mordechai, too, and took him screaming out the door and across the street to the hastily constructed public gallows on nearby Lenin Street.

People were gathered around the square where the makeshift wooden hanging platform had just been constructed. Other soldiers were busily untying nooses from around the necks of two Jewish boys who they'd hung minutes earlier. The soldiers shouted orders to each other as Zeb and Mordechai were dragged toward the gallows.

Reb (Mr.) Dovid Moshe ben-Levi, Berdichev's only *Chasidic* undertaker and *chazzen*[6] of the *Chasidic* synagogue, was quickly summoned to the scene, but he arrived too late to stop anything. There were Zeb and Mordechai with startled expressions on their lifeless faces, swinging above the street from ropes soaked in brine. Mordechai had wet his pants. His breath was not yet entirely gone. He whimpered,

"Reb Levi, I don't want to die now."

Zeb's neck was already broken and he could not intervene. Zeb was only thirty-six.

"Stop, stop!" Reb Levi yelled. "These men are innocent. Please, stop the killing, it is against the will of G-d!"

He fell to his knees in the street while the townspeople, seeming to be mesmerized, watched in wretched fear. This was Berdichev's new ghetto, the marketplace, the Yatki City Bazaar where vendors displayed their goods. This small squared-off block of streets where Jews, Gypsies, Slavs and other "undesirables" were forced to live in ancient vermin-infested buildings, was where the Germans relocated the unfortunates in August of 1941. In these crumbling, junk-filled and manure-ridden places were thrown those whom Hitler's army had rounded up less than a month following their sudden arrival in Berdichev. Rich and poor, old and feeble, they were routed from their homes and herded along Byelopolskaya, Maxnov, Grecheskaya, Pushkin, Greater Yuridika, Lesser Yuridika, Semyonov, and Danilov Streets where they had no choice but to crowd together in tiny, cramped quarters of kitchens, bedrooms, alleyways.

A soldier spat at Reb Levi. It hit his *yarmulke*.[7]

"Get up, miserable Jew!" he commanded. "Get up and get away from here or we'll hang you with them!"

He laughed and kicked the Reb with his black boot. Several *Chasidim* saw what happened. They ran to tell the family of Reb Levi. Fortunately, Zych the Gypsy went immediately to Levi's aid as he lay startled in the street and helped him back to his office at the corner of Genizah and Sadova Streets. Business had to continue. There were new funerals to be prepared and grieving families to inform. No one was around to witness the rape and murder of Zebulon's lovely blond-haired daughter, Ninotchka, the love of her father's life. She was attacked by soldiers who raided their home while patrolling that night. Shana Tova, Zeb's wife, now his widow, had just finished her piecework in the nearby Progress Machine Tool factory. Ninotchka was preparing for her seventeenth birthday at the time of her death. Shana Tova, after finding her daughter dead and bleeding on the floor of their small home, ran to Reb Levi's office, begging him to bring her daughter back to life. But this, the *chazzen* explained, he had not the power to do.

"Then tell G-d I no longer know Him," yelled the woman. She ran down the street to the Gnilopyatka River. It was quiet and seemed nearly still alongside the busy avenues of Berdichev. Reb Levi, hearing her screams, gave chase to stop her, but she outran him. When she reached the river the distraught woman simply threw herself in it as if she'd made an appointment and was late. Reb Levi jumped in to save her. Even with his heavy stomach he was a good swimmer. But the persistent undertow quickly grabbed Shana Tova as its victim and he could not find even her *babushka* after a few moments in the water. He had to admit defeat. Shana Toya would have been grateful for that and called his failure a *mitzvot*.[8]

In the aftermath, it was found out that the storekeeper next to Zebulon's furrier shop, Mayer Shepsky, was the one they were truly after, for he had publicly proclaimed that Germans were insensitive beasts. His declaration was made after his parents were shot in their fields. Their small grain harvest had been taken earlier by Stalin's men. In reprisal for the people's unwillingness to surrender their crops to government quotas, the punishments were quick and deadly.

Reb Levi dutifully boxed and buried Shana Tova with deep sorrow in his heart. As her body was placed in its simple coffin he prayed for her soul to be free of its pain and asked G-d to join her spirit with those of Zeb, Mordechai and Ninotchka in Heaven. "They have much to talk about," he reasoned. But he was distraught by the brutality he had witnessed that day. In his prayers that day, he questioned G-d.

"And why are men evil, Eternal One? Who determines the good from the bad? Must there be such grief?"

No answer came. Reb Levi sighed deeply. He again asked G-d for insight and went home to his dinner.

"I'm waiting for an answer," he told his wife.

"An answer? You think the Eternal One, blessed be He, will call you on the phone? The answer, Levi, is that we make our own bed. G-d has other things to attend. Eat your soup."

Anna walked over to the large iron stove that stood as a sort of room divider in their small apartment. The old floor creaked with age and the smells of dinner permeated the place. Anna donned oven mitts and from deep inside the well of the stove she pulled out a handled tureen full of *borscht*[9] and poured it into a bowl. She brought the liquid to the wide wooden table. A loaf of *challah*, a braided egg bread accompanied their soup.

"Anna, it isn't that simple. The Eternal One knows and sees everything we do, yet He doesn't interfere. I think He is waiting to see how we will work it all out."

"Well then, my husband, He must be very patient. We've been here all our lives. What have we known but war, famine and murder at the judging end of rifles and guns? It's a miracle we're still alive, let alone that we're trying to raise two children."

Anna heaped sour cream on her *borscht* and made little circles in it with the spoon.

Levi looked lovingly at his wife. Deep creases of worry adorned her forehead. Time and much trouble had worried

Anna's hair to grey and dimmed her smile. Her fullness was no more. She had grown old while still in middle age. He thought back to their youth together. He met her at a *bar mitzvah*[10] for her nephew on a rare trip to Kiev. He was already thirty. He had never dated and he was the oldest student at the rabbinical college in Lvov. His parents had long past given up trying to marry him off. A lovely young woman smiled at him from across the room, then beckoned him to her. He shyly obliged, bowed before her and kissed her hand. She laughed, surprised by his actions. They danced together twice, that was all it took. Her laugh, her long dark hair, so fetching to him as it brushed her shoulders . . . They married on the eve of the Bolshevik Revolution and several times had to hide from Russian soldiers or run for their lives.

But some things were changeless. They were still together. Every year they celebrated another year of their marriage, dancing to the same music that had caught them in its melodies those many years past. Another thing was constant, too. They had sat on hard benches across this old wooden table from one another in just this way for more than twenty years.

"We must have more faith, Anna. We must not doubt the Eternal One's plans for us."

Anna said nothing but her sigh was deep and her eyes watered just a bit. Reb Levi watched her rise to fetch him another bagel.

"This is good soup", he remarked as though he hadn't supped on it uncounted times.

~

Ester shuddered. Tears flooded her eyes and she looked at Zeb's tombstone. He was a man full of life, and so proud of his son Mordechai who was *bar-mitzvahed* with honors. She could not forget their bloated faces as they hung in death. She recalled her Papa's words:

"Grief knows no time or place, it is everywhere at once, hidden and waiting; one could never know at what hour his or her nights and days might be filled with mourning, and for this reason each person must be ready for trouble."

Ester Levi learned that well and decided to live as though each moment was precious. It was the only defense against the serendipity of her experience. She was born in Berdichev, a town set gloriously against the Ukrainian Steppes. In this breadbasket of a troubled land she took cold breath in the icy blue dawn of 1919. Her birth came just as the new Ukraine republic was separating itself from Russia, and barely a month before the Ukrainian army staged a *pogrom* here in protest. Her Mama said those murderers would not dare to invade before the birth of her only daughter!

But new plans for a free Ukraine were going well in 1919. The leaders of the Ukrainian nationalist movement attempted to reach an agreement with the Jews, who held considerable economic power. A national council, the Rada, was set up, but unfortunately the newly independent Ukraine had little power against the force of Lenin's new Soviet state. He eventually absorbed the territory under his Communist leadership. Russification was forced upon the people by decree, with guns and unlawful quotas authorizing government seizure of Ukraine's vast grain harvests.

In the four-cornered battles that ensued between Ukrainian forces against the Red Army, the Poles and counterrevolutionaries who were against everyone, thousands of citizens were killed, mainly Jews. The civil war of 1918-21 saw *pogroms* followed by a famine of devastating and prolonged proportions. Ukraine's breadbasket was nearly emptied of its sustenance. Whole villages were victims of the wasted and burned farmlands trampled by the White Army, the Red Army, the Ukrainian Nationalist army, Polish forces, a German puppet army, and bands of marauders that included anarchists. Youths and babies perished by the thousands. Starvation's vise robbed the grave of many dead. Cannibalism was another silent ghoul. Somehow, those who could still fight began a peasant war that lasted until 1923.

By August 1920 the civil war had ended. More than 150,000 Jews had been slain. The victorious Red Army controlled Ukraine but no one was safe from the brutality of the Communist state. Berdichev, once the center for the development of Jewish *Chasidism*[11] — an enormously popular movement that emphasized spiritual enlightenment — had become by 1932 a place of torment and grief, a target of Russian hatred and later of German anti-Semitism. The resulting sicknesses, successive famines and new *pogroms* of the 1930's took thousands more lives.

Ester often recalled with a shudder the many nights she and her older brother Barak, were hurried off to the safety of nearby pines and oaks when the small group of Jewish resistance fighters warned the neighborhoods of the presence of Russian soldiers in the area. There they would pray for their parents' safety at home. But somehow Ester did not really know fear even then. Trust in G-d, Papa Reb Levi told her.

"G-d sees everything, He knows each heart, prepares a place for every soul. He is mightier than our enemies, my *shayna*.[12] Not only did G-d create the earth and everything in it, but all of the cosmos are subject to His will. He knows our desires, our fears, our hopes, Ester. Always trust in Him to see you through."

And so Ester trusted. But her younger brother Barak, was always suspicious. He never admitted to prayer nor mentioned a desire for G-d's guidance. He strongly disbelieved the "lies and games" the Russian leaders told the people. Anna shook her head in worry over their hotheaded son. But he was strong and protective of his family.

"You are a born revolutionary," his disapproving father told him.

No argument lasted. Everyone had to whisper. There was little freedom of expression in apartment houses of the sort the Levi family lived in. Walls were thin. It was common for neighbors to overhear conversations. Some, it was suspected, reported what to them were statements or activities potentially disloyal to the government. Investigations and reprisals invariably followed. It was best to speak low and not arouse suspicion. There was little privacy and few conveniences. Telephones were rarely seen because few in Berdichev found them affordable. Conditions were overcrowded: Tenants shared each other's kitchens as well as common facilities. In Russian winter a single pane of glass in each window did little to protect from the cold. These did not keep out conversation; a cough might be heard down an entire corridor.

Beside the thousands of Ukrainians, Russians, Slavs and not a few Gypsies, there was a large Jewish population of shopkeepers and city officials. It seemed to a visitor that everyone got along, but there was much hatred of Jews in Stalinist Ukraine. This was actually an outgrowth of political hatred that could be traced to Jewish-born Lev Davidovich Bronstein, known to the world as Leon Trotsky. His demonic devotion to Bolshevism was legend and more than anyone, he was responsible for the popular identification of the revolution with the Jews, many of whom were prominent in the Party. Consequently, in the years following the Bolshevik Revolution of 1914-1917 Russian soldiers were sent by Lenin and Stalin to brutalize Jews in their poverty-ridden *shtetls*[13] and in their businesses throughout Ukraine and Russia following the war.

Barak devised a way for his family to hide when Russian soldiers threatened his neighborhood. He installed a secret shelter below some old flooring of their street level apartment that held the four of them uncomfortably and was a sometime home to wandering *Chasids* who'd become displaced by *pogroms*. Because of their hiding place the Levi family survived many onslaughts during the hard years. They could not be sure who their enemies were because adversaries were everywhere like packs of famished wolves hungry to feed upon the innocent. It seemed to them a miracle they were not discovered.

The Russian people helped each other in those lean years and it was their charity and uplifted hearts that saved them for another day. The *Chasids* of Berdichev often quoted their long-dead revered leader, Rabbi Israel ben Eliezer, the *Baal Shem Tov* (Master of the Good Name) who established the school of *Chasidic* philosophy in Ukraine in 1785. He counseled, "Jews, do not despair". Likening Berdichev to Israel he explained that as the burden of suffering continues to increase, it threatens to turn a soul from the true service of G-d.

"These curses come because we do not serve G-d with joyfulness and true gladness of heart, regardless of our circumstances. Holiness, justice, mercy, *mitzvots*, these things are the regimen of law and what sanctifies a man."

Reb Levi, one of his many grateful disciples, heartily agreed. The Levi family occupied several small rooms in an old block-long communal housing apartment building just off Mira and 9th Streets, uptown from the huge red brick Babylonian-styled synagogue they attended.

Their resident rabbi, Yoel Shmuel Levine, was teaching for a time in Kiev. He communicated often with Reb Levi who, with the help of loyal Zych the Romany held weekly *Shabbat*[14] and holiday services in Jewish homes.

Ester, Reb Levi's first born, came from fine old Russian-Jewish stock. Her mother, Anna Rubenshtein was a woman of *Torah* whose two sisters and a brother resided in Kiev and Moscow. Anna's father, Rav Asher Marvin Rubinshtein, was a *Chasidic* rabbi from Lvov, as his father had been before him. Her mother Selya claimed heritage from the large and wealthy family; de Maimonides of Spain. But Anna was impressed more by character than acquired wealth. At 25 she married a gentle, guileless rabbinical scholar after only a brief courtship. They felt impressed to name their daughter for the biblical Hebrew woman who saved her people from mass murder by risking her own life.

When Barak was born several years later his angry, reddened face seemed to say, "I will set this world on fire". When Reb Levi suggested Yitzhak for his name, Anna thought to change it slightly to Yatzakh. "Then it will be as the word 'burn' ".

But as he grew, Yatzakh proved also to be swift of foot with an unusually quick and independent turn of mind. He seemed to absorb his father's teachings rapidly, but often came to different conclusions. He joined rebellious groups and campaigned for free rights. Local government disdained him; he was lucky to escape sometimes with his life. In time his nickname became "Barak", meaning, lightning and this name fit him best of all.

Ester was as mild as Barak was mercurial. She grew to young and proper Jewish womanhood in the post civil war period of Ukraine's slow rebuilding. Despite the many hardships Jewish families were subjected to in Berdichev, she enjoyed the bustling environment. She was devoted to her parents who taught her *Talmud Torah* and encouraged thoughtful daily study. As Ester grew she reasoned that G-d expected obedience and constancy. She clung therefore to simple hobbies and pleasant things, not letting herself be too concerned with the troubles of the world or even the city around her. In this way, by keeping herself aloof from the travails of others she endeavored to retain her purity of character and freshness of outlook.

The rush of wind through the grassy meadows of the Steppes was their energy force. Bright, clear light seemed to be all around and beneath the sky, accentuating the land and blessing the landscape. Inhaling the smell of rich earth brought a feeling of permanence and invincibility while plentiful stands of pine, alder and oak seemed to provide an impenetrable refuge. Both fields and trees glowed in the light that illumined the air around them. Barak learned to play harmonica and tried to imitate bird sounds with it. He and Ester knew by heart the songs of bullfinches, robins and owls and would answer their music with mimicked chirpings. During summers they spent hopeful hours with string and bits of strong cheese trying to catch any of the plentiful fish in the Gnilopyatka River. Sometimes Ester caught her own light-complected reflection in the water's wavy mirror. At these times she felt lucky to look more like the Ukrainian and Russian girls; full bodied, straight brown hair, gentile features. Having distinct physical *Ashkenazic*[15] traits was a guarantee of trouble.

Barak was Ester's opposite, a champion of street justice and bully to the bullies. He sought out ruffian leaders and challenged them, invariably winning bouts through strength and determination. Potential enemies learned to give him a wide swath wherever he was sighted. Crime in Berdichev reduced to an all-time low. Barak seemed afraid of nothing, but this filled his sweet-natured parents with fear and much embarrassment. They feared for his life, but Ester secretly admired him and was glad for his presence beside her at market and on walks through the Steppe forest. Ester and Barak remained on good terms until the raids and *pogroms* seemed to create in Barak a lust for Russian blood.

Long ago, as children, they had often journeyed down Karl Leibnecht Street past the old Polish-style brick buildings to the site of the old Latin cathedral. They played hide and seek within the half-ruined walls of the city's old *krepost*[16]. In later years the *krepost* would become a ghetto of death and a monument of sorrow to Fascist (usually, *Nazi*) brutality. Many Jews would be murdered nearby on the brow of the steep valley overlooking the swift and silent Gnilopyatka River.

The children loved to play in the glorious Ukrainian glow of the wheat fields that shone golden in the sun. They romped through the dark forests of the Steppes in pure joyousness and when they thought no one could see them, they tanned on the riverbanks and skipped along the bridges that crossed the river. On the eastern shore were shops, crafts houses and markets. The flatlands on the western side were reserved for agricultural planting, referred to as the Zalgrebalny district.

Ester's father, Reb Levi was Berdichev's homegrown, humble *Chasidic chazzen* and main Jewish mortician. For over two decades his mortuary's darkened front room had been filled with mourners while caskets came and went to the large Jewish cemetery in a rebuilt Russian bakery truck purchased from the local confectioner. Reb Levi loved his work because of the joy it brought him to pray for the deceased and to send the sons and daughters of G-d back to Him with the proper introductions. At each funeral that Reb Levi held he took a few minutes to address the family of the departed.

"Their spirits are not dead, though they are not any longer here with us. We must wish them well in their journey back to G-d. He will reunite them with loved ones who have passed on. Isn't it wonderful?"

Then Reb Levi would sing in a sweet voice from the Book of Psalms, ancient melodies taught him by his father. Finally, he would relate the story of Rabbi Levi Yitzhak who in a dream found the Adversary making great trouble in Heaven. When the

Adversary was not looking, Levi tried to undo the evil that had been wrought. Rabbi Levi was taken before the Bar of Justice where many who wanted to see him punished, bargained for his life. But the Lord of Heaven Himself cried out that He would claim Levi's soul and work for His own purposes.

"Now this is an example for all of us to follow. The Eternal One, blessed be He, has purchased all of us to serve His many purposes. From time to time he reclaims one of us to finish our work in the Heavens, so we must all be ready. We must be pure of heart and always willing to do good for our fellow man. We must attend regular *Shabbat* services and attend High Holy Day services without fail! If we are worthy, we may be invited to read *Torah* with G-d when He calls us home. How can we grieve for our departed ones when we know they are in Heaven reading *Torah* with G-d?"

Many of his customers thought Reb Levi's beliefs strange, but he was quick to point out that hundreds of *Talmudic* scholars preceded him in these thoughts. He was a well-loved man of *Torah* with a reputation in Berdichev and surrounding towns as one who feared nothing but G-d. Another rumor had also circulated for years that Reb Levi had a healing gift, for how else could you explain the time he raised Maisel Rabinovitz from her sickbed when no heartbeat could be found? Or the occasion when the circulation in Vasily Popov's legs was so terrible his moans could be heard throughout the apartments? Reb Levi simply and shyly put his hands on Vasily's feet and closed his eyes in concentration. Within a few moments warmth returned to Vasily's legs and he felt the sharp pains dissipate. Reb Levi refused any sort of payment for this seeming miracle.

"Glad I can be of help", he smiled and told Vasily to praise the Eternal One instead.

Hundreds in Berdichev knew Reb Levi, who himself seemed to know every Jew, Gypsy and not a few Ukrainians by their first name. He greeted all who passed with a wide smile and a "*shavua tov*."[18] Most evenings, before Stalin closed the churches and synagogues in Russia during his purges of 1937, Reb Levi could be found at his synagogue in prayer and study before walking the few blocks home to dinner with his beloved family.

As Ester grew to young womanhood her mother taught her the *Yiddishe kosher* kitchen, the biblical laws of *kashrut*.[19] Anna sent her to purchase flour, eggs, fish and vegetables in the Bazaar along busy Reenok Street on the day before the Saturday *Shabbat* and to look in on the widows of their congregation. They had enough to eat in Ester's early years. There was always bread and potatoes, though sometimes no butter or milk. But after the famines of 1933 passed, their store of food grew smaller and smaller. This was partially because their pantry was communal and many came and took more than they needed. Ester and Barak rarely knew gnawing hunger pains, but they noticed their parents growing thinner as the months passed. Always though, there was the *borscht* (beet soup) or *schi* (cabbage soup) with *khlyeb* (Russian bread). Sometimes to forget their hunger they sang old songs and danced while Barak played old Hebrew and Russian melodies on his rusty harmonica. Several times every day they gathered before the iron stove in the kitchen to pray long and fervently for protection against enemies who might invade at any moment. Reb Levi kept nightly watch with the neighbor men and the *bar-mitzvahed* young men while the women and children slumbered.

Ester was a placid child disliking of change, content with predictable daily life and happy to be at home with family. Her Mama said she never had to discipline her sweet-tempered daughter because she always minded with a smile. When just able to walk, Ester danced for her mother who provided the songs in Yiddish and Hebrew. She was also a dreamer, often visualizing that the lush, meandering Gnilopyatka River that coursed swiftly through Berdichev would obligingly overflow and wash the streets clean of fear, of sorrow and death. She trusted that her family's soulful, passionate prayers of deliverance would overflow the whole world and spill into the Eternal One's presence, blessed be He. Barak thought Ester foolish and laughed at her romantic ramblings. But Reb Levi assured his naïve daughter that her fantasy was "a wish for the peace that *Torah* brings".

During their family study of *Torah*[19] and *Talmud*[20] many important issues came under discussion. Reb Levi instructed his family thus:

"The Almighty One can hear everyone's prayers, for He is a part of and has a claim on each of His children. Some of us live by the plenitude of faith, and some by power. *Chasidim* believe in following and praising G-d who is the maker of all things good. Our dear master, Rabbi Levi Yitzhak of Berdichev years ago taught this. He was a student of the first Baal Shem Tov who founded the movement. His life was perfect, his love of G-d and his fellows unsurpassed. My father, Moshe Levi, told me of the master's great works among the people here in Berdichev."

The *Chasidic* community of Berdichev thought their Reb a brilliant scholar and mystic, for he spoke knowingly of the *Shekinah*[21] and the greatness of the human spirit. Even in the midst of the fires of *Nazi* hell, they marveled aloud that Reb Levi could see the white holy flames of the Eternal One standing before him! Reb Levi daily read the words of ancient sages and prophets. He was a man of peace, inspired by his faith in G-d. In synagogue on *Shabbat* he spoke to his congregation many words of hope. His favorite theme was that faith triumphs over resistance and opposition. He taught that faith is not to have a perfect knowledge of things, but to hope for things that are not seen that are true. But after services, on their walk home, red-haired Barak often challenged his father's teachings.

"Those old wise men, how smart were they? Teaching tolerance while Syrians, Germans, Communists, and Europeans were overrunning them! If I were around then, they would have fought for their freedoms. Apathy never won a war."

Reb Levi tried not to become frustrated with his son's short-sightedness.

"My son, the Jews have outlasted all their enemies. How did we do it? We believed in our G-d, we called upon him to save us and He has always preserved His chosen. We owned the money supplies, we were lenders to nations., We educated ourselves and built empires. We moved around the world integrating into hundreds of countries but continued to study *Torah* and *Talmud*. We never forgot our heritage; we have kept the mark of the Jew, the circumcision. We have not changed our names or denied who and what we are. Barak, my dear son, if the Jewish people had made war every time they made enemies, even our parents many times deceased would not have survived their generation."

"But Papa," Barak insisted, "we are at the hands of murderers. We will all be victims! If we do not defend ourselves, we will be massacred. Even one man who revolts . . ."

"One who revolts gets everyone murdered. Listen, Yatzakh the angry one, we have always been witnesses to evil. Isn't that what the Eternal One demands of us? Remember Masada? Remember the Exodus from Egypt? Our people had to leave their fate in G-d's hands... Don't worry, my son. Our testimony of evil men will condemn them before G-d who will consign them to eternal misery. It is we Jews who have power, my dear son. We Jews who will finally triumph as a people. You must believe that. Just believe, just exercise your faith, watch it grow until it enlarges your soul and one day your faith will be so perfect it will be as knowledge itself!"

Ester, who always listened to her father's words, felt she understood. But Barak could not arrive at peace within his soul. He seemed to be waiting for a chance to make his mark upon the future.

"We'll see, Papa," he said. "The time is coming for another war. Choose sides now, do not wait until we are surrounded!"

In 1932 Barak, then seventeen and long since *bar mitzvah*-ed, went to work helping his father in his business as one of Berdichev's three morticians. He sometimes accompanied Reb Levi to *Chasidic* councils where they discussed the serious threats of purges and famine to the people of Berdichev. In his heart of hearts he did not want to inherit the family business, or even to remain in Berdichev but he felt he could never make his father understand that action was needed to protect the people of Ukraine. Barak had studied the philosophies of Trotsky and Lenin. He found them threatening to the freedom of the world. He became consumed with hatred for Russia's leaders and their programs. Whenever Ester tried to cheer him he became agitated.

"We're doomed here, Ester," he would say, his large hands gripping her shoulders to make her pay attention. "The Russians continue to starve us! Do you not see how the Russians starve even their brother Slavs? Do you think they'll be patient with us? The news from Kiev—Stalinist ploys! Planning to ask for all our wheat for his henchmen! Then they'll kill us because we are Jews! You, only thirteen! You can't understand. 'We have to leave Berdichev, move to Moscow or even to Kiev. I told Papa but he does not listen to his son!"

"Shhh! You will be overheard! Barak, why do you fear? Stalin says collective farming will bring more grain to every farmer. He says it will be a great success."

"Stalin lies. This year will bring us to the brink of starvation, Ester! You will see, you will see."

Ester was at a loss to understand, but her brother proved right and as time progressed his predictions of trouble materialized. That year Stalin raised Ukraine's grain procurement quotas by forty-five percent. As it turned out there was not enough grain to feed the peasants because no farmer was allowed to eat or store any grain, much less to sell it at market until Stalin's troops and secret police made sure government agents harvested first. The confiscated grain was usually stored under guard in a closed church or warehouse. The starving growers received only empty promises of renewed seed at sowing time. In that disastrous year millions of Ukrainians starved.

The Levi family's food portions decreased furtherdue to non-payment of funeral debts. Barak set traps for fox and rabbit, even trapping some of the wolves roaming the forests nearby. He had some good success at this. Levi planted potatoes, lettuce and carrots behind his store. Anna did sewing for several of the shops in trade for bakery goods. Ester obtained work cleaning offices for day old bread and root vegetables. She tried to keep a cheerful mind. Reb Levi's business increased so much he and Barak became like visitors to their own home, but many services went unpaid for. What time was not dedicated to praying for and burying the dead while comforting families was spent at the homes of other *Chasids* conducting services for the many who starved. The years following the Bolshevik Revolution, especially the 1930's, were spent trying just to survive.

～

The search for tombstones was exhausting and Ester paused to rest. Many years had passed since the German invasion of Berdichev but memories of those hard and hungry times clouded her mind. Many of these dead had been family friends who were not so fortunate as the Levi family. Midst this small city of silenced voices, Ester gave thanks to G-d for the treasure that awaited her here. She had only this day to search and find. The evening was set aside for reunions and the re-dedication of a treasure hidden somewhere within this damp, cold earth.

---

4 Pious ones. Eighteenth century Jewish movement emphasizing dance and song in worship, opposing rabbinical emphasis on formal learning
5 Wise men
6 Trained singer hired by the congregation to assist rabbi is synagogue services
7 Yiddish word for the Jewish skullcap signifying that the wearer is a Jew. Worn by males
8 Charitable act. Commandment, good deed. A meritorious act that expresses G-d's will
9 Beet soup
10 Jewish boy's coming of age ceremony
11 Expressed in praise of God, simple joyous worship practices and personal prayer
12 "My dear one"
13 Villages. In particular, the impoverished Jewish communities of Eastern Europe
14 Period of rest
15 Group of Jews who live in the area between Western Europe and the Baltic Sea
16 Castle
17 A good week!
18 Kosher. Use of correct dietary laws, the laws of Kashrut
19 Torah: Pentateuch. The five books of Moses is the root work of Torah
20 Talmud: rabbinic commentary and teachings on Mishnah and Torah)
21 Divine presence

He who does one precept has gotten himself one advocate, and he who commits one transgression has gotten himself one accuser.

— Talmud, Abot 4:13

2 — Garden of Deceit

Berdichev, split in two by its broad and scenic river, is not far from the borders of Volhynia, the governing region. For over one hundred years until 1941 it was an important center in western Ukraine because of its large concentration of landowners, factory owners, bankers, teachers, and carpenters. A great many of these people and their families were Jewish. For this reason the town was known to Russians and Ukrainians as the "Yid's capital", with more than a fifty percent Jewish population. Jews also filled the roles of craftsmen, artists, doctors, druggists, engineers, bacteriologists, chemists, and exporters. Even women worked in the trades and apprenticed to the arts and sciences. So, as Jewish entrepreneurs essentially came to control the land, the arts and much of the money, their enemies also increased because of the control the Jews came to exert over commerce and government. Many attained positions of power, even prestige, and many were more than a little arrogant.

Berdichev had been an important world center of Polish culture and *Chasidism* for more than two centuries. Many of the wealthier families in town attended the many synagogues where deals were made and paper floated. At its edges were scattered some *Tsigani*[22], living in their trailers or makeshift tent towns. There of course were also the Jewish poor in the Oblast region, but many of these families owned and worked small farms in the countryside around the cities and throughout the valleys. They brought their goods to daily market, bartering and dealing their wares to anyone who could pay. Itinerant lawyers offered dubious services to the unfortunates unable to obtain a competent attorney. Actors gave impromptu performances for bread and cabbage. Street magicians, fortune tellers and rag merchants from other cities buying and selling fabrics were in those days common fare. It was a curious circus of daily life.

Generally, Russians, Poles and Ukrainians lived in harmony with the Jewish population. Small wonder that when the Germans invaded Russia from the west in June 1941, few moved away. So intertwined were their lives with their livelihood that even while friends and family were at the mercy of German death squads they called out one to another their plans to reunite in the afterlife.

As the 1940's began, Germany's *Fuhrer* eyed the bustling, expanding community as a prime target of his anti-Semitism. Berdichev was a burning waiting to happen.

~

But now it is 1985. Ester moves on past another six rows of markers. Of the three old abandoned Jewish cemeteries, only this largest — where the famous and beloved Berdichever Rabbi Levi Yitzhak sleeps — has survived. The enclosure has abandoned itself to wild overgrowth of trees, weeds and shrubs. No paths wind through the maze. Many markers are broken and barely readable, all of them coated with dirt, moss and slime. Ester finds numerous tombstones dating from the eighteenth century. A local guide had told her the land holds an estimated 10,000 dead, many without stones to mark their passing. Further, many bodies were, in haste, interred on top of others and are therefore forever lost to location by relatives.

Ester has come to this dank, overgrown place in 1985 with a sacred purpose, a duty to perform that was agreed upon by her father and his trusted friend long before. She hasn't counted on the conflicting feelings that overcomes her. Forty-three years has passed since German troops left Ukraine in 1942. She feels like a stranger, standing in this roadway of death. But, too, it is as if time has rolled itself back to her days of youth and her nights of terror. It seems she is once again a child in Berdichev, waiting for her parents to come and take her home.

It had not been hard to run away from here. Following World War II, Ester, a new wife pregnant with her first born, emigrated with her husband to America and tried to make a peaceful life far away from the memories of the Hitler years. They wanted to let the tragedies of death and destruction fade into the past. As they struggled to raise a family and to gain a formal education, opportunities to teach in a university setting became available. They were grateful to America for their success and their freedoms but they could not forget their Ukrainian heritage and the promise that had been made.

That duty could only be tackled in Berdichev. When still a child Ester and her brother made a promise to their Papa that had to be kept. Following the war, Barak moved to Finland where he became an activist for free rights in Eastern Europe. He had recently been appointed to a post in the Global Coalition Against Terrorism where he served in the Ukraine office. Ester wrote him and suggested they meet in Berdichev to carry out the task their father had assigned them years before. Barak instantly agreed. He would be joining her and Avram later that evening. It would be a grand reunion.

Ester pushed hastily through the bramble; she did not see the spider's web until her face almost met its sticky film. The wispy silken loom, fastened securely between two alder twigs more than half a meter apart, shone as silver. It was backlit by the morning sun that lazily spread itself over the vastness of central Ukraine. In the center of this intricate network its spiny owner sat quivering in anticipation of new prey. The web in its delicacy was a Heaven-sent artwork.

But it was also a trap. Ester was reminded of other traps of death as she lurched hard to the left to avoid the webby thing. Suddenly she tripped over an upturned headstone hidden in the brush. Like many others in Berdichev's cemetery it was of an ob-long sausage shape and lay flat. Others here were semi-cylindrical or boot-shaped or made of a thin granite material. Some were of granite, rounded, with a Star of David above the Hebrew charac-ters. Others lay sprawled, their ornate lettering covered in vines and dirt. There was no order to their placement or appearance. With a heavy brush and rag Ester painstakingly cleaned away some of the gritty residue overlying a large marker in her path to discern the morbid essentials:

Murdered in cold blood by Stalin's beasts
Peh-Nun[23]
Berger Kolodvych, ben (son) Israel Kolodovna
Nun peh 14 Shevat (Jan-Feb) 5689 (Hebrew year)
Belza Ivanivna, bat (daughter) Moshe Ivanovich, ha-Rav (rabbi)
Nun-Peh 14 Shevat–5689
Tehe nishmatah tzerurah bitzror hachayim[24]

A wave of remembrance washed over her: Ester visualized again the petite Belza Ivanivna and her husband Berger Kolod-vych the jeweler and sometime town crier. They were Russians. In the 1930's they and their four children lived just outside town on a very small farm. Belza's parents lived with them, as well as several children whose parents had been killed by Russian soldiers in a random raid upon Berdichev in 1932, at Stalin's orders. They had little to wear or eat and were always hungry and cold, but though they were not Jewish the Kolodvyches were sympathetic to the Jew's plight. Reb Levi told Ester that Belza's family hid Jews from the Russian army in their wheat fields during the famines and pogroms of the early 1930's.

Belza's daughter Alexa had been Ester's childhood friend. One summer evening in 1929 they were in town playing a skipping game near Ester's apartment. Suddenly they saw Berger, tall and gaunt. He had left his shop to cry out the message that Russian soldiers had been spotted across the river. They would be coming into the old part of town via the bridge that connected west to east Berdichev. He was running down Reenok Street at top speed, his jeweler's eye bouncing on the white smock he wore over his suit at work. A Russian soldier was just behind him, astride his horse. He must have thought Berger was stealing or running from some crime because he aimed his pistol at Berger's back. A shot was fired. Berger jumped forward and hit the street, his moans strangling in his blood that spurted onto the warm pavement. There were other people on the street. They all screamed and ran into the stores to hide. The soldier stopped and shouted something in Russian at everyone. His eyes were wild and he was waving his pistol. Berger died that day. So quickly it was over!

Alexa had run to her father, throwing herself upon his bleeding body. She'd yelled to Ester to run and warn her Mama.

"Tell Mama to hide, Ester. Hurry, they may be coming for her, too!"

But Ester could not move. She was fastened to the spot in horror.

"Hurry, hurry", Alexa shouted again.

Ester remained pinned to the spot. Fear stopped her mind. She nearly fainted in terror.

"Alexa, I'm scared," Ester cried out. Alexa was holding Berger's bloody head in her hands. For Ester the world had stopped moving. Somehow, her feet leaden, she forced herself to rise and move down the street around the corner to her home a few blocks away. She felt the unforgivable coward, falling down, willing herself to rise again before falling forward as if she was being pushed. She threw up her breakfast on the three steps leading to her door. She cowered in terror on her bed. It was Mama who finally shook the story from her and sent Barak to tell Belza her husband had been murdered in the streets. Belza stayed with Reb Levi's family that long, mournful night. Ester was too shamed to look into her

44

eyes, but they were soft when the new widow finally smiled and she took the child to her bosom. Ester could not believe she was forgiven.

Reb Levi found out later that the soldier was only looking for Belza's grandfather who was a protestor against Stalin. The authorities interrogated Alexa who refused to tell them anything. She was taken away. No one saw her again. Later that week, Belza was shot while harvesting wheat in her field. She was accused of violating the quota of 100% of harvest for Stalin's coffers. The penalty was death. Belza explained to the soldiers that she was only getting a little for her disabled Mama to bake with. Belza's mother was unable to walk She was half starved and unclean when a neighboring farmer found her a week later. She was never told of the murders but soon went into a depression, calling out for Belza day and night in her raspy old voice. One day she simply rolled off her bed and crawled toward the window of her room where she was found dead that evening.

Few knew it then but the Jewish future in Ukraine was being second-guessed: Germany's Adolf Eichmann was made head of a Special Section of the *Gestapo* to study the concentrations of Jews in Ukraine, especially in the town of Berdichev which had a wide, paved road to Zhitomir, thirty kilometers to the north.

Ester remembered the funeral for Belza's mother. There were hundreds of mourners in attendance. Reb Levi had spoken words of comfort and hope but still the town grieved. Ester took part in the mourning, standing with the women young and old, while the men chanted prayers of eternal life over mortal death.

Through the trees and brush, Ester could see the large monument to Rabbi Isaacson, her great, great grandfather. It, too, was in disrepair. Reb Levi's mother, Malya Avigdor, had been a fervent *Chasidic* wife of formidable intellect. Her brother, a prolific writer and publisher of Hebrew literature was known throughout the Ukraine. But it was Reb Levi's great-grandfather, Rabbi Levi Isaacson, the Ukrainian *Chasidic* master, a *tzaddik*[25] to his congregation and one descended from famous *Chasidic* masters, who actually built the largest synagogue in Berdichev before the turn of the nineteenth century. His name was worshipped among the faithful of the region and he was a contemporary of that most esteemed and legendary *Chasidic* master, Levi Yitzhak of Berdichev.

It was said of Levi Yitzhak, this "holy one of Berdichev" that his heart was pure. So sublime was his fervor in prayer, so deep was his love of the people of his city, so radiant his holiness that one could question if such a man truly lived at all!

Rabbi Isaacson told stories of Levi Yitzhak; how his words struck fire in the hearts of his generation. How his dancing and song gave them hope and brought them joy. He was a teacher deeply aware of his heritage, a *Talmudic* scholar, to say nothing of his knowledge of mysticism, for did he not nightly light a candle and read in Hebrew from the secret work, the *Kaballah*?

Many of Rabbi Isaacson's best traits were passed on to his favorite great grandson Reb Levi of Berdichev. Many *Chasids*, knowing his esteemed heritage and reputation, came to the Reb for wisdom, blessings and shelter. They were never turned away. He was a most compassionate man. Yet Ester alone believed that next to his love of G-d, blessed be He, her father reserved his most special attention for his only daughter.

"You spoil me, Papa," she would often teased him, waiting for a smile to part his heavy black beard and moustache. "I am so proud to be your daughter, but if you love me too much, how will you have enough for Mama and Barak?"

Reb Levi would laugh and put his hands across his ears. "Do you know, little one, that the intense longing of a parent for a child is spoken of in the *Talmud*? We are instructed to desire *banim*[26], for they build the structure of the family as well as the community."

Ester remembered her *Talmud* teachings also. "But, Papa, it also says in Talmud "happy is he whose children are sons."

Reb Levi made an astonished face. "What? Only because females require careful guarding. A father's love is for his children, and their love is for their children. It is written. My Ester, my love for you grows greater each day! Come, Ester, and give Papa a hug!"

These precious memories of her father stirred Ester's heart this day four decades later, as she foraged through the ravaged, forgotten cemetery. We are separated from life by only a breath, Papa, Ester thought. Somewhere in this garden of the dead was their memorial stone. The bodies themselves lay with thousands of others in the bloody, hastily dug trenches in a field to the north, near the airport where the paved road to the village Romanovka began.

She moved on past other tombstones. The lush growth of trees and vines were strangling. It was like a jungle. Time, neglect and mildew had worn away many Hebrew and Slavic names, making identification very difficult. Except for Zych the Romany, the Gypsy dead were not here. Their bodies lay beneath unfenced ground along the wide, free hills of the Ukrainian Steppes to the west and south, wherever possible facing Romania, their former home.

None of the nationalistic Ukrainian citizens were buried here, either. Their hatred of Jews, Russians, Poles and Communists made them overwhelmingly choose the state cemetery on Boklovna Street. Ukrainians resented the overwhelming network of Jewish traders and businessmen, many of who had derived family wealth from business deals with the Polish in years past. Berdichev, beneath the veneer of daily commerce among its thousands of busy residents, was essentially a town divided. Then there were the *Politzei*.

After the first six months of the 1919 invasion some Ukrainian men who were once Red Army soldiers were treated by the Wehrmacht as prisoners of war. They were a continuing and constant threat to Jews, Gypsies and Slavs because they were slavish servants of the Russian local police and later the German *Wehrmacht*. These soldiers passionately hated Jews. They sought to ambush the *Chasidic* community by any means possible. They were loyal to the Red Army and had no thought for the lives and property of anyone. The *Wehrmacht*, seeing their advantage, armed and paid these malcontents and enlisted them as auxiliary police, or *Politzei*. They were issued white armbands and special peaked hats, then turned loose to patrol the streets like avenging hunters. When the German army came to town it was the *Politzei* who herded Jews into the makeshift ghetto in the old market section and followed orders to weaken and starve them. They then invaded the ghetto at will as thieves and rapists. When the Jews were later marched to the pits outside town it was the *Politzei* who identified them, rounded them up and who, in the massacres of 1941, were in charge of making sure no one survived.

This day in 1985 Ester again walked among these old, massive trees that shaded so many dead. Frightening memories rushed upon her. She remembered the beatings of old men and women by the Russian police, commonplace in the bazaar while she shopped for her family's supper. As a child she would run into the forest to escape, or to this very cemetery where she hid behind the ancient stones. She was like the hope of the people themselves, sometimes dark and brooding yet somehow optimistic, wanting only to live in peace; to become dead to the misery of those memories. But when the massacres were finished and the German army had marched east in September of 1941 — their brutal acts of carnage buried in blood-sogged earth, Ester agonized that perhaps a beating or murder that she had witnessed might have been thwarted by her bold interference. She knew Papa would have ignored his own mortality and run to the rescue if he had been in her place. Should she have done the same? If I had been brave, she wondered, looking at the mass of headstones and half-dug graves, could I have made a difference? These thoughts made her stop and take new stock of past actions. Can one always know good from evil?

Ester remembered suddenly another time of sorrow in her family. Near her 17th birthday in 1936, several of the Nuremburg Laws were passed against Germany's Jews. All, including those of one-quarter Jewish extraction were deprived of rights of citizenship. Intermarriage with Jews was strictly forbidden. This meant the Jewish people were now being defined by their bloodline and/or their religious and cultural traditions. Stories of Jews being beaten, humiliated, robbed and thrown into concentration camps leaked into newspapers and broadcasts. Reb Levi reacted to this news with intense pain.

"That could be us before long," Reb Levi agonized when he heard of the laws. These German Jews are left with no alternative but to leave their country. Where will they go? Who wants them?"

"And they are leaving their possessions behind for the Germans to confiscate," Anna added. "We are hated by our own government, Levi. And what will Stalin do? Where will we go? We must pray for these poor people. Ester, Barak, come and let us all ask the Eternal One to be merciful. Your father will lead us in prayer."

Fear of capture and death had come to haunt every Jew in Berdichev, except perhaps Barak, who wanted now to invade Germany with his friends and lead the Jewish population on an exodus to Israel via the Black Sea. Ester listened just to be polite, but eventually agreed to consider it if her Papa would order it. Talk of capture and concentration camps seemed to her far away and completely unreal. As a girl she would have determined not to think about it further, but now as a young woman aware that she and her family could be murdered, she began to be more than a little frightened.

---

[22] Romanian Gypsies
[23] "Here lies..."

[24] "May her/his soul be bound in the bond of eternal life"
[25] A righteous person; one with more good deeds than sins on his or her record
[26] Daughters

And thine eye shall not pity; but life shall go for life, eye for eye, tooth for tooth, hand for hand, foot for foot.

— Deuteronomy 19:21

3 — Innocence Stands As Witness

The fall breeze seemed to echo old Hebrew melodies as Ester crawled on hands and knees through the bunched grass reading the tombstones. White dogwood blossoms drifted down upon the stones like quiet snow. She felt the dead were there with her as she pushed through this forgotten land of cold finality. Crawling around the cemetery underbrush seemed to be the safest way of avoiding more falls, so Ester crept through the tangles of bushes and around the many mossy reminders of loss, searching for the marker with the inscription she had come from another country to find. Some of the stones were so close together Ester scraped her knees trying to squeeze through the maze. Slime attached itself to her jeans. Sounds of scurrying in the brushy grass made her wince and catch her breath. She hadn't thought this task would be unnerving. Now she cursed herself for refusing her husband's offered help.

Thinking back, Ester wished she could have prepared for what was soon to befall the townspeople in 1941. In her mind the rifle shots were around her again and panic enveloped her. Here another memory assaulted her. A scarred, broken gravestone coldly noted the deaths of Ferga and Yankel Shapiro, the *motl*[27], married forty years and parents of ten children. Before the Nazi occupation in Berdichev in 1941 Yankel was a dedicated *Chasid* and one of her family's dearest friends. He was irrepressibly happy and comical. It would be wrong to say that the *Chasidic* men of Berdichev did not appreciate his happy romps up and down Lenin Street in the early morning hours after prayer meetings, but many, including Reb Levi, thought him somewhat crazy. They worried he was making the devout *Chasids* look like fools. Yankel would shrug it off.

"Live life to the fullest", he said. "Eat *strudel* and be happy, for the love of G-d is in our souls!"

Yankel charmed the women and children with his antics. He loved to dance in the streets and sing Yiddish folk songs with a boisterous voice. When it rained or snowed, Yankel would waltz in it alone or with Ferga if he could grab her. Ferga just accepted her husband's easygoing behavior.

Yankel remained positive. His old funny fur cap he wore backwards. It bounced up and down while he played tunes on his rusty mouth harp.

"The Eternal One blesses us with His tears of joy, his holy white tears!"

Ferga was a quiet woman given to much worry over her children who were often taunted at school because they lived such a different lifestyle, spoke an ancient, odd language and called themselves Jews. Ferga was the town's finest maker of cheese *strudel*. She usually won the Berdichev baking contest. The exhibit was held in the city's only *rynok*[28] district. Here many vendors sold a great variety of articles including antique buttons and other paraphernalia, coins from the Austro-Hungarian empire, silverware, miniature silver and gold crosses that Orthodox women wore on their necks. Ferga joined the produce farmers at their stands. They greeted each other in joy as they laid out their wares: potatoes, carrots, beets, herbs of parsley and dill. In summer, there were red and black currants on the stem, sweet cherries (*chereshnya*) and on. Ferga taught Ester's mother that exacting and tasty art. How they enjoyed those delicious desserts! But after the Germans came to Berdichev, everything changed. Yankel seemed to never realize that his madcap actions had also drawn the attention of the Ukrainian *Polizei*.

One bright morning in August 1938, Yankel's high voice was heard at Reb Levi's door.

"Ester, Ester, a *bissel*[29] of *strudel* have I for the birthday girl and Reb Levi's family!"

Ester rushed from her room to the door of their small dark apartment and in danced *motl* Yankel with a fragrant pan of cheese *strudel*.

"Welcome, Yankel, Mama says to just set the pan down. She has something also to bring for Ferga."

Yankel tipped his hat onto his long, humped nose and bowed ceremoniously.

"*Mazeltov*, a happy birthday to you, your 19th year."

He looked at her quizzically, his brow furrowed beneath the backwards cap. For a moment he said nothing, then put his hands into the air with a flourish. Yankel spoke in Yiddish whenever possible, as did most *Chasidic* Jews in Berdichev, though Russian was the then authorized language.

"Ester, my friend, when will you marry? Go find your husband-to-be and start having babies or your body will dry up!"

Ester blushed, her cheeks burned. Yankel had read her thoughts. They were filled with dreams of marriage. Instead of answering Yankel she nervously picked up a *strudel* and began to eat. Yankel laughed. Reb Levi came into the room carrying a large package of fabric.

"For Ferga," he said, pushing it at Yankel, who promptly bowed and said "*Tov m'od, tov m'od*[30], my *tzaddik*."

"*Shalom*, Yankeleh, how are you? I see you have brought *strudel* for my Ester's birthday. May you and your family be blessed of G-d for your *mitzvot*."

"Thank you, Reb Levi. If I am not mistaken, Ester is today a woman of nineteen years. May she marry soon and start having babies, or Ferga and I will loan her our three youngest to practice on!"

Yankel thought this idea so funny he began to titter, exposing brown teeth speckled with cheese. Reb Levi obliged Yankel a grin. He threw Ester a long loving look.

"Yankeleh, my friend, your ten children are a blessing unto the Holy One Himself Who is Father of us all. He will send your children into the world soon enough to make their fortunes. Give this child her due, my friend. Ester will marry for sure. Is that right, my *madele*, my girl?"

Ester blushed again. "There is no one to marry, Papa."

"Whenever he comes to you it will be too soon, Ester. I am jealous of losing you to a husband and lots of babies."

But his eyes were full of mirth as he turned to Yankel and beckoned him to the door.

"Let me walk with you home, Yankeleh. We will say hello to Ferga and your ten children and perhaps they will accept a blessing of love."

Yankel bid Ester *shalom* and they left the cottage to walk the half-mile to his home. As they turned the corner and passed Yigdael Schlomo's haberdashery, two Russian *Politzei* were talking across the street. Reb Levi immediately grabbed Yankel's arm and whispered to him,

"Yankel, the *Politzei*! Now do nothing to attract their attention or they will be on us like dogs!"

Yankel received the information with dumb goodwill and smiled in accord. He was so happy Reb Levi was with him that he raised his feet and took larger steps. Reb Levi immediately tightened his grip on Yankel's arm and sought to pull him out of the street and into the shadow of the stores. Yankel began to hum a Jewish song in a voice high and soft voice and out of key. He labored to find the tune as the two moved along. As they neared the *Politzei* turned toward the pair of Jewish men walking toward them and, noting their *yarmulkes,* hailed them to stop immediately.

"My G-d in Heaven, Yankel, they want to harass us. If we turn around, they'll run after us. Say nothing. These men have the souls of murderers, may the Eternal One take mercy on them."

Yankel saw the guns on the policemen's hips and suddenly realized his situation. He whispered,

"I'm scared, Reb Levi. You will guide me. My wife, my children! Are we going to be killed here? Will these mongrels follow us home?"

But Reb Levi was already in muttered prayer as the pair slowly approached the *Politzei.*

One of the policemen stuck out his palm and halted the travelers.

"*Kuda vy, Yevrei?*"[31] Why are you on the streets?" he demanded loudly. He reached for his holster, withdrawing slowly a large black revolver. He cocked it and pointed it at Yankel.

Yankel tittered in fear but said nothing. His mouth began to emit saliva. Reb Levi smiled accommodatingly, trying not to show concern before his enemies.

"We are taking a walk in the afternoon, that is all. There is no law against two friends walking, is there?"

"None at the moment, but that again depends on whether we   believe you, and I do not believe you." He looked menacingly at Yankel, whose eyes were on the ground, his mouth emitting saliva from its corners.

"You Jews, you are dirt, you are the reason for our wars. Lovers of the Polish dogs! You think you can make all the money in Russia? You are nothing! Because of you *Chasids* we Ukrainians were captured. You thought your Rada (transitional) government would give you special privileges. You don't deserve anything but death. Soon you will all be murdered!"

Yankel began to whimper. Reb Levi gripped his arm tighter and shook him. He said nothing, hoping for a chance to negotiate their passage to Yankel's home. The second policeman looked at Levi with hatred. His eyes reminded Reb Levi of a hawk swooping down upon his prey. Unleashing his revolver from its holster he pointed it directly at Reb Levi's nose.

"Get down, filthy Jews. Down on your hands and knees. Take off your stupid little hats."

His arm shot out and smacked Reb Levi to the ground. Yankel fell with him, huddling in fear. Saliva poured from his trembling mouth. Reb Levi raised himself to his knees. Later he told Anna and Ester that he felt no anger rushing through his blood but only surprise and sorrow. This kept him from confronting his accusers. He took off his black silk *yarmulke* his head and held it near his breast. Yankel followed suit.

Eternal G-d, Reb Levi prayed in his heart, *if it is Thy will, we ask Thee to preserve us from these madmen. We are humble servants, we pray to be charitable to all and Thou knows we are not new to suffering, O G-d in Heaven, but these men are from Gehinnom, so we must humbly pray for salvation.*

The policeman shouted, "Sweep the street with your stupid hat, you stinking Jews. Clean up the filth until we tell you to stop. You are now the official street sweepers of Berdichev!"

Both policemen laughed heartily at this pronouncement, their guns remaining leveled at the Jews kneeling before them. The first policeman studied them a moment.

"You, Yankel, is it? The *motl*, the town idiot? See that dog dung? Go and clean it up with your silk hat. If you refuse, you will eat it! We will teach you damned *Chasids* to obey the *Politzei*."

Yankel, trying not to cower, crushed his *yarmulke* to his heart and kissed it. He began to mutter unconnected words punctuated with strange gurgles that resembled choking sounds. But Reb Levi, knowing his fate was in G-d's hands, showed no fear. He looked up at his accusers, from one face to the other, then slowly proceeded to attend his task. Yankel watched him nervously and did the same. Trembling all over he crawled after Reb Levi up the cobbled street, scattering the pebbles and rubbing out the dirt of horse droppings with his silk *yarmulke*. Shopkeepers and their customer peering out of shops to watch moved quickly away to avoid being noticed. Many of them were members of Reb Levi's congregation.

"Look at Reb Levi and Yankel out there, the frightened onlookers said to each other. "Any day, that could be us." Then their gaze changed to amazement, for the two *Chasids* on their knees sweeping the street with their *yarmulkes* had begun to sing *Havenu Shalom*

Aleichem[32] while *Politzei* guns were still levelled upon their backs.

In the haberdashery, Michel Steinerson sent a non-Jewish seamstress secretly to Reb Levi's home to inform and comfort Anna until Reb Levi should return. Anna then went with the woman to Yankel's home.

The moon had risen high when Reb Levi and Yankel, the motl were allowed to leave the street, each heading for his own home and family. Ester spent that day deep in prayer with her mother and brother, though it was very hard to restrain Barak from going after his father. Reb Levi, his only suit ruined, knees smeared with blood and street grime, walked calmly into their apartment and smiled tiredly at everyone. Anna took his hands, bleeding and torn, in her own. Ester hugged him and cried with relief. Barak had blood in his eyes and a very red face. He shook his Papa's hand, then stalked outside. Ester begged him not to go after the *Politizei*. It was the worst birthday she ever had.

～

Who can speak for those who lie in the soft mother Earth, their heads upon the pillow of Heaven? Much time had passed and this day also was hastening. The cold dampness of the cemetery ground made Ester's body ache. She trembled as she scrambled to find her parents' burial stone. She and Barak had the memorial made twenty years previous but she'd not yet seen it. Remembering his recent letter giving directions, she hastened to a coordinate just south of the rear of the cemetery, 30 meters by 100 meters, near the edge of the brick and concrete mausoleum of Levi Isaac of Berdichev that faced Lenin Street. Its fancy grey and white walls supported a green pointed roof. Standing before the imposing structure, Ester saw that the memorial was still relatively clean. Some of the wild brush had been cleared away so the inscription could be read. Ester stood quietly on the consecrated earth where lay two of the most famous *rabbis* in all Ukraine; Ish-Horowitz and Ze'ev of Zhitomir. Her beloved Papa's memorial shared hallowed ground with these revered sages of Israel.

Finally, toward the right corner of the cemetery, she saw it, the only clearly designated marker in the group. The shapes of these memorials were unusual; oblong stones with rounded tops and raised backs. They resembled the heads of women wearing long scarves trailing the dirt behind them. Their marble faces were flat. The headstones were arranged in rows at the south end of the mortuary, like a mute audience of wives in silent perpetual mourning for their men. Ester knelt to read the inscription written in Hebrew.

Peh-Nun

Reb Moshe Dovid Levi, ben Moshe Levi, ha-Levite

Nun-Peh 22 Elul 5701

Anna Rubinovna bat Asher Marvin Rubenstein, ha-Rav

Nun-Peh 22 Elul 5701

Tehe nishmatah tzerurah bitzror hachayim

Ester caressed the stone. She let her fingers trace the letters of her mother's name and felt her comforting presence. Remembered smells of chicken soup, the sour, lingering odor of molasses in *chyorny khleb* (black bread) made with rye and wheat. These mingled with the perfume her mother wore: Reb Levi had bought his beloved a tiny bottle of it from St. Petersburg when they courted. Ester imagined the comfort they must have been to each other during their final moments in the synagogue pyre. She felt their spirits were at peace, but she could not keep hot tears from falling upon the cold stones. Her fingers moved across the inscription to her father's name and she imagined him again standing before her in *tallis* and *tefillin*. On his bowed head was the white *yarmulke* he wore except to sleep. Reb Levi never cared in life that his only good suit was too small for his small, portly frame. He would rather eat his fill of Ferga's *strudel* and Anna's *challah* than watch his weight. Mama said her husband resembled a chubby angel of light come to visit the earth in its direst time of need.

Lovingly, Ester cleaned the accumulated of years of dirt from the stone. Tears came profusely. She wished her brother were with her now to share with him her memory of their Papa's fervent songs praising G-d as he danced and swayed in ecstasy of devotion. The memory of his bushy beard, his laugh of delight when Mama tickled it, the sound of his soothing voice as he comforted them in times of trouble, these things she cherished. She thought of the many blessings she and Barak had received beneath his hands. *Papa, here is your madele, come to do your final bidding, to restore a precious inheritance to synagogue!*

Next to Ester's parents' stone a smaller one caught her attention. It was inscribed simply,

Zych the Romany

Beloved Friend and Gabbai.

A Chasid in his heart

Barak had ordered this memorial as well. He and Zych had

been good friends. The Gypsy was in synagogue with Reb Levi and Anna Rubinovka when they were trapped by German soldiers that fateful day.

Zych had been taller by half a foot than Reb Levi, as were Yankel and many of the men of the congregation. But Reb Levi did not worry for his lack of height. He was too absorbed in reading his *Talmud Torah*, the Prophets or the Psalms. His black-rimmed glasses, which he usually forgot to lower from his forehead while he read, were his only adornment. He had to read everything up close to his broad nose. Anna would slip a note into his scriptures to remind him of daily things, for his concentration was so great upon the words of the sages that the world around him seemed not to exist.

Ester sat a long time before the memorials. How she missed her family and the many friends and neighbors whose lives were taken through senseless atrocity! All these years of silence . . . Yet tears still came as memories — pushed aside through years of trying not to feel that pain — seemed now to rise out of the names etched in stone. Were the dead calling out to her to be heard? For justice? She felt increasingly that they desired a chance to speak to the world in their own behalf.

Please, G-d, help me now. Lend me Thy strength to finish my mission among these many dead who cry out for justice. Lead me to the place where Papa's treasure lies. And let those who must speak out from the dead be heard!

In the silence of the cemetery, bowed and fixed in prayer, Ester seemed a living testament to that human hope that is born of grief, a hope of sure redemption.

---

[27] Fool
[28] Open bazaar
[29] A little bit
[30] "Very good, very good"
[31] "Where are you going, Jews?"
[32] "Heaven's peace be upon you"

Journal of the Dead — Rosalia

I am Rosalia, a Jew from Vilna, Poland. My family lived there in Berdichev from 1902to 1941. We were a small but loving family who met every night for a dinner of *matzoh*[33,] carp and vegetables and we were happy until the German army invaded Berdichev in 1941.

We had many happy times in Berdichev. We trafficked with the other Jews there. Every Friday night we would hold *Shabbat* services and come home from the *Beit ha'Midrash* synagogue with happy smiles in the loving arms of one another. My father sang in this synagogue and my mother's voice was rich, also. I was young but very wise for my age. My brother, Zevi, was only 6. He loved his father and wanted to be like him, to inherit the land and work it with love and care. My mother was fifty. My father was a farmer who loved his land and his wife and children.

I was only 18. I had just started my life. I was good at sewing and all needlework. The Russian and Ukrainian neighbors came in and pilfered everything from us. They hated the Jews and did all they could to ruffle us and scare us intro compliance with them. They would follow us home and taunt us:

"Jew, hated Jew. We want to be rid of you."

We were the descendants of *rabbis*, of chieftains in our town who owned the businesses and made the rules, kept the money and made life generally bearable for the many who worked with them. They were of great number in Berdichev. They were close keepers of everything valuable and did not like to share with non-Jews. These prideful rich Jews earned a reputation for hatred of non-Jews who eventually wanted them dead.

~

We were eating dinner the night after the German army arrived in town. They had come in during festivals and were playing the instruments of those in the town, showing how smart they could be. That night they entered the homes of many people, pretending to be friendly, then asking people outside. They were herded into the forest. There they were shot in the back of the neck. In the nighttime they came for me and my father and mother. My brother escaped and lived until the actual wartime when he enlisted as a soldier and was killed in the war.

They raped my grandmother, who was ninety then. I was younger and married to a gentleman farmer. We had very little to eat at that time, living on roots and berries, potatoes and home grown things which we hid in the cellar as soon as the plants told us the ground had given us fruit and we would steal it away during the night so the German soldiers couldn't claim we were using our own food to sustain ourselves.

But we were cut down in the pits that were dug by the Germans in a way so terrible that the blood of that day still rises in my nostrils, and though I am now alive in a spiritual way, we mourn for the death and destruction of that time. My parents and I were taken to the forest and mother watched as my father was bound and stripped and shot in the back of the head. She was next and she screamed and held me and both of us fell into the pit to be with our father. We were shot at that time. We were all murdered by the German army.

---

[33] Unleavened cracker

"Be a lover of your fellow-creatures."

4 — The Land of Havilah

July 12, 1939

Dearest Anna and Reb Levi,

Shalom Aleichem! I trust my letter finds your family well. Have you received the few shekel notes I sent you? More comes next month, hopefully.

You remember Poland, Reb Levi? I trembled when I read in 1933 of Hitler's goal of "Lebensraum" for the Aryan race. He said: "We want ruthless Germanization." He meant to kill us all off!

Good news from press reports. If you have not already heard. Hitler The Crazy One signed a non-aggression pact and trade agreement to exchange food and raw material supplies with the Soviet Union! At long last we Jews of Zhitomir feel hopeful! We've been so worried — Hitler's hatred of us — but seemingly he has thought better and doesn't want to butcher us!

Freedom is the cry, now, my friend. The way to freedom is to alert the people to the evil that is being worked upon them. We must inspire them to act!

I am writing articles calling for an independent Ukraine. Many are taking up the cry. There is hope here and promise, too. I hope to visit you soon with more news.

Your rebellious friend,
Avram Weitzmann of Zhitomir

Avram was the unmarried 24 year-old son of Anna Rubinovka's school friend, Khana Ostrovskii. He had moved to the growing city of Zhitomir, east of Lvov, to find more opportunities for scholarship among the Jewish population there. Ukraine at that time held one and one-half million Jews, almost five percent of all the Jews in Russia. They were employed in hundreds of trades. Their families had toiled for more than four hundred years in this agriculturally fertile and accessible region of the Volhynia. Avram also visited Berdichev on occasion to speak to the workers and storeowners. He was fast becoming well known in the towns along the Steppes.

When Ester's parents read Avram's letter, their faces paled.

Reb Levi was solemn for a moment. He looked at his wife and asked, almost in a whisper,

"Do you think Avram is right? Will they come here?"

Anna's eyes began to fill. "Moshe, they can come here any day they choose." She looked up at him with wide eyes, spreading out her arms in a kind of surrender.

"What defense do we have against that kind of thinking, that kind of hatred?"

They looked at Ester and at Barak who was eager to speak, but for the moment held his peace. Reb Levi turned the letter over and over in his hands.

"He has not said we are in trouble. Why would Hitler come here? He would go to Leningrad, to Moscow. We have no indication he wants to fight the Red Army. Hasn't he made a peace agreement with Stalin? Why would he want little Berdichev?"

Anna was silent. She rose from her chair by the small furnace and went to the window that looked out over other apartments. Glimpses of a graying sky above the tops of the apartment building reminded her of the coming night.

"We are truly defenseless, Moshe," she intoned softly. "Against the Russians, the Germans, against the world outside this door. We are Jews... I worry for myself only a little, you know, Moshe. But for you, for our children, I am already afraid."

She could not supress a small sob. Reb Levi went to her. He took her in his arms and rocked her gently. Ester had never heard her parents speak like this. Tears came to her eyes. She looked at Barak for help but his face was angry, his eyes full of emotion.

"We are not defenseless, Mama," he said loudly with such emotion that Reb Levi started.

"We can fight back. I know a way, People in the Resistance, they believe in freedom. They are the underground of Ukraine's lost freedoms! Papa, I joined them a week ago. I can protect us now, do you see? I'll fight! Against the Russians, against the murdering Germans, against anyone. I —".

Reb Levi turned to face his son.

"What are you saying, Barak? You have joined the Partisans? You must stop immediately! Those men are mercenaries, murderers, criminals. They live in hiding like wolves, The Russians are always hunting them. Barak, please, you will be killed doing such a dangerous thing!"

Anna sank heavily on the wooden bench and moaned.

Barak insisted. "Papa, I am not a killer but a watchman, a go-between. We fight for the sake of Jewish honor, to avenge the Russian *pogroms*. The Partisans will be your rescuers when the Germans attack. I know what I'm doing. Tomorrow, I go north to join with them."

Barak went to his mother and took her limp hands in his own. Reb Levi sat motionless.

"Mama, please understand,'" he implored. "We must do something. Our government is evil. Why, on the street the *Politzei* harass us. Remember how they treated Papa and Yankel?"

Barak looked at his father, whose face was full of grief.

"We have to take action, Papa. We have to know what they're planning to do to us so we can be ready. Partisan intelligence has informed our soldiers that the German army will soon invade Russia. We must now leave Berdichev. Even Avram agrees."

Reb Levi stood and crossed his arms. He paced the bare old wood floor.

"No, Barak, my son. We cannot leave our home. We will stand our ground here. I am a *chazzen*, I am depended upon as the leader of the *Chasidim* until *Rabbi* Levine returns again from Kiev. Also, Barak, we are in business. How can we pack up and walk away from our obligations to our dead? It is out of the question. Please, my son, give up this Resistance nonsense!"

But Barak would not listen. "Papa. It *is* truth. Those who stay here will be murdered! Do you hear me?!"

He turned and stomped out of the apartment into the coming darkness of evening. Anna was sighing. Reb Levi's sad eyes fixed upon the door his son had shut angrily behind him. Many minutes passed before he read Avram's note again. He threw it aside. Tears flooded his face.

"My son, my son. I pray for my son, for his young impulsive life. May our G-d in Heaven keep a watch over him and protect him in his madness. Resistance? Partisans? How can such a thing in happen in Berdichev?"

"But Moshe, if he is right, what?" came Anna's soft voice. "What will happen to us? Can it hurt to have defenders?"

Reb Levi walked around the room slowly, his hands clasped behind his back. Finally he said,

"No, I won't believe those monsters will come here. Anna, we will remain here and serve G-d. You are right, we have no real defenses against those crazy men, so we will carry on and bury our dead. G-d is in charge, not the Germans. The Eternal One has promised that we will know a time of peace and that the Jews will be redeemed as a people. It is so, the prophets have predicted. G-d Himself will liberate the captive and resurrect the dead."

But how and when this was to take place, no one could say, though they wanted fiercely to believe it. Ester rose unnoticed and walked silently from the room, passing a small mirror nailed to one of the walls. She tried to look past herself, to see into the future, but she could not. That night she lay awake wondering where Barak had gone and fearing for the first time that they would all hear the measured tromp of *Nazi* boots on the street below. She made a vow to remain with her parents at all costs but she could not shrug off this new feeling of dread. What if they were attacked? What if the town was occupied by German forces? Where could they hide? How much success could a few Resistance soldiers expect to have against an army? We should move, she concluded, and right away. Her brother had spoken truth. She felt more than ever that the warnings he gave were going to come to pass.

The next morning Ester implored her father to change his mind, but Reb Levi would not be moved.

~

It was February 1941. Ester arose this day with new anticipation. She was to meet Avram who was coming from Zhitomir for a short visit. She had not seen him in several years. The weather was uncommonly warm for winter. It was giving way to spring and Ester delighted in the new buds of the fruit-bearing shrubs. Wild grasses grew in vacant lots that dotted the town, lending a park-like atmosphere. Linden and chestnut trees lined many of the roads and in private gardens the citizens were talking of last fall's crop of apples and this spring's planting of carrots, squash and beans. The sun shone gloriously through billowy clouds across the Steppes and upon Ester as she walked down Reenok Street to the market Bazaar with Rakhel, her good friend from Hebrew school.

Rakhel and Ester often met to shop together at the many informally set up stores in town. They spoke of finding the "perfect one" to marry. Rakhel was a milliner's daughter. Her mother had died of liver disease during the famine of 1932. She lived with her father and his parents in a beautiful home on Chudnovskaya Street. Rakhel's father tried to make up for the loss of her mother by dressing her in fine clothes, even to walk in the market or meander through the park. But Rakhel's passion was her garden. Every year it boasted fragrant peppermint plants, plenty of azaleas, rose bushes and currants. Borders of colorful pansies lined the walkway to her front door.

This market day Ester's list included cabbages, *kasha* (buckwheat groats), potatoes, eggs and bread. Street vendors selling *shaslik*[34] were busy and the pungent aroma of frying lamb filled the cool air. Women stood at tables on the roadside assembling sandwiches and pastries for eager shoppers waiting in line to order meat at vendor stands. Ester loved the happy strains of a lively Ukrainian melody that resonated from accordions played by street musicians, most of whom were ethnic Ukrainians. Many shoppers were milling around a small blue vehicle hooked to a reclaimed railroad tanker parked off to one side, on which the word *KVAS*[35] was painted in yellow. A woman sitting in front of the tanker was selling the barley based drink through the tanker's spout and tap.

They were near the buying booths now. People stood in long queues calling out their orders in Russian, Ukrainian, Polish and Yiddish. As they burrowed their way through the noisy crowd of people, horses and other farm animals, a well-groomed young man in a gray overcoat tripped over a woman's shopping cart. He dropped his parcel. She shouted at him in very basic Russian and hastily pulled her cart away. He looked up sheepishly at Ester and their eyes caught. Ester noticed his were soft but full of energy. She was struck in that moment by his good looks; his dark hair and light skin. His mouth, full and smiling, appealed to her. He seemed somehow familiar. Then she realized she was looking at Avram.

"I'm sorry," he shouted after the woman, but she was already lost in the crowd. He rose to his feet and shrugged with a smile. Ester sensed he was a gentle soul. She and Rakhel laughed and he joined in as he retrieved his package.

"I love Berdichev's rye bread," he shouted to the girls over the din. "I take it home to Zhitomir tomorrow. Everyone there loves it, too." He looked at Ester again, grinning broadly. She found herself smiling back at him.

"Ester, Ester, how good to see you again! I have been looking for you since I arrived here on the train an hour ago."

He bowed slightly and extended his hand to her and then to Rakhel. His smile was disarming. Rakhel blushed furiously. Ester made the introductions.

"I'm afraid I'm the reason for our lateness," Rakhel demurred. "I am so glad to meet you. Ester has told me about your letters, Avram. Your cause is a true one."

"Yes, *spasibo*[36]. I am teaching Russian history to the youth of Zhitomir. But whenever I can do so, I print articles and leaflets in support of a free Ukraine. Everyone in Russia wants freedom from tyranny, is it not so? Say, let's get out of this crowd, can we?" He took Ester's hand as they moved through the milling crowd.

Soon they found a quieter spot at a table. As they reminisced, Ester felt a new kinship with this intense, well-spoken man. Rakhel was eager to tell him all about herself, but Ester noticed that while Rakhel spoke, Avram's eyes spoke to Ester. She remembered him as being shorter than herself, but he'd grown quite tall. His countenance, once full of teasing fun, had become serious. Worries about Germany's invasion into Ukraine are probably responsible for that, she thought.

"Avram, what concerns you most about the threats of war in Ukraine?" she asked.

"I fear, as do many Ukrainians, that Germany is close to war with us, but that Stalin will do nothing. He trusts the treaty of peace that was made between them. He does not know that Hitler wants to conquer the world, but many citizens know it!"

"Yes, Barak, too, is deeply concerned about this problem, and our parents fear the worst may be coming, but we hold onto the hope that Hitler will not break that treaty. Oh, Avram. How I hope that peace can be kept in our country."

They spoke a long time. Avram made many convincing arguments. At these times, his eyes fixed upon Ester and his hand touched her own. It was as if they were alone in the world together.

By the time they had finished their conversations and shopping, Ester knew that Avram was someone she wanted to know better. Rakhel liked him, too, but with reservation. Later, when they spoke again, Rakhel confided in her friend.

"He lives a dangerous life, Ester, printing articles against Stalin. He is brave but perhaps also foolish, you think? Oh, well. A husband with millions of *shekels* and a *dacha*[37] on the Don. A life of ease, yes?"

They laughed at that. Their chances of marrying above their educational or social status were slim, especially for Jewish women. Further, any Jewish daughter who married outside her religion could be assured of swift Jewish justice: family ostracism, rending of garments and often a serious mock funeral for the traitor. A Jewish female who chose a Gentile husband was cut off from her family and community in shame. Jewish men who chose Gentile women did not fare much better and were often ostracized in their community, depending upon their families' professional and financial status. Typically, young women were promised by their fathers to families of well-situated shopkeepers or property owners. Many of these, after 1932, were no longer prosperous, but were nonetheless Jews. These arrangement were worked out with great care years before a woman's marriageable age of 16, or upon her *bat mitzvah*[38]. Reb Levi, however, did not in his heart agree with the age-old custom of marriage brokering. He believed that a woman should let her heart lead her to the husband the Eternal One had chosen for her, even if the man chosen was a non-Jew, (though he prayed mightily (and secretly) that his future son-in-law would be a Jew descended from *Chasidic rabbis*).

Avram didn't fit the pattern. He was not a *Chasid*. He thought their rites distracting and silly. He preferred instead to attend a small Conservative congregation in Zhitomir where worship was sedate.

"With respect to your father, Ester, the *Chasids* think they can dance to God's palace in Heaven," he told Ester. "The truth is, seriousness is more pleasing to the Holy One. They allow Him to concentrate on the thoughts of the heart without distraction."

"But does not the Eternal One love all of us," Ester asked? "If we come before him in song and dance, is He not well entertained by his lively children?" She laughed delightedly, loving his strong opinions. Avram frowned and shrugged. He looked very serious until Ester took his hand in hers and said,

"Avram, maybe you are a better music critic than a dancer?"

Transportation to Berdichev was not easy for Avram and was often a problem. Avram had no car or horse, so he would buy a ride with merchants coming to the Bazaar or ride the train when he could manage to sell some of his pamphlets. He distributed his articles and flyers wherever he went, asking a few *shekels* for the paper on political freedom. He was often asked to speak at rallies in Zhitomir where he was already well known. Whenever Avram could come to Berdichev he visited Ester. They walked in the woods, feeling close and happy. Evenings they took supper with her parents. Parting became quite difficult. After several meetings they knew that love had blessed them. How difficult it was to say good night!

During family evenings over suppers of cabbage, corn and *challah* egg bread, Avram shared with Ester's family many current issues. He was a well-respected member of several organizations formed to protect farmers, craftsmen and intellectuals, Reb Levi then related their discussion to the *Chasidic* council of elders.

The night was cool. Following his discussion with Reb Levi, Avram and Ester sat on the steps outside her apartment and Avram told her of his family. Leonid, his father, had married young and left the family home in Lvov when he was his son's age, to join the fight against Tsar Nicholas in the March 1917 Revolution. When in November of that year the Communists seized power the Russian empire was divided. Soon after, the Ukrainian National Republic was formed. Leonid was of Polish birth. He had inherited land and some wealth from his father. Being a man of strong principle he hated Lenin's so-called reforms. When Joseph Stalin came to power in 1924, many people refused to honor his decree of farm collectivization. In 1929, Leonid shot his cattle and burned his fields in protest as did many Ukrainian farmers. He was labeled a *kulak*[39] by the Soviets, arrested and summarily shot as a traitor. His land and wealth ruined, Leonid's wife and son were forcibly moved to a *kolkhoz* collective farm miles from Zhitomir, much against their will. They nearly starved. Between 1932-33, more than seven million Ukrainian peasants perished in their own land from starvation and disease because Stalin controlled the country from seed to soul.

"I was an angry child. I knew before I was 14 the role I must play in life," Avram mused. "By the time I was 19, I had a book full of tracts on freedom."

To make a living for himself and his mother, Avram obtained a grant and began an apprenticeship as a teacher of Russian history. They lived near the school on his small stipend. During the long nights, unable to settle in his mind the misfortunes of his father, Avram continued his articles of protest against the Stalinist regime. By 1940 he'd gained a reputation for fearlessness, but his concern was not for himself.

"Mother was once a strong, vital woman, in love with life. Those Russian murderers took that from her. Whatever they do to me I must endure, but my mother... " Avram's voice broke as he thought of his parents' misfortunes.

Ester tried to change the subject. She told him about Barak's hatred of their Stalinist government and his recent alliance with the Ukrainian Partisan movement.

"Avram, I fear for you. You are so much like my brother. "

"But the history books are filled with lies, Ester. When I became a teacher I promised myself I would always preach truth! Every day I am given lessons to teach from the school administrator. The lessons are filled with lies. Every day my truths infiltrate their lies. I must teach the truth about Lenin and Stalin, even if I am disciplined for it. You know, Stalin sent millions to their deaths in Siberia. He stamped out the artists, the writers — exiled them. His thugs murdered them so truth could not be known. But people forget. Children in school are being fed lies!

"Trotsky, Lenin, Stalin, those pigs ruined our country, destroyed our nation's future. Jews could not speak to each other in Yiddish or Hebrew because Stalin decided that Russian should be the only language! He closed the churches; the synagogues he condemned. My friends and I are printing material to be distributed among the faithful, those who want Ukraine once again to be a free nation. We must tell the truth about these traitors so people will know what they are up against."

"You and Barak agree on many points, Avram," Ester pleaded. "But please, don't fight. We must endure many of the evils thrust upon us. Papa says there will always be those who would kill us. I am afraid for you to speak out… Stalin is a tyrant. He will crush any opposition. My father teaches us to thank the Almighty for what we do have that is good."

"Ester, I cannot believe you are saying this! To endure tyrants? We only invite more evil. I cannot teach lies! I will not be still while tyranny reigns! Your brother fights for revolution. I also plead for it. I know well my enemies. With educated protest, with truth, we can overthrow. My heart tells me — rebel, rebel, fight hard against the evil propaganda! I must teach freedom and self-determination."

They talked on into the night, comparing beliefs and trying to predict the impact of war upon the future of Ukraine. But finally, Ester bid Avram good night. He was to return to Zhitomir the following afternoon with a wealthy furrier who had a shop there and in whose home he would spend this night. Avram smiled at her, gently took her into his arms and held her to him a moment, then slowly kissed her cheeks. Ester had never known a man's touch, but Avram's closeness seemed natural and reassuring. They lingered on, not wanting to separate.

"I will see you again tomorrow, Ester, may I, before I take leave?" He stroked her long hair. Ester felt faint to answer.

"I… I would like that. You are always welcome here, Avram."

Their eyes met shyly. Avram turned slowly toward the street, taking her hand as he did so. He softly kissed her hand before parting.

"Tomorrow," and he was gone. Ester touched her lips to her hand, as if to seal his kiss. She stood as one entranced, feeling the breeze glide across her arms until her mother called her inside.

~

In the quiet of the Jewish cemetery Ester smiled with joy recalling the first weeks of Avram's presence in her life. How magical was that night! He was the answer to her prayers. She was so grateful she could rely on him through their trials together. His strength and courage was desperately needed in those frightening times. She recalled also Avram's first exposure to Reb Levi's *Chasidic* meeting that Saturday morning and found herself laughing out loud…

The rooms in the mortuary were filled with the *Chasidic* men of the congregation this Saturday morning. Avram had agreed to delay his departure to accompany Reb Levi to services and he told Ester of what took place that morning when he saw her next. Women were not allowed at these services, but they would congregate in another room and hold separate prayer services. Ester often attended these.

There were nearly seventy men in attendance. Most wore long black suit coats and black fedoras or fur-fringed hats. The *Torah* scroll cabinet was handcrafted, gift of a member from Kiev. Reb Levi carefully removed the scrolls from their inlaid wooden home and carried them triumphantly but reverently throughout the room. Another member read a *Talmudic* portion on the nature of mankind after which there were numerous questions to answer. This took up a length of time.

"Now I tell you that simple, sincere, intuitive devotion is the best way to experience the Eternal One", said Reb Levi. "Where do we get our joy? It comes only from feeling the presence of the Eternal One. He is holy and he has planted in each of us a spark of His holiness. One can even have this spark in the face of all things evil and corrupt! We must not be distracted from good by evil… Do not forget that purity of heart is more pleasing to G-d than learning."

Avram spoke up.

"Excuse me, Reb Levi, I am a mere visitor to your synagogue, but wherever sadness and loss take place, how can one be joyous? Where is *HaShem*[40] at that time?"

Reb Levi laid out his worn *Torah* and *Talmud* while he spoke, referring to each in turn as he made his point.

"In *Torah Shebsikav*[41] we are given the commandments which our great teacher, Moshe *Rabbeinu* (*Rabbi* Moses) received from *HaShem* on Mount Sinai. Here, in *Shemot*[42] of the *Nevi'im*[43] Moshe spoke with *HaShem* forty days and nights. Upon his descent from the mountain with the two tablets, the skin of his face shone. Aaron and the Israelites were afraid to come near him. He had been with G-d. Now in *Talmud* we read,

'Ye shall be holy, for I, the Lord your G-d, am holy.'

"I ask you, my friends, what is *HaShem's* purpose for creating mankind? Ah, you are right, Zych, my friend. We are to have joy! We are to love one another! *HaShem's* glory is increased by our love for His kingdom and for one another. Our humble teacher and spiritual guide, *Rabbi* Israel ben Eliezer, the *Baal Shem Tov*, may he rest in peace, he knew this. He taught us to express joy through prayer and dancing and singing. Another question?"

Meier Levin spoke up.

"Reb Levi, which is better, to follow always *Talmudic* law or to be swayed by the Holy Spirit, the *Ruach ha-Kodesh*?"

"Why, Meier, how can we be blind to what moves us to action? *Talmud* contains the reasons behind the Law, but the *Ruach ha-Kodesh* is the holy essence of the Eternal One, blessed be He. The *Ruach* gives us enlightenment, comfort, ideas, the wisdom of our G-d of Abraham, Isaac and Jacob. He is the teacher and testifier of our faith. When he speaks to you in that still, soft voice, you must listen! The ear of the Eternal One is close to your heart. He knows your destiny. The *Ruach* is given G-d's message to bring you, to teach you. Meier, read always *Torah* and follow always the *Ruach ha-Kodesh*.

"We are Jews. We love to study *Talmud Torah*, to use our intelligence, to question all things. Our intellect is a gift from the Almighty but our sages and prophets tell us moral responsibility is better. Meier, make sure your body and spirit are operating together!"

Meier laughed with the others. Rev Levi continued in a spirit of goodwill.

"We must pray always, my brothers. Prayer is mystical.

When we show appreciation for the Almighty's creations and praise His holy name in all things, we are clinging to Him, showing that we are unceasingly aware of His Presence. And when we sing and dance — ."

Abruptly, Reb Levi rose from his chair and began to wave his arms back and forth in the air, like a man reaching for clouds. His portly body swayed as he shuffled in jerky rhythm around the room. He motioned for the others to join him, which they did with joy.

"Now we can begin to experience *hislahavus*, a spiritual exultation, as our souls are elevated toward G-d Who reveals our destinies to our hearts. We have but to ask, only to listen."

Reb Levi began softly to sing a letter of the Hebrew alphabet, remaining for a long time on the repetition of one sound, the Hebrew "*d*": *di, di, di,* or *la, la* or even *bim, bam, bim.* Earlier he had prepared Avram for this portion of the meeting by explaining that *Chasids* disregard ritual formalities of prayer, preferring the simplest sounds or words or even whistling, to bring in the spirit of G-d and uplift the soul. The congregation followed their *chazen* in familiar singsong. In a few moments the room seemed to brighten. Reb Levi began to chant other letters in Hebrew: the "L" and "G": *lamed, lamed, lamed, gimel, gimel, gimel.* The men all followed his lead. Hands on hips, they danced to the music of their own sounds, hopping and swaying through the small rooms of the building. Zych the Romany clapped his hands excitedly and swayed in unison with the others. One of his many duties at these functions was to make sure everyone had wine in his cup. This night he had filled each one to the brim.

Avram later related his experiences to Ester. He actually partook in the song and dance and liked it! Even the women in the adjoining room heard the loud chanting sounds and the stomp of men's boots on the wooden floor as their words rose in the air, becoming shouts of unanimous acclamation. Hats were thrown high in the air. They bounced off the ceiling. Wine goblets dipped precariously. Everyone was filled with love and joy — the brotherhood of *Chasids.* Finally, what seemed like hours later, the exhausted congregation enjoyed more wine with cakes. Everyone had communed with G-d and their fellows. The troubles of the moment melted into sweet merriment, and why not? The war for German *lebensraum*[44] was yet four months in the future.

~

Reb Levi was very tired but also exhilarated after the meeting; it was one of the best in recent months. Even Avram was blushing with wine and good cheer. The family had just prepared for supper when there was a heavy knock at the door. It was not yet dark, they were expecting no one. Reb Levi cautiously opened the door. There stood their letter carrier, the Ukrainian Pyotr Smilovich. One of his two sons was a member of the *Politzei*. Smilovich did not like Jews. He handed Reb Levi the letter, nodded curtly and pulled the door shut behind him. The envelope was addressed to Avram in Zhitomir but had been marked for forward to "Berdichev" by a neighbor who that morning had sent it.

May 15, 1941

My friend,

Shalom aleichem on this Shabbat night. I have bad news. Even as the German Foreign Minister flies to Moscow to sign the peace contract with the Soviets, Kiev Radio is broadcasting Hitler's address to a Nazi gathering. He has vowed to crush the Soviet Union! He calls it Operation Barbarossa.

I am worried for all Jews! You should be aware of the plans brewing in Germany! Herr Hitler screams about more "lebensraum" for his so-called "Herenvolk". I fear he means to take over the world. Russia in his path of worldly conquest. It is quite conceivable that this madman may attempt to invade us before it's finished!

Avram! Your leaflets have been noticed by the Politzei here. They want to speak with you! You would be much safer in Kiev. Almost half of the Jews in Ukraine live in only four cities, Kiev being one of them. You'll be better off there than in Zhitomir or Berdichev, Avram. Please consider. It is not be safe for you here anymore.

— Your friend Abe Chudnov, Zhitomir

Avram folded the letter. A grave expression came over his face. He looked at Ester, then at Reb Levi, reading the curiosity in their faces.

"My friend, he is concerned for my welfare," he laughed gently. "Seems I am becoming known as a dissident in Zhitomir."

His tone was light but his eyes belied his concern. Ester took the letter from him and read it. The look in Avram's grey eyes was thoughtful but bore no trace of fear. She grew very worried.

"Avram, if you go back to Zhitomir the *Politzei* will arrest you! Don't you think it would be better to hide here?"

"I cannot hide, Ester. There is much work to continue; I will not give in to fear. Of course, there is also my poor mother. I must be sure she is safe… I will leave for home this afternoon."

Avram took Ester's hand in his. She felt she was falling in love with him. He was so positive in all he did and he seemed old for his twenty-four years of life. She felt a security with him that she'd known only when in her father's presence. But what if trouble lay ahead? Suddenly Ester felt fear in her throat. Barak seemed to have disappeared; now Avram might be caught, beaten or jailed. How would she find him again?

The world was an increasingly dangerous place and it seemed to Ester that peace was no longer possible for anyone.

Years later, here in Berdichev amongst these unlucky ones, Ester recalled that difficult day. So many emotions… They were unsure of everything; the war, their livelihoods, enemy invasion, their future as lovers… even their individual survival. Some of those fears were realized, but throughout all their experiences they remained in love and kept the hope that one day peace would return to Ukraine and they would be together always. But the future was not to be as bright as she imagined it.

---

[34] Marinated cubes of skewered lamb
[35] A sour, but refreshing drink with barley and hops
[36] Thank you
[37] A country home
[38] A Jewish girl's rite of passage at 13 or 14 years of age
[39] rebel
[40] The Name. Indirect mention of Hebrew word for God
[41] Portion of the Talmud containing words of prophets
[42] The Book of Exodus
[43] Portion of the Talmud containing the writings of Jewish sages
[44] German word meaning "living space"

There is no death without sin.

— Torah, Shab. 55a

5 — Thresholds

Reb Levi's mortuary was not in the main part of Berdichev, but across the river and quite close to the train depot on Karl Leibnecht Street in the northeastern end of town. Some of the deceased were to be buried in cemeteries in other locations. Since immediate burial is a Jewish tradition, simple pine boxes were provided as a convenience for quick interment or same day shipping to families in outlying areas. The mortuary was small and nondescript on the outside, as with many Jewish businesses in Berdichev. A small, darkened street front window bore the thought-provoking inscription:

Mortuary
Yekara D'Schichva[45]
Reb Moshe Levi, Funeral Director
Orthodox, Chasidic — or what have you
No First Day burials on Shabbat or holiday

The interior of the store was simple but respectful. A large rag rug covered cracks in the concrete floor. There were several small lamps adorned with dusty shades adorning them, uncomfortable straight back chairs (to keep the *shomer*[46] awake), and old, plush couches. This was the 'reposing room' where the body, once in its casket, would be placed until burial or until orders for pickup or shipment were received. The relative accompanying the body sat *shiva*[43] in this room because sitting *shiva*[46] with a body until its burial is Jewish law. Mirrors were nowhere to be seen, even in the large bathroom. Copies of *Torah* also were not in evidence. On some occasions Reb Levi would remind his customers that death is, for the survivors, a time of grief.

"The reading of *Torah* is considered a pleasure. So how can we have grief and pleasure at the same time?"

To the rear of the building Reb Levi laid his only suit on caskets, piled up against the wall. In the room there were crates of packing material, boxes of shipping and receiving forms, a desk, a phone limited to a 50-mile radius in any direction and the paraphernalia of Jewish death. This included shovels, candlesticks and holders, *menorahs*, shawls, tissue, clean white shrouds and scissors for garment rending. Since the Lord is no respecter of persons regarding their stations in life, a quick, simple funeral is considered most appropriate.

"All of us are equal before the Almighty," Reb Levi would advise the family. "He has no more respect for a wealthy man than for a poor one. That is why the dress and the coffin must be simple."

His customers were usually orthodox Jews, though he would gladly help anyone who desired it. Because he was *Chasidic*, all the *Chasids* used his services. There were thousands of *Chasidic* Jews in Berdichev, so business was steady, but payment sporadic. Famines and occasional purges by the Russian army broke the backs of many Jewish merchants. As war with Germany drew closer, more and more families paid with IOU's which Reb Levi always received with as much grace as he accepted *shekels*. Few of these were ever collected.

"Pay me when you can," he'd remind, gently patting the grieving relative on the shoulder. "Remember us in your prayers, if you will be so kind, and with your extra grains. Your dead will be grateful to you and speak well of you at Heaven's gate."

Barak, until he left home to join the Partisans, worked with his father and drove the groaning hearse that was always in need of repair. A gurney and white shroud were always carried in the back of the van. Usually they met the *rabbi* or family member at the deceased's home. From that point forward, rituals thousands of years old dictated everyone's actions: The *rabbi* made sure the deceased's eyes and mouth were closed and the body laid flat and turned so the feet faced the doorway. Mirrors were instantly covered. In homes of the ultra-Orthodox the deceased was placed upon the floor within twenty minutes following death. Water was poured around him, slowly, and allowed to leak beneath the front door of the home to the street, as a symbol to watchful neighbors that a death had occurred.

Generally, candles were placed near the deceased's head in memoriam, then the body was surrounded by grief stricken family members, known as *onens*. These sat *shiva* with the dead in respect (*kavod ha-met*) for his life, for this ritual helped to preserve family unity. Comfort (*nihum avelim*) was offered. Often, when Reb Levi and Barak entered a home they were detained until family and friends asked formal forgiveness of the dead. The *rabbi* or *chazzen* then recited Psalms 23 and 91 before calling to obtain medical certification of death. As president of Chevra Kadisha, the burial society, he also helped with plans for handling of the remains. Finally, he and his helper placed the shrouded body on the gurney and collected their fee, if possible.

At the mortuary the body was outwardly cleansed and dressed in a new white, pocketless shroud of muslin, cotton or linen. If the dead was a male, a *tallis* or *tallit* was placed around him with one fringe cut off. At this point the *rabbi* and/or Reb Levi performed ancient *taharah*[48] rites. Finally, forgiveness was asked of G-d, the body was cleansed and wrapped for its presentation to the Eternal One. The wooden casket held its new prize until burial or until the body was refrigerated briefly awaiting interment. The shomer accompanied the body, reading constantly from the book of Psalms throughout the day and night, for the dead must not be left alone until placed in the earth, where it returns quickly to the elements.

Zych the Romany worked daily with Reb Levi now that Barak had joined the Partisans. He proved a quick, reliable assistant. Ester liked his thin graying black moustache. It seemed like a second smile.

Today, Ester came to visit unannounced. Reb Levi was in his office preparing paperwork on a sudden death of a child. He was engrossed in his work as she approached.

"*Shalom*, my *shayna madele*," he said, wiping his eyes with the back of his suit sleeve. "What brings you here now? I am just leaving for the Glasser home."

"Father, why do you cry?"

He stood up, embarrassed to be seen with tears. He blew his nose hard.

"This little girl who died, she was Saul Glasser's only daughter. Such promise she had, such promise. Your mother is there now, sitting *shiva* with the family today."

He sat down again, staring at his desk. "You know, Ester, I believe that G-d loves children so much that when they pass on, they are taken by angels to Him, to live in His presence."

"Yes, Papa, that is a wonderful thought. Their hearts, of course, are pure. But why does He sometimes take them from us so early?"

"Maybe to keep them pure, or to save them from great tragedy. But do not worry. Our G-d knows your heart, blessed be He. I will implore Him to let you keep all your babies, but first you need to marry!" He laughed and hugged his dear daughter. "What brings you here today?"

Ester took a deep breath, anticipating her confession. Surely this would be news to her father. Would he disapprove?

"Papa, I... I wasn't going to tell you or Mama yet, but... I think that I love Avram...

At this news Reb Levi started. For a moment he stared at his daughter, for she had caught him off guard. Then he rose up and gave Ester a bear hug.

"*Mazel tov! Mazel tov!*[49] He is a good man. He will be a good match for you, Ester. But... does he return your feelings?"

"Yes, I think so. I see love in his eyes when he looks at me... but this is so new to both of us..." Oh, Papa, he is so much like Barak. His revolutionary ideas, they sound like Barak's words. I wonder what kind of life we can have together?"

Reb Levi turned away and sat down heavily in one of the three tufted chairs. His eyes once again grew sad.

"Come and sit by me, Ester. Come, sit here." He patted the arm of his chair and Ester moved close to him.

"Avram is an honest and worthy young man, but he is too rebellious. He takes many chances by thumbing his nose at Stalin. We can only pray the Eternal One will preserve him for you. But if Avram is falling in love with you, he will want you to be safe at all costs. We will have to wait and see. Ester, have you told your mother of these feelings?"

"Not yet, Papa, but my heart tells me Avram is the very special one . . . one day soon I may come and ask for your blessing."

"Ester, you must search your soul before you make any decisions about this young man. I think that Avram's actions will determine his fate. He is of the new generation that advocates changes in the old ways. I think that he and his mother may already be in danger from the Stalinists. You see, we Jews have become accustomed to thinking of ourselves as victims. But Avram is a scholar. He understands well how our government has lied to us. Many people in Ukraine do not want to face the responsibility of letting Stalin know they think he is a tyrant! "

Ester did not reply.

"Ester, listen to me, I want to discuss with you something very important. Remember the *Torah* scrolls in synagogue? If the Germans do come to Berdichev they will burn the synagogues. They will burn our *Torah*... I cannot let that happen." Tears again came to his eyes. Ester had a sudden vision of seeing their precious *Torah* in flames.

"Can we hide the scrolls, Papa? Hide them where they will never be found?"

Reb Levi searched her face. "Yes, yes, but then we will have to do without it on *Shabbats* and holidays.

"But, Papa. We must take the chance! Do you suppose that in Lvov there are scrolls that we can borrow?"

Reb Levi's face screwed in thought for a long while. He stroked his beard. Then he looked up. A smile lit his eyes.

"I've got it, " he said. "I've thought of a plan. *Torah* will be preserved. Go now, Ester, I have much work to do."

Berdichev was just coming to life the day news of Hitler's breakthrough of the Russian border came to the city. These spring mornings were free of mist and fog, but a gentle diffused illumination fell across the streets and seemed to breathe a calm into the air. The town crier this time was the Ukrainian Sergeyevich. His usual route was to begin on Reenok and run along a grid that led to Leibnecht Street and further east to the streets bordering the river. The sunrise cast a rosy glow upon the eastern sky. After a short rest Sergeyevich would run east around the Sherentsis Theater and the obelisk commemorating the Russian Revolution of 1917. His wind would begin to ebb as he rounded the outskirts of the Friendship Hotel and by the time he passed the Progress factory and the train station he was ready for a light repast. This was daily provided at the bread factory where he celebrated the end of his run with rolls, beer and sausage at the *Pyvnytsya Ukrainka*[50]. The name was appropriate. It was famed outside Berdichev for its numerous brands of ale and also for the six kinds of Russian bread it sold, including *chyorny, khleb, kulich, mchadi, lavash* and *ukrainka*. These were all baked daily at the bread factory northeast of town.

The town crier's awesome message this day was one that would soon close the tavern and the bakery to all but the German army, who would eventually burn them both. The day was Saturday, 21 June, 1941. Ester remembered Sergeyevich's hoarse announcements woke her at dawn from a restless sleep. Weary with worry, she had fallen asleep in a fevered state. Now, hearing the news, fear again took her heart: and she moaned anew.

"The German army has invaded Ukraine! Today they have crossed our borders to the north and the south of Ukraine! They will free us from our enemies, from Stalin, from famine and *pogrom*! Welcome the German army, they are at our doors!"

~

But the town crier had severely misjudged the situation. The German *Wehrmacht* and *SS* were not liberators but invaders from Hell, as people soon discovered, and it was feared they were now inside Ukraine headed toward Berdichev. No one expected them, so no preparations for defense were made until the German troops were more than fifty miles inside the Russian border.

Reports were circulating in Kiev that Stalin was unconvinced of the attack even after his spies confirmed communiqués. Barak's Partisan unit was unsure why he hesitated to believe. Busy with restructuring Ukrainian politics and food allocations in June of 1941, Russia's leader refused even to believe the frantic reports of his generals. He was shocked and unable to act when he heard Germany was at war with its Russian ally. Consequently, the Red Army's war machine was immobile when the *Wehrmacht* crossed the Russian border. Almost too late he discovered that for Hitler the pact had been nothing more than a ruse and a stall, until his armies could be readied for war.

Ester and her family read of Stalin's error in underestimating Hitler's motives and marveled at his naiveté. Russia and Germany had signed a non-aggression pact in 1939, expected to last indefinitely. During this time, Ukraine was duly absorbed into the USSR. Communism reigned, churches were closed, the upper class eliminated. No one in Russian government had taken the lunatic Hitler's words of conquest seriously, yet knowledge of his intentions were aired in European political circles years before his invasion of Russia. In letters and speeches his ambitions for her conquest were common knowledge, duly filed in government offices and in Ukrainian newspapers.

Avram was interested in the strange sounding "Operation Barbarossa", Herr Hitler's initially secret mission. Barbarossa was the Italian code-name for "Red Beard", nickname of Frederick the First, Germany's 12th century ruler. The fact that Hitler longed to rid Eastern Europe of the non-Aryans and the non-Europeans was no surprise to any Jew in Ukraine! He had a pathological hatred of Jews — he thought them the dregs of humanity; misshapen, ugly and dangerous because of their economic success, their legendary intellectual abilities and financial acumen. Hitler's feelings were based partly upon fear and partly upon a jealousy for power because Jewish prosperity in Germany and neighboring states had grown tremendously before World War I. Jewish banking houses were still financing world powers by the late 1930's. Hitler believed Bolshevism to be a Jewish plot toward world domination and he often declaimed that the economic achievements of Bolshevism were due to Jewish power grabbing. Jumping on the bandwagon of renewed anti-Semitism in his homeland and in Russia, he seized the moment to promote his own cause.

"Hitler also thinks the Slavs are an inferior race because of centuries of mixing with Mongoloid stock," Barak told Ester on one of his visits home. "His hatred of anyone not Teutonic extends to the Gypsies of Eastern Europe. In his deranged mind that's enough reason for him to plan the extermination of the millions he figures are unfit to live."

Barak shared much with his family relative to Hitler's motives. He gleaned them from the Partisan's intelligence reports. These reports told how Hitler's dream was to build a German "Master Race", the Aryan *Herenvolk*. To achieve this end, Hitler's armies were carefully and unceasingly indoctrinated with the heretical propaganda that Jews, Slavs and Gypsies were to be eradicated — the "Final Solution". In a speech given a few months earlier the *Fuhrer* told his army generals that the "struggle" was one of ideology and race and that it "must be conducted with unprecedented, unmerciful and unrelenting harshness." To that end, all Soviet territory was to be made free of Jews — *judenrein* — so that the *Endlosung*, the "Final Solution" of the Jewish problem, would be achieved. To Adolf Hitler and his entourage of murderers this meant the annihilation of all European Jewry.

"The rebel forces in Germany say the military there believes the *Wehrmacht* to be superior to the Red Army," Barak told Ester. "Even the most serious German military thinkers believe it. After all, Soviet armaments were old, antiquated and out of date. It is only their immense population and physical size that is for the moment stopping Hitler, but he and his generals believe a surprise attack will balance Germany's inferiority in numbers."

Avram, too, had extensive knowledge of *Reich* activities. In his classes he taught that the riches of Russian agricultural real estate and prized resources were also jewels that attracted Hitler's greedy eyes. In his book *Mein Kampf* (My Struggle), published during the 1920's and at the core of *Nazism* Hitler expressed his desire for *lebensraum* in Europe because he believed the Aryan nation he was trying to create must expand its territories wherever possible. *Mein Kampf* was obligatory reading for *Reich* members.

Hitler decided that conquering Russia in 1941 would help to fulfill his plans when added to the territories he'd already claimed: the Rhineland, Bohemia, Moravia, Latvia, Estonia, Lithuania, Slovakia and Poland in 1939, Austria, Romania and France, Norway, Denmark, Holland, and Belgium in 1940. His armies invaded Crete two months before attacking the Soviet Union and they had Bulgaria on its knees a month prior to that! His troops marched triumphantly into Italy in September 1943. Hitler even declared war on America on December 11, 1941! Barak could only shake his head in amazement that anyone could do so much damage in so little time.

Now, at the borders of Ukraine, Operation Barbarossa had begun. German troops three million strong were advancing on four fronts along a 2,000-mile frontier, from the Arctic to the Black Sea. The Partisans were busy tracking the moves. The attack's objective was a line running from Archangel to the Caspian Sea. All four advances began at the borders of East Prussia and Poland, moving east, then branching north and south like a horrid creeping insect infecting all it touched on its way across the continent of Eastern Europe. Hitler's northern objective was to pass through Lithuania to Leningrad. Another line of attack had Smolensk as its objective. Moscow was the target for *Einsatzgruppe* B. A fourth wing would follow the Dnieper River east to the Caucasus range. This strong southern thrust would capture Kiev in the process, September 19th. Moscow, Hitler reasoned, would capitulate quickly thereafter.

Ester often listened to Barak and Avram discussing this war. It was so personal to them and they had formed a fast and strong friendship in the little time they'd known each other. But these discussions also brought fear to her heart. The terrible final cost was the loss of many innocent lives. What if they awoke to invasion with the coming dawn? Barak himself knew early of the German attack upon Ukraine. He had been privy to a conversation overheard by another Partisan; this to the effect that the day previous, 21 June, 1941, Russian Col. I. Fedyuninsky interviewed a German soldier who approached a border guard. The German had been drunk when he struck an officer. Facing court martial, he asked for asylum in return for divulging information about Hitler's planned attack. The soldier's father was a Communist and the young man liked Russia. He told Col. Fedyuninsky that the German army was soon to be the enemy of Russia and that

Hitler's soldiers would attack at 4 a.m., 22 June, the shortest night of the year when only a few hours of real darkness would give them cover.

"That's ridiculous," Col. Fedyuninsky told the German soldier. "The Russian news agency TASS has issued a statement stating that Germany is unwaveringly observing the conditions of the non-aggression pact with the USSR."

Nevertheless, wanting not to believe what he had heard, Fedyuninsky phoned Major General M.I. Potopov, commander of the Russian Fifth Army. Potopov said that a German in fear of his life "would babble anything." He did not respond further.

Ester laughed loud and long at this revelation. Barak could hardly continue the ridiculous story he was telling.

"Barak, how can this man Potopov be so arrogant that he refuses even to suspect this is true?"

"Yes, it's crazy, but what is more unbelievable is that the Kremlin received a similar warning that same day from a secret agent. The message was received on June 18. The Foreign Minister Vyachaslav Molotov, when told that German freighters and cruise ships were hurriedly pulling out of Soviet ports, harumphed and said: 'Only a fool would attack us.'"

The attacks were to be made on land and in the air. The German *Wehrmacht* and *SS* units planned to coordinate activities in Ukraine. They intended to commandeer the Zhitomir-Berdichev Highway, to enter those towns on foot, on tanks, and on motorcycle to surprise the Russian defense before they could detonate any demolition charges. The highway was paved and therefore ideal for German transport. In this way, Berdichev — the seemingly insignificant town of 60,000 — eventually became a vital target for the *SS* and the *Wehrmacht* in the early months of the invasion. The ensuing devastating war, one of the most costly in human history, was to bring shame upon the German nation and rain down upon ill-prepared, innocent populations, evil unimagined.

It is fact that within six months after the German invasion nearly 800,000 Jews were murdered on Soviet territory alone, almost all of them by the *Einsatzgruppen*, a shooting unit of several thousand men who followed the *Wehrmacht* into Soviet territory with the single goal of killing every Jew they could find.

~

It was now 1985, yet the memory of those few days before the invasion of this territory settled upon Ester's mind with an aching reality. The horror of the war that followed left no life untouched and filled the cemetery she stood in. The tragedy of her own parents' death cast a shadow of deep sorrow upon her even after all the years that had passed. The grief she had so carefully tried to put behind her was now resurfacing. She moved on toward another sector of the graveyard.

The prize she sought was somewhere in the hard clay ground beneath her feet. But the information left by Reb Levi was not exact. He'd written it in Hebrew on a scrap of paper that later Ester discovered hidden in his *Torah*. She and her brother deciphered most of it, but some investigation was still necessary. With a heavy but hopeful heart, she continued her search.

---

[45] "Beloved laid to rest"
[46] A watcher. Sits with the deceased from death to burial
[47] Means "seven." Process of mourning death includes seven days of following internment
[48] Preparation of the remains of the dead for burial
[49] "Good luck!"
[50] Ukraine Pub

*For wickedness burneth as the fire: it shall devour the briers and thorns,
and shall kindle in the thickets of the forest…*

6 — Cast Thy Net On Hope

"Hurry up, Barak, we haven't time to go back!"

Grigorii was certain Elena was behind him as he and the other Partisans made their way through the bristly thickets of the Steppes. When he reached the safety of the underbrush he turned back to find the others. Elena, her wide Russian frame hindering her speed, came up panting a few moments later.

"Barak is gone," she whispered, catching her breath. "He left the trail to visit his family again. He'll meet us tonight at the river camp."

"Barak is always choosing his own times," Grigorii growled. "One day he will be found alone and shot if he continues. No one is with him, he works too much alone. Does he think he is protected by God?"

Three Partisans were all who were left of their original seven. They continued carefully on the new path to a lookout point near the northwestern thrust of the Gnilopyatka River. From this vantage they would be in a position to see the first German troops coming from the west. They managed to secure the safety of the town through 24-hour surveillance, always moving from the previous day's location, until they had circled Berdichev. This took about two days of almost constant momentum. Barak was a central part of their operation. As they moved, hunger pangs tore at their stomachs. The night before they had been fortunate to find potatoes in bins behind a burned out store. No choice but to eat them raw, and that had been their substance. A week earlier the fresh carcass of a Russian soldier's horse had provided enough protein for several days of running, and for ambushing several Russian troops who were pistol-whipping a Jewish landowner for hiding a 25-pound bag of flour.

But Barak worried for his family more than for himself, so on this afternoon he made his way through the forest that lined Berdichev on the west and waited in some brush until nightfall. As he sat, vivid pictures came again to his mind of Partisans Nicolai and Alexa. They had been recently captured by the Red Army whose

85

hatred for Partisans was legend. Only the approaching German army would learn to hate these freedom fighters more.

When the main avenues emptied of storeowners and tradesmen returning home to their suppers, Barak stole through quiet streets to the old, dark apartment on Mira Street to pay his family a clandestine visit. Not expected, he stopped to play a soft tune on his harmonica outside their door. Ester jolted awake and with a cry of joy ran to the door, pulled it open and threw her arms around her brother's neck. His thinness surprised her. His uniform smelled of the earth and grass and other things Ester identified with the outdoors.

"Barak! You're here! I missed you so much!"

"Hush, hush. We must not alert the other tenants. Go, wake Papa."

Later, a very serious Barak related the frightening news that Hitler was masterminding the murder of all of European Jewry. He begged his parents to leave for the Black Sea with him and others who were at this hour fleeing towns near the German and Polish borders.

"You must leave now. The German army will come soon to Berdichev. Many will be murdered. Hitler's orders are to cleanse Ukraine of Jews, Gypsies, Slavs, old people and babies. Berdichev has a reputation as the 'Yid capital' and that alone is a great enticement to Hitler. He will continue his *judenrein* here and across the Russian frontier! Please, Papa, Mama, Ester, come with us. Our men have a place to hide you until we can get to our hideout."

Barak hurriedly whispered his information about a Partisan cooperative plan for the saving of Berdichev, Zhitomir, Bela Tserkva and other nearby towns. He was part of a group whose task was to knock on doors of Jewish families to warn them of the danger. They were being asked to leave their homes as soon as possible. They would gather at the southern edge of town near the Vinnitsa highway and be escorted to a hideaway near the Black Sea.

Reb Levi considered his son's words carefully. He felt in his heart now that Barak might be right. If so, his family must move to safety. But how could he be sure?

"Barak, my beloved son, I do agree with you that there is cause for worry. However, the Germans cannot be worse than the tyranny that has kept us here. The *Politzei* are beasts and Stalin is a murderer, like Lenin, like Trotsky. But I wonder . . . how can we suffer more than we have? Perhaps these invaders you speak of will pass through as friends, not conquerors... Have they not come to liberate us from our government? Can they not live here in peace with us? Barak, I think that our G-d will protect us; we must praise him in joy, Barak. Do not let these rumors of war distract you from worship."

Barak's face tightened. He shook his head in disbelief and paced the room. Reb Levi motioned for him to speak quietly, fearing the neighbors would hear.

"How can you think that? You condemn yourself and our family to death! Papa, they are coming to kill you in your bed!"

Turning toward his mother, he implored her to change Reb Levi's mind. But she only shrugged, not wanting to make the situation worse. Ester winced as she saw the pain in Barak's face. She looked hard at her brother and realized he'd changed before her eyes. It was his new lifestyle; his red hair was already thinning, his body was wiry beneath his torn, slept-in uniform. His face had lost of its former youthfulness and taken on the stern demeanor of one who is dedicated entirely to a just cause. He had grown used to living by his wits, eating what he could steal, beg or kill while on watch. Days were times of desperate action. Nights were spent sleeping in forests with rifles by his side, ready at a whisper to rise, grab his weapon and return fire.

"I'm sorry, my son," Mama said, trying to smile. "I cannot go against your father's wishes. But if what you say is true, we can hardly prepare here for defense against the monster, Hitler."

She turned to her husband. "Moshe, you are the leader of our family, but consider, please, your son's words. What if he is right?"

Ester saw her opportunity. She had no further doubts that Barak spoke truth.

"Barak *is* right! Papa, please. *Rabbi* Levin would want you to go."

Reb Levi walked back and forth across the floor, intent upon his thoughts. He knew a decision had to be made quickly, but still... there were issues.

"No, I cannot leave. *Rabbi* Levin has left me in charge of the *Chasidic* movement here. I have responsibilities to these people. Who will hold services for them, who will minister to their needs? How can I run away? And what of my business? Who will bury the dead?"

"Papa, if you all remain here, there will be more dead to bury than you can say *yahrzeits*[51] for and G-d forbid, what if you are in the path! At least come with me to tell them, please. Help me warn them that their lives are in danger. Tell them there is a way out if they act quickly."

Reb Levi paced. Finally he sat down and stared out the window into the night for a time. He heaved a mighty sigh and turned to Barak.

"Okay, I will warn them, yes, okay. I see maybe you are right. This work of notifying will take time. There are many in our congregation. We must act carefully and quietly. And . . . Barak, take your mother and sister with you tomorrow."

Barak let out a long breath while Ester found her voice of protest.

"What! Papa. No. I am not leaving you. I am waiting here for Avram to come. I cannot leave!"

"He will find you. You cannot stay. If what Barak says is true, your life is threatened. You and your mother will go with your brother to safety. We will send Avram after you."

"But Papa, please. I don't want to go, I must stay here with you!"

But her father raised his hand to stop her. She knew that meant the question was closed. Her mind raced. How would Avram find her? What was happening to him in Zhitomir? Had he been jailed?

That night Reb Levi and his son directed the fate of many. They made plans, discussing almost until sunrise. Ester fell asleep on the floor and when she awoke from a fitful sleep, Barak was gone. Reb Levi, heavy of heart and woozy with sleeplessness, hurried to meet Zych at his apartment. They went first to Reb Zitsler's apartment to warn him. Ester accompanied them. She brought strudel for his wife, who was ill before returning home to pack. Reb Levi and Zych continued on to join with the many other *Chasidim*. Following their daily worship service a posse was formed to alert the congregation of impending German army attacks on the Jews of Berdichev. Meeting places and times were chosen for an exodus from town. It was hurriedly scheduled for late the following night. Hopefully they would be able to get out in advance of all attacks, but no one could be sure.

Barak was to arrive with Partisans from the central Steppes organization to accompany the massed groups southward. They agreed to meet in Nicolayev, a small town just north of the Black Sea. Each person was to bring no more than what could be carried on his or her back. With the plan firmly in place Reb Levi started homeward, thinking of ways to tell his wife and daughter that he would not be leaving. Zych had also refused to join the exodus.

"This is my home," he told Reb Levi and then laughed. "Where else can I be a *Chasidic* gypsy? Reb Levi, I have a most important issue to put to your wisdom." He cleared his throat and hunched his thin shoulders in Reb Levi's direction.

"Now, is it conceivable, even possible, that these Germans will be friendly? After all, they haven't declared war on Ukraine, let alone stated any intentions to enter Berdichev."

"True, Zych, my good friend, but they have declared intent to overtake us by the sudden crossing of our borders with their army. That does not bode well. We can hope they do not come here to fight for territorial gains. But true or not, we must tell every Jew to warn his neighbors of the dangers we will all face."

"Well said, Reb Levi. But Hitler has spoken of re-establishing an independent Ukrainian state. That would free us from the tyranny of Communism, would it not?"

His large brown eyes widened. They fixed upon his *chazzen's* face, ready to agree or disagree instantly with him.

"We will see," Reb Levi replied. "Remember that Stalin's Communism has closed up the churches and synagogues. Perhaps the Germans will allow us to worship again in our holy places, but Stalin will quickly send his army to push them back across the border. My son, Barak, believes with all his heart that the Germans are not coming in friendship. He says we are the target, the only target."

Zych shuddered. "It is true we must consider every alternative. But if we are wrong, if the Germans come to kill us, it will be too late to run, will it not?"

Reb Levi looked long at his friend. "We will do as we must," was all he said.

Zychoslov Petrovich Romanov was an orphan. He had met Ester's father years ago and took a great liking to him. "Zych", as he liked to be called, claimed to be a prince descended from Russian royalty. He confided that his parents had gone into exile in 1881 in Romania following the death of his great grandfather, Pavel Petrovich, grandson of Peter Ist The Great of Russia. He had no religious training as a child and so the happy world of *Chasidism* appealed to him. He prayed and sang the Hebrew songs in his native Russian, and in that way he embraced Judaism. Zych was along in years but had never married nor fathered children.

Because Zych was sure the Russians would kill him if they knew that any Romanov descendents were still alive, he begged Reb Levi to never reveal his true identity.

"My parents and I became gypsies, sleeping and eating wherever the wind took us. We never told anyone who we really were. When I was merely 15 my parents were murdered. I knew Tsar Nicholas, the emperor, before he and his family were murdered. And once I had occasion to look into the eyes of Rasputin."

Whenever Zych would talk about his royal bloodline his rounded back straightened and his hands went to his head, automatically forming an invisible crown. He lived with a *Chasidic* family. For a pittance, he would perform on the street juggling loaves of bread or potatoes or whatever anyone gave him on the streets and in the marketplace. Over the years he and the Levi family had formed a strong bond of friendship.

When the pair reached Zych's door once again, Reb Levi took his friend aside and pressed *shekels* into his palm.

"My dear friend, we need to know what our Rabbi Levine desires of us in this situation. When is he returning? You are my liaison to him. Alert your kinsmen and go to him quickly in Kiev to seek his advice. Shall I continue as *chazzen*? What precautions to take? Tell him we are informing our congregation of the danger here and asking them to leave Berdichev for Nicolayev with the Partisans."

Zych was visibly surprised at this sudden request, but showed no hesitation in following his *chazzen's* orders. He smiled at Ester as she offered him a pastry.

"Very good, Reb Levi, well said, indeed. I shall leave by train tonight for Kiev."

"Yes, yes. Let no one know your mission and travel quickly. We need this knowledge before Hitler's army reaches us."

---

[51] Prayers for the dead offered yearly upon anniversary of death

But now the Temple no longer exists. If they practise charity, well and good but if not, heathen nations come and confiscate their property by force.
— Torah B.B. 9a

7 — Where Heaven and Earth Meet

It was nearing noon. A large rat raced past Ester as she moved through underbrush seeking to follow the coordinates that would lead her to the buried prize she sought, that sacred symbol of her Judaism. She screamed in fright. The animal jumped through the weeds in fear. Ester realized she'd frightened it as well as herself. Her clothes and shoes were badly stained with earth and slime from the forest floor, but part of her work was accomplished: She had promised Barak that she would find the memorials he'd provided for her parents, and this she'd done. But there was the other task to carry out, the task they had returned to Berdichev to complete. Hurrying past the log-shaped markers to the northwest of the cemetery, her attention was drawn to a small object half-buried in the tangle of foliage. She reached for it. It was a miniature *Shabbat menorah*, made of brass and quite green with oxidation. How it got there was a puzzle. The candle cups were badly scratched, as if they'd been used as tools.

Holding this new found object, Ester remembered the *menorah* symbol that adorned the windows of *Beit ha'Midrash* synagogue in her youth. Within those walls her parents were murdered, but from within that precious house of G-d her father had also performed a great *mitzvot*. She recalled his telling her of that night…

~

In 1941, the streets of Berdichev were always quiet after the businesses closed, for nothing was offered to the public at night except in the various Russian beer halls along Lenin, Sverdlov and Liebnecht streets. A single light cast long shadows. Reb Levi walked quietly alongside the buildings, hugging the darkness to him until he reached Sverdlova Street. In a moment he was at the elaborately etched wooden door. Above it in Hebrew was the name *Beit ha'Midrash*[52] synagogue. He remembered that beneath the black paint smeared across the windows a *Mogen Dovid*[53] was glazed into the window glass above the door, carrying out the theme of two *Mogen Dovid* configurations atop a golden *menorah* that were etched into each of the unbroken curvilinear windows around the building. The exterior itself was a faded, dirty white. Numerous bullet holes pockmarked the synagogue walls, grim memoriam of years of Russian purges.

Reb Levi's old key, the very one he'd kept as a sacred responsibility for twenty of his forty-five years, slid easily into the lock. With a single turn the heavy door creaked open. Stale, freezing air greeted and unnerved him; the stench of dust and dankness was choking. Quickly he closed the heavy barrier behind him, hoping he hadn't been detected. The Red Army had smeared all the windows with black paint two years earlier. At the same time they extinguished the Eternal Light fixture near the *Torah* cabinet. Reb Levi had not in his lifetime been in a synagogue in darkness. He felt a sneeze build inside his nostrils. His throat constricted. The blackness was overwhelmingly abysmal. He could not see his hand before his eyes. He became panicky as his body stiffened against the fear his sudden blindness brought him. He immediately began to pray for peace in his heart so he would not fear the blackness.

Concentrate on the *Mogen Dovid*, he told himself. He remembered *HaShem* in Hebrew written into the center of the six-pointed star painted upon the high whitewashed ceiling in gold and white.

The *chazzen* felt his way cautiously toward the congregation seats, walking toward the rear of the interior. Seats creaked as he touched them. He counted the dozen rows that led him deep into the room. He stood there, experiencing for the first time what it was like to be blind with eyes wide open. He decided to ponder the German problem until the prayer should take effect and he found the courage to continue. He had decided to accept fully that the Germans were coming to Berdichev and now he needed a course of action. There was his family to look after, his business and his humble home with barely enough room for the few hearts that beat within its thin walls. How could he protect them from the terror that might come at any time? When might the soldiers come? In the night? During *Shabbat* prayers? While they were at dinner? He had no weapons, no means of defense other than his belief that G-d would be their protection. And what of Barak, his only son, the inheritor of the mantle of *rabbis*? Barak the freedom fighter! Every day he was in danger of death. Who, in the face of destruction would carry on his name and his work?

Reb Levi sank into a bending position before the *Torah* cabinet. He realized suddenly with a laugh that his eyes were closed. Now he straightened slowly, sighed and then sat down heavily in a creaking seat. He was very cold there in the blackness. He had seen so many in death, and he thought of how it might feel to experience that new and final coldness. He had often wondered at the process of dying. In his preparation of the dead for burial, he sometimes had an awareness of the deceased's spirit freeing itself of its earthly vessel. He "felt" that they lingered a moment, as though to bid goodbye, before departing to other realms. Upon question, Barak confessed a similar sensitivity.

Gradually, Reb Levi began to make out the outlines of the pulpit ahead of him as well as the *Ner Tamid*[54] lamp. He murmured his thanks to G-d and wondered suddenly if the lamp could be relit without anyone noticing it from the outside. He thought: the oil. Was it still in the old place, near the lamp of the Eternal Flame?

What was this synagogue to him, to his *Chasids*? Was the building itself sacred? No, but it was a house of the Eternal One, the Father. These cold paint-smeared walls had been His holy house, the "knot that tied Heaven and earth together", a place where man could commune with his Creator, or at least approach His bench.

Now look at it. Reb Levi began to cry. How many years had these happy *Chasids* danced up and down the aisles chanting and singing and *davening*[55] in praise of *HaShem*? The *Ner Tamid* burned with the fervor of passionate love for Him who chose them and gave them *Torah*. A man who reads *Torah*, Reb Levi knew, longs for more than synagogue. He is ready for an essential point of harmony between the mortal and the celestial, the "living" reminder of what once was cherished by the faithful — the Temple! This meetinghouse was a mere bookmark in time between Solomon's Temple, destroyed by conquerors of another time, and the one to be built in Jerusalem after the *Mashiach's* return. But, Reb Levi had told Ester and Barak, there were always conquerors, there was always destruction. He sniffed and wiped his eyes in the dark. These fools, these murderers, they could murder the body but G-d would never permit them to murder a Jew's love for *Torah*, his synagogue, his sacred lost Temple.

Reb Levi recalled the day when he heard the news that all synagogues in Ukraine would be closed. He'd discussed this often with his family. His gut ached with fear of losing his holy home!

He saw again his congregation of *Chasids* standing across the street from their meeting place, their cradle of Judaism, watching in sorrow and gulping tears as their beloved synagogue was boarded up and heavy paint smeared carelessly across the hundred year old stained glass windows that bore the symbols of their faith.

"Sing," he told them. "Sing of our love for our G-d who will redeem us from this tyranny and help us to take back our synagogue one day! Be brave, my fellows. Did the Eternal One bring us this far in history to let it end now? Did he not bring us from Egypt and from the hands of many conquerors? This is not the end. We will be saved from this injustice, too."

But many did not take up his song or talk of hope. They turned away in sorrow and dejection, shaking their heads like a lot of old goats. Now they would have to meet secretly, keep constant watch and be careful not to alert the many enemies of Jews in Berdichev who would quickly report them to the traitorous *Politzei*. They would have to cover the windows and dance in stocking feet, lowering their voices while whispering fervent prayers. Perhaps, they worried, they could not sing at all their praises to the Eternal One!

"We can always read the *Tanach*,"[56] their *chazzen* told them.

"My father, the Reb Moshe Levi was a lover of goodness, a friend to all, Reb Levi told his children on this occasion of sadness at the behavior of the *Chasids*.

"He was filled with compassion for everyone he met, his good deeds were legendary, his presence in synagogue a wonder to behold. I, his son, I also come to the synagogue filled with love for G-d."

His prayers were loud, filled with ecstasy and joy that lit his face like a candle. His songs and prayers rang with passion, his boundless energetic clapping and singing seemed to shake the thick concrete walls. Ester loved to hear her beloved father pray at home. Her heart exulted in the sing-song wail of words sung a capella that ascended through the roof to the ears of the Holy One. At synagogue, his exuberance seemed to overcome all else.

"Do we not love our G-d and Master?" he would shout, grabbing worshippers by their coat sleeves and smiling intensely into their faces. "Whom do you serve?" he would ask each one.

The trembling *Chasids* would answer "The G-d of Heaven, the G-d of earth, my G-d, my Redeemer."

"Yes, yes, that is right!" Then, looking skyward, Reb Levi would address his Maker as if the Eternal One were standing in the air just before him.

"My exalted G-d, do you see how your people love you? Let us all dance with joy before you."

Reb Levi then pulled the men into a traditional dance circle with him. Their feet pounded the floor in rhythm with the songs and chants. The noise of so many ecstatic voices rose higher and higher until their songs and prayers were like the sound of the *Shofar*[57] itself as they brought to all of Berdichev the joy and passion of unrestrained devotion to G-d.

~

The memory of that day was buoyant. Ester laughed in joy recalling her father's stories of the *Chasids*. She stuffed the little *menorah* in her duffel bag and continued on through the brush in search of the prize that awaited. Her mood had lightened somewhat. The great gulf between past and present was becoming more easily bridged here in this garden of silenced but living spirits. *You live in the hearts of those who love and remember you*, she said aloud, knowing that many were here with her now, guiding her in this most urgent journey. She came to a ornate fenced enclosure containing two monuments, side by side, painted in white with blue trim. The inscriptions were of a man and wife, murdered in the shoah by "Fascists". Another, smaller stone was behind the first two. No weeds cluttered or intruded. Someone obviously visited this site and kept this small enclosure maintained. Small family plots like these were common in Ukrainian and Russian graveyards.

As she moved on, she recalled a long letter her father had written about his own youth. She'd read it many times and made a copy for Barak, who also treasured it.

"In that synagogue that day, I wiped tears from my eyes in the cold dankness and contemplated my own short life. At birth, in my grandfather's home on Brodskii Street the Levite Levi Isaacson took me, his tiny great grandson, from my mother's bed. He held me at arm's length before the whole family and pronounced:

'This day we are blessed with a son, a son of G-d who has given us the greatest gift of all, the gift of continuing life. L'Chaim! He shall be named Moshe Dovid ben-Levi[58]. He shall be taught Torah and raised in love and fear of his G-d. I bless my great grandson with the will of lions, the insight of Solomon and love for his

Father in Heaven so strong it will remain within him at night to arise newly born each day. Let us shout for joy! *L'chaim*[59]. *Mazel tov!* "

But with such a welcome, Reb Levi's childhood was not spectacular in any way. He spoke of his fondness for his sister, Tova and his nieces and nephews. But he was fonder still of the readings in *Torah* his father gave him each night and morning. He grew up a quiet, serious and loving son who was humbled by the human sorrow and toil he saw others endure. He was dutiful in helping his small family provide for themselves. Often the boy gave his bread to his sister when she cried with hunger or fell on the small, sharp stones in their yard while at play. His large brown eyes seemed to take in all the experiences that life had to teach him, yet he never complained. He seemed to know the value of suffering was to deepen his understanding of life.

One day in the quiet of a *Shabbat* afternoon, Reb Levi's voice took on a serious tone.

"Ester and Barak, my sweet children, I will tell you a most unusual tale. In synagogue a remembrance came to me. I recalled my neighbor's little dog, Feifel, a whitish mongrel that searched all day for scraps of food, following his sniffing nose around the neighborhood's gutters. One day Feifel received a kick from a horse that was startled when he ran in front of the carriage it pulled. The little dog yelped in pain, then fell lifeless in the street where it soon began to bleed from the mouth and nose. I was very little, but I saw the accident and understood. I was only nine, but I felt that I understood the animal's plight. I brought it to the curb. Shutting my eyes tightly in concentration I prayed over its body. In a while the animal's bleeding ceased. It began to whimper. In another moment it struggled to its feet and sat dazedly looking at myself there kneeling. I kept praying and moving rhythmically over what I thought was a dead dog. Then Feifel licked my knees, he turned away and limped unsteadily toward his home. When I, his benefactor opened my eyes I found only large spots of blood on the pavement. I thought the dog was still lying dead before me while I prayed for its delivery from pain. That is how I, little Moshe, discovered I had a gift for healing."

He told no one of the event for many years, but several neighbors had observed him and they quickly passed the story around, embellishing it with each telling. Within a few days Moshe found himself a very popular child whom all his schoolmates and not a few of their parents wanted to shake hands with. Several newspapers called his home for interviews. This outpouring of interest embarrassed him to the extreme. When Moshe's parents heard the story they knew their child had been blessed by G-d Who, of course, did the actual healing. This they explained carefully to a very worried Moshe, who was relieved to know he did not himself possess that "frightening" power. He never mentioned his experience again.

From that time, Moshe began to feel drawn to the problems and pains of those around him. He liked to speak to people he met in his daily travels within Berdichev, drawing them out, discerning their worries and concerns. He would quote revealing *Talmudic* passages as a way of bestowing support and giving hope, making metaphors and inventing short allegories to dramatize his points. By the time he was only seventeen, Moshe's father knew he had an exceptional child who should study for the rabbinate and follow in the footsteps of Rabbi Israel ben Eliezer, the "BESHT". But the money to send Moshe to rabbinical college in Krakow never materialized. His father's disappointment at not being able to see his son achieve that honor depressed him deeply and hastened his early death. Moshe sat *shiva* with his father's body, telling him over and over that he was not to blame.

When Moshe turned thirty the Berdichever *tzaddik*, Abraham Saul Levine, heard his lyric tenor voice and chose him to be *chazzen* to one of the largest *Chasidic* congregation in western Ukraine, with 750 members. This appallingly humbling responsibility Moshe faithfully and joyfully carried out, though he was always worried that his efforts were not sufficiently pleasing to his *tzaddik* or to G-d. To deal with his insecurities he decided to go before the Lord daily upon rising and nightly upon retiring to repent of his inadequacies, a practice he never forsook. Now, fifteen years later, his life and the lives of thousands might be in quick and awful jeopardy. He felt helpless in the face of the coming onslaught. He thought of going home to Anna's arms. She was the practical one, always thinking ahead, decisive and efficient. But if the town were invaded by marauding Germans, not even Anna's quick thinking would avert or influence the outcome.

Reb Levi rose from the hard wooden seat. He had grown somewhat accustomed to the cold now. He discerned the layout of the synagogue. Its dimensions were thirteen meters side to side, by sixteen meters. On each side of the hall were a dozen desk-rows, simple wooden chairs with seats folding upward. A long dark table occupied the center front of the hall. Reb Levi remembered that years ago during *Shabbat* it was covered with an ornately embroidered tablecloth embossed with silver threads. A storage shelf for *tallith, siddurs* (prayer books) and the like had been installed for convenience around the room.

Near him at the rear of the hall was a lectern and just to the right of it was the *bimah* table which on *Shabbat* held the *challah* shewbread. Reb Levi better discerned the outlines of the *Torah* cabinet to the left of the lectern. He knew the *Ner Tamid*, a branched candlestick with three light bulbs protruding from it, was above and to the right of the cabinet near the *bimah*[60]. Slowly and with great caution, he stole toward it, being careful not to make unnecessary noises on the old parquet flooring. His breathing became labored as he felt for the rickety wooden railing that separated the seats from the stage. He found it and felt along it until he was within touching distance of the tall, wide cabinet that held the sacred *Torah* scrolls.

"Ah, here you are."

His hands found the small hidden drawer that still held the key that would open the doors of the heavy mahogany piece. He inserted that key in the lock. In a few seconds the doors were opened. From his pants pocket Reb Levi extracted a wooden match that he struck on the worn heel of his shoe. Light suddenly flared in the darkness. Reb Levi saw that the three bulbs remained. Heaving a sigh of relief, Reb Levi began to whisper the ritualistic litany of prayers that were said before the lighting of the *Ner Tamid*. He quickly twisted the small bulbs… they responded with a dim glow. Because of the blackened outside windows that ringed the synagogue, light from the bulbs near the rear of the synagogue would never be seen outside the building.

With the faint glimmering light he could now reach into the cabinet's heart and touch the papyrus skin of the *Torah* scrolls, so cool and welcoming.

"Come here, my love, my beloved *Torah*, thou stick of Judah."

Slowly he reached around to secure the wooden rollers. Then, carefully balancing himself against the bench at his back he pulled them as one from their secure wooden womb into the cold, stale air of the synagogue. Setting the heavy scrolls on the bench, he wrapped them in the blanket that had covered him on his trip from home. With a fervent prayer to the Eternal One for safety under the cover of night, Reb Levi found his way back up the aisle and around to the back door's exit. Holding the *Torah* scrolls over his right shoulder, he left the synagogue, carefully relocking the old door. He almost stumbled under the weight of the walnut rollers, like huge sticks, as he flattened himself against the wall. Then, while inching toward the rear of the building, he was startled by a movement in the grass.

"Please, let it be him." Reb Levi muttered under his breath. A quick whistle of wind passed his ears. The signal!

"I've got it, come help me," he barely whispered to the bushes across the empty road. The grass rustled again and a short, slender figure stepped out of the darkness. Soon the two men with their precious, weighty bundle headed into the back streets toward the cemetery under the protective gaze of the star-filled night.

Reb Levi did not return home until after dark but said nothing of his whereabouts. Ester thought it unusual that Anna, who knew his daily routine was unchanging, asked no questions when he left again after supper. The next morning Ester noticed her father's large brass synagogue key was missing from its place near the door. The synagogues had been closed for two years. She remembered the conversation in Reb Levi's store. Had he moved the *Torah* scrolls? When she inquired, Anna said only,

"Do not ask questions, Ester. Go to market for me, we need bread for tonight's supper. Then you must pack. We are soon to leave." She looked so worried, Ester went to her Mama and held her close.

"Are you afraid, Mama?"

"Oh, Ester! I fear for my dear husband and my only son. What hell will befall them?"

"I fear for them, too, Mama. We must be brave. Barak says change is necessary now. I hate change, I hate war. I want to have peace so we can all be together and happy."

"Yes, peace. But when have we ever known peace to last?"

～

The weather was balmy this day in 1985, and Ester was glad for the shade of the many trees and bushes. Suddenly she saw something gleaming in the brambles. It was a plain silver ring, somewhat smaller than her own, and now quite scratched. How did it get there? She retrieved it, remembering the similar token ring that Avram had given her the night they became engaged.

He later replaced it with an heirloom ring his mother had saved for many years. To give her that simple round of silver he had gone for many days with little or no food. She loved him for that sacrifice. The both cried when he put the ring on her hand. Within the first month they dated she knew that this quiet, serious young man was the one she wanted to spend her life with, yet when his proposal came suddenly she was overwhelmed with surprise, which quickly gave way to joy…

The visits of Avram to Berdichev had taken on increasing frequency between February and mid-June, 1941. With the weather bringing warmer days, Ester would walk up the highway to meet him as he walked down to meet her. They laughed together until they reached her home and sat at the table laden with that night's bread, *matzoh* soup and spiced cabbage. Avram's mother occasionally sent *hamentashen*[53] with him. On two occasions Avram was able to borrow a cart and horse so his mother could meet Ester's family. But thoughts of the burden of a new war with Germany brought urgency to their time together and hastened the seriousness of the love growing between them.

One evening following their meal, Avram took Ester's hand and led her to the porch of her apartment. There, sensing her feelings for him, he lifted her chin and gazed deeply into her eyes.

"I love you, my dearest one," Avram said quietly. "You are my Queen Ester." Ester's eyes began to moisten. With a lover's sigh, Avram took her in his arms and kissed her deeply. He felt in his pocket for the simple silver band, the engagement ring he'd purchased the day before. She gazed at it in wonder and joy. It slipped on easily.

"Marry me, be mine forever. Will you be mine, my queen, my love?"

Ester was speechless. She had secretly dreamt of this day but never suspected it would happen so soon! She recalled that first day at the marketplace when the wind seemed to tell her that she and Avram were already old friends. Somewhere between then and this moment she had already given her heart to him.

"Yes, my darling, I will be yours," Ester told him shyly, "with all my heart and soul, yours forever!"

"Ester! Oh, my dear one! " They held each other a long time, then announced the happy news. The wedding was planned for July. But now, with the expected arrival of German troops and Ester's suddenly leaving Berdichev before she and Avram could make definite wedding plans, their future suddenly became temporal as the wispy winds. When and where would they meet again?

---

[52] House of study

[53] Star of David

[54] Everlasting Light. Olive oil used originally. Usually near Torah cabinet in synagogues

[55] Orthodox Jewish prayer style. With head covered, prayers are uttered thrice daily while rapidly bending knees and/or neck forth and back. Practiced by Ashkenazim Jewry

[56] Acronym for Torah, Nevi'im (prophets), Ketuv'im (writings). The inclusive Torah

[57] A ram's horn ceremoniously blown on Jewish High Holy Days

[58] Moses David, son of Levi

[59] Wishing you many lives!

[60] Table in a synagogue upon which the showbread is placed

[61] A 3-cornered pastry used during Feast of Purim

Journal of the Dead — Maisel

The Germans pillaged our homes, our crops and our businesses. Our lives became their lives, and our will became their will.

My name is Maisel. I was one amongst the murdered of Berdichev in 1941. On that day the German soldiers came up behind us and herded us from our ghetto into the no-man's land at the end of Brodskii Street. They lined us up alongside the pits they had dug. We were stopped there and interrogated as to who else we knew who was hiding out. None of us spoke to them. They spoke to us in German and sometimes in halting Russian. We would not give them names of those of our families who were hiding in the streets, the cracks and corners of houses, beneath shrubbery or in the fields, among our crops.

I will never forget those ending final moments of my life. I am a young woman. I stand at the brink of certain death awaiting a rifle shot to my brain. I call out upon my G-d in Heaven to save me from the wrath of these strangers, these devils in men's clothes. But no voice returns to me, no hand comes to lead me away. I am shot, oh, my head! I fall heavily into the pit before me, on top of other bodies writhing in death agonies. My blood chokes my throat, my eyes are covered with blood and my life flows away through my back, thorough the hole in my head. I cannot live more. Oh, my life is over. Instantly, I see a white light before me. It is the light of angels, so bright I cannot see past the brightness. A voice at the other side calls to me in Yiddish; it is the voice of my mother and my father.

Maisel, my darling, come to us, come to your mother and father. We await you. We love you and bring you home to us, my dear child. You shall live forever here with us, Maisel. Come and be happy. All is not lost!

I go through the light to my parents at the other side. Oh, it is beautiful there among them and my relatives, my friends from school, those who are dying with me are there, also, transported to the other side in health and vigor. We do not rest in death. We are taken home to that G-d Who gives us eternal life with our families. Praise to G-d.

Hence today I believe that I am acting in accordance with the will of the Almighty Creator: by defending myself against the Jew, I am fighting for the work of the Lord.

— Adolf Hitler, Mein Kampf, p. 192

PART TWO
THE FATHERLAND
THE HIRSCH STORY

Journal of the Dead —
Marta Avromovich

When I was born there was fierce fighting in the area. The Russians were not our friends; they often came through towns purging and murdering. They came to Berdichev often and purged there, also. My parents were their victims, so an aunt raised me. On the morning of September 17 we were in the ghetto the Germans had made with the full consent of the Russians who abandoned us all to the invading forces. They came for us there and herded us out to the edge of town, to Brodskii Street. It is or was to the north, around the corner from a large factory. The street was dirt with wooden sidewalks. It was dug up and trenches a mile long were laid in that street. They received the bodies of the dead as they fell from the bullets. We were taken *en masse*. Everyone knew his fate was to be executed. We traveled slowly despite orders to move faster. We were then stopped and lined up. The men went first as their women watched.

I was married but my husband had run away so as not to be caught by the Germans. I stood in front of their guns with my back to them. They took many of the women after the men fell into the pits; people I had known all my life, in school and on the street, at the market buying bread for the day's meal. When it was time for the women to follow, we were turned backward to the guns, brought to the edge of the pit and shot in the head so we would fall directly into the mire of bodies and blood. Many of us did not die instantly but fluttered around in life as our bodies realized they were about to die and began the awful process of shutting down from the top down and the bottom up. My own death was hardly felt because I was shot in the neck and felt little pain. I had only fear that my body was losing consciousness from limb to limb. I was fully dead in minutes and I joined with the other women of our town in that attitude; fully dead in sight of the German soldiers.

I was not touched, only murdered. The Germans were in no mood to rape. They were trying to kill as many as possible to get the job over with as quickly as possible to move on to other towns and other massacres. They were under orders to murder as many as possible in a short time and hurried about it. We were like pigs and goats to them, not human and not worth messing with.

After my death I felt the bodies and spirits of those who had gone just a few moments earlier. I heard them wail for unrepentant sins and unfinished work on earth they knew they could not now complete. They knew each other and commiserated before leaving the scene of their death. We went immediately to a heavenly place where we rested from our earthly toils and gradually our concerns with earthly things fades away.

Here is knowledge: *We lose consciousness after death for a few moments, and then we are revitalized in the spirit which is freed from the body and has to ascend, lest it linger too long near earth and become lost or afraid that it will be unclaimed.*

"First their synagogues or churches should be set on fire, and whatever does not burn up should be covered or spread over with dirt so that no one may ever be able to see a cinder or stone of it...drive them out of the country for all time."

— Martin Luther, Of the Jews and Their Lies. Pamphlet, 1542

8 — Harvest of Wild Fruit

The year was 1890. Professor Isidor J. (Judah) Hirsh was a longtime professor of religious education and philosophy at the Jewish Theological Seminary in Halberstadt, Germany. He read in the newspaper *Germania* that conversion to Christianity was thought to be a "social salvation" for Jews. The article also stated these demi-converts rarely adopted the changed religious practices that accompanied baptism. This compromise was reminiscent of the first converts to Judaism in the time of Jesus Christ. Traditionalists of Jewish social circles were deeply indignant of the "traitors" among them who had themselves baptized. The Orthodox especially despised a lack of loyalty. Conversion for any reason, the consensus went, showed astonishing lack of character. Professor Hirsch's succinct reply was often quoted:

"To be a Jew is a condition. Pride is no matter, nor shame a part of it."

Sitting at his desk in the comfortable mahogany office provided for him by the Seminary Board, Reb Isidor Hirsch contemplated this latest of many insults to the long, arduous history of European Jewry, He scoffed into his elegant, professionally trimmed gray beard, muttering epithets into the cool, vasty air above his tri-cornered fur hat. He himself had been raised with the specter of the movement of Jews toward conversion to a Lutheran or a Catholic way of life in Germany. It had increased tenfold since the descendents of the hunchbacked scholar genius from the Desau ghetto, Moses Mendelssohn, set the pattern in the mid-1700's by seeing that his children converted to Christianity.

The professor was used to being tolerated. During the mid- to late nineteenth century Germany was increasingly liberal toward the contributions of Jews to German industrialization, the arts and literature, philosophy and religious thought. Anti-Semitism had not yet captured a popular mindset and Jews were taking advantage of the social and financial possibilities. Conversions to Christianity became essential to their role in cultural "enlightenment". It was the "entrance ticket to European culture". Just in the past week Hirsch read that between 1812 and 1845 more than 3,500 German-speaking Jews were baptized. This figure included many women who found an acceptance in a broad social milieu otherwise inaccessible. Fashionable intellectual circles of Christian society now lay invitingly exposed to them. It was a freedom the ghetto could never promise or hope to deliver. While young Isidor was studying for his *bar mitzvah* in 1840, friends in his Hebrew school, those from "refined families" (meaning flush with money and/or title) attended Christian dance classes and other social occasions. Their children intermingled while the parents shared liquor and lunches with well-to-do *goyim*. These nurtured habits were quite beneficial for business, commerce and increasingly, a blending of familial roots . . .

Hirsch still could not understand these "*galuts*"[62]. He lived in the elegant Grunewald district of Berlin. He was an intellectual. His fortunate life had been filled with *Torah* and *Talmud*, with daily synagogue attendance and Hebrew study from age nine through his early manhood. He knew his religion and his languages. Hirsch and his four younger brothers were schooled in Judaic practices by their late father, a French Jew and student of Rav Sechel Yehudah. The *rabbi* was one of the few men permitted to be called Rav because of his erudition and his strength of character. By the time Isidor reached forty his contemporaries referred to him as a *chachan*.[63] Isidor enjoyed nothing so much as reading a *HafTorah*[64] portion at the end of *Shabbat*, kissing the *Torah* scrolls as they were carried around synagogue on High Holy days and hearing the soul-raising sound of the *shofar* (ram's horn). He had belonged to the Society for the Scientific Study of Judaism in 1819 and was a longtime friend of the renowned Rabbi Abraham Geiger until his friend surprised him by declaring himself a moderate. In the following months Geiger's ideas on reforming the liturgy of Judaism were published. Hirsch refused to have anything to do with him after that.

Rav Isidor Hirsch was only following faithfully in the footsteps of his illustrious rabbinic ancestors who had taught in French and German universities, and who had campaigned assiduously against the revising and modernizing of many European *siddurs* (Jewish prayer books). His fame as Hebrew scholar and researcher, teacher of philosophy, even charitable minister to the poor of the German streets, became known throughout Berlin. He inherited money from an uncle in the de Reuter family and used it to establish a large Hebrew school — a *yeshiva* — in Berlin, where he eventually moved his family homestead. Industrialists came to him for business savvy. Those without immediate means appealed to him for quick sustenance. His spacious and bustling elegant home, presided over by wife Elena, was a known welcome mission to Yiddish-speaking pilgrims emigrating from surrounding countries. Rav Isidor even researched everyone in his patriarchal and matriarchal line that had brought him to this day and to this spot. He traced his mother's line to the time of Germany's Teutonic age and knew his father's line of succession back to the 15th century, when Emperor Sigismund granted land and titles to Frederick of Hohenzollern.

This lust for marshalling the past and capitalizing on every opportunity Professor Hirsch passed on to his two sons and four daughters, who sought to emulate their brilliant father. But Hirsch's favorite and eventual heir was his oldest son, Aaron, who unwittingly and unwillingly would inherit the Rav's heavy mantle of intellectual prowess, cultural philanthropy and unfaltering *zeitgeist*.[65]

His hero was Prinz Otto (Eduard Leopold) von Bismarck, Germany's prime minister. He defeated France in the Seven Weeks War of 1866 and emerged victor of the Franco-Prussian war in 1871. Bismarck was due credit for founding the German empire and husbanding a peace for nineteen years as Germany's chancellor. His success in annexing duchies, principalities and cities through straightforward and unequivocal methods earned him the faith and love of his people.

In 1885, five years before the aging statesman left office, Aaron Yehudah Hirsch began his own life as an underweight, waiflike thing. His lungs, not fully developed at birth, took their time coming to maturity. He went home with his anxious mother two months late and continued to convalesce for the next several years. Proud papa that he was, the elder Hirsch sat beside the white wicker crib and read to his infant son about the master politician who had achieved political unification of a Prussian-dominated empire. Professor Hirsch thought Bismarck a true king, even a man of prophetic proportion. He quietly nicknamed him "Lord Otto". Here, after all, was a crafty, manipulative ruler who never seemed to doubt the veracity of his judgment. He was called the master of *Realpolitik*.[61] He was practical, opportunistic and often not above using cutthroat tactics with anyone in his way. Perhaps Isidor thought that Aaron would somehow inhale the story of this self-vindicating genius. What pride he, Isidor, would have — as father of Berlin's most revered Jewish sage, Rav Aaron Yehudah Hirsch!

But by 1891, after much pressure upon German citizens by the new government a petition was circulated and presented to the *Reichstag* with a quarter of a million signatures demanding that immigration of Jews into Germany be halted. Somehow this largely escaped the elder Hirsch who saw only miraculous progress toward a strong, independent nation.

"At last we will have a united and strong Germany that no one can take apart ever again," boasted Rav Hirsch about Bismarck. "He is creating a new Germany. We will become the strongest economic power in Europe. He is the father of the Fatherland!"

Little Aaron looked at his father with love and pride as he spoke glowingly of "Lord Otto". How glorious to be confided in! How thankful was the boy that his wise father read him these thrilling tidbits of the ministrations of power at their supper table. Neither suspected that their Iron Chancellor would step down from office in 1890 leaving behind a nation without political will or an internally unified people. They could not know the citizens of their homeland were destined to submit to whatever was decided for them, or that Bismarck's legacy would become the Jews' misery: in that fateful year the Pan-German League was founded and the old idea of Teutonic supremacy again surfaced in their meetings.

The influence of the German League spread rapidly across Germany. Gradually stories of anti-Jewish demonstrations began to appear in the newspapers. Stories of shops broken into and desecrated and Jewish families ousted from the better neighborhoods. Anti-Semitic articles appeared with some regularity in the various presses around Berlin and the larger cities. Editorials complained that Jewish businesses were swindling their customers. By 1892 the consensus was that Jews were to be considered a corrupting and negative force. The Second German Empire (*Reich*) had begun like a felling sledgehammer.

These political changes brought much worry to Rav Hirsch as well as to all the Jews in Germany. Even little Aaron felt the pressure. When he was eight, Aaron took his small bike from his family's garage and rode through the Berlin streets while his mother was at the hairdresser. He was found late the next day playing happily on the steps of a local Lutheran church. The cleaning ladies gave the boy food and asylum before calling on Hirsch to come get his wandering son. Though there was nothing to fear from this episode, Rav Hirsch took little Aaron aside and with little regard for the boy's feelings, demanded that never during his life or his eternity must he be found anywhere near a *goyishe*[67] establishment upon pain of paddling and other serious privations.

"If they find you are Jewish, there is no telling what can happen, even to a boy," he said. Great worry wrinkles creased his broad forehead. Aaron trembled as he gazed tearfully at the strained expression of concern and fear on his beloved papa's face. He promised to never stray again.

During his first ten years, Aaron's mother spoke mostly Hebrew to him. German was his second language. Yiddish was *verboten* (forbidden). It was the language of the streets, not of scholars. Rav Hirsch gradually introduced his sons to *Talmud* tractates. Though he was too young to attend synagogue except on *Shabbat* and holidays, Aaron quickly absorbed the Jewish culture and language. On High Holy days he and his younger brother Schmuel, accompanied their parents to one of the largest synagogues in Berlin to learn the customs and prayers. Aaron loved these occasions. The rumblings and mumblings of the devout in their *tallith* and phylacteries fascinated him. His father taught him to *daven*,[68] and to join the chanting of prayers that echoed around the immense inner building.

By the turn of the century, 1900, Aaron had become well-versed in *Torah* study. He was taught that being one with G-d meant living the stringent Law of Moses every waking moment. This had a dual effect upon his mind. On the one hand, Aaron was pleased to be brought up amid wealth and scholarship, bathed in the light of *Torah* and fueled further by his father's stern but loving attentions. In play with school chums he was deferred to. At his parents' social gatherings Aaron's every desire was evaluated, then ministered to with a solemn efficiency. Even Schmuel did not mind the occasional burst of anger or violence that shot from the prideful mouth of his elder brother. Aaron's mother sought to spoil him with food, his father with exacting, endless drill.

It was in this situation that Aaron felt trapped. The birthright of the firstborn was his. It rested upon his thin young shoulders squarely as a burdensome yoke he must carry without help or relief. While his parents looked upon him with pride, he shuddered in shame at his own feelings. He was expected to follow his father's path, to achieve wealth, to absorb and exude scholarship and philanthropy. While these goals were admirable in any son, Aaron chafed beneath their rub. He wanted to be a normal, carefree child. He aspired to a life of common achievement. But Aaron knew he must never utter his rebellious feelings to his parents and so he came to know a private anguish within himself and a guilt he was never to lose.

Daily life in Germany was at the crux of chafe and change, too. Quiet for perhaps a quarter of a century, the year 1893 was one in which words of anti-Semitism were again shouted in the streets and the lecture halls, this time with far-reaching consequences. The financial crisis twenty years earlier had been immediately blamed upon Jews. Stories of Jews accosted and spit upon in Germany's city streets became daily fare in newsprint. Famed German composer Richard Wagner, a virulent anti-Semite, wrote to King Ludwig II of Bavaria that he regarded the Jewish race as "the born enemy of humanity". The Pan German League announced its intention to rule the world. The well-regarded writer Paul Anton Lagarde, disappointed in Bismarck's *Reich*, wrote: *There is no racial purity here. We need a Fuhrer who will somehow educate the nation in its needs.*

By 1903 and now 18, young Aaron Hirsch the *mensch*[69] had obtained part of his inheritance from his father to study *Torah* in a well-known *yeshiva* in central Poland. A week before he was to depart Berlin, *The Protocols of the Learned Elders of Zion* appeared in the Russian press and was quickly picked up by news media around the world. The *Protocols* tract, of uncertain authorship, was a supposed attack on Napoleon the Third. It was written in 1884 to the effect that he sought world domination. No mention was made of Jews. But somehow the text had been altered, though the culprit was never determined, and in the place of Napoleon's name the words "Elders of Zion" were placed, this concocted title referring to a mythical council of Jews and implying they were involved in a plot to take over the world. Many, including Tsar Nicholas II, rejected it as pure fabrication, which it certainly was. But by then it had been published in numerous languages and circulated around the world. One effect of this happened on the eve of Passover that year in Kishinev, Moldavia, when forty-five Jews were murdered, 600 injured and 1,500 homes of Jews destroyed.

This news and greatly alarmed Professor Hirsch to the point that he began to worry for his own safety. Coupled with the steam of Jew-hating articles and diatribes still brewing in Germany and elsewhere, Aaron's parents determined he should remain with them and seek his fortune in local businesses in which Professor Hirsch had investments until the climate of hate should dissipate into a passive tolerance. Aaron acquiesced without argument. He had long since determined to break free of his father's plans for his life as an Orthodox Jew and looked at this change as a fortunate opportunity to make something of himself in the professional world until the time was ripe to break out on his own.

---

[62] Strangers
[63] A Hebrew scholar
[64] A reading section from the Torah
[65] The trend of thought and feeling in a particular age of society
[66] Practical power politics
[67] Non-Jewish
[68] Pray
[69] Gentleman

Deliver me from the oppression of man: so I will keep thy precepts.
— Psalm 119:134

9 — Wanderers in a Strange Land

Aaron chose the accounting field. His father was very pleased and availed his son of excellent instruction and internship in a well-known German firm. When he became thirty, he met a beautiful, educated Aryan-like German woman of his same age and fell passionately in love with her. He had never dated, but when he noticed the slim, well dressed young *fraulein* transacting business in his father's bank one morning he was instantly taken with her. Aaron shyly introduced himself. When the woman smiled at him he asked her to dinner. Before dessert arrived, he knew she was to be his mate. Her name was Fredericka von Metternich, the only daughter of a minor German official who wanted to see the Aryan race a reality and accordingly despised Jews as "intruders" into German society. His virulent frame of mind made Fredericka sincerely empathetic with the romantic and rebellious young man who called her his "princess" and courted her with great energy and an almost *Talmudic* devotion.

Fredericka was fair-minded, independent and gracious, spoiled but amenable, and no ingénue to refined German sociality. She was preparing for a career in design and still dependent upon her parents for sustenance when Aaron found her. She saw in Aaron the Jew a strong spirit and a talent for self-determination. Her parents had never seriously practiced their declared Catholicism, so Fredericka interviewed him about his Jewish beliefs and then allowed herself to accept her lover's religious background with little more than a wince and a heavy shrug.

"The burden of your Jewishness will fall on me, too, I imagine." Fredericka philosophized to Aaron. "We will work around it somehow. Germans plant their misfortune on the backs of those they secretly admire." Her opinion became prophecy.

Aaron hesitated to tell his parents of his love for this Gentile woman, not because he would greatly disappoint them but because he feared being disinherited. Thus their love was hidden from both families, but they devised a plan. Aaron would tell his father he was being moved to his firm's office in Baden. Fredericka's ploy was that an aunt there had requested a visit. Their ruses carefully planned, Aaron and his German "princess" quickly eloped. They were married by a *rabbi*. Fredericka at first wanted also to be married by a Catholic priest as a nod to her family but during the initial interview in the local diocese, Aaron became upset when he was asked if he would consider giving up his Judaism. He rose in anger and walked out of the church. Fredericka, who had never truly embraced her faith, quietly followed him out.

"We're already married," Aaron said. "For better or worse, for Jewish or Catholic... What do you think, my princess? I cannot become a Catholic."

Fredericka turned and looked up at the imposing edifice they had just left. It seemed the whole world was against their union, perhaps even G-d. But was G-d in the Church or in the synagogue?

"It's up to us, Aaron. Have we not just made our vows? Let us go now and live them."

They settled in the north country, in Hamburg. Aaron obtained a position as a minor official and each Sabbath he attended one of the quaint synagogues there. Fredericka resumed her studies and waited for him at home. When at last they wrote their parents an apology for their marriage and circumstances, the worst they feared came true. Fredericka was disowned for marrying a Jew. Professor Hirsch, reading that his son had married a Gentile whose father was an anti-Semite, had a sudden heart attack. The news shattered him. His attained wealth and success lost all meaning. Aaron was summarily disinherited. Frau Hirsch accused him of having grossly overindulged their son. They mourned Aaron as if he had died and vowed to never see him again. Hirsch grew progressively melancholy and took to wandering through the Berlin streets at odd hours in his oldest clothes.

Aaron, now 36, had by marriage forfeited an important means of support; his father's trust funds. He waited anxiously for letters, but received only one, from his mother. She would pray for his soul. His father was a broken man. Aaron added this new guilt to the old; he understood he must pay the price of his choices. Thereafter, when he went to synagogue he wept silently for his father's pain but also for himself, so deep was his guilt and so intense his longing for forgiveness.

In 1921, Aaron and Fredericka's first and only child, Gerhardt Israel Hirsch, came into the world without a cry, as if he respected his father's guilt more than the burden of his own new life. He was born in his parents' bedroom. The neighbor who helped out expected shrill report. She was amazed at his tolerance and sweet patience but worried that he was not fully comprehending. So she swatted his behind with nervous gusto until finally the babe gave angry voice. When Aaron saw this as he gazed for the first time at his firstborn male child sleeping in its mother's arms, he vowed to raise a strong son of the Abrahamic Covenant. Fredericka, seeing a family in the remaking, told Aaron she wanted more children as soon as possible.

At eight days, Gerhardt, the first born and heir to the Hirsh intellectual legacy, was ready to be circumcised by the local *mohel*.[70] This Levite was recovering from a heart attack and his hands were unsteady. When Aaron saw how both hands shook as the knife reached the tender skin he grabbed for it, but was too late. The slice penetrated the organ and the baby screamed in agony. The *mohel* apologized profusely but his deep cut caused many infections and consequent pain as well as permanent disfigurement of the baby's organ.

When the bloody cut was cleaned it was discovered that the organ's foreskin was still halfway intact. What to do now? The *mohel* said he'd not had a knife slip in thirty years of circumcising and would not accept payment. Aaron was beside himself with grief. He went to synagogue that night to ask G-d not to be angry with him and begged forgiveness for his choice of *mohel*. He also asked G-d to accept the ritual as symbolic of the covenantal mark. When he returned home, Fredericka swore no one would ever take a knife to her son again. She called the whole affair "pagan" and spent the night swearing in German beneath her breath.

By age two, Gerhardt was lovely as a German poster child; golden haired, blue eyed and sweet of disposition. He had his mother's tender smile and her way of laughing with her eyes. He did not possess his father's independent but melancholy turn of mind. Gerhardt was instinctively his mother's child; he was slavishly devoted to her. He followed her everywhere. He was taught German and some Polish at her knee but Aaron worked harder at teaching him Hebrew. At age eight, young Gerhardt began to accompany his father to synagogue on Saturday mornings, waiting in the hard black seats until Aaron finished his *minyan*[71] duties. There the love of Judaism and respect for the traditions of the ages old culture seized his impressionable mind and he felt he'd come upon a second home. On these occasions Gerhardt was deeply happy. He loved the huge old building's ancient tapestries and stained-glass windows. He would point these out to his mother, who admired them, also. The synagogue walls were two feet thick. Gerhardt felt G-d loved him. He was protected from the world.

At first only the sounds of Judaism attracted him. On High-Holy days he tried to mimic the alerting summons of the long, white ribbed *shofar* that reverberated off the massive walls. Gerhardt listened in fascination to the bearded old Jewish men, the way they spoke to each other, the wails of their somber and penitent prayers. He loved the musty scent of olive oil in the *Ner Tamid* as it burned in its container above the *Torah* cabinet. A year later, Gerhardt had learned to sing many of the prayers and songs of the holidays. His Yiddish knowledge was extensive because Aaron spoke it to his son almost from birth. Gerhardt even knew the ritual for welcoming the "bride of *Shabbat*". He was by then well known to the members of the congregation, who called him by his middle name, pronouncing it Yisrael. Occasionally, one would remark on Gerhardt's blond hair and fair skin. Aaron, not wanting to admit his wife was a *goy*, let it be discreetly circulated that she was a Nordic Jew.

"Oh, of course, of course", they said, and stared at the child's straight, well-formed nose and wide chin. "Nordic, okay, but a Jew nevertheless, a son of the Covenant of Abraham. *Mazel tov.*"

~

Aaron was becoming increasingly uneasy about current events in Germany. A student of history, he'd witnessed in 1918 the birth of the Weimar Republic. With the abdication of Emperor William II just before Christmas season began, the German passion for rigid efficiency dissembled into a mad dance of anarchy. Soldiers refused to obey their officers. Workers called general strikes and marched on the capital. Aaron watched from the sidelines. He saw how flare-ups in opinions became outbursts that often ignited unchecked lawlessness and violence. But he approved of the patriot Friedrich Ebert, a former harness maker. Only 47, he'd lost two sons in the First World War. In an overnight coup Ebert emerged as the new, strong leader of the Social Democratic party. The German people missed their chancellor, but they commiserated and decided to accept him as one of their own.

But the taste of revolution was turning into a lust for power and even new Chancellor Ebert couldn't hold back the tide of Marxism. Germany's new leaders favored immediate socialization of industry and empowerment of workers' and soldiers' councils.

In truth, the nation's economy was on the verge of collapse because they were slowly being starved to death by the Allied blockade. Finally, two days after Ebert took office, Woodrow Wilson's personally engineered armistice agreement was secretly signed in a railway car placed for the occasion in a French forest. The new German republic was simultaneously begun, defeated and humiliated.

But talk grew rapidly that the army hadn't been defeated in the field. Instead, it was stabbed in the back by so-called subversive elements at home. Named as culprits were pacifists and liberals, Communists, socialists and especially Jews. Field Marshal Paul von Hindenburg was a proponent of this myth. "We are invincible", he wrote, and Chancellor Ebert also propagated the fiction of German invincibility. Aaron and Fredericka were in the crowd that day, December 11, 1918 when the German legions returned home from France and Belgium. At the Brandenburg Gate, Chancellor Ebert welcomed his men. He told them:

"I salute you, who return unvanquished from the field of battle."

Stirring though his words were, they absolved the general staff of the responsibility for defeat while at the same time condemning Ebert's own revolutionary republic. From that point forward, internal political wars and contentions saw Germany divided and her government reduced in power to an unruly militia. Aaron's employer, reading his morning *Volk und Zeit* (People and Time) observed,

"We might as well volunteer, ourselves, Aaron. That way we can keep the militia from our *own* doors!"

But Aaron was more concerned about the rise of the Volunteer Rifles, a force of 4,000 well-equipped men from all walks of life including fanatical nationalists and demobilized soldiers. Dubbed the *Freikorps* (Free Corps), these "thug" groups were organizing all over Germany. The soldiers glorified nationalism but were hostile against socialism, democracy — and Jews. Referring to themselves as *Landsknechte* (Freebooters) they formed the early crux of the men who would later become the focus of the forces seeking to undermine and destroy the republic. Many of the Nazi party would be recruited from members of the *Freikorps*, which soon boasted 400,000 men under arms.

By the following year, any new strength of nationalism the German people might have felt was crushed with the signing of the Treaty of Versailles in June 1919. The treaty, as American President Woodrow Wilson presented it, limited the mighty German army to a force of merely 4,000 officers and 96,000 men without an organized reserve. The navy was also severely cut and the merchant marine fleet was almost wiped out. Germany was also made to surrender some of its provinces and colonies, with hard-fought for land going to other European and Nordic countries. German goods were effectively barred from Allied markets for a period of five years.

But perhaps the worst blow was spelled out in Article 231 of the Treaty. It was the death knell to Teutonic honor. *It was required that Germany take sole responsibility for causing World War I and pay reparations.* Knowing that armed resistance was hopeless, Chancellor Ebert accepted the inevitable. His acquiescence brought on a period of national mourning. The sword of defeat cut deeply into Germany's proud psyche. She was crushed. She had lost face.

Only one year later a vast plan for revenge was laid by a penniless, rootless 29-year old Austrian expatriate named Adolf Hitler. The night this army corporal read the famous Twenty-Five Points that would become the basis of Nazism, a wolf was born. By August of 1921 the German public was already receiving the preached dogma of Teutonic superiority and the racial inferiority of Jews. Gangs of Storm Troopers roamed the streets, pummeling faces and cracking heads. Jews were beaten in the streets. Synagogues were desecrated. The country had become a trap for businessmen and families alike. Many Jews hurriedly fled Germany for the Americas and any other port offering sanctuary from this new terror.

One day, after much thought and careful observation, Aaron announced to Fredericka that it was no longer safe to be a Jew in Poland, in Germany or anywhere in Europe. He had decided they would quit the synagogue and forgo all outward worship as a Jew. His wife was startled but after some reasoned discussion they agreed that measures had to be taken to secure their safety as a family. Without his father's money to help with essential needs, Aaron had barely enough to support his family. They packed and moved again to a quiet, anonymous looking apartment in Stuttgart where Aaron obtained a minor position as a state auditor. He registered with the local authorities as Karl Schell, of no particular religion. When Aaron submitted his resume to the auditing firm the clerk looked at the certificate and other forms Aaron had signed. His certification application noted no children in the household.

"Your salary will little permit having a large family, Herr Schell," the magistrate said with a small laugh, for times in Germany were very poor.

"My wife and I have no plans for children, magistrate. We do sometimes care for my wife's brother's boy. Her brother was killed recently in an auto accident."

"Oh, that is so? Kindly list his name and age here, then." He pointed to a line on the form. Aaron carefully wrote Gerhardt von Metternich, aged 11.

Their new residence proved to be worse than in Hamburg. Twice the synagogues in Stuttgart were bombed. Aaron feared someone would decide he had a "Jewish" face and make trouble. He kept to himself at work and did not make friends easily. To protect himself and his family in case of invasion he buried the artifacts of his religion — his *Mogen Dovid*, his *mezuzah*[72], his *Torah*, his phylacteries. His *tallis* and his undergarments, which he had never relinquished, he burned. Fredericka, knowing children tell what they see, sent Gerhardt to the store while Aaron was busy in the yard with his tasks, but the child returned in time to see the thick, black book he knew so well vanish into a box and laid to rest in the soil beneath a pile of rocks. Aaron's face crumbled in sorrow as he buried his beloved *Torah*. He looked up to see Gerhardt watching him.

"Come here, son." Gerhardt ran to his father's embrace.

"You must never tell what you are seeing. Promise? Promise me!"

Then Aaron explained that to be a Jew in Germany was an invitation to trouble. They could all be murdered, anytime, anywhere. The boy tried to understand. His father explained calmly that they were no longer to be Jews. They could have no Jewish friends or acquaintances because their lives would also be in gravest danger. They would, probably for their lifetime, have to live and think only as Germans, as Gentiles. Gerhardt would not be going to synagogue again. He would not have a *bar mitzvah*. Worst of all, he must now refer to his parents as Karl and Fredericka. He was not even to tell anyone he was their son, but a nephew whose German father had died in an auto accident. His mother, Hannah, had long ago deserted the family.

The child was devastated by this last decree. Tears rolled down his face, merging with his father's as they held each other. In that moment of sacrifice a new birth occurred bathed in a destiny first of war, but then of prophecy. Gerhardt cried often in those days as he walked alone or played in the yard near the buried *Torah*. He felt the torturous separation from his parents, even though he knew it to be untrue. Fredericka tried to console him; she assured Gerhardt that the outward appearance of things was only to save their lives. But the child began to wish he could murder those who wanted to kill Jews so he and his parents could be a true family again. He would find those responsible. He would search them out and bring them to repentance.

During the next year, Aaron and Fredericka began to quarrel. They argued over the lack of money needed to pay raised taxes, over lack of time available for togetherness and over the lack of family worship. Fredericka was accustomed to an active intellectual and social life. She had little in common with Aaron's few business associates. After they argued, days and nights were spent in cold silence. These trying periods increased. Gerhardt also felt the tension. He became unsure of his parents' love. He began to cry at dinner as he ate. Aaron's absences increased. He seemed to be at work all the time. Fredericka opened a small designer consulting and home goods store and worked there seven days a week. She, too, was rarely home. They had little in common beside their son. One day Aaron returned from work to find scrawled on the door:

"Pity Gerhardt, he has no home."

Who had written it? Gerhardt eventually confessed. He felt unnoticed, insignificant. These changes fostered a lack of family unity. The spirit of peace that had once been as a fourth entity in the home, disappeared. There was no prayer, no synagogue, no *Torah*. The house became an empty shell. Gerhardt felt it. It made him sick, but he loved his parents so dearly he tried to bring them back together with good deeds and thoughtful ways. On rare occasions the family took small trips to the park or to the lovely towns outside Stuttgart, but his parents usually quarreled over money or available time.

Gerhardt returned from school one day to find his mother crying in the bedroom.

"My *leibchen*, Gerhardt, my darling, I have something to tell you."

Gerhardt felt he knew. They were going to move again.

"Your father has left us today. He is not coming back, so we will have to move again."

Fredericka reached for her son. He was in shock. The world

124

had just crashed onto his heart. He collapsed in tears at his mother's feet. At that moment, in his 12-year old mind he wondered how a loving G-d allowed these things to happen. Then he knew. G-d didn't care about his parents' troubles or his shattered family. It was G-d's fault. He determined that G-d must answer for the hatred of Jews that was responsible for the breakup of his family and the abandonment of their precious religion. A new resolve grew in his heart. He, Gerhardt, would avenge it all. He would have his parents with him again in a Germany free of hatred. If G-d wouldn't help, Gerhardt would do it alone.

A week later, Gerhardt and Fredericka moved across town into a small and dirty *pensione* with other poor part-families. One of the women there took a look at tall, blond Gerhardt and said to Fredericka:

"That boy belongs in the Hitler Youth. They'll take him. Is he 13 or 14? They'll teach him to be a man and to defend Germany against its enemies. Why don't you enroll your son in the Youth League program?"

Fredericka had never considered being parted from Gerhardt, but the more she mulled over the woman's suggestion, the more she wondered if it would be the best thing for her sober, sensitive child of 12. She was told the Youth League was accepting boys as young as ten. She was told the boys grew tough and self-reliant, that they exercised ferociously and were healthier than other German youth. That sounded good to Fredericka. She saw an opportunity for her son to find and fill his potential and serve his German state. Perhaps she would consider it. The year was 1934.

---

[70] The man who circumcises the male baby at 8 days of age in the ritual called Brith Milah.

[71] A group of ten Jewish males over 13 years of age who gather as a constituted group for public Jewish prayer

[72] The oblong container affixed to the side posts of a Jewish home containing scrolls from Deut. 6:4-9; 11; 13-21

[73] Lower class pension or retirement

"My program for educating youth is hard. Weakness must be hammered away. In my castles of the Teutonic Order a youth will grow up before which the world will tremble. I want a brutal, domineering, fearless, cruel youth. Youth must be all that. It must bear pain... That is how I will create the New Order."

— Adolf Hitler, 1933

10 — Dark Assembly

In the jungle of German politics, the nature of the menace went undetected, but its prey trembled. Sensing entrapment it was, alas, too late when Adolf Hitler the Austrian was appointed Chancellor of Germany in January of 1933. The Jewish population in Germany at that time lingered around 566,000. anti-Semitism had long since become a severe Jewish problem there and in other western European countries. Hitler was furiously building upon any opportunity to implement his master plan to exterminate all Jews from Germany and nearby countries. He immediately swore in 40,000 SA and SS men as auxiliary police. The deceptive power of evil was a stalking beast in Germany's midst. The German Workers' Party name was changed by Hitler to include the term "National Socialist". Thus the full name was the National Socialist German Workers' Party (*Nationalsozialistische Deutsche Arbeiterpartei* or NSDAP): For short, *Nazi*.

A few days later the *Nazis* burned the *Reichstag* building to create a crisis. Hitler was granted emergency powers of government to combat this and the uprisings that followed. A month later he was made dictator. He became suddenly the most powerful man in Germany, though Paul von Hindenburg was still president. Hitler immediately began building concentration camps. Soon Dachau came into being near Munich, then Buchenwald, then Sachsenhausen and Ravensbruck for women. In April of the same year his *Nazis* boycotted Jewish shops and businesses. Hermann Göring, a war hero who joined Hitler's party in 1922, created the *Gestapo* in Prussia. Then the official state youth organization of Hitler Youth was born. The holocaust of unfortunate souls had begun.

Before 1933 receded into scarred history, the *Nazi* Party was declared the only legal party in Germany. Anti-Semitic meetings were held in public places. Because of Hitler's obsession with Jews and his constant reference to them as "a great hindrance" to the rebuilding of Germany, they were increasingly singled out. In fact, anti-Semitism was legitimized after 1933 as a government priority. Jews were defined as "non-Aryan"; they could not own land in Germany or participate in the arts, they were in danger of forced sterilization and they were eventually to feel the effects of the terrible Nuremburg Laws. [See Appendix 4]

Fredericka kept up with the news. Jewish businesses were being boycotted. They were excluded from parks, theaters, public transportation, and swimming pools. A new national act prohibited farmers from inheriting land if there was any trace of Jewish ancestry going back to 1800. They now considered individuals with even one-eighth Jewish ancestry as full Jews. This affected any individual with at least one Jewish grandparent. A civil act of April 11, 1933 dismissed Jews from the army and from civil service. National Socialist extremists also advocated the dissolution of mixed marriages and advocated Jewish sterilization.

Fredericka grew increasingly concerned and worried for Gerhardt. She recalled ironically that Aaron had seen this coming long ago. One day she purchased a copy of Hitler's *Mein Kampf* (My Struggle) from a small bookstore. On the first page she turned to she read the words: "The Jew is a maggot in a rotting corpse; he is a plague worse than the Black Death of former times; a germ carrier of the worst sort . . . the people's parasite; the people's vampire."

She shut the book in horror. He was speaking of her son. "*Gott in Himmel,*"[74] she exclaimed to the walls around her. "How can I protect him? What if he is found out?"

The month was May, her vacation permitted four days to use as she saw fit. They went on a hiking trip into the aspen forests and meadows of southern Germany, accompanied by friends from Fredericka's workplace. It was a wonderful time for everyone. Gerhardt's grief at not seeing his father had diminished somewhat because Aaron wrote short letters monthly from his apartment in their old neighborhood in Hamburg where he had managed to find a stable but low paying employment with an accounting firm. He wanted Gerhardt to visit in that week, but Fredericka won out, she had custody. Aaron could have him twice a year for two weeks each. So Aaron sent pictures of himself, his apartment and views of the city. He often called Gerhardt and they commiserated across the miles.

"Be strong and loyal to your mother", Aaron told his son. "Remember your roots (but be careful not to let anyone know who your father came from). We cannot be too cautious. There are great dangers around us. We must wait until Germany is once again free so all her citizens may once again enjoy their natural freedoms. Then, I pray, we will be together again."

Gerhardt, fearing spies upon the Jews might intercept his letters and phone calls, replied honestly that he missed attending his "church" and reading "their book". He felt somehow amiss without the practice of his faith. He missed his "Shbt" observance. Aaron replied that he also missed these things, but time would bring the advantages around again, and perhaps they would one day be reunited. He called every few weeks but these calls often left Gerhardt lonelier than ever for his father's nearness. This vital portion of his life was gone forever.

Gerhardt often visited his mother's store after school. She had to work long hours to support the two of them, though Aaron sent what he could. Gerhardt also took to long walks in the city's streets. He was sometimes so deep in thought that he didn't arrive home until late.

Fredericka worried deeply for her son. At the same time she was ashamed to be a German citizen. What could justify this fanaticism with Hitler? Was no one safe any longer? In the increasingly threatening atmosphere of hatred she began to consider a dangerous plan: Gerhardt was an attractive, healthy boy, blond and blue eyed with regular features. He didn't look "Jewish", and this was in his favor. Also, he was not truly circumcised. Perhaps no one would check further. But then she hesitated. What sort of things would he be exposed to? What would Aaron say about it? Fredericka knew that answer, she knew Aaron. It was inconceivable he would allow his son to be dropped, as it were, into the midst of murderers! He might even withhold parental support . . .

As for Gerhardt's emotional acceptance of German military life, he was young and very malleable. He (almost) always obeyed his mother happily and with a charming acquiescence. He liked to work, to figure things out. He was bright, even scholarly in his schoolwork. Again, his gentle disposition would save him from becoming a front line soldier. This fact appealed greatly to Fredericka.

But what kinds of horrors would he be exposed to once enrolled? Hitler's officers would be unrelenting in their mission to preach hatred to the youth. This would harden them. They would become unrepentant murderers. How would this affect her sweet-natured son and his love for his Jewish heritage? A thought came to her then, but it was so outrageous and foolish she immediately discarded it. *What if he turned against his parents?* No, he could not turn traitor without giving himself away as well, thereby hanging a noose around everyone's neck!

No, that was not Gerhardt. She knew her son . . . a loving, loyal child of high moral character. But one ugly and frightening thought crept into her mind, just below the surface. Given his German looks and quiet demeanor, and given her careful preparation in "recreating" his German parentage — even if she were able to successfully enroll her son in the Hitler Youth — *what if somehow, someday, they found him out?* There was no doubt he would be killed, by one or by many.

Then what to do? The choice, she felt, was hers alone because she had read that Baldur von Shirach, the man responsible for the recruitment and training of the Hitler Youth program, was in favor of laws requiring ALL German youth who had reached the age of ten years be recruited into the program. Of course, if they were suspected of being Jewish, they would not be accepted. What would become of the Jewish boys and eventually their families?

Gerhardt was trapped: join or die!

So Fredericka's decision was forced upon them both. They had no real choice. There was no longer any way to protect Gerhardt from Germany's malignant cancer, the Third *Reich*, and its evil enterprise, the Final Solution. She would have to entrust him to his Maker. *Protect him, mein Gott,* she prayed, *save my darling son from the very bowels of Hell . . .*

But there were qualifications. Upon arriving at the recruiting office, Fredericka was given a sheet of four essential guidelines that Gerhardt had to meet. She was told to read them carefully and to bring papers if requested for proof of her statements, which she and Gerhardt were required to swear to under oath. As she read the first requirement, fear gripped her heart. It read:

All Jewish youth are denied entry. This includes any child with a Jewish ancestor. Parents will be required to prove that their son or daughter is racially pure.

Fredericka had not expected this. Was not Hitler himself an Austrian of dubious birth? If these Nazi dogs found out her son was half-Jewish, Gerhardt's penalty would be swift and severe: he'd be barred from any future employment, he would be ostracized in public, followed and reported on by spies, and eventually he could become a hunted man. He might even be murdered. Carefully she went over the details of Gerhardt's ancestry. He was born at home without a midwife to report the birth and the event was never recorded in Germany's Vital Records Bureau. All anyone had been told was that her only and somewhat older brother Von had given the child he sired out of wedlock to Fredericka to raise. He was dead now and Fredericka's brother's wife had disappeared. Would the Party seek out the woman Fredericka claimed to be the actual mother? Let them try. She was likely across the world somewhere, married and with another surname. Anyway, Gerhardt's looks favored the German side of the family. They would never suspect. She read on:

There can be no hereditary disease in the boy or girl's family.
The child can have no objectionable political opinions by Nazi standards.
Each child must be physically fit or able to become so.
There will be no exceptions to these standards.

For the first time since Aaron had left them, Fredericka was concerned. She showed the paper to Gerhardt when they arrived home.

"Why don't they want Jews?" he asked.

"*Leibchen*, dear one, these people are deluded. Jews are not inferior, only different. Perhaps these people will see that and not pursue this path. You are as good or better than any other boy. If they cannot find a Jewish strain, they must admit you."

"But how will we pretend I am not Jewish? We'll have to tell them about Papa."

"No, no! We cannot ever disclose your father, they may decide to hunt him down. I am thinking of a plan. We must protect you from your father's heritage, *leibchen*. Germany is no longer safe for the Jew. Remember, we have no birth certificate for you as Hirsch and Aaron registered you as a von Metternich. This, our family name, has been in German records for two hundred years. Don't worry, we will find a way."

Fredericka remembered the eighth day of her son's life, the *mohel's* accident, and the results. She was grateful now for the slip of his knife.

On the morning of March 25th, 1934, papers and plan intact, Fredericka and her son walked into the pristine offices of the Youth League. Gerhardt was surprised to see hundreds of boys his age and general appearance. Men in brown uniforms with *swastika* patches on their shoulders and epaulets were interviewing. They sat at long desks that lined the four walls of the spacious room. Fredericka signed in. They were ushered to seating. Gerhardt felt himself slowly relax. He studied the posters of Germany that were nailed to the walls of the office while his mother enrolled him in the program. The posters were at least twelve feet high, he thought. One in particular caught his attention. A rosy-skinned blond boy like himself but many times magnified, wearing dark shorts and a brown short-sleeved shirt, topped off with a smart black tie and a Nazi cross for insignia. He was gripping a Nazi flag and smiling broadly. Light was upon him, radiating from his triumphant smile. He looked unbelievably proud and happy to be German. The words alongside his head said *Der Deutsche Student*. The bottom of the poster read *Kämpft Für Fuhrer und Volk.*[69] Looking at the poster, Gerhardt realized his own dream image. *If I can become as he is, I'll help free the land for Jews again, and bring my father home to us.* Tears came to his eyes but he quickly wiped them away.

Fredericka was speaking to a woman she knew in the neighborhood. Gerhardt looked at the others waiting to be interviewed.

"What will we be doing?" he asked the boys next to him.

"We'll be going on trips," one of them replied. His eyes shone with anticipation.

"Yes", said an older boy next to him. "We'll be learning camping, athletics, many things, you know. My parents are excited about it. They are grateful to Hitler for this program."

Gerhardt noticed some boys who were in his schoolroom classes. One parent accompanied each. He counted 217 boys and parents. Girls would be interviewed the following month for a separate League.

"Do our parents get to come with us?" he asked, hoping he wouldn't have to leave his mother for any length of time. They had never been separated. The older boy spoke up again.

"Oh, no, this is for us, just us. Parents aren't allowed. We'll have trainers and leaders, I guess you could say... they're going to be like our parents."

Gerhardt frowned. He didn't like the idea of leaving Fredericka alone. They'd always been very close. He couldn't imagine being without her firm hand for more than a few days. The other boy sensed his hesitation.

"Oh, you'll see, it will be okay. We'll get to go home for visits. It's kind of like a mission, becoming the Chancellor's youth."

He extended his hand. "I'm Horst Werner. What's your name?"

"Gerhardt von Metternich."

"Gerhardt? Glad to meet you. I hope we'll be pals." He turned to the man beside him, portly and ruddy faced.

"This is my father. He owns factories in Berlin."

Gerhardt extended his hand to Herr Werner, who shook it generously and laughed a hello. Horst rose from his chair.

"Come and meet my friends. The interviewers won't get to us for awhile."

He took Horst's hand and they went throughout the room acquainting themselves until Fredericka called him. Within another hour, the interview for *Hitler Jungend* (Youth) was completed. Papers had been submitted for verification. The oath would be taken at the swearing in ceremonies to be held the following month. Gerhardt von Metternich was to report for indoctrination and uniforms. A strange new excitement came over Gerhardt as he contemplated how his life would change. He wanted to pray and ask G-d if he was doing the right thing but he was still angry with Him for the increased reprisals against Jews. He remembered his vow to undo the wrongs that G-d had let happen. He would stick by that promise and his parents would be proud of him and their little family would be together again. On that hopeful note, Gerhardt made a resolution to overcome his loss. He would become a successful Youth. He would fight for the freedom to restore his family's lost faith. He and his father would again attend synagogue, read *Torah*, study *Talmud* commentaries and attend High Holy Day services without reprisals. It would be his oath. He would do it or die.

Gerhardt came home to his father's message that all Jewish and Protestant youth groups throughout Germany had been ordered disbanded by Hitler Youth leader, Baldur von Schirach. The pretext was that they were "public nuisances".

"The Catholic institutions are still alive and well," Aaron laughed on the phone when Gerhardt called him back. "I guess they have some arrangement with the Nazis, but I'll bet it won't be long until they fall, too. Have you been given any assignments yet?"

"No, but I know I belong to the *Jungvolk* (Young People). They call us *pimpfs*, little fellows. When I'm 14, I'll become a *Hitler Jungend* (Youth), an HJ member. My interviewer said that if I show myself well I could become a leader of others."

Aaron was silent a moment. "Gerhardt, my son, you know I don't approve of this move of your mother's, to get you into Hitler's world. Promise me you will never, never mention your family background. You must appear to be 100% German. If they investigate us, they'll find we are Jews and we'll be marked. Your life in Germany will be in danger.

"Maybe they'll never find out, Poppa. Maybe they'll overlook us."

As Gerhardt hung up, he thought about the interviewer; the cold efficiency of his manner, his ironed appearance, and his haughty, penetrating look. Gerhardt felt that the man knew every corner of his mind. He felt small and foolish beneath the huge posters and flags that hung on all the walls. They seemed to demand his every breath and thought. He wondered if the man who gripped his hand when the interview ended suspected the hard knot of fear in his stomach. Was it fear or was it anger? Gerhardt knew only that his mother wanted him to be happy and safe, to grow into a worthy man, even a Gentile, the only fruit of her loins. She was the love of his life. He wanted to make her and his father so very proud. He wondered how little he would see of her once his training began.

Three weeks passed. The time for the inauguration ceremony had arrived. There was always an elaborate yearly ceremony when young people were admitted into a single branch of the HJ: the *Jungvolk* or the Air Corps (*Luftwaffe*), the Motor Corps, the Naval Corps or the Equestrian Corps. Many of the prominent members of the Nazi party attended and the chance that Hitler himself would make his presence known was the great expectation of all the recruits. The day was April 20, Hitler's birthday. This year the festivities were held on the grounds of a castle near the Rhine. Gerhardt was excited to be inducted in the *Jungbann Fuhrer* ranks. At the *Hitler Jugend* office he was issued the required uniform. Hesitantly, he signed for it. He slept little and arose very early to be ready for Horst's father to pick him up. They were going in a caravan of army trucks. His mother could not take time from work to attend but she pressed his new regulation brown shirt, tie and slacks and made him a large breakfast of sausage, eggs, bread and cheese.

As he dressed, Gerhardt could think only of his secret dream. He would rise in the ranks and make his parents proud. He would become a fighter for freedom. He would sacrifice to make Germany great again and secure freedom for his Jewish brethren. He checked himself in the mirror. His short black stockings were new. He had a trench cap and a *swastika* armband. *Jungvolk* insignias were on his shirt and shoulder strap. He did not carry his scout knife or his German army bayonet knife. When he became a certified mechanic and was promoted to the regular HJ league, he would bear them proudly.

The ride was fun. All the boys tumbled together in the truck beds, laughing and enjoying their rides. When they arrived at the castle grounds the Leaders ordered them to form lines of fifty and gave them instructions on entering the vast grounds behind the walled fort. The day was overcast but dry. Clouds hung high above them as if watching the proceedings at a respectful distance. Thousands of people were gathering to watch and cheer. The new recruits marched in solemnly as entry music began. Banners and lighted torches were carried by older boys who were the first ever entrants in the HJ when it began in 1933. Each of the thousands of recruits wore the same uniform. Those who would be making presentations and their lieutenants were *Wehrmacht*. Their manner was stiff and proud, their uniforms spotless, their heavy black shoes reflective in their shine.

The first speaker opened the ceremonies and reminded the youth of the significance of their roles in the National Socialism party. He introduced the man behind the idea of the Hitler Youth, Baldur von Schirach. He was tall and formidable looking. He spoke for an hour of the role of youth in Germany's revival.

"We must rise again to power. Youth will have a great deal of influence and power in their movements. We want all German youth to be Hitler Youth. We want you to be the new privileged class of Germany. The world will be open to you; people will bow before your superior training and your Aryan heritage. You are the hope and ideal of the new Germany, the Third *Reich*, and the Third Kingdom. You are the knights in armor. Long live the *Reich*!"

Following this stirring speech the stadium rocked with thunderous applause. Every recruit took an oath of allegiance. When it came Gerhardt's time, he stepped forward with his company of five hundred and in a trembling voice recited carefully the words:

"I promise in the Hitler Youth to do my duty at all times in all faithfulness to help the *Fuhrer* – so help me G-d."

As if shot from cannons, military bands began playing loud-

135

ly, everyone saluted, and the audience of thousands cheered. This new membership would last two to six months while individual backgrounds were checked and family commitment to Germany ascertained. Upon completion of these inspections it was rumored that deeds of valor would be performed in full dress uniform. Gerhardt was unable to learn what those were. Horst said they would have to jump out of windows with only pavement below, but all the boys laughed at him, all except Gerhardt. Looking at Horst's earnest face, he had already begun to be frightened.

During the following months the boys were introduced to war games, a requisite for new recruits. They chose sides and red and blue armbands were issued. Each platoon of boys wore one color on their right upper arm. Leader Frommer decided his team of two hundred boys would wear blue. Across the campground area, Leader Verhoven passed out red armbands to his group of two hundred boys. The colorful fabric stood out against the camping uniforms of black and brown. These "competition" trials were to be common in the HJ and *Jungvolk*. The boys were told they were participants in a "hunt" for "the enemy", color against color. When the enemy was "found", their armband was to be ripped off. This game often resulted in fistfights and outright brawls between platoons. The Leaders encouraged rough play, they approved of total immersion in games to toughen up the boys. Gerhardt instinctively hated these games. He often got the worst of it for not moving fast enough out of the way of the boys attacking him. Several times his shirt got ripped and his tie became a noose from which he was dragged along the rocky terrain until he managed to break loose. He discovered in himself a reluctance to fight or to risk bruising, but he was more fearful of attracting Leader Frommer's anger and so kept his reluctance silent.

Horst was different, he loved the games and knocked as hard as he was shoved.

"Come, Gerhardt, fight! Show your colors for your Fatherland! You are not weak, only hesitant. How will your Performance Booklet look to our leader? Watch me, follow my lead!"

He bounded ahead, screaming vengeance. Gerhardt, summoning all his might and courage, raced behind his friend into the fray, forcing himself to forget his apathy. Bodies slammed into each other. Screams filled the air and the fight was on! Gerhardt grabbed at armbands, twisting out of reach, feinting and moving quickly. He became amazed at himself. Horst was at his side now.

They ran together after red-banded boys.

"Bring him down," shouted Gerhardt "This one, now grab and run!"

"Got 'im, go after that one, on your left. Look — 12 o'clock, trip him, trip him!"

Hours later, at final count, Gerhardt's team had captured 120 red armbands, but Verhoven's "men" had 160 blues. Gerhardt and Horst were bruised but not badly. Three boys had to be hospitalized; many had bruises and were crying. These last were spit upon by their leaders in full view of the other boys.

"You must be heroic! Hitler has no use for sissies and cowards. Fight to win, play to win. You are German, a member of G-d's Master Race! No weaklings are allowed here!"

But new directives had been issued. No one was allowed to leave the HJ. Schirach's orders were to recruit all German youth and keep them occupied in activities of the Third *Reich* for the remainder of their lives. When Gerhardt told his mother this, she caught her breath in horror.

"They have said this? *Mein Gott*, you are not to be a savior of Germany, *leibchen*, but a slave. This I never suspected. All the youth of Germany are now trapped!

"I will be safe as long as it is not discovered that I am a Jew, Mama."

"True, Gerhardt, true. But can you pay such a price as the loss of freedom?" She held tightly to her son and regretted her decision to put him into the way of these wicked people.

"We must pray to Gott that Hitler is destroyed, my son, before he destroys Germany."

Gerhardt closed his eyes and remembered his vow to unite his parents again.

"Yes, Mama," he said quietly.

~

Gerhardt reported to his regular school early each morning and his HJ classes in early afternoon. They lasted until nightfall, when he walked the two miles home. Upon arriving at HJ headquarters he joined with his classmates to salute the German and *Nazi* flags, reciting the oath of allegiance before it:

I promise to do my duty in love and loyalty to the *Fuhrer* and our flag.

Then the slogan:

We believe in the indomitable strength of National Socialism.

We are the future, we are on the march.
We will destroy everything in our way.

As the months wore on and in spite of the charged atmosphere, *Nazi* Youth school became routine and for Gerhardt, dull. He exercised with his group for the first hour and at the end of classes each evening. History lessons were filled with *Nazi* propaganda and diatribes against the Slavic and Jewish peoples. Former German leaders were glorified. A study of the early Teuton tribes, precursors of the so-called "Aryan" race was stressed daily. A huge portrait of Hitler hung in every classroom. The Leader's pronouncements were as law. Everyone had to write them down and recite them. Leader Frommer's uttered epithets were the new Gospel. There was no room for disagreement or discussion. No research was permitted; there was no library because intellectualism was discouraged. There were only posters and copies of Hitler's speeches.

But the worst part was the anti-Semitism lectures. The National Socialists had figured out that the Nordic or Aryan race (as Hitler named it in *Mein Kampf*) was a race of "culture founders", the principal ingredient of the German people. Therefore, life was a struggle between bloodlines as well as individuals. The *Nazis'* ultimate goal was the preservation of this *Nordic*[76] race. The HJ were told they were in a race war to eliminate the "culture destroyers"; Jews, Slavs, mental and physical misfits of the country, and eventually the world's non-Aryans.

"This is how to spot a Jew," Leader Frommer would say, pointing at a picture pinned to a board. It showed a boy walking with his parents. Leader Frommer would point out the salient physical characteristics of the faces, ears and body types. Of course, there were no Jews in these classrooms to bring forward as an example. The picture remained in front of the class every day. Derogatory remarks about Jews were encouraged.

"These Jews are a threat to the German people," Leader Frommer often said, while he jabbed his pointer at the picture. "They have no place in the *Reich* or in this world. We will not tolerate them. They want to destroy the Nordic race, to pollute your heritage, to bring back the dark veil of time. Remember, people may be put in categories of species or races. The History shows us that all true advances in the world have been made by the Nordic or Aryan race. Other races are inferior to us and these must be destroyed. They must not be allowed to pollute the Aryan race of people. Jews are not racially pure, they are inferior as a race. Beware of them! They are culture destroyers. Remember, you boys are the dream of the Teutonic race, the Master race! You will overtake the world! Now the oath[77]:

"In the presence of this blood banner which represents our Führer, I swear to devote all my energies and my strength to the saviour of our country, Adolf Hitler. I am willing and ready to give up my life for him, so help me God."

The first half dozen times Gerhardt heard Leader Frommer's speeches against the Jews he became sick. He broke out in cold sweats and had to be excused to the bathroom when the diatribe began. Sitting on the toilet seat, he forced himself to stop shaking. What if these crazy people discovered he was half-Jewish? What if they thought his disfigurement was a circumcision? He was terrified someone would find out. He feared that scarred reminder would give him away. Was there any truth to Frommer's statements? How could he accomplish his goals in this repressive and dangerous atmosphere? My G-d, what if he should try to escape! Would they find his mother and murder her in reprisal? So many thoughts raced through his mind.

Gerhardt was so nervous he promptly threw up, but after a time pulled himself together. He made it through the rest of his classes, then ran the two miles home. He called his father that night. Aaron was deeply worried for his son but he knew he could do nothing against the *Nazi* machine. In Yiddish he quickly counseled: "Now you understand why we had to bury those sacred things, Gerhardt, why I changed our names and residence. Now you know firsthand that we are a hated and hunted people. I love you, my son. Never let them make you forget your birthright, but protect yourself at every turn. Never let them turn you into a beast, Gerhardt. The *Reich* is evil. These men live to destroy the free will that G-d has given each of us. But it cannot continue forever. Learn and grow as productively as possible while you are there. I know we will be free again one day. Be wary, be careful, my precious child, I pray to our G-d for protection."

When Fredericka heard of the dangers Gerhardt was facing, she admitted it was all her fault for enrolling him. But she knew her child would not be safe anywhere in Germany as long as the HJ existed. She began fasting every week and attending a nearby church, where she cried and prayed for her child's safety and for her own forgiveness.

That year the new *Nazi* labor leader Robert Ley initiated the

National Vocational competition for HJ members. Every boy was to learn to work in various trades. For this they would be judged and rewarded, with winners getting to meet Hitler. Gerhardt wanted to learn gardening but this was not offered. He was given tests to determine his abilities, which were decidedly mechanical. There was also an initiation phase in which his I.Q. was measured and determined categorically according to mind-hand coordination, conceptual understanding, linguistic comprehension and problem solving abilities. He did well in all of these. Finally, he was screened, interviewed and strictly counseled about accepting any field of endeavor he would not be willing to embrace with total purpose and commitment for the *Fuhrer* and the future of Germany.

He was told his aptitude qualified him as an apprentice mechanic. He felt he had no interest or talent at it, but Leader Frommer told him,

"The *Reich* needs good mechanics for its tanks and trucks. You will learn all you can of the value of hard labor. You must be ready to sacrifice for your country, Gerhardt. This will earn you the smiles of your *Fuhrer*!"

Everywhere Gerhardt turned he heard a constant refrain: Sacrifice the self for the leader, the *Reich*. Think of yourself as one of a group of heroes inseparably tied to one another by an oath of faithfulness. Stand your ground, even when surrounded by superior foes. Your group may be reduced to the last man. The leader who audaciously and bravely defends the dead soldiers lying around him becomes the victor! He is a superhero whose unparalleled bravery brings about change for the better.

Gerhardt shrugged. He was quickly learning that his life was being decided for him at every turn. Individual choice was abandoned if it didn't fit the program. It was stifling. Absolute obedience was required; no amount of deviance from orders was tolerated. Everyone was taught that the Germanic peoples were meant to be godlike. Everyone was trained for leadership, but the realization of this honor would go to those chosen by his or her physical abilities.

Gerhardt thought of the bicycling trips that were a part of all camping excursions. The boys loved this chance to compete in trials as they pedaled along the German roadways. Gerhardt enjoyed casual riding but he was urged on at every opportunity to exert himself as much as possible, to keep up with the others. Team play meant everything; individualism had no place in this juggernaut.

"Become drenched in sweat, Gerhardt! Give it your all! None of us must be a comrade who loses heart or gets tired and asks the way."

It was the same with drilling, swimming, calisthenics, cooking or playing SS officer and Jew. Compete! What mattered were the groups of boys, the vitality and expertise, group strength and obedience. The rule of the stick: get bruised, accept it, hit back showing no mercy. Be tough, be cruel, become invincible. When stressing this principle, Leader Frommer often quoted from Hitler's famous speech: "*I want a brutal, domineering, fearless, cruel youth. Youth must be all that. It must bear pain.*"

But Gerhardt was not a competitor. He didn't want to bear pain, he wanted to study and learn. He wanted to attend synagogue and pray with his father on High Holy days. Daily he practiced translating German books into Yiddish so he would not forget his first language. This lifestyle suffocated him. He felt his insides slowly dissembling. He had hoped to become brave and successful in the HJ, but he was no more than a speck, a cipher. And he was always lonely. His plan to become a proud, poster-like Hitler Youth failed miserably. He just wanted to go home. He rarely saw Fredericka now, though they wrote long letters to each other. She left food for him at night but he was often too exhausted to eat and went immediately to his bedroom, trying not to feel the weight of separateness that came over him every night when he came home to a dark house and found her asleep. He wanted to ask her permission to leave the HJ. But she would have told him there was no way out of it. The HJ was now law for all German youth, male and female. They dare not disobey if they valued their lives and wanted to protect their families from severe harassment, loss of employment and, perhaps, even murder.

⌣

Three years passed. It was 1937. Gerhardt's 16th birthday came and went. Gerhardt read that Jews were now banned from many professional occupations, including teaching, accounting or dentistry. The official ranting against Jews had increased tenfold in the camps. Daily he heard the haranguing of his officers about the evils of Jewry. He was very careful never to confide his childhood secrets and memories to anyone. He found that when he jammed his mind with remembered *Torah* prayers he was able to blot out some of the noise of *Nazism*. But there were still times he had to hold himself back from shouting: "Enough! We are innocent, we are only people; trying to live our lives!"

Gerhardt had to tell himself that these men and women so passionate with hatred were obsessed with their own feelings of importance and were really impotent to carry out their blind, perverse attacks upon humanity. anti-Semitism was official policy of the *Third Reich*. It was like a nest of vipers, the lies and innuendos of Jewish inferiority and evil, injecting into every mind and heart its dangerous venom, until an unreasoning hatred of Jews was as essential to the philosophy of the *Third Reich* as the *Nazi* salute.

At night, Gerhardt prayed to G-d. *"I am in a fallen world. Chaos and horror are all around me. Please, build me a ladder in the midst of this Babylon. I am struggling and I ache for peace… How can I endure this hell?"*

Gerhardt's adjustment to the unavoidable routine of hard physical "play" was slow and painful, but though his mind was full of disgust for the ideology and rhetoric of the *Reich* and his gentle spirit weaned to a life of hard line toughness, his body had become hard and resilient. He grew strong playing, swimming, boxing (which he hated), marching with eleven-pound knapsacks on his back. Almost in self-defense he became a dedicated and creative mechanic, receiving praise for his thoroughness and completion of tasks. All the while he was careful to keep his thoughts private. This was not difficult because there were thousands of boys always around in the camps and schools. He had few friends. In the group showers he always showered last. To be safe if observed, he wore a cloth truss and invented a story claiming that at birth his "organ" was mangled because he was born at home and delivered by an inexperienced midwife. The ruse worked after a fashion. The other boys laughed at him and called him a liar. They taunted with made up names that embarrassed Gerhardt terribly. They lay in wait for him. When their victim appeared for his evening shower they grabbed him and ripped his appliance so badly it was rendered useless. Fredericka had to purchase him numerous extras. Even Horst was not able to protect him from their cruel words and snickering comments. But eventually, after several weeks, the bullies tired of their demeaning attacks and Gerhardt was generally ignored and left to shower as he wished. For this he was very grateful.

~

Gerhardt's group was scheduled to attend a rally in Berlin that summer, with many other chapters of the HJ. Gerhardt was not interested; he had weathered many of the protracted, intense oratorios from *Nazi* party bosses. Horst, on the other hand was ecstatic because he was chosen a candidate for the HJ *Streifendienst* (patrol force), the internal political police. Their leaders who would present them at the rally chose these young men. Horst had shown special aptitude for intelligence work. His mind was quick though not especially bright, his loyalty to Hitler absolute. He was always looking for approval from his leaders. He gloried in the chance to wear the classy uniforms of the police though the duties were somewhat mundane; keep order at meetings, ferret out disloyal members and to denounce those who were critical of the *Fuhrer* or other *Nazi* officials.

Once, when he and Gerhardt were on a camping trip, Horst whispered a secret: he had recently reported his father to the police for voicing doubts about the policies of the *Reich* to his wife. His father was interrogated and roughed up, his mother threatened with "other" reprisals. Horst's father was straightaway told that his son had reported him, whereupon he and his wife wept bitterly. Horst, however, was congratulated for his loyalty to Germany. He was sorry for his parents' trial and apologized, but he was secretly quite proud of his new honor. He said the short name for the political police would be "*Gestapo*". Gerhardt was too astounded to say anything.

On the day before the trip, Gerhardt was at home packing his uniforms when his mother's store manager called him. She gently informed Gerhardt that his mother, who had been working hard for months without a day's break, had that morning collapsed of exhaustion. She was in hospital for recuperation. Gerhardt was to ride his bike the two miles there and bring her identification papers. The woman was quick to say that Fredericka would be fine, that he should not worry but have a good trip to Berlin. Gerhardt hung up before she'd finished her sentence. Immediately he got on his bike and rode to the infirmary.

He worried greatly for his mother, she was not strong. He knew she worked many hours more than was healthy for her to support both of them and that she fasted to help make ends meet. Aaron's monthly stipend checks were steady but too slim to offer any accumulation of excess. Gerhardt was away so often at Hitler *Yungend* activities that he and Fredericka rarely took supper together or had time to talk. Guilt stabbed at his heart. It was his fault, his mother's pain, her loneliness, her overwork. Worst of all he felt trapped because he could do nothing to change it. HJ was mandatory for all German youth. Any attempt to leave was severely punished. He could not risk subjecting his mother or himself to the dangers of Hitler's cruelty.

Fredericka's hospital room was stark gray, sparsely furnished with a wide, ugly hospital bed, a vanity and one chair. The room was kept dark with heavy curtains across the only window, and through it one could see only factories. The place stunk of ammonia. It's antiseptic stench filled Gerhardt's nostrils. He winced in pain, covered his nose and walked on tiptoe to his mother's side. She seemed to be asleep. Gerhardt looked closely at her. He noticed her normally robust complexion was sallow, her eyes were sunken in their sockets.

She was quite thin now, the light mesh blanket barely disturbed by her frail body. Gerhardt felt tears come. She looked like death. He knelt beside her bed on the cold tile floor. Sobs suddenly came from deep within him. Tears of remorse and loneliness, sorrow for the absence of his father, anger at the breakup of his family. His own guilt at his failure to bring them together again threatened to choke him. He felt a hand gently caress his head. He moaned, then realized that his sobs had awakened his mother.

"Mama", he said, and with a cry he threw himself clumsily across her bosom.

"Now, now, my *leibchen*, my little Gerhardt, now… don't sob so. I am okay. Stop your tears, will you? Sit by me and tell me of your day."

Her soft voice seemed to come from the air above them, soothing and calm, gentle with love of him, quiet with fatigue. He would not let go, he held her fast. An hour later the nurse came into the room and found them asleep, Gerhardt's body slumped across his mother's, her small hand stilled upon his severely trimmed, *Nazi*-style blond hair.

---

[74] "God in Heaven"
[75] Camping for our Leader and the People
[76] Scandinavian people of Northern Europe [see appendix IV]
[77] The Jungvolk Oath was taken by ten-year-old boys upon first entering the Hitler Youth

Journal of the Dead — Abraham Isopovich

My mother was a schoolteacher. The German *Gestapo* came through Berdichev in 1941. They noticed her when she ventured out of her area of the ghetto and shot her on the spot. She was foraging for food for her family but they didn't care and took her out of the group and shot her there in the street. My father grieved for her for many years and it hastened his young death at 59.

I was 5'7", slender and medium of build. I was very strong and did many things, lifted many things. I ate Russian food of all kinds and had lots of fun eating, though I worked quite hard at the Russian fur factory. We made the fur pieces for sale and inclusion on coats and hats and other things. I was very happy. I had no brothers or sisters but went to school with many nice folk who treated me very well.

My life was spent working in the factory around the town of Berdichev. I was a laborer who made what he could at the job and loved a woman who didn't love me and we couldn't be married because she would not come around to my way of thinking, which was that the people of the world should unite in Communism for the good of all. She was a freedom thinker, always wanting to be independent and do her own thing. We didn't get along at all sometimes, yet I loved her spirit and wanted her for my bride. I died before I could get her to come around to accept me for who I was. She became engaged to another man and had his child out of wedlock. She was not a Jew but liked them anyway. I died too early in my life to achieve very much and I am very angry for that.

Outside of Berdichev, on the steppes, there was a field in full view of the world and the mountains to the north and south. There many of us workers were herded like cattle and lined up and shot. I was stripped of my clothes, told to turn around and then shot in the back. The bullet pierced my heart and lung and I drowned in my own blood. It was horrible and I died from the fright of it. I was shot in full view of all the German soldiers who laughed and said "Good riddance to you, rubbish." I watched the German soldiers leaving the area.

Shortly after I passed out I came to life again in a way I don't understand. I saw the bodies around me. We were buried in that field and flowers are growing over our bodies now as we molder here in Heaven's gate awaiting the Judgment that will place us all in our proper areas for eternity. I waited for them to leave and then tried to rise but realized I had no body left to use. I was taken here to Paradise right away so I wouldn't be alone in death. Many who died in the field are here with me now.

We were a happy bunch until the Germans came and shot us. We had one soldier named Mirovsky. He was of Russian birth and had moved to Germany with his parents years ago. He was especially cruel. He had no care for any of the prisoners and spoke harshly to us all. Russians killed him later on in the war before 1942. His spirit suffers greatly in hell, I imagine. It is worse than my own.

"It is almost like a dream - a fairytale. The new Reich has been born. Fourteen years of work have been crowned with victory. The German revolution has begun!"

— Joseph Goebbels' diary, January 30, 1933

11 — A Plague of Locusts

In 1936, a year before Gerhard's 16th birthday the *National Socialist* party passed a law requiring every qualified German youth over the age of 10 join the HJ. Involvement with the HJ usually began at ages 4 through 6 when children were taught about the importance of the Party and the HJ until they were eligible for membership. These organizations of youth were coalesced into *Adolf Hitler* (ah) *Schools* in 1937 for boys between the ages of 12 and 18. It was considered by the Party to be an elite education. The ah Schools were operated by National Socialist party members and did not answer to the Ministry of Science and Education. Over 2 million more were added to the roles in coming years. Some joined out of loyalty, many more out of fear because membership was forced upon their families who were threatened with loss of jobs and severe ostracism. This made for an interesting schism among the groups: some were ardent *Nazi* supporters, others hated it. Gerhardt was, of course, of the latter.

From the first days of recruitment, Gerhard's friend, Horst, fully adopted the *Nazi* philosophy, it defined his existence. Gerhardt could not say what their friendship was based upon. Perhaps it was their very different personalities that complemented each other in unusual ways. Horst, though brash and generally insensitive, was very protective of his quiet, thoughtful friend. Gerhardt, on the other hand, saw through Horst's belligerence to his lack of self-assurance. Both came from broken homes. Neither boy had siblings; both needed a friend who could be trusted with the secrets of teenaged thoughts and dreams.

"An individual is 'the soldier of an idea'", Horst parroted Adolf Hitler's remark. "We are not numbers, we are the future hope of this German land. You, Gerhardt, don't seem like much of an idea to me. You are always glum."

They were resting on the grass just outside their classroom. It was lunch time, the summer sun was deliciously warm. Their black shorts and brown shirts absorbed heat well. Gerhardt's jacket covered his eyes, he was almost asleep. Horst lay next to him. He bit into his apple.

"*Gerhardt, ach tung*[70]!" Then he laughed. Gerhardt moved the jacket away and looked up sleepily.

"What do you want, Horst? Can you not eat quietly and study by yourself?"

"I want to know what you'd do if we were soldiers now." He took another bite and chewed lustily. "We're the SS. We come upon a nest of Russians, we encircle them, our Leader gives the signal and wham! We attack!"

Gerhardt was only half-listening. Horst was always making up war stories. He loved the idea of warfare. His internship with the Gestapo police had been accepted and he'd be attending school in Berlin when fall came.

"What will you attack with, silly? You don't even have a rifle."

"Ah, yes. But I will have a pistol, a Walther, perhaps, or a rifle. I'll aim and fire point blank. His fingers formed a gun barrel, emptying bullets into Gerhardt's chest and legs.

"Ow, ow! You shot me, you lousy *Nazi*!"

Gerhardt rolled over, pretending to be mortally wounded. Horst sprang up and danced around the bleeding body before him. His right arm swung out in a *Nazi* salute.

"*Yavol, mein, Fuhrer*. I killed a parasite, a miserable scum of the earth Jew! Ha, ha!"

His laughter was manic, his joy complete. But suddenly the bloody body rose all at once and with a sour look turned toward the classrooms. Hunching his shoulders, Gerhardt walked quickly away.

"Hey, what… where are you going, Gerhardt? It's not time for class to start. Hey, Gerhardt, let's go find some traitors and shoot them! Gerhardt?"

～

The trip to the Berlin summer rally that month was invigorating. Hundreds of boys clamored aboard the numerous trucks in the motorcade, noisily picking their spots as the vehicles lurched ahead. Gerhardt was worried. Fredericka had recovered well and was back at work. But she developed a nagging cough that disturbed him. Occasionally, she spit blood, but the physician had said it was due to a small ulcer. He'd spoken recently with his father. He wanted to marry again, this time to a woman of Nordic background. Gerhardt received this news with great alarm.

"Wait," he told his father. "I know you love Mama. Let all of us sit down and work it out. I know we can all be together again."

But Aaron didn't think there was much hope for working things out. He was tired of being alone. He wanted another chance to have a family.

"My life here is lonely, son, and I have found a wonderful woman to share it with. Please be happy for me, Gerhardt."

But Gerhardt was not happy. His dream of reuniting his parents was crashing before him. His precious mother would never remarry. And then he realized that it was he who would care for her the days of her life. He was and would be her only protector, though he was away so often she fended for herself. Without Aaron she had no other recourse but her son, whose strength she already depended upon whenever he was home. But when was he home?

Fredericka had other plans. She wanted Gerhardt to marry.

"*Leibchen*, you are not interested in girls?" she teased him. "You are a tall, handsome sixteen."

Gerhardt blushed and found himself painfully shy. The girls he'd seen were all in the League of German Girls, the *Bund deutscher Mädel* (BdM). They were uninteresting in their sameness, in their identical, spotless white blouses, pigtails and black skirts. Those he'd met always wanted to discuss the principles of National Socialism with him or to become pregnant. He was deeply confused over this issue. Though his father had disobeyed his parents by marrying a gentile, Gerhardt wished mightily for someone of his own faith to confide in, attend synagogue with, and be of the same blood. Though he loved, even adored his mother, he yearned for a companion who would share his love of *Torah*, a woman to whom he could give his small gift of love. There was little time, even at the camps, where he was urged to get to know the girls of the BdM. He was tongue-tied and reticent, preferring to study the mechanical journals that were made available to him. At least he could become expert in something other than Hitler's speeches or the rhetoric of the National Socialist party.

These were among his thoughts as he with thousands of young men and women took their places on the huge field in the Berlin stadium. He looked splendid in his formal dress; new long sleeved brown shirt and shorts, white calf-length stockings and shiny black shoes. Hitler had called the boys "magnificent youngsters", and believed he foresaw the final product of National Socialist education. Officers of the *Wehrmacht* also lined up; the hundreds of thousands of men who paid homage to *Fuhrer* Adolf Hitler, their savior of Germany, freer of his people, architect of the Master Race.

As Gerhardt listened he realized it was not so much the content of the speeches he had become used to hearing at every turn. The way in which they were delivered made the difference to an audience who wanted to believe. These men spoke with gusto, with absolute sureness of and adherence to the Holy Grail of *Nazism*. The public attending a rally came to be convinced — and there stood men who lived utterly according to the ideals (*Gedankenguf*) about which they spoke, men who were totally inspired by faith in what they said. It was intoxicating, dominating, unassailable. Germany — the super power — fueled by supermen! Listen as one of these new "prophets" speaks:

"Look at these young men and boys! With them I can make a new world... Weakness will be knocked out of them. A violently active, dominating, brutal youth – that is what I'm after... I will have no intellectual training. Knowledge is ruin to my young men... but one thing they must learn – self command... out of it will come the creative man, the God-man."

But Gerhardt was numb. He heard only the rantings of madmen and his sorrow knew no solace. *He does not speak to our understanding, but to the proud heart of the German people. He tells them they want a renewed nation of warlike people. He convinces them to share his madness. What fools they are!*

And then Gerhardt hated himself because he loved his country. He was as they all were, these millions of faces hoping for a revitalized, victorious new Germany. What was he, then? Traitor or a patriot? Could one be both and still be a Jew?

The afternoon sun was high, beating down upon every head. His group was the *Unterbann*, it consisted of four *Gefolgschaften* (troupes) totaling 600-800 boys. Gerhardt's troup was facing the middle of the vast field. Horst was in another row downfield from Leader Frommer's position. At the podium central to the field, Hitler's security agents and top-level commandants sat admiring the throng of millions who were there to rally the cause of the *Reich*.

Suddenly, as if a windstorm had swept through the crowd, there was a caught breath and quick applause. Gerhardt looked to his left. At the entrance to the field, more than one-quarter of a mile away a touring car with convertible hood drove slowly along the huge cheering crowds onto the arena. A man stood stiffly in the passenger side, right palm horizontal in salute, head erect, commandant cap in hand. They came nearer the far end of the stadium where Leader Frommer's boys stood. Gerhardt's entire contingent struck at once the Nazi salute and froze at attention. Nearer still came the car. The man at attention in the front seat did not move. On his left arm the black armband with a white circle containing the *Nazi* cross. His left breast pocket boasted a black facsimile of the ancient Germanic runic cross. His black hair was slicked against his head. His eyes squinted at the sun. Beside him, five men in dark *Nazi* uniforms were serious and foreboding beneath their gold-insignia hats.

The car came to a halt just past the field's center. Two of the company left their seats and came around to open the door for the man saluting. He stepped out and stood looking at the boys' out-stretched arms. Then he clicked his black boots at attention. His right arm shot out and back in another salute. He shouted to them *"Heil Hitler"*, and every boy and girl in the stadium returned his shout. The response, it was reported later, could be heard through every German wood. It penetrated every household and rang a bell of alarm through every town in Europe. The young voices were a hallelujah to arms, to war and to death. Gerhardt imagined that Fredericka heard his voice from many miles away, and Aaron stopped his work in Hamburg to wonder at the resounding chorus of unholy allegiance.

As the thousands in the stadium watched, the small full figure of the man Hitler walked stiffly along the mile-long rows of his Hitler Youth, stopping here and there to touch a face with gloved hand to adjust a lapel here, a tie there. Gerhardt felt his breathing becoming heavy, for Hitler was coming very near him. The very legend himself!

Then, as in a dream, Hitler stood before him. His intense light blue eyes shocked Gerhardt, who had thought them brown. The thick brush of moustache above his thin, tight lips looked out of place but Gerhardt felt no humor, only that time had suddenly stopped. The man was looking past the youths, past the rows of Germany's best, the country's future. He was perhaps seeing the road to world domination or the next advance of German troops onto foreign soil. Gerhardt coughed nervously. The man looked at him for an instant. His serious face was lined with the stresses of leadership. Straight black hair worn like a helmet crossed his lined brow. Hitler's hard, measuring stares were legendary; they pierced a soldier's soul. Gerhardt felt himself suffocating. No sound was uttered. He suddenly had the feeling he was staring at a corpse. He wanted to throw up, but he held, and held...

The moment passed. The man and the legend moved heavily on, continuing inspection. Gerhardt was left to recover himself. Dizziness made him weak and he started to slump to his knees. Franz, on his left and Horst on his right caught him up sharply, but the rest of the afternoon was a blur. On the trip home Gerhardt was silent, still under the spell of his encounter. It came to him in that summer afternoon that he had been confronted by evil itself, a force so powerful he was immobilized before it. And he knew with a perfect and solemn understanding that he was and would be, so long as that man lived, in the service of the devil.

⁓

Gerhardt rarely saw his home or his mother anymore. He called his parents when he could from the dining room phone that all the boys used to phone their families. There was often no privacy during these calls and a ten minute limit applied. He could say little to her of his thoughts or feelings, but Fredericka knew her son well. Her health was failing, but she did not want to alarm him. Instead, she encouraged him and cautioned him to endure whatever was necessary.

"You are safe there, Gerhardt, for outside your camp walls Jews are being insulted and humiliated in the streets. The *Nazis* make war on these poor people. Soon I fear they will be hunted and murdered in great numbers."

"Yes, mother, but no Jew is safe in here, either," Gerhardt whispered. "Every day I hear how we are hated, how we are foul and dirty creatures, guilty of ruining Germany's world and almost not good enough to kill. We are told to find Jews and make them pay for being what they are. I am so afraid, so afraid they will somehow find me out!"

"Oh, Gerhardt, don't speak like that. Someone will overhear you!"

Gerhardt turned to the wall so his lips could not be read.

"These boys are fed horrible lies every day, mother, and every day they grow tougher, meaner, more hateful and insensitive to everyone around them... they are being trained to kill, mother, just innocent young boys learning to kill. Oh, my dear mother, I am trapped here just as surely."

"Oh, my son, I am so sorry for you, like a trapped animal in that place. I love you, Gerhardt, we will be together again one day and we will be free, do you believe that?"

Gerhardt shrugged and closed his eyes to stem the tears falling freely down his face. Other boys were waiting to use the phone at the lunch table only a dozen feet away.

"Yes, mother. I know that one day we will be together again, and I wait for that day."

Horst's heavy boots were heard on the porch. He swaggered into the room, heading toward the phone. "Hey," he said, pushing past the others at the tables.

"*I'm* next!"

~

It was 1938. Gerhardt celebrated his 17th birthday in a summer camp outing, digging trenches on a local farm. Horst was a newly inducted member of the elite *Gestapo* corps. Gerhardt had developed physically into a strong young man with endurance abilities far beyond his expectations. Days were spent at community service, drilling in marching, pep rallies. Nights he was allowed to study elementary science and the mechanics of farm machinery and transport vehicles. He was rewarded with opportunities to help diagnose and repair camp trucks, a task he greatly enjoyed and which took his attention from thoughts of his mother and father. Within those few years Gerhardt the Jew compiled an enviable knowledge of his subjects. He filled two lockers with copies of diagrams and specifications of the workings of German autos, jeeps, tanks and various farm equipment. His prowess didn't go unnoticed. Several times he was congratulated and promoted by Leader Frommer who recognized in Gerhardt a scholar among the rank and file.

Fredericka wrote him that all Jewish-owned businesses were now required to register with the National Socialist government. She heard of other reprisals to come. Jews were prohibited from selling their services and identity cards were required. Her physician, a Jew, was told he could no longer practice medicine. German Jews were fleeing their homeland as quickly as possible but only the lucky were able to get out safely.

"The United States asked many other countries to take the Jews, but no one would accept them, Gerhardt. They are trapped here. Hitler will fill the streets of the country with their blood… Call me when you can. I love you, my *leibchen*."

In bed that night, Gerhardt pondered his fortune. A day never passed without slurs against Jews, but he had long since

153

become immune to *Nazi* rantings. Here at least and at most he was protected from hatred, search or seizure or murder. His body and mind were prospering and he had hopes of military service, which would take him eventually into battle where he would be free of drills and pep rallies. In battle he would find himself. He would fight for the freedom of all peoples and in his own personal way he would triumph despite the evil that stalked his country and made its people insane.

Aaron's phone messages were full of halts and starts. He had not remarried and would not be doing so. His position at work was unsteady due to the rumors of war. And, oh, yes, he had formed a small group with a few other Jewish men. They regularly held a secret and joyful *Shabbat* service in one another's home.

"We may have been found out, I'm not sure. Anyway, we'll continue unless we know someone has reported us. Gerhardt, these years without you and your mother have taught me to honor my G-d and my religion, even in this small way. I know you understand."

Gerhardt was happy for his father. He, too, prayed secretly without words when around the other boys. He prayed for strength and endurance, for G-d to bless him with the knowledge he would need to free himself from the prison of hatred he had to endure. He prayed for his parents, their health and safety. And he prayed for the survival of his people in this terrible time of war that raged with increasing terror against the chosen of G-d.

On August 11 he heard that the German army had destroyed the synagogue in Hamburg, several kilometers from where Aaron lived. Ten men had been in the edifice, holding a service. They were killed in the attack. Their names were not given. That day Gerhardt fasted and prayed for his father's life. He could not inquire openly, but several times he phoned Aaron's apartment. He received no answer. Fredericka was in shock. She had no means to travel to Hamburg. Neither of them knew the whereabouts of his place of employment, only that it was in Hamburg. They waited for his call but it did not come. By the end of the following week Aaron's phone had been disconnected.

"What will we do, Mama," Gerhardt cried. "He is dead, I know he is dead. The Germans murdered him."

Fredericka sought to comfort her son, but to no avail. He grieved in his heart for many weeks. He was given to suddenly sobbing openly, though he dared not allow himself to weaken

154

while at camp. His grades fell precipitously, but he did not care, he was a prisoner among crazed men. His loneliness and sense of defeat often overtook him. He pondered running away to search for Aaron but the camp was totally guarded at all hours and gates and finally he gave up the idea and steeled himself to the hopeless inevitability that his father had perished.

Gerhardt's classmates heard rumors that every boy and girl of German blood was soon going to be forced to join the HJ. This was expected to add 2 million more youth to the organization. Gerhardt was nearing 18, a veteran of six years in the HJ. He was anxious to leave the camps and become assigned to the Labor Service, the *Nazi* three-pronged armed military-style organization. These were the *Wehrmacht*, the *SS Schutzstaffeln*, (protection squads), and the Order Police (*Ordnungpolizei*). He would be assigned to the *Wehrmacht* division which comprised the army (*Heer*), navy (*Kriegsmarine*), and air force (*Luftwaffe*). He also obtained permission to come home for a week. Fredericka was ecstatic.

Newspaper headlines sped by, each more ominous in their reports of terror:

October 28: *The Nazis arrest 17,000 Polish Jews, sending them to Poland where they are refused admittance.*

November 9, 10: *Kristallnacht — Night of Broken Glass. An assassination of a German official led to attacks by mobs throughout Germany and the newly acquired territories of Austria and Sudetenland. They attacked Jews in the street, in their homes and at their places of work and worship.*

November 12: *Nazis fine Jews one billion marks for damages related to Kristallnacht.*

November 15: *All Jewish pupils are expelled from all non-Jewish German schools. A month later a law is passed to "Aryanize" all Jewish businesses.*

December: *Hitler's commandant, Hermann Göring is put in charge of resolving the "Jewish Question".*

The web of evil continued to spread its silken threads of hatred over Germany.

---

[78] Attention

Only those who are our fellow countrymen can become citizens. Only those who have German blood, regardless of creed, can be our country-men. Hence no Jew can be a countryman.

— Point 4 of 25 Points of Hitler's Nazi Party

12 — "Sweat Saves Blood"

By 1939 Hitler had annexed the demilitarized Rhineland, Austria, Czechoslovakia. His world vision was called *Gross-deutschland* (the Greater Germany). His vision was to create the perfect race of ethnic Germans who would rule Europe initially and eventually the world. His regime worked unceasingly toward that goal. This entailed the killing off of everyone defined as imperfect: the disabled, the mentally ill, homosexuals, the handicapped and aged, the sick, prisoners of war, forced laborers, camp inmates, critics, Jews, Slavs, Gypsies, Serbs, Czechs, Italians, Poles, Frenchmen, Ukrainians, certain religious groups, and on. He thought of himself as the living symbol of Alexander the Great, conqueror of many nations.

On September 1 Hitler's armies invaded Poland, fueling World War II. By 1941 the German military had become an undeniable presence in an area of Europe from Paris to Moscow. The German press boasted of finally gaining revenge for the humiliation of the Versailles Peace Treaty, when Germany finally had to accept responsibility for the war.

Propaganda invaded every home and every ear with testimonials to the superiority of the Aryan race and the inferiority of Jews. Freedom of the press was eliminated, political parties were disbanded and anyone who spoke against the *Nazis* was jailed.

Among the soldiers, however, many were not *Nazis*, but only Germans fighting for their country. Before the *Nazis* came to power, leadership positions were given mainly to wealthy, educated men. Enlisted ranks were filled with working-class men. But the Nazis promoted anyone to leadership who showed ability for it — who could lead to victory. In this way the armies of the *Third Reich* were loyal to their standard and eager to do their best. German recruits were told that "sweat saves blood"; meaning the harder they trained before battle, the better their chances in war.

"If you are courageous, if you are cruel, you will save your life. Simply handling a weapon will no longer be enough," Commander Frink told his men on the the their arrival at barracks outside Berlin. "We require you to persevere, to have endurance and to resist the enemy at all cost."

With that, he commanded all his men to lie prone upon the ground, and with his huge, bulky frame and heavy boots he walked over each of them, crushing bones, smashing faces into the dirt. But not a man moved.

~

The summer days of 1939 were lovely and reminiscent of past successes. Gerhard's visit home was on his mind. He was nineteen. The Labor Service would claim his life for the next six years. His mother's tears did much to wash away his homesickness. They talked for hours and shopped for special foods. Fredericka cooked Gerhardt's favorites; potato *kugel* casserole and cheese *strudel* pastry, and in this way their week together was fruitful, though he desperately missed his father's beefy arms around him and the reassuring camaraderie they had always shared. It seemed there would be no healing for the boy's lonely heart. But how could they find out if he had been killed? Fredericka said she would try to contact his employer.

"*Nazism* will never let you go," Fredericka said, shaking her head in sorrow on that last day. The warm breezes of August followed them as they walked the blocks around Fredericka's small home. "You will be in that damned *Nazi* army as long as that madman lives, Gerhardt. Thanks to G-d they don't know who you really are, but how will you continue when they expect you to kill your own?"

"I will not kill my own, Mama. Somehow I will find a way." He had agonized over this in his heart many times. Perhaps it would not come to that, perhaps he could shoot over their heads. In the heat of battle, everyone looked out for himself. He would not be watched. He didn't know. There would be a way.

"Come on, *leibchen*. Your rifle will be pointed at a Jew, maybe a *rabbi*. Even, G-d forbid, a child. Your commandant will order you to pull the trigger. What will you do? Will you decline? Will you take their bullet? Court-martial, Gerhardt, that's what can happen. Sent to prison to rot. Taken from us forever."

His mother wrung her hands in worry. She'd thought about this many times but not spoken with her son before now. Gerhardt put his arms around his mother. In the innocence of youth he intoned,

158

"As a German soldier I will fight for freedom for Germany. Some deaths will be necessary, but I dream of freeing us from further enslavement. Do not worry, Mama, I will do well."

"My son, your idea of freedom and that of the madman Hitler are vastly different. He dreams of your eradication as a people. He has you trained to carry out his orders, not your own. You will see, Gerhardt, at the point of murder, you will come to your senses and understand clearly."

Gerhardt was quiet a long time. They reached the house again. The boy turned to his mother and with a grin on his young face he said "I will do as G-d commands me."

Two months later, on September 1, German troops attacked Warsaw, Poland. Though his was being trained as a mechanical expert, Gerhardt, radiomen and others in allied lines were told they would be tried in the field if needed for this battle. The news hit Gerhardt hard. First, part of his secret dream of reuniting his family in peace after defeating the enemy – this seemed to be within reach. But Hitler's true enemy was the innocent – the *judien*, the old and young, Slavs and so on. Fighting Russian soldiers, that was a matter of territorial war. He would lift his rifle in defense of his homeland and his fellows. But what if his weapon was ordered aimed at those without reason or desire to oppose?

But there was little time for contemplation. Gerhardt and his new friends were made to participate in a training exercise, learning to fire machine guns. The location was an isolated roadside. A trench was dug, the gun and ammunition were brought to it and the boys manned it. Several army officers accompanied the training session teachers, giving lessons on war tactics. Gerhardt was involved in these exercises and at the same time assigned to a truck and tank detail. He was chosen from the several hundred young men in his company for this assignment because of his unusual scholarly understanding of mechanics and maintenance expertise. Now he would be trained for reserve duty. That meant days and nights spent away from hearing *Nazi* propaganda drone through speakers located all over the camp. For this alone he was greatly thankful. He would have a little peace. Reports of planes bombing Polish towns seemed remote, the German countryside was calm and lovely. The air was clean. Birds sang outside the Service camp where military training exercises took place. It was a new Valhalla, but still Gerhardt was afraid.

By this time he'd resigned himself to his father's death and to his new soldiering duties until the Reich army should let him free — a glorious gift they might never give him. But what if they should somehow assign him to murder? After all these years of hiding who he was… he had worried each day that he might be found out the next. What would he say? What would they do with him… and his mother? These seemingly insoluble problems kept him awake many nights constructing ways of deflecting any orders to kill, but one thing would not fit into place — he could not anticipate his enemy.

Gerhardt's closest bunkmate was Dieter Penske, a rough and tumble 18-year old who had been in HJ since the age of 12. His parents were dead and he had no relatives nearby. For Dieter the HJ was the only family he'd ever known. His current assignment was to help with the collection of metals for the war effort. He and other boys boarded old trucks with the words *Metallspende der D.P.* on the side and rode through town after town collecting various metals, paper, clothes, skis, whatever items families could be cajoled into parting with.

"Its fun to talk people out of their belongings for our war effort," Dieter chided the new arrival. "You should come along, Gerhardt, as our mechanic. We'll pretend the truck has broken down, you can pretend to fix it while we ask for metals and maybe get sausage and bread for lunch as well."

"Yes, but if we are discovered, there will be penalties to pay. How do you propose to handle that, Herr Penske?"

Dieter shrugged, his dark eyes falling upon the manuals and schematics spread before Gerhardt as he labored to fix a truck with multiple problems.

"We can get by with many things here, if one knows how to do it. Lots of us know ways to have fun here. We're the hope of Germany, you know. We can do anything we want to anyone. "

"So long as you're not caught?"

Dieter laughed and slapped on his cap. "You'll see, my friend, you'll see soon enough." He slapped Gerhardt on the back and turned to meet the other boys at the truck. Gerhardt watched them pull away. He heard the engine choke and sputter.

"I'll be fixing that next," he grumbled.

The next week Gerhardt was told to drive to Berlin's outskirts to pick up some parts needed to repair several vehicles. A boy from another building was his passenger, a lanky, quiet youth wearing glasses, something Gerhardt rarely saw anyone wear. He introduced himself as Jürgen.

"Let's stop here a moment, can we?" asked Jürgen as they passed some stores. "I want to find out some details about our invasion of Poland."

They stopped at the small kiosk. Jürgen jumped out and disappeared for a moment behind the stall. He reappeared smiling and they continued on their way in silence.

"What do you think of this war?" Jürgen asked casually.

"I think I'd like to be in it," Gerhardt replied, but he felt increasingly unsure.

"Why, what do you think?"

"Oh, maybe it isn't necessary to make war on the whole world. I mean, I think Germany is a great country and we could all live peacefully together."

Gerhardt turned to look at his passenger. He had never heard a disagreement from anyone in the HJ. It was just accepted that the *Third Reich* could do whatever it wanted and everyone would accept it at face value. Jürgen was smiling.

"You've never heard dissent before, have you, Gerhardt. Does that shock you?"

Gerhardt said nothing. Was this boy a spy?

"Many of us have these thoughts and many of us would like to do something about them."

"Many of you? Who else would dare to speak out? Do you suggest speaking out?"

"Not exactly. But if you love Germany and are her patriot, there is work to be done."

Jürgen said no more. Gerhardt pressed him but he only smiled and said he might be able to offer suggestions the next time they were out of earshot of the camps. When they returned to camp, Gerhardt parked the truck and brought the parts indoors. The bag fell open, the parts tumbled to the ground. A white paper fell out of the bag. It looked like a leaflet. Gerhardt read it. It called for the overthrow of the National Socialist government:

Our present state is the dictatorship of evil. I ask you not to allow these men who are in power to rob you step by step openly and in secret. Your rights as a citizen and a human are taken from you every day. Those who disagree with the system are being crushed. More evil will follow. If you love your country, do your part, in whatever line of work. Crush the evil power that has overtaken our beloved country! Resist, delay, do not help the enemy to rule over you. Sabotage the war equipment, do not participate in any cultural events that glorify the government. Down with Hitler and his henchmen. Freedom is G-d-given. Don't let thugs take it from us. — The White Rose

Quickly, Gerhardt stuffed the leaflet in his pocket and said nothing. He knew that Jürgen had left it behind for him to read. In his room alone later that afternoon he read it again, and the next morning once again. Then he tore it in scraps and flushed it. Who or what was the "White Rose"? He needed to see Jürgen again. He discovered him reading a book in the camp library. Jürgen motioned him outside.

"Who are you?" Gerhardt asked. "You could be punished with prison for your words to me in the truck and for that leaflet. Are you the white rose?"

"I am only one. The White Rose is many. What did you do with the leaflet?"

"I flushed it, of course!"

"Good. Then there is no record of it... what do you think of what you read?"

Gerhardt hesitated. It had been years since he'd allowed himself to think of speaking out against Hitler. He knew his mother would suffer with him if he was suspected of anything irregular.

"Why do you come to me? I can do nothing for you."

"Somehow you are different, unlike the others. What is it? Perhaps you are here also against your will?"

Gerhardt felt increasingly nervous. He wanted to open up, but the risk was too great. What if this person was a *Nazi* spy who had been sent to test him? What if they knew he was Jewish? He tried to look calm. He looked away and said nothing. Jürgen shook his head and chuckled. He knew the stranglehold *Nazism* had upon almost everyone.

"I understand, dear Gerhardt. You are afraid. Many people are so. I approach almost no one, but you are different, you are a thoughtful one, and watchful. I have noticed you these few months. Remember you can come to me any time. I have much to teach you. You have much to do."

Jürgen turned and walked back to the library. Gerhardt's mind and heart raced. It was obvious that Jürgen felt no fear, yet he was careful in his approach. He had judged correctly that he could trust Gerhardt. So there is an opposition to this demented party of madmen, Partisans do exist! Maybe there was hope for Germany yet to live in peace, to overcome tyranny! Gerhardt wanted to sing out, to thank G-d for putting these brave souls in Germany and in the Labor Service! He wished he could tell his parents of this great discovery, but he knew he would keep Jürgen's secret.

Gerhardt tried to imagine himself as a Partisan. How would he be able to help? He had no real freedom to come and go as he pleased. Orders from his commandant straight-jacketed the lives of every boy in camp, determining every hour's activity. Too, his position with the *Wehrmacht* was vital to him now, and the war had begun in Poland. He knew within a short time he would be sent to join the effort. Gerhardt felt deeply that his private victories would be achieved on the field of war where he could fully discover himself as a Jew, a German soldier and a patriot.

When Gerhardt undressed for bed that night he thought as always of his dear mother and father. His whispered prayers were fervent. He grieved for his father. Tears born of a thousand lonely nights watered his sheet, and yet, because of his new knowledge he felt freer and happier than he had in years.

A week later Gerhardt was called up to help move an armored division of tanks and trucks to the eastern border of Poland, near the *Bug* River. The news came to the camp over the loudspeakers, then was attended to by the daily supervisorial staff in the camp. Each boy was told to ready himself for a physical exam the following morning. Most of the boys were uproariously happy, Dieter among them. They gathered in the field following the noon meal and sang war songs and the German national anthem. Gerhardt made excuses that he did not feel well and retired to his bunk where he could think and pray. He tried to phone his mother at work but could only leave word. In a trembling voice, he pronounced,

"They will train me to fight. I will soon be on the field. Please, Mama, pray for Gerhardt. "

He knew she would recall her words to him. Would he find himself a hero or . . . ? His heart held no joy but only a growing regret. He was finally getting his chance to make war.

Though thou hast sore broken us in the place of dragons ... our soul is bowed down to the dust, our belly cleaveth to the earth ... redeem us for thy mercies' sake.

— Psalm 44

PART THREE
THE *KINDER*
ESTER AND GERHARDT

Journal of the Dead — Belza

I was in the *Judenrien*, yes, and I was a problem for the enemy, the Germans. They were after my father and his family who lived with us. We were very poor, living in the *shtetl* there in Berdichev, Ukraine. Let me tell you it was hard. All we had were the clothes on our backs. Our heat was a stove that was always failing us. We never had enough to eat and we were always hungry and sick. I was often sick as a dog from many different causes. My family consisted of twelve people, myself and my husband Berger who was a jeweler. His sons and his brothers who were all married lived there in town with us. My mother also lived with us and our children — four of them, and their friends who stayed with us. Their own parents were shot in 1893 during another pogrom in that town. We often had another person with us for different lengths of time. We were very poor and crowded.

I was one of the murdered people from that town, barely escaping Auschwitz in that summer. My father and his mother were also victims. My husband was taken out and shot before I was killed. He was 55, I was 19. I was given away to him when I was only a schoolgirl. He was a friend of the local pastor. We were not Jewish. We had no great religious leanings but were sympathetic with Jews and often hid them from the *Gestapo*. I think my husband and I looked Jewish and were gunned down just in case.

My death came as I was working in the fields we had. We had several acres and I was still a young woman when I was suddenly taken and shot down. Yes, it was something like that, a surprise. I beckoned to my mother and father to get out of the way. They were sitting nearby on a porch. The German officer came close to me and told me to get away from the harvesting I was doing. The German said I was eating my own harvest and that was forbidden. I was a large woman and only looked like I was eating it. In reality I was trying to grab a little for my poor mother sitting on the porch watching me hoe and weed. I lifted my hands in the air and backed away. He took aim and shot me.

I felt the earth move from under my feet as I hit the ground, mortally wounded. I knew death instantly. My spirit was lifted completely from my body and I saw myself as if I were hovering in air. I felt little or no pain because the bullet pierced my heart right away and passed through me, leaving me without breath. Shock naturally set in right away. I was gone in less than three seconds.

My poor husband called to me from his death spot and we merged in our minds and created our own refuge with each other. He was coming home from his work as a town crier. He warned people of upcoming problems from the German army and bivouacs from the Red Army. He was crossing the street where we lived to come in the front door and he was gunned down by a street patrol of Germans looking to score a hit on this Friday night. My husband fell to his death instantly and he lay there for two days until we could find out where he was and get to him. I loved him dearly and his death filled me with sorrow and longing to murder his assailants.

My children were also murdered by the Gestapo. They were not in Berdichev at the time but were in a nearby town working with others against the enemy. We were trying to form an underground there, near Berdichev, but it was discovered and my children were shot along with many others who were there. I am so sad for them. I have not seen them since. I hope that in the *Millenium* we will be together again.

And I will gather the remnant of my flock out of all countries whither I have driven them, and will bring them again to their folds; and they shall be fruitful and increase.

— Jeremiah 23:3

13 — In Advance of Peril

The ground in the cemetery was wet, and the afternoon drizzle didn't make Ester's journey among these cold stones any easier. The brush was getting thicker toward the northwest end of the huge cemetery where the mausoleums were located. Her father's directions seemed to indicate she should concentrate her search in that sector of the yard. Suddenly, her foot caught on a stone and she fell full length onto the wet leaves. She groaned as the soft wetness of the earth beneath sullied her clothes and hair.

As she rose she felt for a moment as if she were rising from the dead. A vision of faces grew before her eyes. Faces of the occupants in this city of death. She looked into the eyes of innocent children, wistful, full of hope. She looked away but now there were the faces of the executed – their eyes spoke of horror and fear. Other faces appeared: haggard, hungry countenances seeming to rise from the clay earth. As Ester rose she turned to see that she'd fallen into a shallow grave, deep as a wound in the earth, littered with brush. She screamed. The voices grew louder, matching her own: *They have taken our lives from us! Our precious days and nights, gone forever. We are cut down in our prime! There must be justice, there must be restitution!*

～

The date was July 7, 1941. Ester awoke in a sweat. Her sheets were soaked and the room stank of it. She'd been dreaming of war. In a trench, face up and mortally wounded her dead eyes beheld German troops jumping the chasm above her. Their rifles were at the ready. Their greatcoats flapped open as they jumped the ravine in which she lay bleeding. Dirt flew, much of it over her lifeless body as German boots stamped heavily on the soil. In the fray, a heavy artillery troop tripped and fell as he crossed the trench. His heavy body slammed Ester's corpse. Horrified, she awoke beneath him. "No, no", she cried out. But the weight of his body was too great. He turned and smashed her head with his rifle butt to silence her, then saw she was already dead. "Jew bitch" he yelled at her in disgust. He dug his heels into her face scrambling out of the ditch.

With a huge gulp of air, Ester awoke and sat stark upright in bed. She felt the rifle butt against her nose, the huge boots shredding her face. Her hands were full of blood. The blood was in her eyes, all over her bedclothes and filling up the room.

"Save me, save me," she cried out. "Papa, I'm dead."

No one heard, no one came. The dead woman could not move. She sat there, feeling no life within her. Minutes passed. Then slowly she felt the weight of the soldier's body slide away. The blood on her hands disappeared and she realized there was none anywhere. She was alive. She was not dead. The house was dark and quiet.

Shakily, she arose. A few minutes had to pass before her legs were steady. She hurried to the window looking for German or Russian troops. In the pre-dawn mist she saw only Meyer Lushovsky below, hurrying down the street to work at the Ilyich Leather-Curing factory, his little grey dog Svitzl skittering behind. Meyer was whistling as usual. Ester sighed in relief, but then moaned, remembering. Today was the day. She must pack her few things and with her mother and many more of Berdichev's Jews, follow Barak south to the Black Sea enclave held by the Partisans. Ester and Anna were to meet him at dusk near the southern end of the Gnilopyatka where thick stands of hornbeam, maple and oak trees would shield them in the gloom of a dark night on the Steppes. They would move in a column along the highway south to Vinnitsa, then follow a pre-planned route through heavily forested areas, avoiding all roads. They planned to arrive within a week in Nicolayev, a port just north of the Black Sea. Partisan troops had been summoned and organized to lead and protect the refugees. More would be waiting in Nicolayev, but no one's safety could be assured. Anything could happen. German troops were said to be hurrying toward Berdichev. The Red Army was still nowhere in sight. Timing and great caution were essential. How long before Stalin realized Ukraine had been invaded?

In the briefings they gave their soldiers, the German *Gestapo* rarely shared much military intelligence. But they were hungry to take Berdichev because it was significant militarily to the *Wehrmacht*. It was the nexus for a railroad line stretching back to Poland. From there the German army could move its massive materiel with little cost and much dispatch. There were problems involved: the logistical units had anticipated that the land was harsh and frozen, so they were amazed upon their eventual entry to discover the soil was clay. Building roads in the clay soil of Ukraine is very difficult: the land is rolling countryside with a dearth of gravel and stone. Spring and winter rains turn the soil into mud that can literally suck soldiers' boots off and mire trucks and tanks for days.

But Berdichev was also the terminus of a 25-mile paved road that ran south from Zhitomir. That main axis was one of the few highways in the Soviet Union at the time. Mainly for this reason the *Fuhrer*, with his eye on Kiev, decided Berdichev was the ideal staging area for the planned assault.

Secondarily, the "Yid's capital", as Berdichev had come to be called, was a shining light of opportunity for the *Third Reich's SS* division. They envisioned a gigantic German state stretching from the Atlantic Ocean to the mountains of the Urals in the east. A plan of worldwide domination required that each detail be carefully evaluated and perfectly executed so that no time, manpower or materiel was wasted. The town's population, ethnically about fifty percent Jewish and an important center for *Chasidic* enlightenment, gave Hitler' generals a green light. That the accomplishment of the murder of 10,000 or 20,000 or more Jews in a single *Aktion* was possible, even probable, would prove a great victory for Operation Barbarossa and further the *Reich's* dark dream of *lebensraum*.

Those were terrifying days, filled with insecurities at every turn. Ester and her family felt as if the earth were churning beneath their feet, ready to heave apart at any minute. There was no place to run to, no safety in their homes or in their country. They asked themselves why such evil had come to Ukraine and to its Jews. To this question they found no answer, but Reb Levi, who daily read from his *Torah*, said that the Eternal One had promised through his prophets that he would eventually reunite the families of Israel in peace: "*He is aware of our suffering and He knows the perilous times we live in. He is with us always… in life or death. May we praise His holy name and trust in His Plan for us.*"

～

On July 1st, Anna received a letter from her son. Gerhardt wrote his mother:

"*Finally, I am in the field! The commander of our tank unit has picked me to follow these cumbersome beasts across Poland. We began last week and already we have made significant advancement. Of course,*

171

all the trucks and troops are with us, too. I've had little to maintain so far. Our materiel is superior to all opposition forces, we are advised. But we must be alert to all the possibilities. This is so different from my air raid warden work in Berlin.

My friend, Jürgen, is looking forward to peace, but I believe this war has long to go before peace will be achieved. For now, we are heading toward a border (cannot tell you), where our leaders say we will become experienced at using our weapons and our legs!

We are well fed, mother, do not worry for your soldier son. As I write this, I am in the back of a truck looking at the hundred of vehicles that follow us. These roads are rutted and impossible to traverse at normal speed, I am sure I will never run out of mechanical work. There is deep clay and we sink into it. The tanks are looking for firmer ground to the east of these roads so their tracks will not become mired. I hope the new land we are entering has better roads!

Haven't seen any fighting yet. Take pride in knowing your son is well (and not hearing any more you-know-what!). Now I can find my true purpose. Evil must be conquered! (We are only allowed a letter a week.) How I miss Papa. I pray for his soul every day... Perhaps he is alive but has disappeared to save himself!

Well, Auf weidersehen for now.

– Gerhardt

Behold, I have refined thee, but not with silver. I have chosen thee in the furnace of affliction.

— Isaiah 48:10

14 — Satan's Legions

Reb Levi, his dark beard working as he bit his upper lip, was deep in thought as he passed his old synagogue on the way to Zych's apartment. He had risen before the dawn this July 7th to begin the final organizing of his *Chasids* who were leaving with Barak and his Partisans. He ordered his wife and daughter to join the party and this tore at their hearts. Negotiations with the Partisans and with the *Chasids* had taken several weeks. Now most everything was ready: families who would leave had been identified, counted and briefed. They had been cautioned against taking what they could not carry, for though there were wagons available the party could not move swiftly and secretly through the forests unless they traveled unburdened. What caused the most confusion were the things people owned. Many buried their possessions hurriedly, but many sold theirs. Others hid them or gave them to relatives for safekeeping until they would meet again. Few were willing to walk away from all they had worked so hard to acquire. Reb Levi berated them.

"The preoccupation of men with their worldly possessions has been cause for much of the terror this world has endured, is it not so? Have you hunted ones taken time to think, you might suspect your precious belongings will quickly become the spoils of war! It is your lives you must save, understand? Not your things!"

Privately, he complained to his wife.

"Oy, these people, questioning everything, everything! Are they eager to leave? No, they doubt any Germans will come to Berdichev, and then they say, 'Welcome! Can these people be worse than Russians?' "

But finally, after meetings with Reb Levi, Zych, Barak and the Partisan groups, about 1,500 people in all grudgingly agreed in purpose. Many of these soon-to-be refugees were children of parents who chose to remain behind. They had to be appointed adults who would be responsible for them until they reached their destination and the parents could join them. Part of a revised plan included boarding the freight and passenger trains that passed twice nightly through Vinnitsa heading south. Some of the boxcars were usually half-empty. This plan would hasten the refugees' arrival at their Black Sea outpost. Partisans were to accompany them.

It would be a perilous trip. Prayers were said. A time was arranged for departure and the location secured. Runners spread the word to every Jewish business, farm and residence: No one was to divulge the whereabouts of the party. They would simply disappear . . .

Finally, group leaders were chosen. As Reb Levi watched Zych and Barak assemble groups of fifty he remarked it was like the Exodus all over again.

"Only this time we are not leaving together. We have to send back for those who remain behind."

Reb Levi knocked firmly on the door of Zych's tiny apartment, feeling the weight of his hurried breakfast of bagels and butter with warm tea to wash it down. Zych answered the knock in his nightclothes, a long shirt that showed stains of soup. His thin old briefs needed patching in the seat. His scrawny legs trembled in the pre-dawn cold. Great wooly socks looked silly on his long, flat feet. He regarded his visitor with a smile.

"Reb Levi, what finds you here at this hour, before dawn? Has something gone wrong?" He stepped back to let his *chazzen* enter. The wall clock showed 4 a.m. Reb Levi came into the apartment, thinking deeply. He went to the small couch and sat on it heavily.

"My friend, I was recalling how this city, this "Yid's Capital" has never been safe from invasion. It is a true fact, I believe, that the Eternal One has plans to remake the universe. Yes, He is teaching us humility in change, patience in affliction, strength and honor in war."

"Yes, Reb Levi. That is a good assessment. We are certainly learning those things, I agree."

Reb Levi thought for a while, and then looked up at his friend. Tears flowed down his cheeks into his beard. Zych sat down next to Reb Levi. He wiped his eyes of sleep.

"And another thing. Why would He bring the Germans here? When they come they will kill us. All of us. They are a… a killing machine. Who are we kidding? I fear those who stay behind will never live to see their families again. But what can we do? Shall we abandon what we have in fear? Shall we run into their guns? No, we cannot. We must stay and fight this evil together. My good son has made me see that. At least our children will live and be safe, may G-d be willing."

"Reb Levi, I am sorry to see your tears. I, too, fear you are correct in your estimation. The *Chasidim* must remain and face the enemy. Perhaps the Germans will come through here and move right along, do you think that possible?"

Reb Levi arose to pace the room. He walked quickly to and fro and back again. Eventually he sat down again and looked into the eyes of his good friend.

"Zych, my fine Romany friend, I am honored that you have thrown in your lot with the *Chasids*. But after much thought and prayer these few days I am certain the enemy will stop at nothing to gain their objective: the destruction of the Jewish people. Therefore, I want you to leave tonight with the party, on my orders."

The other man twitched in surprise.

"Reb Levi," Zych began after a frustrating minute of silence. "I cannot leave Berdichev when my dearest friend remains behind. Who will help you? Who will see to the remaining families and care for the dead that will surely cross your doorstep? No, no, I cannot . . ."

"Zych, please. Do as I ask you. If you love me, honor my request for your safety. I cannot go to my grave knowing I have kept another from living."

Zych then threw himself at Reb Levi's feet and hugged his knees. Tears wet the Reb's worn suit.

"I will not leave you, my Reb, my *chazzen*," Zych wailed. "I, Zychoslov Petrovich Romanov, the last of the Romanovs, choose to live or die here in my adopted home. Whatever we must endure, that I shall endure at your side. You must not send me away, my Reb, my *chazzen*. Allow me to serve you until the very end. Then this Romany can die happy. After all, what meaning has life without our struggle, without our pain?"

Reb Levi rose and the two embraced. "I am humbled by you, my friend," mumbled Reb Levi. "Let it be, then. And now, let us finish our plans for this day of Exodus."

~

Avram was returning that morning from Lvov where he had posted some of his revolutionary posters. The day was clear, he felt exhilarated. *I shall have a tea before returning to school*, he thought and headed in the direction of home. His mother would be pleased to see her son before his classes were finished.

Few people were on the street at the noon hour in Zhitomir. Most were at their jobs in the factories or small shops that lined the boulevard. As Avram approached the corner leading to his apartment he saw two uniformed Russian soldiers talking and laughing in front of the building. Cigarette smoke wafted upward in the balmy air. Avram grew cold. He stopped short, looked for a place to hide until the men would move on. But one of them looked casually in his direction. Recognizing him, the officer came to attention and gave orders in Russian to his companion. Avram didn't wait. He turned and ran back toward the train station where he hoped he could get lost in the crowds of people and traffic. He could not hear the boots of the Russian officers behind him but he heard their shouts ordering him to stop. "I will be able to outrun them", he thought as he put on all the speed he possessed. He had a one-block lead. The image of a warehouse near the train came to his mind. He determined to hide there until he could safely leave again. When he reached the warehouse he collapsed on the floor, but he made himself crawl out of sight behind crates and piles of ropes.

It was many hours later when Avram finally ventured forth from the warehouse. His mood was dour but anxious. The police had not guessed his hiding place. He'd missed teaching his classes. Who knew what the students were told when he did not arrive? And his mother, she must be terribly worried! But could he return home? Dare he return to his class? With great caution Avram made his way toward his apartment building. He waited in the shadows at the corner where he had seen the officers. The avenue was not inhabited. Slowly he progressed to the door, then up the stairs, quietly slipping his key into the lock. The rooms inside were dark. His hand reached for the switch and the usual dim light illuminated the room.

On the floor before him was the body of his mother. She had been shot in the chest, and then fallen flat backward. The expression on her face was one of pain and surprise. The blood around her had already begun to dry. The smell of death permeated the room. She had been dead for hours.

As Avram gasped and cried out, two figures stepped through the hallway gloom. He turned in time to see the Russian officers behind him but he could do nothing to save himself. They grabbed him and held him fast.

"You — come with us, *balamu*[79]," one of the policemen said angrily. "You are under arrest for revolutionary acts. Traitor to Russia! You will see what we do with traitors."

Avram felt his stomach convulse. "My mother, you killed her! You pigs, lousy Russian pol . . . " A soldier slapped him hard across the mouth and shoved an arm beneath his prisoner's chin.

"You have brought this on yourself with your posters and your *boltani*[80] against Rosiya (Russia). Your mother is long past caring, we shot her hours ago. When you saw us outside your apartment house she was already dead. *Vyso, poshli.*"[81]

The Russian officers laughed in triumph and shoved Avram out the door into the night. His last thoughts were of Ester before he slumped to the ground in a faint.

~

When Ester saw Myer Lushovsky hurrying to work she was faintly aware that the whole busy little city of Berdichev was also on its way to work. Many hundreds had well-paid jobs at the Ilyich Leather Curing factory, one of the largest in the Soviet Union. Others were secure in positions at the Progress machine-tool factory, the Berdichev sugar refinery, and many other factories and shops that produced goods for local and Ukrainian and Russian consumption. Some were sent as far away as Samarkand and other towns of Central Asia. In fact, Berdichev was almost overflowing with goods: soft *chuvyaki*[82] slippers, hats, leather, shoes, metal products, cardboard and much more.

But at Reb Levi's home the least was the most allowed. Ester and Anna were busy deciding what few items to take with them. One of Ester's prized possessions was the photo taken of her parents just after their wedding. The photographic paper had slowly taken on a brownish hue. Her mother's presence seemed to dominate the picture. Anna's long black hair raised from her neck and pinned atop her head gave the appearance of a dark crown. Reb Levi, posed to her right, was stooping a bit as though he were apologizing for his appearance next to the commanding presence of his wife. His beard was not well combed, his *yarmulke* a bit awry. The black coat he always wore had several stains that he tried to hide. The result was one hand just at the left of his suit jacket, while the other rested at his right thigh. But his expression, Ester noted with fondness, was one of simple joy and gratitude, for at the parents' feet sat their two precious children, clean, perfectly dressed, well combed and smiling.

Anna had given her daughter the picture for a birthday memento. It was a gift she treasured. Ester sighed and carefully put the picture at the bottom of her bag. It would keep her spirits up while she waited for her father to join them. By early afternoon the women had packed and were ready to be escorted to the meeting site. Many who were assembled at the southern edge of town were already moving toward the river. The estimate was that nearly 700 men, women and children were in the first wave of the party. Many hundreds more were scheduled to leave by 7 o'clock. Anna and Ester were to be in this second party.

Reb Levi would accompany them as far as the river. He was concerned that the latest news of the German army was not encouraging. The 11th Panzer Division was headed in the direction of Kiev from Lvov, a distance of 480 kilometers (almost 300 miles) to the northeast. Once they reached Kiev only four hours separated them from Berdichev to the south, to take advantage of the paved roads between the two cities. But Partisan activity had not reported their progress in two days, evidently because many of the ranks had been shot, so no accurate information could be had.

By seven o'clock that evening the second group of refuges from Berdichev was gathered at the edge of the city along with family members who were seeing them off. Anna had left copious instructions for her husband to follow at home and inspected her daughter's pack to be sure that only the essential clothing and few other items were taken along. Their goodbyes were hurried and emotional.

Barak arrived late. He went immediately to find Reb Levi who was saying prayers for everyone in the lineup.

"Papa, they are in Kiev already, heading south towards us! We have to leave right away."

"I know, my son. I am just asking G-d to be merciful. Will you be going with them?"

Barak wiped his face with his sleeve and lifted his rifle back upon his shoulder.

"I will accompany them to the trains at Vinnitsa. Then some of us will have to turn back. We have a group leaving from there at midnight to escort." He paused and then took his father's shoulders. "You should be going with them, Papa. We are no match for these murderers."

Reb Levi smiled tightly and shrugged. "I must care for these *Chasids*, Barak. The living, the dead… they will need Reb Levi to pray for them. I have been put in their charge, remember, by our revered rabbi. You go, my son, go and be with your mother and sister. Tell them not to fear. I will join them soon to bring them back when the danger has passed."

Barak hugged his father and kissed him. They parted to their separate tasks.

Suddenly, noises were heard from a distance to the north. Rifle shots. The Partisan soldiers quickly surrounded their group, yelling at those leaving to move out immediately. They had to forcibly separate them from family members who had decided to remain in town. Anna and Ester grabbed each other; they were almost trampled by everyone rushing past. Reb Levi, startled at the noise, was unable to react at first. Then he called out to the people to hurry to the river. Zych was nearby, saying farewell to a friend. Seeing Reb Levi, he suddenly took off his cap and waved it around like a sheepherder amongst his flock.

"Hurry, hurry, hurry. The Germans are coming! Get out, get out!"

The next minutes were chaos, but the Partisans shepherded everyone out of sight into the trees along the river. Reb Levi called out to his wife and daughter to hurry with the group. He and Zych ran down an alleyway to a deserted shop several streets away and hid there. Sounds of gunshots came again, this time seeming closer. Anna saw them running. Ester grabbed her arm.

"Come on, Mama. We've got to get out of here!"

But Anna hesitated, looking after her husband. Suddenly the women were thrown to the ground by neighbors pushing and shoving.

"Faster, faster," Barak urged. People were already running through the trees, yelling to those in front to run even faster. The earth roared with the sound of a thousand feet.

"Hurry, hurry," Barak called to them, waving his arms behind the slow moving people. "Must I herd you like sheep? Why do you question, now, you silly people. Do you want to be shot? The Germans have arrived and our soldiers will die in the fields and in the streets fighting them off. Get on, move!"

As it turned out, no soldiers were behind the fleeing horde of townspeople, and their journey was safe. The invaders were more interested in setting up perimeters and headquarters. Because Stalin refused to believe Berdichev was occupied by German troops, they were unopposed for the first week.

In a few more minutes the meeting area had been almost cleared, but in the city's northern sector there was shouting of men's voices and the ground-rattling vibrations of tanks.

The Germans made their entrance in Berdichev unexpectedly. German tank troops had broken through to the city. The people of Berdichev who remained were finishing for the day and looking forward to soup, cabbage and bread. They put down their tools, turned off their machines, stopped working and sat or stood frozen in confusion. They turned to one another in bewilderment and unbelief. What was this? Tanks invading a bustling, productive little city in mid-evening?

Then they remembered. Rumors had been passed like a virus up and down the boulevards of apartment houses, throughout the business district to the factories and across the river to the west. The town crier had come through two days earlier with warnings of invasion to the north or west, but no one suspected that Germans would invade Berdichev. Is it true? Then, today is the day? The German army has arrived, has it not? And what will happen? Are they liberators or enslavers? Are the Russians coming to fight them? Is it really the German army? Well, we will find it out soon enough!

All in all, only about a third of the Jewish population managed on that day and in succeeding weeks to evacuate successfully. Those who were in the northwest end of town heard the soldiers shout from their vehicles "*Juden kaput!*" They waved their hands and laughed. Almost the entire Jewish population had remained in town. Not until almost mid-July did Stalin send the Red Army contingent to rout the intruders and at the same time assist them in the purges. There were many eyewitnesses to these goings-on.

~

One of the hundreds of tombstone markers Ester passed as she made her way northward toward the mausoleums was that of Gersh Geterman. She'd never known his story until his children inherited his diary after his death years later. Ester was a friend of his eldest daughter who invited the Levi family to share the long diary entries with her. She recalled now many details of the terrifying record:

Geterman the cabinetmaker was an eyewitness to the horrors that happened the first day of the Berdichev occupation. When the German army invaded Berdichev on horseback and on foot, they rode along Glinishci, Greater Zhitomir and Stein Streets. These residential streets were near the Zhitomir highway. The elderly were long time residents. Gusta and Yekaterina Korotkova, sisters of old Meyer Polyak and dearly beloved of him, were among those driven from their homes toward the huge factory vats that lay before them. Gusta cried out when the Germans broke down her front door and aimed a rifle in her face. The three of them were having dinner. Three large potatoes were still on the stove cooking in a weak cabbage juice.

"Jew, we come to murder you and all the stinking Yids here," a soldier yelled at her in German. He motioned for the women to leave the house and shoved them into the street where they met the others who had been rounded up. Within a short time, a hundred bodies were being hustled across Zhitomir Highway toward the open doors of the Ilyich Curing Factory. Most of the people did not speak or understand German. They were amazed to see German soldiers at their doors and windows and even more confused at their own deaths by these foreign uniformed gangs.

The leather curing shop was nearby also, giving off its acrid odors day and night.

The workers in the factory looked up in astonishment. The evening shift had just begun. Maybe 100 workers bustled about readying the fabrics to be dyed, shifting them along huge pulleys toward the acid-filled vats. In walked a hundred old Ukrainians, many of them Jews, flanked by German soldiers with rifles and on horseback.

"G-d in Heaven, protect us", a man said aloud, staring at the spectacle before him. Others said the same thing, and some began to cry softly. Nothing like this had ever happened before in the factories. Always the Russian purges had targeted the homes of residents at night, when there was no opposition and little if any chance to see the victims as more than bodies rolling across floors or falling on their faces as they were shot from behind.

As the workers looked at the poor townspeople and neighbors who had interrupted their processing of leather and other goods through the dye vats, they read terror in their faces, and this made them all afraid. The soldiers then demanded their group climb the few stairs at the center of the building and jump into the vat. There were screams and some women fainted. The soldiers pushed their rifles into the backs of the bodies before them, pushing them toward the stairs. More people fainted, or dropped to their knees to pray. The soldiers were becoming impatient. They shouted commands at these people and kicked them. But no one moved to the vats. Instead they huddled together in fear.

"You must do as we say or you will all be shot!" one of the

Germans commanded. He was a handsome blond man with an imperious air about him. He wanted to get the business done so his men could move on to other conquests. Still no one moved toward the vats. The soldiers stood back, raised their rifles and shot into the crowd. They continued firing until all the people in the room were dead. Then they began the process of picking up each body and heaving it into the pit of acidic extract. To pick up their spirits during this heavy work, they began to joke that they were "curing human hides". This was the first execution by the Germans when they took Berdichev on July 7th, 1941.

---

[79] troublemaker
[80] jabber
[81] "That's all, let's go"
[82] A Russian fur

Journal of the Dead — Reb Katzenbach

My name is Reb Katzenbach. I want the world to understand what happened that day. My story needs to be told.

I was aware of the Germans coming into Berdichev, for the news and the runner had broadcast their whereabouts for several days prior to their arrival. They came shouting "*Juden diet!*" (Jews, die!)! They were many and they came in a rush, on horseback and in tanks, running across the river and stopping at our plant where we were busily preparing leather for the dye vats. We were many, then, neighbors helping each other with the complex vat dying procedures. Six Germans came into the building shouting at us to hurry up and fill orders for them. My *madele* and myself were working there with many others. The Germans dismounted and ran toward us, shouting and waving their arms. Their uniforms were gray with dust and dirt, caked with the mud of Ukraine. They came at us bustling and in great humor, thinking it very funny.

They said "Hurry and make us the order. We want the dyed hats and coats of leather in our hands by morning. One thousand orders. We will not pay you, but we may let you live."

One of our workers, a bustling man who never took no for an answer, decided to challenge them.

"I will not work for no money', he said. 'Give me your order and arrange for payment now.'

The Germans got angry. They hurried over to the man. He stood on the edge of the precipice above the acid-filled vat. They ordered him to jump in the vat. He refused and backed away. He was standing on a high board that teetered above the vat. He had to be very careful not to trip and fall in the soup that was made of very potent dyes and could easily scald the body with sores that would not heal.

"I will not jump into this vat, are you crazy?" he yelled. The Germans laughed, then quickly took to the air with their rifles and shot him out of the sky above the large vat. He screamed and fell, bleeding profusely, into the mix. He sank beneath the hot greenish watery liquid and was not seen to rise. We were all transfixed. Fear coursed through me.

"The rest of you," the Germans shouted, "jump in. Hurry or you will be shot and thrown in it."

We were in shock. The man next to me wet his pants and the floor. We didn't move.

"Jump!' they shouted in German. "*Raus, raus!*"[75] But none of us moved toward the hot waxy liquid. I dived for cover, but was shot in the legs as I did so. The soldiers opened fire and killed everyone in the place. Then they laughed and called us sub-humans. I guessed they forgot to search for me in their great humor and excitement at what they had done. My wife found me there late at night and halfway dragged me home. I bled a great deal but had help from a doctor. I lived to be old because my wife and I ran away from Berdichev after my legs were somewhat healed two weeks later. We were fortunate to be gone when the Germans built the pits on Brodskii Street.

---

[70] "Hurry, hurry!"

The question of what to do was asked by all surviving Jews: but none could know for certain the answer, or by what path life might be preserved.

— Holocaust, p.585

15 — Holocaust

In another part of the city, twelve German soldiers who had been ordered to secure the main marketplace, stood overlooking the Rynok market bazaar. Now this small enclave was the market basket of Berdichev. Peasants and farmers from many miles in all directions felt it their duty and great profit to sell at this downtown plaza every day, for the Jews' *Sabbath* was Saturday, but the Ukrainians and Russians shopped sometimes even on Sundays. This day the market had just closed. The vendors and their trucks and horses had left their stalls barren of goods to return laden with new and day old produce the following dawn.

Captain Fuchs, seeing the bazaar deserted, lowered his rifle and noticed with pride its glistening barrel. He contemplated the makeshift rotted wood selling stalls and saw no reason they should remain. He radioed across the city for two trucks. When they arrived a few minutes later he ordered them to destroy the marketplace. The soldiers laughed in glee as the old wooden stalls and tables were smashed and squashed beneath the heavy wheels of the German trucks.

"Now burn it," shouted the captain. "Burn it down! Let these Jewish bastards go hungry. They're not worth feeding."

Captain Fuchs had exceeded his authority. His orders never mandated the destruction of the market, but he was determined to come off a hero of the *Reich*. This particular bit of destruction, he imagined, would earn him the plaudits of Hitler.

Town leaders were called immediately to session. They had not met when the town crier broadcast the news and now they regretted it because it was obvious they were powerless to stop the destruction unless they could negotiate with the German army leaders.

"This must be done quickly," urged Reb Landrovich, the mayor of Berdichev.

"Who will go to the bazaar to stop this destruction?"

"You go, Reb Landrovich. Your store is nearest there and your livelihood is being affected." The others agreed.

So Reb Landrovich made for his store in haste and worry, but it had already been burned when he arrived, and as the culprits were nowhere to be found, he ran home and told his family they must leave town. They were among hundreds of others who took only what they could carry and left the only home they'd ever known for the wilderness of Ukraine.

People living nearby rushed to their doors and windows, shocked to see the sudden and total destruction of their market-place. Where would their food come from now? The vendors would arrive in the morning to a burned out city market. They would do a hasty retreat. Now the citizens of Berdichev would be forced to buy in secret and to hoard their meager supplies until the misunderstanding could be resolved. To whom could they appeal? Who were these soldiers? Were they passing through or…?

Ziba Stein-Moskovich shielded her three small grandchildren from the sight. She hustled them inside her shack across from the market and told them to hide beneath her bed.

"Here is something new, *kinder*. Pretend a game is being played on us and we mustn't let them find us. When we are sure we are safe, there is *strudel* for each of you."

But these attacks were no accident. Russian troops were nowhere in sight. Berdichev was unprotected from her enemy who lost no time in securing her strategic points. German troops were stationed at the entrances and exits to the city. No one was permitted to enter or leave. The railway station was "cleaned" of most of its personnel while troops patrolled the tracks. All busses leaving or arriving in Berdichev were confiscated, the passengers herded into the forest and shot. The airport was shut down indefinitely and the occupants locked inside a hangar to starve or freeze. Phone lines were cut.

None of this was lost on the citizens. They heard the rifle reports. People fleeing the opposite direction of gunfire were so confused they didn't know where to go, and were seen hiding behind trees and buildings, only to run into streets and find other places to hide. The scene was chaos.

"What's happening? Who is invading, Germans, Russians, who?"

"*Oy, oy*, how can such a thing happen here? What have we done to deserve this?

Almost as if to answer, the military commandant slowly and

confidently rode upon his horse south into town followed by his large contingent, also on horseback. It was a scene unique in all of Ukrainian history — mounted German soldiers riding almost as if in parade down the colorful old streets of Berdichev. Captain Fuchs stopped in front of what looked to him like a city edifice and shouted in German to the people sitting on broad steps. It was in fact a newly constructed building for the administration of benefits to factory and railroad workers.

"Find me the man in charge of this place. Do it now if you don't want to be shot."

One man, short, wide and dressed in the old work clothes of a factory worker, rose from his rest to run into the building and in a few minutes another man in a worn, worsted brown suit, appeared on the front steps. He wore a *yarmulke* on his head and a *tallis* beneath his coat. The German officer spat at him and spoke in German. The smaller man hurriedly interpreted for the man in the suit.

"Jew, We have taken over your town and your people. You are subject to the German army and the *Third Reich*. I hereby put an indemnity on the Jewish population of this town. Here are my demands. First, one hundred thousand rubles must be delivered in three days. Second, fifteen pair of patent-leather shoes. Then, six oriental carpets. Make them immediately. If they are not all ready in three days, you will be shot. And from now on, take off your stupid little hat in my presence."

With that, the captain wheeled his horse around. His troops followed him back up the wide street, kicking up dust as they went. The men on the steps stood still as ghosts. Finally, they turned to each other, still in shock.

"What are we going to do, Reb Chelmikov? Who can fill a quota like that in three days?"

The taller man shrugged and scowled.

"What are the Germans doing in Berdichev anyway? Who does he think he is, this *meshugah* horse rider? Go find the honorable Reb Levi. Tell him to get everyone ready. Always we have had Russian thugs to murder us. This time comes a German *pogrom*!"

～

A few blocks to the south of the exodus site, cold and stiff in their hiding place next to the meat lockers in Reb Zemelmeir's butcher shop, Zych the Romany painfully flexed his cramped back. With effort he peered through the grease-smudged front window. It was dark now, the shopping area was deserted. Reb Levi raised himself up just enough to view the entire street. Only a single light across from Melman's apothecary lit the shadows along the empty boulevard. The street was empty as a Sabbath evening.

"OK, let's go!" Reb Levi whispered. Careful to keep a low profile, the pair moved stealthily around the meat cases, lowering themselves almost to the floor as they crept behind the tables set for pastries and *kvass*. Eventually they reached the entrance to the shop. Reb Levi thought fleetingly that Zemelmeir and his large family would at this moment be on their way to the Black Sea refuge with Anna and Ester and many of the town's other *Chasids*.

The two men listened for German boots or running feet, but heard only their own shallow breathing. Carefully they entered the avenue and paused, wondering which way to turn. Reb Levi grabbed Zych's arm and pulled him northward.

"The synagogue," he whispered. "We'll be safe there. Those *Chasids* who are still in Berdichev have been instructed to rendez-vous here if the Germans should come. I have the key with me."

The two men flattened themselves against the buildings. In the twilight they could not be seen. Slowly and carefully they made their way along the buildings, taking shortcuts through dark alleyways, turning westward at Ekaterina Street, until they were almost in sight of the *Beit ha'Midrash* synagogue on Sverdlova Street. There they paused to rest and evaluate the situation. From a distance, they heard voices of men and women wafting past them in the dimness of evening from the direction of the synagogue. The *Chasids* were arriving. Zych estimated he was within five minutes of the voices.

"G-d in Heaven," Reb Levi muttered, hearing German spoken. "Are those devils at my synagogue, too?"

Zych looked at his friend with trepidation. Now they heard the shrill voices of women crying out — the enemy must be desecrating their precious tabernacle!

"But let us draw a bit closer," Reb Levi whispered. "Perhaps we can help without being seen."

Zych gulped. He knew Reb Levi's forthright nature, but perhaps their stealthiness in the deepening darkness could be of some avail to the captives. He stayed close behind as Reb Levi's portly figure in its faded old black suit moved swiftly against the darkened buildings.

In a moment they'd reached the corner of Ekaterina and Sverdlova Streets. Ahead of them lay the beloved monument of their synagogue, its painted old wood walls faintly aglow even in darkness. In front of it were two German troops on horseback. Huddled on the steps of the entrance were about twenty Jews, their hands waving in the night air, their backs to the soldiers. Reb Levi recognized most of the captives but it was too dark to see much. He caught his breath. Were they going to be shot on the synagogue steps? Zych whispered a favorite curse in Romanian.

"We haven't any rifles, Reb Levi. How can we help them? If we had rifles we could pick these maggots off their horses."

Reb Levi pondered the next move. In his heart he opened a prayer to G-d, thanking Him for His mercy.

"Please, *HaShem*, if You will be so kind, let my people go," he prayed, fingering his *tallis* fringes. "If You will be so kind, what shall we do?"

Zych, whose eyesight was keen, inched a few feet further toward the group. Suddenly he gasped. He sank to his knees and groaned, his voice a furtive whisper.

"Reb Levi, my dear friend, oh, G-d in Heaven..."

He pointed toward the group of distraught men and women.

"The woman there, on the right, do you see? Is that --"?

Reb Levi strained his old eyes ahead in the mist of darkness, wishing he had his eyeglasses. Most of the shapes were indistinguishable, but with careful attention he was able to discern his wife's timeworn blue and green *babushka*, a loving husband's gift on their last anniversary. It was askew and clotted heavily with blood. He choked in shock and surprise.

"Anna! My Anna! What are you doing there? Didn't you leave with Barak? My G-d, they'll kill her. What can I do?"

Reb Levi held his head in grief and shock, forgetting altogether that he was in hiding. Zych threw long, comforting arms around his friend. They cried silently together. Suddenly, action at the synagogue entrance increased. One of the two soldiers opened fire upon the massive front door of the synagogue. He and his companion laughed. The door fell with a shudder and splintered upon a bench of gray stone. The captives were immediately ordered inside. Reb Levi saw with relief that Ester was not among the group, and for this he gave thanks.

"We must get inside, we must get them out."

"How can we do that? The Germans will capture us, too."

"We'll distract them. If they'll come after one of us, the other can lead everyone out through the back door."

Zych stared at his *chazzen* who he had never before questioned. He saw that Reb Levi was desperate, not thinking clearly. He knew very well that plan would not work. They would be shot on sight or herded into the synagogue with the others.

"Reb Levi, my dear friend. Of course I understand, but we also have to save ourselves! A few more steps forward and we will surely be discovered. How can two unarmed men...?"

The older man fought to think calmly. Zych had stood by him through many trials. They had enjoyed wonderful times together. But he was not a Jew; he had no wife or family. He was not in a position of responsibility for the lives of others. There was no need for his sacrifice.

"Zych, my dear and faithful friend. I am your *chazzen*, am I not? And now I implore you, go and find my Ester. She would not have left town without her mother and thank G-d, she is not among those poor captives. Go find her and tell her I will meet her at the river's edge tonight, where the Partisans met us. May G-d be with you, my great friend."

Reb Levi embraced his friend to seal the bargain. Zych was taken back at this request. He started to resist, then realized argument was useless. Reb Levi now turned away and took a determined step into the street toward the whitewashed walls of the synagogue. Zych grabbed at his coat and pulled but the old man shook free.

"I must go now," he said calmly. "I must meet the others, to lead them... and to be with my wife." The other man watched in horror as his *chazzen* walked into his death trap. Tears flooded his eyes. He reached out, pleading.

"Reb Levi, my friend, what are you doing? How can you order me to go? What shall I do without you, *chazzen*?"

He looked away, seeing through his tears the empty streets before him, knowing in his heart he would never find Ester. He was a fool, prince of a dead dynasty, a man without a country or a king, penniless and now, friendless. How could he desert the only one who had given him refuge and hope?

"Reb Levi, wait!" he shouted, running into the street. Reb Levi turned. The mounted German soldiers turned their horses to face the men coming toward them. One of them snickered and raised his rifle to his cheek. Zych, seeing this, slowed down, put his thumbs into his belt and pushed out his chest. Tears choked his voice as he raised it to a shout.

"Do not shoot! I am Prinz Zychoslav Petrovich Romanov of Romania, great grandson of Pavel Petrovich, esteemed grandson of Peter the Great of Russia! Also I am *gabbai* (helper) to this esteemed *chazzen*, Reb Levi, my truest friend. We are together. We demand asylum!"

The two men reached the synagogue. One of the soldiers dismounted and ushered them inside to join the others. He was intrigued. Suddenly a shout came from inside the synagogue. Anna had seen her husband.

"Moshe! Moshe! Run, run away, please, Moshe!"

She was ignored. The soldiers were intent upon Zych. Reb Levi grabbed him and stood with him.

"Papers!" he demanded of Zych. "Let me see your papers if you are a Romanian Prince."

"Ah, you Germans are nothing if not methodical! They are with the German consulate in Romania. My word is good enough."

The soldier laughed. "Your word is nothing to us without papers." He looked the man up and down. "You say you are a prince? A Jewish prince, then?" He laughed with hilarity. Zych said nothing.

The soldier sobered quickly. "You are nothing but dirty trash to us," he snarled in German. He raised his rifle and slammed its butt across Zych's body. Zych fell to the floor, gasping for breath. Reb Levi instantly threw himself across him. The soldier kicked him off and spit at them both.

"Get up, Jewish prince and take your *rabbi* with you. *Raus!* Get inside. We have a surprise for all of you. Now move!" The soldiers motioned them inside.

With difficulty the two men rose to their feet. Reb Levi entered the dark synagogue and instantly began searching for Anna, who, with a scream of joy and then sobs of sorrow, found him first. They embraced in tears. The group was herded further inside where they were forced to kneel before the *Torah* cabinet.

"Now, conduct a service here! We of the *Third Reich* order you filthy Jews to pray to G-d to forgive the sins committed against the Germans."

He spoke harshly and in German. Only two men understood

him. One of them was Yefim Elyash, a carpenter in the trades of the city and a weekly *minyan* participant in the Saturday morning *Shabbat* services. Yefim repeated to the others what the soldier said. They looked at him in disbelief but no one said anything.

"Go ahead," the other soldier demanded. He pointed to a box at the edge of the pulpit. The box contained a store of *tallits* and *kippahs* (skull caps).

"Put those on and get on your knees and pray for G-d to forgive the sins against the Germans!"

When no one moved, he shoved his rifle butt into the group. A woman screamed and fainted. Reb Levi and others moved to pick her up, but the German soldier hit them and they fell against the rough wooden seats. Blood spurted from their wounds upon the floor and onto the clothes of the captives, eleven of whom were males. The women cried out. Reb Levi found Anna and hugged her close to him. He wanted desperately to know where Ester was but there was no opportunity to ask. He rose to lead the other men.

Yefim again translated the German into Hebrew. Slowly ten of the eleven moved toward the boxes, removing the *tefillin* and *kippahs* from them. They did not speak. With sure knowledge they would never escape their captors they slowly donned the garments and came to stand at the lecturn, facing the *Torah* cabinet. The Germans were joking between themselves, laughing as they made fun of the shawls and the small black round caps adorning the heads of the men. One of them noticed that Zych was not among them and yelled to him.

"You, prince of the Jews. Get over there," he said, pointing to the boxes containing the garments.

"I am not a Jew," Zych said. "But I will die with my friends."

"You are not a Jew? You think I care if you are a Jew, a prince or some other bastard? Today you are a Jew. You will pray with Jews and then you will die with them. Now move!"

Zych did not move.

"They want you to wear the *tallis* and the *yarmulke*," Yefim told him. "You'd better just do it."

Zych slowly rose. More soldiers were entering. They had brought pieces of wood and wooden objects. One of them had a can of diesel fuel. He began to methodically empty it around the inside walls. He sloshed fluid upon them and upon the *Torah* cabinet and the *bimah* stand where the shewbread is lain. Reb Levi let out a cry that sounded of his own death. Suddenly, flaming pieces of wood smashed through the windows, scattering around the room, some landing on the wooden seats, others on the cement floor, even upon some on the prisoners scrambling around to dodge them. The soldier with the diesel fuel hurried to safety outside the synagogue. He turned and threw a lighted match behind him. The other soldiers hurriedly followed him out.

That single match ignited with a deafening crash. The synagogue walls were quickly engulfed in roaring flames. Reb Levi, holding Anna, thought suddenly of the rear entrance to the synagogue, but how to get to it? He looked in that direction, then yelled to Zych who ran toward the only other exit. It was locked but not bolted. Having no key Zych grabbed the old handle and yanked it repeatedly, but the door was stuck. Suddenly a shot came through it, hitting him and splitting his left shoulder. He fell to the ground in agony.

More flaming pieces of wood came flying through the air. The prisoners scattered. The air was poison; the heat coming from the burning walls had begun to buckle them. Reb Levi knew the roof would soon collapse. Outside, the Germans lifted up the broken front door and set it firmly again in the doorway, separating finally captives from their captors. Inside everyone was coughing. Six had already passed out from smoke inhalation. The deadly fumes were becoming unbearable. Around them the walls were on fire as well as many of the seats, and now the *Torah* cabinet was burning. It was a funeral pyre.

Anna collapsed from the heat and smoke. Reb Levi, choking and coughing himself, knelt over her and pulled her as close to the altar as possible.

"Anna, my love, where is our Ester?" he yelled to his wife, but she was beyond answering. He motioned the others to join him. Those who could crawled together to surround the altar, the only thing in the room not on fire. Outside, the soldiers heard the cries of agony and laughed.

"We are a *minyan*," Reb Levi yelled against the noise of crackling flames. "We must thank *HaShem* for bringing us to Him this day. We must also pray for our families, then for our enemies and ask a quick death for our women so they will not suffer longer than necessary. There is little time! The ceiling will soon crush us!"

Massed together, duties given and understood, the men praised G-d for His goodness and then asked for His blessing.

They did not cease to pray as long as they had life.

The smoke climbed the walls and quickly obliterated the unique ceiling paintings showing a twelve-pointed design — interlocking Stars of David colored red and purple. The design was encased by a thick gold border. No one knew when or by who this design was drawn, but there were old *Chasids* in Berdichev who recalled its shining presence from their first encounters with the synagogue.

Outside, the German soldiers celebrated their victory. It had been a successful first day for *lebensraum*. Tomorrow there would be new opportunities.

~

It was in a smuggled diary printed in Ukraine months after the war that Ester and Barak finally learned all the details of their parents' death. Since no one inside the synagogue survived, the report of their last hours were revealed by the conscience-stricken German soldier who admitted pouring gasoline inside the building. He was captured by Russian infantry and eventually confessed to multiple Jewish murders. He was never executed.

Barak refused to ever again discuss the tragedy. In his grief he could not bear to speak of it. He and Ester decided to carry the sadness within their hearts as a memoriam to their parents.

For the Lord your God is he that goeth with you, to fight for you against your enemies, to save you.

— Deuteronomy 20:4

16 — The Russian Delusion

Shadows lengthened on the tombstones as the sun progressed across its sky. Ester was making progress. She paused in her task of cleaning away some of the overgrowth from the stones with tools she had brought along. This would help her to read clearly the Hebrew inscriptions on the monuments and to locate the one she so urgently sought. As she worked, more memories imposed upon her mind. She recalled the microfiche records she and Avram had read before traveling here from their home in America. In an effort to understand those times and the significance of the events that took her family from her, she'd made a collection of the reports and brought them to share with those she would meet on this journey. She decided to read from the notebook while she rested:

June 21, 1941

The first casualties of Operation Barbarossa are Soviet frontier guards. Just as the Moscow-Berlin express passed through the border at Brest, the German army opened fire. Guards, half-dressed and taken completely by surprise, rushed to and fro, but to no avail. The Nazis have invaded Mother Russia!

This invasion is the largest in history. There are 3.2 million German troops. They are deployed against only 170 Red divisions. Comrade Stalin has forbidden opening artillery fire on the Germans. Moscow Radio today woke the capital at 0600 with Keep-Fit exercises and weather.

By this evening two Soviet fronts have been broken through. German tanks are moving with great speed.

June 28-29, 1941

On the 28th a prong of the German advance invaded Minsk. Next day, in an unexpected attack, another division conquered Lvov. They're heading east toward Berdichev. Several thousand Ukrainian nationalists are being held in Lvov prisons. Relatives of the prisoners are surrounding the jails and wailing with grief.

Maria Spiridovna, our national hero who assassinated a Tsarist police chief in 1906, has been captured and murdered in her cell by NKVD guards.

June 30

The brave Russian soldiers of Minsk have fought back but finally the city fell to the German army. The Red Army's Western group broke into two German encirclements at Bialystok and Minsk. They lost 3,785 tanks and 440,000 men.

July 9

The German 11th Panzer Division has broken through and occupies Berdichev in the Ukraine. Russian troops finally overtake them in a ferocious counterattack. Stalin has initiated a Scorched Earth policy. Everything is left burned in the wake of battle.

July 16

Smolensk has been captured by German arms. Within 200 miles of Moscow, the citizens are now prisoners. Reports have estimated there are 30,000 Russians in the hands of the Nazis. It seems the Baltic states have been overrun. But church bells, flowers thrown by girls in national dress greet the advancing German columns. Country women greet with salt and bread. They make the sign of the Cross! They do not know: the NKVD guards are murdering their prisoners by the thousands! Russia is dying!

But Russia did not die, Ester thought. True, the 1940's were very desperate times. Her country was in chaos. Hitler's "scorched earth" policy destroyed much of the land and ruined millions of lives, but through the courage and strength of its people Russia and Ukraine survived. Ester was proud of that fact; it gave her hope for the future and filled her with the certainty that those who died here would in time be vindicated by an independent Ukraine whose citizens welcomed all people in peace and fellowship.

She read on:

Operation Barbarossa made Hitler a Judas to the German-Russian peace pact. There were plentiful warnings of betrayal. German planes were spotted flying reconnaissance missions over Soviet territory. In Leningrad, officials of the German consulate suddenly canceled their tailors' orders and headed back to Germany. The final tip off was received June 22, 1941. Soviet secret agent Alexander Foote reported to the Kremlin he'd discovered Hitler had planned a surprise invasion upon the Red Army from which he would emerge the ruler of all Soviet territory west of the Urals. None of these communiqués were heeded.

Blind bravado and political blunder were the greatest stumbling blocks in the way of Soviet readiness following the Great Purge of 1937 when Stalin arrested, tried and executed most of his top officers and subordinates in an effort to remake his army. Thirty-five thousand of his most talented commanders and other subordinates were murdered in that year. This, in effect, broke the spirit of the Red Army. Servility became the new watchword. Fear of a misstep stifled any innovative thought. Few of the new commanders had any battle experience, yet yesterday's battalion commanders now headed divisions and former divisional commanders were put in charge of whole armies. If Stalin had intended to destroy his entire army, he couldn't have done a more admirable job.

But the Red Army was deficient in modern equipment as well as leadership. The war with Finland in the winter of 1939-40 was responsible for the decrepit condition of the Soviet forces. The USSR committed more than one million men to that effort which lasted only four months. Eight million bullets later they admitted to 200,000 Russian casualties (though the true figure was probably much higher). Now, trying to modernize the armed forces the Russians realized their many mistakes (one was the disbanding of their mechanized corps) and hastened to rebuild by the end of 1941.

According to reports, much of the motive power still depended upon horses. Thirty divisions, or 210,000 horsemen accounted for a large section of warfare preparedness. Of the 24,000 tanks, all but 1500 were small and obsolete and three-quarters of them were inoperable. That meant three of four motorized divisions had no tanks.

There were no armored personnel carriers and a great shortage of trucks. Few staff cars and motorcycles were available. The situation in the skies was no better. Of the 12,000 planes, 80% were obsolete and the fighters could go no faster than 300 mph, while German Messerschmitts flew at over 350 mph. Few of these planes had radios!

Other problems were a lack of coordination in train timings, motor transport, petrol supplies. But Stalin overlooked these things in favor of misplaced confidence in his army's ability to fight and win a war effectively. Certainly there was plenty of manpower. The Soviet population, 190 million at the time, was three times that of Germany. In army personnel, there were at least 360 Russian divisions by August 1941. The Germans thought there were only 213. Small wonder the Russian commanders saw their army as invincible!

But on June 22, 1941 the Russians found themselves suddenly engaged in a defensive war on their own territory, totally unprepared. All their shortcomings became evident on the battlefield. Their western special military district was in shambles, six to seven thousand men short of a wartime establishment. This was because the soldiers had been hired off to build new tank and aviation units. Shortages of experienced personnel suddenly showed up everywhere.

Stalin, because he had not listened to the rumors of Germans break-
ing across the Russian border, was deprived of anti-Russian informa-
tion. Operation Barbarossa hit him like a maelstrom. Finally, upon
being advised of the immediate situation and broad scope of problems, he
bemoaned:

"All that Lenin has created we have lost."

Deeply depressed, he promptly went into seclusion for two weeks
while the German hurricane of destruction rampaged through Ukraine.

On July 3, Stalin had recovered enough to address his besieged
nation by radio. He vowed "the enemy and all his accomplices must be
hounded and annihilated at every step, all their measures frustrated."
But whereas the Luftwaffe had minutely planned their tactics, the Red
Army had no plans at all. In truth, they were fifty to one hundred years
behind the Industrial Revolution in all areas.

By late spring of 1941 the Germans had a clearer picture of Russian
preparations for war in their western areas. There was the oil situation
to worry about. In a war of any length the Soviet threat to Romania and
the Wehrmacht's oil supply would become great while Germany's might
could only decline as war dragged on. This concern easily overrode the
abstract idea of "living space" or a grander concept of a Greater German
Reich that would ideally stretch from western France to the Black Sea.
None of Hitler's generals endorsed these grand theories. They agreed
that removing the potential threat before it could be realized called for a
surprise attack.

Part of the plan for conquering the Soviet Union involved a
"scorched earth" policy that would be disastrous for Russian homes, live-
stock and terrain. At war's end the Wehrmacht had burned more than
one million tons of grain and murdered one-half million livestock. The
price: 80,000 German lives.

Ester closed the book and leaned back. History contained
much irony. Would the well-oiled German machine have labored
so furiously had they guessed the war's eventual turn? Would
they have slaughtered with such righteous fervor had they known
their beloved Fatherland would be reviled in the eyes of the civi-
lized world? What if, in the midst of pointing a rifle at the neck of
a mother hugging her child to her breast, the executioner received
a vision of future news reports: his beloved *Fuhrer*, when he was
sure Germany was defeated, ordered the *Luftwaffe* to bomb Berlin
and then blew his own brains out...

War, Ester reasoned, is caused by men who are spiritually

bankrupt. They lust for territory without regard for the people who inhabit it. How shortsighted are the philosophies of men! How blind their dreams of power!

---

[84] NKVD — People's Commisariat for Interior Affairs was the name for the USSR agency that handled a number of state-related affairs in the in a certain time period. It is mostly known for its state security and police functions,

And it shall come to pass in that day, saith the Lord God, that I will cause the sun to go down at noon, and I will darken the earth in the clear day.

— Amos 8:9

17 — The Wolf Shall Vex the Lamb

SS-Oberschutze (Private First Class) Gerhardt the Silent, his fellows called him. Gerhardt the Thoughtful, the Ponderer. He had just turned twenty. They laughed at him for his dour sobriety, his lack of amusement at their wicked jokes about Jews, Slavs, cripples and fools. They knew enough to stop their jibes when his face flushed or when he stared at them for long moments. And then, seeing his seriousness and sensing his hurt — though they did not understand — they would begin to apologize, clumsily, in the way men sometimes divulge their feelings. Gerhardt finally would shrug and manage a one-sided grin; everyone would visibly relax. In some way he was a barometer of their group conscience. But he knew not the extent of their potential for brutality. They knew not the limit of his benign tolerance.

On the first day Gerhardt entered the war, he had no feelings except exhilaration at being free of his camp and the seemingly constant anti-Semitic haranguing. Hitler and his henchmen had as their standard the goal of uniting all those in Europe who were ethnically German into a *Grossdeutschland*. To achieve this goal those who did not belong to Germany's legacy had to be removed. The German community was to be protected at all costs from the Asiatic-Jewish influences out to destroy the *Reich*. The young men in Gerhardt's unit were convinced this scenario was inevitable. They gloried in the romantic belief that they, shining examples of Aryan strength and promise, would soon be tested in battle. They would wage a memorable war, suffer privations and overcome them, find hope in their fellowship and patriotism and finally win for their *Fuhrer* the long hungered-after fruit of German *lebensraum*.

Gerhardt hoped for many of these things for his Germany, but he did not see the murdering of Jews as necessary. If we are soldiers fighting for our country, he reasoned, then I must do my duty as they do theirs. We each must be true to our beliefs. But if we are taken prisoner, we will have to suffer some privation, for this is a war, and after war comes the peace. He imagined his army would take many thousands of Russians as prisoners of war.

Perhaps they would kill some Jews in the process (if they were armed), but he hoped fervently that it would amount to little (and he would have no part in it) and that it would be done quickly and forgotten. How else could it turn out?

Of course, Gerhardt was deluded. He had no knowledge of the German army's orders. Troops were always the last ones to know their fates, they were cannon fodder. The boys of the Hitler Youth heard only the swift, helter-skelter rumors of fighting and longed to participate, to use their rifles, to know the lovely hell of war. Would they remain unaffected when they shot bullets into bodies of the living?

Too, thanks to their indoctrination the German army expected (and for a time received) little resistance to their march into Ukraine and onto Russia's terrain. It was reported to all *Wehrmacht* personnel that except for occasional Partisan ambushes, German troops were unopposed the first two weeks following their invasion. Gerhardt and his fellows nicknamed it "the peaceful war" and moaned that they would not be fortunate enough to do any fighting. No one anticipated the Russian attacks that finally materialized. The reality of the slaughter of the innocent went for the most part uncontemplated and unnoticed.

But Gerhardt did not have time to dream. He was given orders to spearhead the move of materiel and trucks from the Polish border to the Berdichev-Zhitomir highway. These details absorbed his time and he was not able to study developments on the battlefield ahead. His commandant was pleased with the health and energy of his men. He predicted an early, easy win. To the Hitler Youth boys this was to be a war that would fill history books — men on the field of battle.

The German troops were superbly conditioned fighting men. In the Polish campaign their predecessors had walked over 40 miles per day. Now, every man also carried a Mauser rifle weighing 11 pounds. Every troop packed hand grenades, a mess kit, gas mask and shovel. Their method was to *blitzkrieg*, to strike swiftly and without warning, take few prisoners, then move on to the next target. These brief but intense wars were quite successful. Their technical and organizational superiority made it possible to move quickly and respond efficiently to changes in battlefield circumstances.

This highly dynamic *blitzkrieg* lasted four years but cost the lives of well over one million German soldiers, not to mention the many more millions of their victims.

The troops were not without complaints. Gerhardt and Klaus Hauptmann marched across vast stretches of ground in their trek across the Russian border. Gerhardt wrote to his mother:

We are always trudging along on our tired legs. Our equipment is very heavy, it almost conquers us, but we are made stronger by each step that brings us closer to our targets… but the cost! This agonizing heat brings sweat and a lust for more and more water. Oh, mother, the despair of fighting these fields of dust clings to us. We sing to relieve the thoughts of our endless steps… why are men sent to die in these fragrant summer fields while our leaders sit in their cool offices and plan wars to keep themselves in power?

But Gerhardt did not falter. His training had well prepared him for any eventuality, though he and the other troops were usually unsure of their mission until the final moment. A favorite conversation among his fellows was the taking of Poland in only twenty-seven days, an astonishing record.

"We will take the whole of Russia in two months," boasted Klaus on one occasion. "These Russky peasants will fall before us like wheat before the sickle."

"They will surrender as they see us coming," Gerhardt replied, visualizing himself as a *Rotten Fuhrer* (corporal). Steel helmet beneath his arm, his *Waffen-SS* tunic spotless, he and his battalion would lead a hundred thousand prisoners to Moscow. He would bang on the palace doors, demanding entrance. Stalin himself would open them. He would scream in horror at the sight before him. Gerhardt the Victorious would announce the end of this doomed war. Stalin would be humiliated before his generals, before the Russian people, even before G-d Almighty. Stalin, that beast of a thousand heads would sink to his knees in defeat. That night he would be hung in Red Square. Russia and Ukraine would annex to Germany. Fatherland and Motherland would be united finally in *lebensraum* without bloodshed, and Gerhardt, child of war, his work accomplished, his family together again would reclaim his father's *Torah* from the worms and return to his synagogue to pray in peace. Let the truth be restored.

He shared this dream with no one but it was in his heart and he returned to it often as the march of time led him toward his destiny.

～

As the days and nights wore on, the army's footsteps

spanned many miles but nights were warm, the Steppes were vast and the mood of the soldiers anticipatory. A contingent had been sent into Lvov. Gerhardt's group of one hundred troops from the 11th Panzer Division were being spearheaded to Berdichev to commandeer it, secure the rail lines and begin the monitoring of all foot and motor traffic heading in and out of the city. The haze was high across Ukrainian skies that 9 July, two days following the arrival of the exploratory unit that had converged on the dye vats. Gerhardt's unit was to reconnoiter with them and establish a base of operations until transportation arrangements could be secured for the Occupation troops moving eastward to Moscow from Berdichev. The roads were massed with Panzer tanks, motorcycles with their sidecars and at least fifty horseback units flanked by trucks carrying more troops.

They approached the defenseless town from the northwestern edge of Berdichev across the northernmost bridge over the flowing Gnilopyatka. Lenin Street led them past the hospital, just south of the Berdichev Jewish Cemetery. At that point the *Wehrmacht* infantry rode along the eastern edge of town past the airstrip and train station just off Karl Leibnecht Street. Their captain, *SS-Hauptsturm Fuhrer* was Heydrich, a distant relative of Gottlob Berger, Chief of Recruitments in Berlin. Heydrich had taken part in the occupation of Austria and Czechoslovakia several years before, earning high marks in combat. This was his first "civilian" assignment.

The three small children of Elya Romberg peeked through the curtained window of their small cottage at the northern edge of town. They saw an amazing sight. A parade of dusty but well-dressed men were coming down their street. They rode horseback and motorcycles. They laughed and joked. The children were astonished.

"Mama, Mama", cried 7 year-old Sofya. "Come, look at the horses!"

Mama Romberg, her hands full of doughy flour from kneading this night's bread, ran to their small cottage window. She saw rifles, black boots, SS epaulets, metal helmets of war, and gasped.

"G-d in Heaven, Sofya, Elena, Ya'akov! Get away from the window. Quickly, we must call father. They're here. The Germans are here in Berdichev! Quick, run and get the bread and salt!"

Across the way on Pushkin Street, Fanya Moishievna Blumstein was combing her long black locks before the house's only long mirror. She admired her image, remembering that she wanted to wear her mother's wide earrings because Herschel her sweetheart was coming to visit. She heard the whinny of horses outside her bedroom. A look of puzzlement crossed her face. She ran to her window. Before her eyes were numerous men in handsome, decorated uniforms on horseback leading a cotillion of troops and tanks down her avenue. Most of them were young, blond and fresh. They were smiling and laughing between themselves, shouting hello to every curious face that popped out from behind frilly curtained windows.

Fanya opened her window and waved to the troops. They saw her and promptly whistled. In German they praised her dark beauty. Gerhardt saw her and thought he would like to know her, to stroke her lovely black hair and feast on her radiant smile. *Hauptsturm Fuhrer* Heydrich, the world at his feet, smiled curtly. He made his steed do a little sidestepping on the cobbled thoroughfare. His men laughed and cheered him.

"Death to the Jews," he swore beneath his smile as he waved to a group of people outside a family meetinghouse bearing a Star of David in the window. Mentally, he noted the location for future reference. The men rode confidently onward, letting the townspeople get a good look at them. More people came out of their small homes and offices to stare and wave at the advancing Germans.

"Have you come to save us from the Russian army?" one shouted. "Where are the Russians?" another asked. "Hooray, our saviors are here, we bring you the bread and salt of Mother Russia," said an old woman crossing the street with packages beneath her skinny arms.

Another asked in confusion: "Are we at war in Ukraine?"

To these remarks and questions the men answered nothing, but laughed and smiled widely while riding in regal style upon their steeds. They continued in an easterly direction through town toward Karl Leibnecht Street, where the old movie house stood. Many Berdichevers assembled to wave them on and throw small flowers upon their tanks and horses. It was like a parade. The Germans smiled, fully participating in the welcome. *Hauptsturm Fuhrer* Heydrich, his charm a smooth veneer was ever courtly, bowing on his steed, extending an arm behind him to introduce his armory. This morning he had dressed in his regiment's formal attire for this occasion. Belt and dagger were clearly in evidence on his "walking-out" semi-formal uniform. His straight shoulders urged the epaulets on his gray cotton tunic into perfect horizontal bars. His helmet bore the S-rune decal of the *SS*, monogrammed in a thunderbolt style. The German *Mauser* handgun at his side was cold and silent for now, but fully loaded. He was the picture of a confident conqueror who knew his enemy had already been vanquished.

"Are you our heroes?" a voice shouted from a doorstop. "What are you doing in Berdichev?"

"We are here to save you from your Russian enemies," *Hauptsturm Fuhrer* Heydrich proclaimed with confident aplomb, smiling at what lay ahead for their inquiring looks. The men behind him chortled. Crowds came to their front porches and shop sidewalks to cheer them on. Girls dressed in Ukrainian dance costumes fresh from a performance in the nearby park ran over and presented them with woven wreaths and bright smiles. Hauptsturm *Fuhrer* Heydrich beamed. "Thank you," he said. "You are too kind." Heydrich assumed the Russians had not yet massed for attack nor would they know for several days that German troops had arrived in Berdichev. Then the fun would really begin.

Upon coming to Karl Leibnecht Street he halted his men in front of the Sherentsis Theater marquee. Its scarred white board bore the legend "Wednesday Matinee Cancelled" in Cyrillic letters. The theater was an imposing stucco structure built around the turn of the 20th century. Its entrance beheld a wide portico. The theater, still in use in 1941, showed weekly movies from Ukrainian and Russian archives of history. Its outer walls were painted a light blue, making the building easily visible from the streets around it, but its walls were thick to offer protection against the freezing Ukrainian weather. A dank loft above the auditorium was used for storage and posters of movie stars. It would make an excellent machine gun post.

The captain gave instructions. He and his lieutenant circled the area slowly to determine their best defense possibilities, the extent of their safety and vulnerability. Troops were quickly posted around the perimeters. Soldiers commandeered the building and its grounds for temporary offices and garaging. Existing phone lines were checked. Within two hours the familiar family theater became a working *Nazi* installation. From this vantage point the business of cleaning the town of "undesirables" could be efficiently waged. The already resident one hundred troops had taken over the rail station. More Division troops were leaving Lvov for Berdichev on the morrow. Their orders were to erect military checkpoints at every major city entrance and exit. Heydrich laughed at the ease of his assignment. In a few more hours Berdichev would find itself inescapably surrounded by *Wehrmacht* troops. All that remained to be done was the "cleansing".

*The Lord shall bring a nation against thee from far, from the end of the
earth, as swift as the eagle flieth; a nation whose tongue thou shalt not
understand; A nation of fierce countenance, which shall not regard the
person of the old, nor shew favour to the young.*

— Deuteronomy 28:49-50

18 — Bouquets of Good and Evil

Ester had spent hours in the cemetery but still had not found
the key monument that would disclose the place to dig. Barak's
instructions were to investigate the northwest portion first, but the
exact area was uncertain because Reb Levi's original note contained only the destination of the buried items. This made the task
very difficult in addition to the thousands of tombstones that were
jammed together. Many hundreds could not be read at all. It was
as if the earth had gone crazy and pushed up a million jagged,
odd-shaped granite teeth!

As she examined the headstones for clues, the names of two
more old friends were revealed:

Benderskaya, Zenya — Vasily

The marker bore the date of 1942. Seeing this, Ester moaned.
She figured they were probably murdered helping someone else
to escape. Both people were in the prime of their lives with a
growing family.

"You were also my saviors," Ester said gently. She recalled
Zenya's love for flowers and decided to return the next day with
a spray of them to lay before this unkempt grave. That first day of
the German invasion was again before her eyes . . .

Zenya Ilyaevna Benderskaya was a simple Ukrainian woman
who had resided on a large lot along the entrance to the Vinnit-
sia highway. Zenya was known for her front yard flower garden
which she fiercely protected from man and beast. In addition to
the several varieties of roses and lumen sold in Berdichev, Zenya
grew all manner of colorful plants. A carefully laid row of odd-
sized rocks and stones were piled high to protect her enterprise.
Every evening as Zenya's family of six ate supper at their wooden
table, she would make an entrance with a loud "Ahh!" and de-
posit a vase full of fragrant wonders before them. Due to the long
growing season in the Steppes region, not many weeks passed
without a bouquet at the supper table and in the rooms of the

children, who were forbidden to touch them. Zenya' family knew by sad experience that their mother's filled flower vases were off limits. The few neighbors who visited also knew to throw only admiring glances, all the while sitting on their hands. They became familiar with Zenya's baleful reprimands to a stray hand or a curious poking nose.

And so Zenya was horrified the evening of July 7th when masses of people congregated on the street just outside her home and garden, tripping over her rocks and trampling on her azaleas in their eagerness to leave town. She ran from her house waving her apron above her head, screaming epithets in Russian.

"Get out. What are you doing here? These are my babies, my lovelies! Get away or I'll throw these rocks!"

Unfortunately, Zenya's wild shouts came at the same time as rifle shots were heard in town. This is what really began the stampede of the Jewish citizens of Berdichev out of the area. In the confusion Zenya sought refuge behind her door. In the wild push of bodies, many were thrown down and trampled. Everyone was shouting. Anna, fearing to leave her husband, called out to him but she was shoved hard onto the pavement, nearly fainting. Blood gushed from a head wound.

"Ester, Ester," she screamed. There was no answer. With great effort, Anna broke loose of the crowd. She ran down the street in the opposite direction shouting for her family. Her blue-green *babushka* was soon colored in her blood. Roving German soldiers found and arrested her. They captured others running to freedom and herded them at rifle point toward the synagogue on Sverdlova Street.

~

Ester regained her consciousness amidst a bevy of flowers in vases. The room around her was dark and quite small. Cobwebs were formed on the bedposts. She looked up from the pile of bed sheets beneath her and beheld vases of ferns. They smelled like cinnamon and mint. She was disoriented. This was not home. Trying to sit upright she moaned in pain and fell back. She felt as though all her bones were broken. The room was windowless, the place quiet. Where was she?

A heavy-set woman entered. She wore a no-nonsense expression. Around her head was the traditional Russian *babushka*. Under one arm she carried a small child, whom she deftly deposited in a crib. Turning to Ester she spoke in a quick stream of Ukrainian.

"Ah, you are awake. Good. You were almost crushed in the street. Those screaming people — terrible! I picked you up from the flower beds. You were lying on new bulbs. What were you doing out there?"

Ester's mind was clouded with pain. She tried again to sit up and moaned.

"With my mother. We were leaving for… Where am I?" How long have I been here?

"Your mother? Who is your mother? I am Zenya Vasilevna Benderskaya. Where is your home?"

"Mira Street. I am Ester Levi. My mother is Anna Rubinshtein. My father is Reb Dovid Moshe ben-Levi, the *Chasidic* undertaker of Berdichev. Are they here? "

Zenya inhaled quickly. She put a hand across her lips. Her demeanor instantly softened.

"Ahh, ahah! You're the daughter of reb, reb . . . Reb Levi? I have heard of him, he is a saint in Berdichev, a saint. Well, then, you must rest, dear. Your parents are not here. My husband says Germans are here already! All over town! We will hide you. You will have supper with our family — we will be seeing to your welfare."

Zenya came around and busily plumped Ester's bed sheets. She poured a cup of water from a spare vase for her and smiled broadly.

"Rest now, Ester. We will talk later. I go now to gather my children." She patted the bedclothes and hurried out.

"But I must find my parents. And Barak. I cannot stay," Ester called after the departing woman.

She rose unsteadily to her feet and fell back again at the sudden sharp pains in her legs. Escape would have to wait.

Two days and nights later, Zenya's husband Vasily accompanied a limping Ester to her house at nightfall by way of a secret route. Vasily was a clever tradesman and agent who did business with many Jews of Berdichev. He had access to people in diverse walks of life. When Zenya told him of Ester's plight, he immediately sought help from a contact in the Ukrainian lower bureaucracy who hated both the Russians and the Germans. This man, Nicolas Mayakovsky, put Vasily in touch with a Partisan group whose leader knew of Barak and quickly offered to care for Ester's safety home and wherever else she determined to go.

This done, and knowing they would be protected by the

Partisans, the pair made their way to Ester's family apartment on Mira Street. They found the entrance ajar. The whole place had been scrupulously ransacked. Contents of drawers, food supplies and warm clothing were missing or strewn across the floors and into the hallway. Adjoining apartments, many now empty of tenants, had also been vandalized. Important papers, Ester's private mementos, even hers and Barak's socks and boots were missing. But her only picture of Avram had been overlooked by the raiders. She pressed it to her heart. Tears filled her eyes.

"It might have been anyone, Ester," Vasily told her sadly as they began to repair the mess around them. "If not the Germans, then ruffians from the street hoping to sell your things to barter for food or perhaps guns. Let us salvage what we can."

Ester sank down on her parents' bed and wept.

"No, Vasily. Our home has been ravaged. I cannot stay here. Where is Barak now? With my mother? Are they safe? What of my father, he would not leave Berdichev. Where is he? I must find him. I am so afraid for him."

By this time, dawn was only a few hours away. They decided to go to Reb Levi's mortuary. They found it closed, the wide, heavy doors double locked. Zych's small cabin was empty. Most of Reb Levi's *Chasidic* congregation had been in the crowd escaping south. Ester was at a loss where else to look.

"I can do no more here, Vasily. I must now try to find Avram," Ester determined. "I will leave for Zhitomir tonight."

"Ester, the Germans are on the lookout for Jews. It is very dangerous for you now, especially on the roads. Stay here tonight. We will continue to look for your family. Please, don't be foolish."

But no amount of advice swayed her. Finally, Vasily gave up and led her to the Mayakovsky cottage. His wife Fedya greeted them. She obligingly offered bread with salt and soup. As the morning light shone upon the fields and forests of the Steppes, Ester and Ilya, her new Partisan guide began their swift journey northward to Zhitomir.

～

The fields of wheat in Central Ukraine wave at the sky for miles and one can walk them all the way into central Asia. It is a vast sea of grassland punctuated by long dark stretches of deep alder forestland. Geographers of this area call it a "wooded steppe". The Steppes are broken here and there by many small rivers that have avoided flooding the plains by diverting through canyons and river basins. These mighty rivers flow throughout, making central Ukraine a region of intense fertility. During summer, sunflowers and wildflowers also fragrance the breezes. This refreshing bouquet encouraged Ester's hopefulness as she and Ilya began their trek north along the Gnilopyatka. They saw neither German nor Russian soldiers but used great caution nonetheless.

At a junction just five miles north of the Berdichev rail line they suddenly noticed exhaust smoke to the west.

"It's the Germans," Ilya said. "They are probably coming through the highway from Chudnov. We'll have to detour east through the open fields. Perhaps we can find cover with Partisans at Nikonovka."

They left the cover of the riverbank and cut east through the fields of tall wheat, alternately crouching and running, then lying flat and crawling. Ester's knees were soon bruised, but there was not time for complaint. Where were her parents, her brother? What had happened to Avram? She fought her anxiety, trying to assure herself that all would be explained eventually, that she would find everyone well and safe.

When she mentioned this to Ilya, he replied with a smile that all would be well.

"After all, the 'world famous' Red Army is probably still to the east! We are not yet even in their sights!"

Nightfall came. Ilya ran ahead, his gun cocked and ever ready. The steady rhythm of his boots upon the dry ground was soothing. They were in sight of Nikonovka. They stopped to rest and refresh. Ester lay in the grass while Ilya kept watch. She fell asleep.

It seemed only a moment before rough hands shoved her awake. She was pulled rudely upright. Night sky masked her assailant.

"Stand up, *raus!*" came a hoarse voice. She saw a gray helmet above angry blue eyes and a wicked scowl.

"What doing here?" the soldier demanded in Russian. He smelled of sweat. Ester could not answer. He shook her hard and asked again. She felt herself fainting. He hit her across the mouth. She tasted blood in her teeth and choked. The soldier threw her to the ground. He shouted orders to a man behind her. This second man laughed and kicked her.

"*Judien?*" he asked. "*Judien?*"

Ester did not respond, though she knew he was asking her if

she was Jewish. Would they kill her? Where was Ilya? Again, she was pulled to her feet and shoved in the direction of Berdichev. A rifle barrel slammed into her spine, thrusting her forward onto the ground. Shooting pains went through her entire body. Then the blackness of relief overcame her.

"There is no Ukraine. We must remember we are the master race."
— Erich Koch, Nazi Reichskommisar, Ukraine

19 — Beseiged

Ester awoke in darkness hours later on a cold, damp floor. She started to rise but searing pain ripped through her jaw and back. She screamed for help but then stopped, fearing further beatings. No one seemed to hear her yell. From nowhere then it came; she remembered her father's admonition whenever she was in trouble: Pray. Ask *HaShem* for protection.

She began: "*HaShem*, I praise thee, O my King. Help me now, I beg Thee, in my hour of need..."

She must have passed out again. Hours later she was shaken awake. Daylight shone through a partly opened door. A tall figure walked toward her slowly. He wore a German uniform. Ester looked up into the handsome face of a young soldier, staring intently back at her. Concern filled his blue eyes. He bent over her body, putting a proprietary hand on her brow. Noticing its heat, he clucked and withdrew his hand.

"You have somewhat of a fever, *fraulein*. I will bring you a blanket."

His voice was kind. Ester recognized a few German words that are in common with Yiddish. He rose and left the room, returning in a while with a large shawl, which he placed over her and continued speaking in his native tongue as though he assumed she understood him.

"If you are hungry, I will bring you food... you are a prisoner of war here. I have been put in charge of our prisoners for the day."

His voice was impersonal, though kind. Ester did not understand him but she sensed they were alone in that room and that he was not going to hurt her.

"*Essen*," she whispered, knowing it was also a German word. She wondered if he spoke or understood Russian. Her body was filled with pain. She found herself able to turn on one side and to lift her head. Her back ached and her mouth was caked with her blood.

"Oh, don't move. I see you are truly hurt. Can you try to sit up now?" he asked, taking light hold of her shoulders. Ester screamed against the pressure, falling back against the concrete floor. The soldier winced.

"Uh, oh. Sorry. You wait."

He stood and walked quickly out the door, shutting her in the dark once again. Within a few minutes the door burst open. Other voices were suddenly all around, sounds of screaming and women crying. A harsh, commanding voice demanded them in German to stop.

"*Judien!* We will murder you tomorrow. Don't scream and make us shoot you sooner! We have our orders!"

The man who had spoken appeared very tall and threatening. His hands waved at them. They were like fat hams. He stood huge in the doorway. What resembled a ball bat waved in his right hand. Ester moaned in fear, knowing he could kill her with that bat. He did not look in her direction but at two women who lay at her left, those whose voices she'd heard. They were frail and appeared to be quite old. Blood spotted their clothes and they were crying. Ester wanted to go to them but she dared not make an attempt while the soldier remained in the room. Instead she tried to push herself deeper into the shadows, trying to see through the gloom. Beside her was a mattress. She was in a bedroom; probably in a home the Germans had overtaken on their march through town. She saw curtains on the darkened window. Small framed pictures were on a nearby dresser.

The German officer turned to look at Ester's prone body lying before him. He smiled at what he saw.

"*Sie! Sie sind blond. Jung. Sind Sie Judien? Nein? Was ist Ihr Name?*"[85] he demanded, pushing at her with the toe of his boot. He still held the bat.

Ester struggled not to faint with fear. She had to answer him. In Russian she whispered:

"*Ya tolka bednii Russkii krestyaniin.*[86] Please, I need help."

"*Russkii?* Where are your parents? Are they in government here? Never mind, we have already identified and shot most of them. We will still put you in the group that we will shoot at dawn. You will first be registered. "

He turned and briskly left the room, shouting what seemed to be orders at someone outside. Ester had not understood him. One of the women began to cry afresh. After a while the younger soldier reentered. The room seemed to brighten with his presence. He had brought several blankets. He moved quickly to the two women and carefully covered them with the blankets. They

216

groaned in pain.

"Rest," he offered in German. "Tomorrow it will be better for you."

He rose then and moved over to Ester. From his pocket he took a flask of water. Removing the cap, he motioned her to lift her head and put the flask to her lips. The delicious taste of cool water flowed down her throat. She cried with relief and drank all she could.

"You were thirsty, *fraulein*. If you can eat, I have brought something to give you."

From another pocket he took something bulky. It smelled delicious and Ester determined it was part of a loaf of hard bread. She took it gingerly from him, pressing it to her lips. The smell of rye and yeast awakened her senses. She tried to bite into it but the pain in her jaw stopped her.

"Oh, you cannot eat it just now. Here, keep it with you. I will see if there is more for the others."

He stood to leave her. Ester tried to find her voice.

"Please, who are you? Are those women hurt? Thank you for helping us."

The soldier shrugged. His face showed he did not understand her.

Did she dare speak to him in Yiddish and give herself away? Would it matter now?

A soft, unsteady voice spoke up, one of the other two prisoners. In a halting, broken German she translated. The young soldier smiled in acknowledgement.

"Oh, yes I help you now. I am *Oberschutze* Gerhardt von Metternich. Many others will be added to your group tomorrow. I am sorry but you are our prisoners for this war."

While his words were being translated into Russian, Ester thought he seemed unsure of himself around them, as if he was waiting for someone else to relieve him of this unmanly duty of looking after women. He looked about her age. Perhaps he was not a German butcher of Jews.

"*Ester. Ich bin Ester.*" Then in Russian she thanked the old woman for her skill with German. The woman said "*dahnke*" (thanks) and continued on with her translation.

The soldier studied her.

"Ester, what were you doing yesterday in the fields? My captain said you were captured with a Partisan soldier. He has been silenced. You are also a Partisan, yes?"

Ester caught her breath as the old woman's words unveiled this new information. Ilya! They murdered her gentle guide! Again she felt fear clutch her throat. This kind-natured German soldier would probably be the one to take her and everyone else they captured into the wheat fields and shoot them!

"*Nyet. Ya ne Partizan, tolka Ruskii devushka.*"[87]

"Not a *Judien*, not a Partisan. Well, well. What were you doing then in the fields? Running away from the Germans?" He laughed. "We are here for awhile, Ester. Even the Red Army doesn't seem interested in making us leave."

"The Russian army is no more welcome here than you Germans," Ester said beneath her breath, echoing the words her brother Barak had told her so long ago. She bit her lip, hoping they would not be translated.

But the old woman did not speak more. There was silence in the room while Gerhardt looked at the attractive girl before him. He recalled a picture on his dresser at the camps. One like this; young, blond and small but of strong build. That memory had been temporarily forgotten with the preoccupations of war. But it came again to his mind with new force as he stared at Ester. His mother's photo, taken in youth. He suddenly felt inclined to tell her, but then thought better.

"I will go now. You are being watched, so don't attempt to leave this room."

Ester heard him depart. She knew the next day might well mean death for her, but somehow she was not afraid. Russian troops were already in the city; perhaps they would murder her murderers! Had her parents died at the hands of this soldier, not knowing the fate of their children? Did they run for their lives? And Barak? Was he alive? What then of her beloved Avram? Would they ever find each other?

~

SS-Hauptsturm Fuhrer Heydrich preened himself in his full-length mirror, a found prop from the Cinema's backstage collection. He adjusted his spotless officer's uniform and stiffened his lower back to see how authoritarian he looked. The *Fuhrer's* demands were on his mind this morning. "Eliminate European Jewry!" The phrase rang joyfully in Heydrich's ears; he was the perfect henchman. During his earlier campaigns those in his command secretly referred to him as the "mechanic" because of his

218

attention to details of planning and execution. His disregard for humanity was already a legend in the SS. He took an eerie delight in carefully orchestrating each and every maneuver of troop deployment and execution techniques, but his expertise had earned him high marks from his superiors. Information from the Commandant indicated a Russian attack was imminent. More *Wehrmacht* infantry units were on the way. This time, though currently short of desired manpower he decided to become creative in his use of available troops. Russian invasion or not, Heydrich firmly believed German forces would prove to be superior.

Gerhardt, on the other hand, was in shock; his loyalties were fast changing. Already, their first few days in this town had brought several hundred deaths, many of which he had seen but managed to avoid. It had made him sick. He wanted to go back to Berlin and hide in his mother's house. He'd heard another unit of soldiers bragging about their "human hides" escapade a week earlier, and he knew Heydrich planned mass executions in the coming week. Gerhardt was deeply worried. He could not concentrate. While he studied routes for the transport of vehicles, his mind wandered to the scenes of death he had witnessed. When he slept he was witness again to murder. He saw himself running away from the screams of victims, afraid for them and for himself. He couldn't decide if he had been confused or just terribly stupid to think he could avoid the horrors of this war. He did not know what to do about it. At times he felt his body was tearing apart! When he looked at his weapon, it made him sick with fear to think he might have to participate in the extermination of his own people! How could he have been so stupid as to think the army would not want to kill all the Jews!

He prayed mightily for guidance, for courage to do what was right, as he had told his mother he would do. But all that came to him was a sweet calmness, a mild but insistent feeling like his mother's gentle kiss upon his cheek. He did not understand. Where were his instructions from G-d? Then he remembered that he had decided G-d was not concerned with the breakup of his family, or with this war. Why, then did he pray to a Deity Who did not care about his desperate dilemma? He *must* depend upon himself.

Gerhardt tried to find courage in this decision. He would make it all come out right somehow. His dream might have to wait, but he alone would work it out. And from this meager hope he took courage.

His nights had not been restful in the makeshift bunks within the dark bowels of the cinema-turned-war office. Thoughts of the young blond woman, the Russian speaking Ester — he could not erase them from his mind. She was not his first female prisoner but he felt very drawn to her. She was lovely, and he guessed she was near his age. He couldn't bear to think of her bleeding to death in a trench. But how could he save her? If he dared she would still hate him, maybe spit on him as others had done when he passed them in the makeshift prison. She would not see his loneliness and fear for her own and she could not know that he desired her.

By July 9th Heydrich had assembled some of the men to dig the pits up on Brodskii Street, just south of the railroad tracks. Maps and layout showing depth and breadth of the area involved were provided. The railway embankment would be the "bullet catcher", just ahead of the prisoner kneeling at the brink of his yawning death trap. The ditches were modeled on the execution map used in Zhitomir. They were dug by Ukrainian and Jewish prisoners.

"The pits have been marked off for digging. We will commence shooting when the pits are ready," Heydrich told his men. "We have new orders. We must see that these tasks are carried out immediately. All men who are not immediately needed for transport or communications will be part of this work force. You and the others will round up the prisoners and see that they do not cease their digging. If they run, they are to be shot immediately. The pits are to be ready in two days. If the Russians invade, we will invite them to lie with the Jews in our trenches!"

Gerhardt was now face to face with this most reprehensible aspect of warfare. His chest tightened and he felt weak. This was unexpected. He hadn't really been tested as a soldier. His specialty was mobile transport, auto and heavy equipment repair, not murder.

Too, these new orders were a deviation from normal procedure. It was true that his work, for the moment, was completed. It was true also that there were limited troops available to man the mile-long ditch that was Brodskii Street. A Red Army contingent had just been spotted, so there was need for more soldiers at the town's perimeters. Evidently Heydrich was testing these non-infantry troops, finding out what they were made of while taking advantage of the available manpower.

Gerhardt's new orders were to transport the few prisoners to the northern checkpoint site so their names could be taken. Others who had been rounded up the day prior were being held in a quickly constructed holding cell near the town's original marketplace. They would join the registration party. The *Aktion* that would follow was to be privately held; no filming or written record of the events would be tolerated. At the end of the day, all prisoners were to become permanent residents of the pits in which they had so diligently labored.

As he dressed, Gerhardt trembled. He could not calm himself. He was not a killer. True, he had not been asked to shoot anyone, only to supervise the digging of ditches. No reason to be afraid or struck by conscience! He would not be told to kill, that was certain, even if they made him drink *schnapps* (liquor).

Drugs and *schnapps*. That was what the soldiers were given to help them murder. Gerhardt did not know what drugs were used but they made the men fearless. Then they would be driven to the countryside to round up Jews and other undesirables. Gerhardt saw how the powdery substance brought madness into the eyes of his mates. The concoction gave the German soldiers courage to rape, beat and even murder their victims. In the few short weeks he'd been a part of this war, Gerhardt had seen babies tossed into the air and shot. He was witness to body searches that were really rapes. He'd seen more animal-like behavior among his fellows than he imagined possible and he was sickened by it. Under the evil influence of these drugs the men experienced an odd elation: They seemed to truly enjoy the carnage they produced. Gerhardt was grateful he was never called to participate in this debauchery.

But was he not an indirect contributor to the murder of his own people? The Jewish prisoners were unarmed, they did not resist their captors. To the contrary, he had observed their downcast faces submitting quietly to the bestial punishments of their torturers. Why did they did not fight back? Their regal stoicism stung his heart and deeply troubled his soul. He could not sleep; he increasingly found himself unable to look his fellow officers in the eyes or to behold his own image without distaste and guilt. His mother's letters, full of love and fear for her only child did not belie the foresight she must have possessed when she cautioned him so many months past: he might be *forced* to kill Jews as a part of his life as a soldier.

Outside, captain Heydrich spoke harshly to an associate. Gerhardt flinched. He looked again at the rectangular mirrored image before him and set his jaw. He reprimanded himself. Steady! This is war, *Oberschutze* von Metternich. Prisoners are taken, prisoners are shot. The common spoils. A soldier endures, he hardens himself and does his job as directed. Paramount in his mind and heart is the command of the Fatherland and the father of the German people! I am a man of honest devotion to my country, my fellows and my destiny!

Suddenly he remembered Ester and the two women prisoners. He sighed. They must be weak from lack of food and drink. He would feed them before "escorting" them to Brodskii Street. But on the way to their "cell" he suddenly felt to make a run for it. He had the keys to several trucks in his pocket, he could be out range in a few minutes . . . he would say he was chasing a runaway! Yes, he knew he could get away with it. He would drive to Zhitomir, up to Kiev or west to Chudnov; it would be easy to get there. His mind raced ahead. Abandon the truck, change clothes . . . but then what? German troops were all over the western Ukraine, and soon the Russians would become their hunters . . . he would be found out, shot as a traitor. No, there was really no place to hide.

And what about Ester? If he left her to her fate, how could he live with himself?

He found the women together holding hands in their misery. Their cries had stopped, their bloodied hair, hands and faces had dried but they were in obvious discomfort. He warned them, then allowed them to seek relief outside the room at gunpoint while he turned away.

Ester was in obvious pain from her wounds but she held herself well and did not complain. Her face, when he searched it, held defiance; the kind he had felt in himself when his roommate teased him or spoke angrily of the "Jewish problem."

"Will you feed us?" asked the woman who spoke German. "We are so hungry."

She put her bony hands together in the form of a prayer and touched her lips with them. Her eyes were misted over with cataracts, her sagging sallow skin was more than he could look at. The second woman seemed to second the request in Russian. Ester was quiet but her stomach's rumbling gave her away. She flushed, turning her back on her captor.

"How do you know German, woman?" Gerhardt inquired. She did not answer immediately. Then she shrugged. "My Poppa, he was in Germany before the war began. Selling machinery. Spoke Yiddish and German at home."

"Your father was a Jew? And your mother?"

The old woman slowly rose up on an arm and steadied herself. In a voice low and filled with pain and not a little pride, she carefully replied,

"My Mama-le was killed by your SS men. And I? I am one of G-d's children, as you are. I am a person and also a Jew. Understand that though you murder my body today, my spirit you will never kill."

So saying, she spat at his feet and looked into his astonished face. Gerhardt was stunned at her words. He looked at the saliva on his black boot. He took a step toward the woman, then turned uncertainly around and walked clumsily from the room, leaving the food and water at the door. Ester immediately moved toward it and the three women partook in a moment of silent joy.

Two hours later Gerhardt returned. With as few words as possible he commanded the women to follow him. He helped them into the rear of his jeep and told them to hide behind the equipment it carried. He drove them hurriedly north into the woods beyond Brodskii Street.

When he had reached the forest's edge he parked out of sight. Calling the women from the vehicle, he gave them each a small bag of bread and fruit and told them to keep walking. Without a word he jumped back into his truck and headed back to Brodskii Street. He did not look back but in his heart he suddenly felt a strong urge to drive all the way to Berlin where he could feel again the longed for safety of his mother's comforting arms.

～

The old women chose to go south toward the farms, casting their fate among Berdichev's older migrant Jews. This set Ester free to continue her journey to Zhitomir. But though her will was strong, energy was lacking. She realized that walking to freedom would take her a very long time, so she chose to crawl and walk for short periods, then rest a third period. She would eat bark and roots as necessary. The forest cover was thick with pine, beech, oak and ash trees. From these she obtained an essential sustenance. She continued in this way for two long days but her progress was small and her young body betrayed her more at every step. Increasingly, Ester found sleep more appealing and she dreamed each time that she had almost reached her goal of finding Avram. His welcoming embrace quieted her fears and filled her with the certainty of a sure and comforting love. Often Ester prayed for help and protection. At these times she felt her father's presence with her, quelling her fears and strengthening her mind. She felt G-d was also with her, guiding her steps with His sure Hand.

It was almost without effort that another German patrol happened by and arrested her while she walked in the wheat. She was nearly faint with exhaustion and exposure and was unable to run or resist. The convoy was on its way to Berdichev. The Germans were laughing and drinking in the front of the truck and Ester was grateful they didn't bother with her until they'd reached the railroad checkpoint. Her efforts to escape the area had been useless; her captor's allowance of freedom was now remanded. She was once again in the way of certain death.

The soldiers handled Ester roughly when they reached Berdichev's Brodskii Street. They made her sit on the ground at the edge of the pits while they ordered a large group of male prisoners to dig trenches. She could observe each man from her vantage point. The Germans had gathered them up during daily raids in the town's central district. All the men were ordered to doff their hats in the presence of German officers. They were then commanded to fall onto the pavement, put their hands behind them and wait to be bound. Those who did not comply this regulation were beaten, forced to crawl on the sidewalk on their stomachs, collect garbage with their hands and pick up manure from the pavement. If it was an old man, his beard was cut off. Then they were herded through the streets by soldiers on horseback or taken in trucks to the railway site where they were held in the station until the pits would be ready. The women and children were in a separate holding barn apart from the station house. Most of them were Jews.

Ester found that from her vantage point at the edge of the line of men, she could search the many gathered prisoners for her parents and brother, but she had no success. She noticed a number of people she knew in Berdichev. There was Samuil Oizerovich Zemermeil. He was without his wife — was she shot beforehand? Also Reb Genrikohovich, an old Jewish man given to mutterings in Hebrew beneath his breath. Her father's neighbor Leizer Zelmanovich, an old *Chasid*, was shoveling slowly. His tears watered the holes he dug. The younger Yaakov Borisovich attacked the ground with gusto, stepping on his shovel with passionate intensity. Ester guessed he was acting out imagined reprisals upon his captors. Duvid Shekhterman the Tailor was also there, and the town crier Moishe Yakovlevich Shtrikmakher, not yet forty, known for his avid defense of factory workers against their bosses. He had a sick wife and seven young children. Ester felt great sorrow for their plight, even more than for herself.

German soldiers kept watch over the prisoners, pointing the barrels of their rifles from one to another. At the far end of the trenches, Ester saw with a start that the young soldier Gerhardt was one of these. He was about 15 yards away. She felt her throat catch. How could she get his attention? Would he be able to save her (and the others) again? Finally, several of the soldiers left their posts to bring in new prisoners. Gerhardt moved to the front of the line of diggers. They were very near each other. In a moment their eyes met — Gerhardt's showing great surprise. He began to speak, then turned away. But he had seen her. There was still hope.

"*Fraulein, Judien?*" said a soft voice behind her.

Without thinking, Ester turned around to say yes. It was Heydrich. He had set her up; now he knew. Heydrich slapped his knee in triumph. He laughed harshly.

"I thought so. You are Jewish. *Wo sind Ihre Eltern, Judien?*"[88]

Ester said nothing. He was cunning; an animal seeking prey.

"I would speak if I were you, *fraulein*. Several days ago many of your kind burned to death in their precious synagogue. Your family may have been there."

Heydrich began to laugh again but Ester rose instantly, whirled around and grabbed blindly for his throat, screaming into his face. Quickly, soldiers grabbed her and held her back, but not before she had wounded his cheek with her nails. He slapped her and she fell. Blood came from her mouth.

"You murderers," she screamed in Yiddish, sobbing. "Where are they? What have you done to my parents?"

Heydrich recovered enough to kick her in the stomach. She moaned in pain.

"*Judien!* What is your name?" he shouted.

"I am Ester! Ester Levi," she screamed through the blood and tears choking her. She was not afraid of this man. "I am the daughter of Moshe Dovid ben-Levi. What have you done with him?"

Heydrich unholstered his Mauser. Its slick black barrel glistened.

"Ah, yes, I recall the name Levi. He died in the synagogue days ago with many others of your kind. We burned them while they prayed. They — "

Ester's screams drowned out his words. She tried to rise but was held down. The prisoners ceased their work. Several started for her but were shoved back by the soldiers. She did not notice a young soldier coming to her side.

"Permission, *Hauptsturm Fuhrer*. This Jew is worthy of death, yes, it is true. Permit me the honor, my captain. Release this one to me... for my own purposes, yes?"

It was the young Gerhardt, pushing himself in front of Ester's young body, bowing and removing his hat, his face stern, his gestures purposely sharp and broad. He scowled at Ester, knowing Heydrich was watching. Heydrich looked hard at *Oberschutze* von Metternich a moment, seeing mettle in youth. Then his shoulders relaxed. An aide brought him a towel and he held it against his torn cheek.

"I should kill her now," he growled in pain while spitting upon the body of the girl at his feet. He looked hard at Gerhardt, then he smirked.

"Take her, quickly, before I change my mind. But do not think to countermand my orders, *Oberschutze*, or you will suffer her fate. She dies at dawn. You may not leave this compound with her! That is an order! *Heil Hitler!*"

The *Heil* salute was returned. Gerhardt picked Ester up and carried her across the pit area to the rear of the station. He found an isolated bench and set her down. She grimaced and spat out blood. He brought her toweling and pressed it against her mouth. Gerhardt remembered some Yiddish, but he'd not spoken it in years. He hoped hers was much better, and that she could get the gist of his words.

"You are crazy, do you want to die?" he gently chastised her in German, wishing fervently now that he could speak Russian. Speaking very slowly, he used many hand motions with his words.

Ester, trying to comprehend her captor's words, responded in Yiddish, a language used by Jews but based upon German.

"Let him shoot me. He killed my parents. I am sure you will finish the job."

Seeing new grief overtake her, Gerhardt looked away, feeling helpless. He knew nothing he could say would help now, but he felt he must try to explain.

"Fraulein, I don't want to kill you. I am not a murderer. I did not come to the army expecting to kill Jews. I don't hate them . . . you should only know . . . I am in charge of the motor pool and mechanical accuracy of our vehicles. But I must . . . must try to do what my captain tells me."

"Even when he commands you to murder? Are you an animal, a heartless animal? Did you kill my parents, too?"

Gerhardt raised his voice. This was not what he expected to encounter. How could he make her understand his position? How could he defend the wholesale murders that were taking place? Did he dare speak to her in Yiddish now?

"*Fraulein*, I did not know about this killing. I have never shot anyone! Please, I am not an animal, but a soldier! I have responsibilities to my captain, my unit, my leaders. In every war there are prisoners. They are guilty only of being in the wrong place at the wrong time! It is always so. You are a prisoner of war. Can you understand that?"

Ester looked at Gerhardt in amazement. "How do you know to speak Yiddish?"

"Never mind . . . Answer my question."

"I understand that your army has come to our home and brutalized our people. We are unarmed non-aggressors, defenseless against your weapons, and you know it. Why do you hate Jews? We have done nothing to you! We thought you had come to save us from the Russian thugs, but you are no better — you are worse!"

Gerhardt turned his back and walked to the window. There was much commotion because the latest truckload of prisoners had just arrived. They were taken into a room next to the train depot to await the morrow's execution. Gerhardt watched the men and women help each other out of the truck. They held their heads high. Some even smiled. Did they suspect the fate that awaited them?

Ester motioned toward the new prisoners.

"Why have you arrested these people? They were only living their lives, caring for their families. What are they to you? Now they are digging their graves! And why do you keep me? I am of no value to you. Your captain treats me like vermin. Let our murderer Stalin fight your crazy Hitler! That is an equal war. You and your armies are monsters!"

She turned away from him, cold, trembling and very hungry. Gerhardt stared at the floor. She was right, this whole thing had gotten out of hand. Prisoners of war were one thing, but murdering the innocent? He felt trapped in a situation he could neither halt nor believe in. He, too was a prisoner. Heydrich had given orders to take the life of this young Jew but Gerhardt knew even as she spit out her words at him that he would not be able to shoot her. He would have to face Heydrich. What horror would be his reprisal, his punishment? If he did not carry out Heydrich's orders, his captain would finish the job. Night was approaching. Frantically, he searched for an answer, but it was even then becoming obvious. Somehow, he had to save them both.

"*Fraulein* . . . Ester. I will take you to a safe place where there is food and water. Come with me, quickly."

He led her out into his truck, hiding her beneath a tarp that covered some auto parts needed by a convoy due soon at the outskirts of Berdichev. Her tears continued to come as she mourned her parents' death. Gerhardt drove quickly out of the yard and headed north on the Berdichev-Zhitomir highway.

It seemed that he drove a long time. Ester was tucked safely out of sight in the rear of his vehicle. He found a small food market near Ozeryanka and quickly purchased food and drink from the startled storeowners. Only a few hours separated her from the hour of certain death. He wanted desperately to share that time with her though he did not really understand the urgency. He had been her savior twice, yet she had nothing but insults for him — his uniform was to her the German army, his face the visage of evil. Through his language were given the commandments of death. She was a Jew, and he? What was he?

For the first time in many months Gerhardt thought about his life in light of these new circumstances. His dream was crumbling around him. The grandiose plans to liberate his country, bring his parents together . . . these seemed impossible now. And this Jewish woman hated him. What if she knew he was fully a Jew in his heart and that he wanted to help her as one of his own!

If only she knew . . . would she hate him even more that he was beginning to hate himself?

～

Many miles north of Berdichev, Gerhardt parked off the road in an area of dense forest. Ester was ravenous. She ate all he offered. They sat in silence, neither willing to begin another conversation. Any words exchanged would have to be in German and Yiddish and he knew misunderstandings would add stress to their time together. Nevertheless . . . Gerhardt half-covered her with a blanket and helped her from the truck. Her face was gaunt and tear-stained. He watched her walk ahead and wondered how to begin.

"I am sorry for your parents. Heydrich thinks only of executing the *Fuhrer's* orders."

"Your captain is a beast," Ester whispered, turning to face the young soldier. "But I know he would have killed me . . . *Spasibo*. What will you do with me now?"

Around them was silence but for night sounds of animals settling in. He removed his cap and placed it in the truck. He found another blanket for them to sit on. Her eyes searched his, but he did not answer her question.

"My mother is also blond, " he said softly. "She is very beautiful. I write her every week."

Ester looked at her captor, surprised at this personal revelation. He seemed quite young. His blue eyes were friendly, his expression unsure but kind. There was a sense of something different about him, a quality of resigned sadness somehow deep as her own.

"At least your mother is alive. And your father, is he also of the *SS*?"

"My father, no, well . . . of course, they are divorced. My father is probably dead. I want my mother to be safe, that is all I ask."

Gerhardt blushed beneath his collar, which he loosened a bit. Speaking this way with a woman was difficult for him, but he felt somehow comforted by her presence.

Ester remained silent. She looked away from him, but she was listening.

"They were so in love, *fraulein*. It was really the *Reich* that separated them, the hatred and the fear that they would be found out . . . "

Ester turned, a look of puzzlement in her eyes.

"Found out?"

Gerhardt took a deep breath. He had told no one until now. This great secret locked deep in his heart . . . he yearned to confess it. Dare he share it now with this Jewish woman in the few hours before they parted forever?

229

"Yes, uh, you see, my father told us we would have to hide our books, change our names…"

Ester said nothing. He could tell she did not suspect.

"My mother is German, you see. And my father, he . . . he was raised — "

Ester whirled around, suddenly comprehending.

"Jewish? You are a JEW!?"

Gerhardt began to cough uncontrollably. He choked out the words.

"Yes, yes! It is out, finally! I am half Jewish. You see, I — "

Ester jumped to her feet.

"You're a Jew and betray your own people? How can you? G-d cannot forgive you that. Traitor!"

"No, no, you must listen. Mother put me into the Hitler *Yungend* to protect me. She was advised that Hitler would make it mandatory for all German boys over ten years to join. She didn't know how else to keep me safe. Oh, listen to me, *fraulein*. All those years of hearing how we are hated, how Germany is only for the new, pure race… I had to hide who I am. What could I do?"

"But why didn't you run away? How could you live among these murderers?"

"It wasn't like that at first, just a lot of boys having a good time. Then they began to teach us physical strength — how to fight and to hate all other groups of people, especially the Jews. I despised it, shut my ears to it. Over and over they preached blind faith in the *Third Reich*, in Hitler, how he was rebuilding Germany to conquer the world!"

Ester shook her head in disbelief. She walked off a distance, looking at the hazed moon above them. A soft breeze blew. Why was he making this confession to her?

"But now you are here, in war. You have been trained to kill your own people. How can you do that?"

Gerhardt pleaded. "There is no place else to go, *fraulein*. I had to go alone . . . in this way my Mother and Father would be protected also. This was the only way . . . But I did not choose war. I learned instead about trucks and cars, transports, maintenance. I chose to keep myself away from the killing, but I was sent here and then Heydrich told me I must be ready to — ."

"To murder the innocent? What did you expect? And now you have orders to take my life."

Gerhardt came to Ester. The two stared at each other in frustration.

"I have no intention of harming you, *fraulein*, you are free to go. I will take you out of the danger area to protect you. As for myself, I must go back, there is no other choice . . . Oh, it has been so hard for me, pretending, waiting to be free of the camps, the interrogations, the brutal men. I needed to tell someone . . . all these years . . . I have to hide my real self."

"You have never told anyone? My G-d. How could you live such a lie?"

"Please! There is no place to run in Germany. If I ran away, these crazy men would kill my mother. I had to endure it but I had hoped . . . well, hoped that somehow by going to war I would hasten its end . . . see Germany at peace, put an end to anti-Semitism. There is so much hate in this world . . . But I was a fool, I see now. A fool. It can never be."

Gerhardt turned away and walked to his truck. He fought for control.

"I am the son of a German mother and a Jewish father. I am Gerhardt Israel Hirsch, a Jew descended from revered *rabbis* and teachers, forced to live with my enemies, to endure as a captive the horrid Hitler Youth propaganda of hate until I am numb. Yes, I am Gerhardt the Fool who lives each day with the dream of reuniting my parents and studying *Torah* in peace. But I think my father was murdered . . . I don't know . . . I'm so confused now . . . "

Ester was silent, trying to assimilate this information. She realized now that he would not harm her. A wave of pity came over her. He was not the enemy.

"I'm sorry, I did not know . . . How terrible. What will you do, then?"

"I must go back and plead for mercy. Several of our group refused to join Heydrich's murder squad and I was one of them. He finally ordered them back to Berlin to be reassigned. Maybe I will be lucky, too."

"I hope you're right. But . . . what if they come looking for me again?"

"I will tell Heydrich you are dead, that I killed you and threw your body in the river. He can't prove me wrong."

"But he can reprove you, even jail you?"

"Tonight I would welcome jail . . . But I'm young. They will let it go."

Gerhardt wiped his face. Quickly, he opened the cab and seated himself in the truck. He started the engine. He was deeply embarrassed.

"Get in," he said. "A regiment is coming to Berdichev tomorrow. The roads should be clear tonight if we hurry. I will drive you to Zhitomir's interior, where it is still safe. We are near there now. You must find your own shelter until morning."

⁓

Years later this incident with the German soldier was still strong in Ester's memory. She could not forget him and the terrible choices he faced. What had happened to him after he left her at Zhitomir? He was so tormented, so torn apart between his duty and his heritage, between his dreams and the reality of the firing squad. Many times since that night she had asked G-d to bring peace to his soul. Was he still alive?

This young soldier had saved her life with great risk to his own. Who was he? In her hurried rescue and overwhelming desire to find Avram, she could not even be sure she'd heard his name correctly. Was it *Ober* . . . ? Hirsch? Ester tried to locate a soldier named "Hirsch" in the aftermath of the war, but the German government said they had no information. What if someone here in Berdichev who was a witness to the shoah in 1941 could shed some light? She determined to find out as soon as her task here was completed.

---

[85] "You! You are blond. Young. You are Jewish? No? What is your name? Answer me!"
[86] " I am but a poor Russian peasant."
[87] "No. I am not a Partisan, only a Russian girl."
[88] "Where are your parents, Jew?"

Journal of the Dead — Helmut Kamper

I was in the air force in Germany in WWII. I was raised in the Hitler Youth, the HJ. There were a lot of bad years. We were trained to kill and to hate. I rarely saw my parents or family. I fought in the air with planes, I did very well but I was killed in action by a US plane toward the end of the war. Hitler himself made war on Germany from the air before he died. He was a bad man, a murderer. He is in a purgatory from which he will never arise. He is dead to all who are not evil but filled with good and the love of G-d. My G-d, the Eternal One, took me home after my death and I learned once and for all of the goodness and majesty of the G-d of Abraham, Isaac and Jacob, my *Mashiach*, whom I have learned to love as my father and my brother and my savior. I am in a peaceful place until the coming of the *Mashiach* upon the earth.

I remember many things. First, when I was young, a Jewish neighbor boy lived just across my street. We were good friends until one day his parents were taken and murdered. He was an orphan and he ran away to his grandfather's house. The grandfather took him in and hid him. This little boy grew up to be a martyr for his country. He joined the Air Force and was shot down trying to help me out of a predicament in the air. I shall always love him and be grateful to him for his actions in my behalf.

In the Hitler Youth program there was little to break the routine of training, eating, playing, and feeling as if we were special and loved for our youth. We were happy there in the camps but we had no parents or friends who could understand us.

One day a friend of mine came to me and told me we were going to war against the Russians.

I said "Oh, boy, a chance to fly against their Air Force." I couldn't wait to get aloft. When finally I did fly, it was for the love of my country, not because Hitler told me to do so. I flew many missions and wrought havoc upon the Russian soldiers and the towns below my plane. I heard or saw none of the misery or death upon the ground. I was secure in my plane; that I was doing my *Fuhrer's* bidding was an extra reward.

When I discovered how evil he was, I was aghast. I reneged upon flying again and I never took wing again. I was never court-martialed but would have been if Hitler had stayed in power.

You must believe that I was a good soldier. I knew nothing of the massacres and murders being committed in the name of Germany. I rest here with my parents who are full of love for me and for the German people. We are so sorry "your people" were murdered by "our people" and that I had to fly above them to murder them from the air. All that is over now. I am alive in the spirit and glad to be finished with the earth and all its problems.

"Earth has no sorrow that Heav'n cannot heal."
— From The Spiritual, "Come, Ye Disconsolate"

20 — Shoah on Brodskii Street

Dawn crept over the darkness but did not erase it. This day many would look upon the light of the world for the last time. Hopelessness was like a heavy, sinuous wind that blew upon everyone in Berdichev. People barricaded themselves in their homes, but there would be no escape. The vast, efficient German machine had come to blow the Russian earth clean of its Jews, Slavs, the aged and the infant, the sick, the dissident and the insane. But today the first onslaught of the Red Army invaded Berdichev's northern border. German troops were holding them off near the airport and along the highways leading to Zhitomir. There were tanks everywhere.

The town was in an uproar. Anyone seen on the streets was foolish and in imminent danger. This seemingly insignificant town of 50,000 or more souls had become a vital target for the *Wehrmacht*, the *SS* and the Red Army, but for different reasons. The *Wehrmacht* was most interested in conducting a short, efficient war. To this end they were responsible for defeating Soviet forces on the ground and in the air. The *SS* was set upon murdering as many Jews as possible everywhere they went in pursuit of lebensraum. The Reds had to reclaim Berdichev, protect Ukraine from further penetration and from the eventuality of a German victory on Russian soil.

People passing through Lvov in July of 1941 would note there was murder with abandon, an evil circus. And to think, there was an atmosphere of joy when the Germans first entered Lvov. But now, thanks to a People's Court held by the local Ukrainians, many were condemned to die, taken to the woods and shot. These actions were encouraged by the German troops who offered the local peasantry rewards of vodka, sugar or salt, cigarettes and even money to turn their neighbors over to the *SS* police. It was later estimated that within the five weeks of the German invasion of Russia on June 22 the number of Jews killed exceeded the total number killed in the previous eight years of *Nazi* rule. Many were children, many were new mothers.

So, devastation was the town crier this day. Everyone breathed it in like prophecy.

The condemned, huddled together inside the train station stoically waiting their turn at death. From the station windows they could see the finished furrowed pits along the dirt road that had been Brodskii Street. Shovels still lay on the cold, damp ground. Why did they go politely to their deaths without screaming or weeping?

The busy craftsmen hurrying to their livelihoods — "Here, wait, you come with us, Jewish swine! On your knees, lick up the garbage — now get in the trucks. *Raus!*"

The farmer folk going to market were suddenly rounded up and herded from their homes to be ordered hurriedly by armed soldiers into German transport trucks.

Those who watched the undesirables shuffle solemnly to the brink of their lives, what could they do, run into the street and grab back the condemned? *Nyet*, but many secretly praised G-d they would live to see another day!

The many Ukrainians, Slavs and Russians who tipped the Germans (and later the Red Army) about Jewish identities, workplaces, whereabouts stood on the wooden sidewalks snickering while watching their tips pay off, seeing the "vermin" marched through town to Brodskii Street with carbines at their necks.

Some hesitated. They asked: What is the price of a man, or a child and its mother? How valuable to us and to *HaShem* is the skinny old woman or the madman? Where is it written in *Talmud* that we should carry the living upon our backs? When will the *Mashiach* come? How can we answer these questions without our *rabbi*, and where is he now? We must wait for his judgment.

But others prepared; those few saviors who hid their fellows under floors and under wheat stalks, in potato cribs and in damp-floored closets. If the hidden were found, everyone would die. *Nyet*, they told the hungry wolves. We have seen no one. It was chancy, no one openly begged to be saved, but *HaShem* sent angels to Berdichev in those days . . .

⁓

Heydrich was busy, it was morning of July 10th and there were hundreds, maybe a thousand bodies to be shot. No names were collected before the massacres because mass shootings sometimes had a deleterious effect on the soldiers' "fighting spirit". For this same reason no filming of the shootings were allowed. The logistics of war had kept Heydrich awake much of the night, along with two of his most trusted officers. His commanding officer, Major Rozler, was occupied with new troops dispatched throughout the suburbs of Berdichev. Intelligence reports indicated that masses of Russian troops were already at Berdichev's eastern perimeter and heading for German headquarters. There was no time to waste.

Drawings had been made and followed in the digging of the pits. Heydrich checked every detail before giving the go ahead.

Area A was the railway embankment which would serve to catch stray bullets. Area B, the ditch, which was approximately 4 meters (12 feet) long and about 3 meters (9 feet) wide. Area C was really a mound upon which the unshackled but not blindfolded victims would have to kneel, facing forward into the pit. Bodies in number would have to fall upon each other. From a distance of approximately 10 meters (30 feet) Areas D and E were the places where the Execution Detachment would stand, aim and fire. In Zhitomir's killing field this detachment included a commanding officer and two NCOs as well as 15-30 shooters from the lowest rank of troops. Approximately twenty people could be killed at once with this arrangement. No one would be able to flee. Powdered lime could then be poured over the bodies. Another layer of dead would be added before the pits were refilled with dirt.

Heydrich approved of this plan for Berdichev and followed it generally throughout the war in Ukraine. Though he had instructed that no photos of the massacres be taken (of if taken, shown to others), there was always a "possibility" that some of the more graphic scenes would find their way to the *Fuhrer* . . . Heydrich carefully let it be known that he could be induced to let this happen. Heydrich was omitting no factor that might earn him another star on his cap and commendation for service in "battle".

Heydrich hardly noticed Gerhardt's haggard appearance when the young soldier gave the *Heil Hitler* salute before his captain that morning. He had slept in his truck outside Berdichev until dawn. Racing back to his post he saw in his rear view mirror an advancing Russian tank! He could hardly believe it! Immediately, he knew they would all be in a pitched battle and Heydrich would have no time to recall his promise of death to Ester or to take revenge. Finally, Gerhardt the Weary would have his chance at the Red Army!

By the time Gerhardt reached his post near the trench-diggings, Heydrich was already on the phone to his subordinates in the field, instructing them on warfare with the Russian troops which had evidently massed outside the town the previous evening. According to intelligence, there appeared to be only 500. This was an incredulously low number and Heydrich suspected he was being duped — thousands more were surely coming upon the town from other locations! Heydrich hung up and motioned to Gerhardt.

"Gerhardt, get on the line. You will watch this shooting and be prepared to assist. Here, back off the trenches 10 meters. That's it. Now stand your ground. Use your rifle, not your pistol. Extra ammunition will be brought. We will begin immediately."

Before Gerhardt could object, he was placed on the shooting line. His mind was whirling. He began to tremble, his legs were weak. He was grateful that Ester was out of harm's way. There was only himself to deal with now. His rifle fell from his hands. He scurried to pick it up. *I cannot do this!*

It came to him then, clear and clean. He saw himself in the mirror of his own history.

I have lived a lie. I cannot reunite my country. I cannot bring my parents together again . . . I am only a victim in Nazi uniform. Papa's dead. What kind of son am I? A mechanic in charge of vehicles. Vehicles! How stupid my dreams! A cipher carrying out the orders of insane men. A soldier in the service of murderers! Mein Gott, forgive me! Help me, Eternal One, help me!

Captain Heydrich gave orders to have the prisoners brought out of the hangar and from behind the station house. Many of these people had been rounded up on tips from the local populace who were quite willing not only to tell the Germans who and where the Jews were hiding, but to murder them as well. Standing with them in line were numerous Ukrainians who had hidden Jews in their fields, their homes and businesses and who refused to give them up or answer the inquiries of the SS soldiers. Those who were not immediately shot were hanged with those they sheltered.

Slowly, quietly, the condemned came forth: shopkeepers whose wives called out to them from other places in the lineup; mothers carrying their babes; teen-aged boys who were on their way to *yeshiva*; small children being led by their grandparents; the dissident with complaint; the many resigned; handsome young men who would have married and fathered families and fortunes in Ukraine; sisters holding hands; visiting *rabbis* who were arrested at a Sabbath worship; bankers in the midst of trading financial paper upon which the town depended for its credit; ambulatory patients from the hospital to the north of Berdichev; several well known Jewish physicians and their nurses, and on. They were feeble, barely able to walk after the several days they had spent without food or sleep in extremely crowded conditions in the hangars.

Still the Germans prodded and spit on them. They coughed and sputtered. Many smelled of excrement and blushed with shame. Some prisoners owned businesses in town. Some were not Jewish — they were made to get into line nevertheless. The assembled cadre of bodies extended for a mile. Everyone was soiled, sick and lethargic, though few but the children uttered cries. Their cries were quickly hushed. All around the captives, the Germans were shooting at Russian soldiers. Occasionally a bullet hit someone in line waiting to be shot. The first victims of the trenches were claimed in this way.

They were given the order to undress. An *SS* man walked around them carrying a riding whip. He used it when responses were too slow for his liking. The soldier ordered everyone to put their clothes in fixed places, sorted according to shoes, top clothing and undergarments. This the people did without screaming or crying. Then they stood in family groups saying farewells.

There was no complaint or plea for mercy. The largest group was a family of eight persons; a man and woman both about fifty with their two daughters and sons-in law who held their two children. An old woman with snow-white hair was holding a one-year-old child in her arms, singing and tickling it. The child cooed with delight while the parents looked on with tears in their eyes. The father held the hand of his young son and spoke to him in a soft voice. The boy tried to hold back his tears. No one made an effort to escape. It was as though they all believed G-d had brought this about as a part of His Grand Plan for the end of the world. His Chosen must now do their parts and this they accepted, for His knowledge was far greater than their own.

At that moment the *SS* man at the pit started shouting something to his comrade. The latter counted off about fifty persons and instructed them to go behind the earth mound and kneel facing the pits. Soon there was a row of prisoners spanning the length of the trenches. Everyone complied quietly. When they were lined up the riflemen were instructed to raise their rifles and to shoot with an economy of bullets. Gerhardt was one of the squad of shooters. He looked at the naked bodies before him; the child, the grandmother with her charge, the father holding his little boy's hand.

"*Schiessen sie!*" the order came. "Shoot!"

Bullets exploded into bodies, instantly piercing their targets who fell forward into the pit. Their blood gushed and splattered everywhere. Deep red stains ran into the dirt beneath the dying and dead. It spurted up and backward and sideways like fountains gone amuck. Some of it even landed on the polished German boots of the shooters. The little boy lay dead, the white-haired grandmother's face was unrecognizable. Many people were not killed instantly. They writhed in agony, their brains no longer intact. Several others lay at crazy angles with broken spinal columns. Others were still alive. Babies howled. How they screamed out their pain.

Suddenly, one of the soldiers dropped his rifle. He had not fired a shot.

"I cannot," he screamed. "I cannot! *Gott in Himmel*, how can you allow this?"

Everyone was suddenly quiet. All eyes turned upon Gerhardt. One of the shooters, an *SS* man, sat at the edge of the narrow end of the pit, his feet dangling into it. He laid his rifle on his knees and lit a cigarette.

Gerhardt stumbled toward the pit. His eyes were large, his face contorted. He stared at the writhing, broken bodies in horror. He began to cry, gulping huge gasps of air. Seeing several victims still alive Gerhardt reached into the pit, trying to grab at the bodies.

"You, here. Why do you go quietly to your death? You are alive, let me get you out! And you, little girl, you have to live! Let me take you home, *madele*."

The other soldiers looked shocked at their comrade's crazy behavior.

"Hey, Gerhardt, what are you doing? Get away from there," they called to him.

Heydrich was immediately summoned. He came down the line with other officers in tow, roaring orders at Gerhardt who began singing in Yiddish to the living and dead in the trenches. Their blood stained his uniform, his face and hands. His tears fell upon the pitiful and he wept openly.

"*Oberschutze von Metternich! Shtup!* Stand at attention!"

Gerhardt could not respond. His heart was filled with grief.

His mother's voice rang in his ears. Heydrich reached him and yanked him upon his feet. His hand shot across Gerhardt's face, sending him backwards upon the dirt. Everyone watched, including those waiting to die.

"*Oberschutze von Metternich!* Have you gone mad? Get up!"

Heydrich reached for Gerhardt's clothes to pull him to his feet, but Gerhardt pushed his captain away.

"Beasts! Beasts! You must not kill these people, they are innocent. They must live!"

"They are Jews, misfits, Slavs, human waste," Heydrich shouted back. "Our *Fuhrer* has ordered them removed."

Gerhardt spit at his captain's feet.

"The *Fuhrer* is crazy! Damn your *Fuhrer*! Damn your war, Damn you all! It is you who are mad, you who should be shot! I will not be a part of this!"

Gerhardt motioned to the hundreds waiting their turn to die. His mind was spinning. He felt exhilaration, even joy in his anger. At last he was being true to himself. Every fiber of his body testified to him of the rightness of this moment.

"Let them go! Let them return to their lives and families! I demand it!"

Heydrich watched his soldier in amazement and horror. At last he acted. He turned to his lieutenants and barked the order to arrest Gerhardt. They grabbed at him, but he resisted as they wrestled to pin him down.

"Gerhardt, listen to me," Heydrich shouted. "You are young, new to battle, you are not trained for these squads. We will reassign you. Step aside now. Leave this area, I order you!"

But instead of following orders, Gerhardt broke free of his captors and ran to the edge of the pit. He put his arms around a young victim reaching up for help.

"Gerhardt! Step aside!"

But Gerhardt pulled the bleeding child out of the pit and turned to face his captain. Wait! Was that Aaron's ghost behind Heydrich? Gerhardt blinked to be sure. The image persisted.

"Jews are not human waste, captain, they are G-d's chosen . . . I know this because I, too, am a Jew. Yes, it is true! I am Gerhardt Israel Hirsch, a descendent of the great *rabbis* and intellectual Jews of Germany!"

Heydrich froze in shock. "What? von Metternich, *Judien*? Impossible! You cannot be. We would have found out! You'd never get away with such a lie! I don't believe it! "

Heydrich reached out and grabbed Gerhardt's jaw. He turned the young man's face left and right, quickly examining bone structure; the blue eyes, the fair hair and complexion. He shook his head in disbelief then slapped Gerhardt smartly across the face, drawing blood.

"Jew or not, you're a coward! I will have you shot! Take him!"

Soldiers again grabbed Gerhardt. Again he wrestled away. He pushed the saved child into the line of condemned people. *Now I must save them all*, he thought. He ran back toward the pit to grab another prisoner, but a bullet ripped through his chest and another hit his left leg, tearing open his body inside his uniform. Gerhardt fell forward but he was not yet stopped. In agony he dragged himself toward the pit. *Got to get to them*, his mind said. He was pulling desperately at the ground. *Can't die now, got to save them all* . . . But he could not rise. Then four more bullets exploded into his body. He lay finally still. *Mama, Mama, I have tried, but too late* . . .

As he died, Gerhardt Israel Hirsch saw his father, Aaron in a halo of bright light.

"Gerhardt, my boy. Let the *Shema* be on your lips."

"*Shema, Yisroel, Adonai Elohenu* . . . "[89]

Heydrich stood over the dead man and shook his head sadly.

"Throw him in the pit with the other *Judien* waste," he ordered.

~

With Gerhardt out of the way, the carnage continued. Fifty others were herded to the pit from the line and the same routine followed. Soldiers had to pull them from one another. Over the sound of rifle fire the naked doomed were calling out their good-byes, promising to meet again. There was no resistance. The trenches continued filling with bodies and their spilling, spurting blood. People were closely wedged together, lying on top of one another so only their heads were visible. Nearly all had blood and guts running over their shoulders. Some of the people shot were still moving. Some were lifting their arms and turning their heads to show that they were still alive. They were put quickly out of misery.

More condemned were ordered down steps cut in the clay wall of the pit. These were ordered to clamber over the heads of the dead to the place where *SS* men directed them. They lay down

242

in front of the dead or wounded people. Some caressed those who were still alive and spoke to them in low voice. Then a series of shots. In the pits, bodies were twitching. Blood spurted from their necks. The next batch of the condemned was called. They also went down into the pit, lined themselves up on top of the previous victims and were shot. In this way three hundred people were quickly done away with. Then a halt was called. The soldiers took their scheduled lunch break while everyone else waited.

---

[89]From the Jewish Creedal Prayer. "Hear, O Israel, the Lord our God, the Lord is One."

Those who sow in tears shall reap in joy. They who go weeping, bearing their sack of seed, will yet come home in gladness bearing ample sheaves of grain.

— Psalm CXXXVI

21 — Voices From the Dust

Summer dawn came over the Steppes like a bright cleansing beam. First it shone upon the alders and maples and they shimmered with dew. Squirrels scurried to find food in disappearing shadows. Then the clarified light fell across broad meadows, searching through the wheat for the littlest grains lying cold and fallow. Almost at once they moved with new life; the warmed ground received them. Rays of gold illuminated the air and bounced through the forest with abandon as sunrise gave a filmy backlight. It burned off the steam from the cool pre-dawn in preparation for another day of heat.

The ground in the pits on Brodskii Street was still covered with morning chill. The day's killing squads had not yet arrived nor had there been any cleanup of the previous day's massacre or quicklime poured into the pits. The soldiers had dutifully murdered everyone scheduled. They were then dispatched to join the fight against the Red Army troops outside the town's wide perimeter. Now new light illuminated the pits and the many hundreds of freshly killed bodies that filled them. Great amounts of blood had congealed on and around the victims. They lay in various attitudes and positions; many completely naked, some only partially. A few had tried to crawl away but they had later been discovered and shot again. Their final expressions were vivid in death. Some had died in horror, eyes wide. Others with eyes tightly closed against the rifle barrel that pushed at their neck. Some were in an attitude of prayer. They had fallen upon one another in layers. It was impossible to see the bodies on the bottom of the piles or to count them. This was the scene as far as the eye could behold.

The beginning heat of a new day on Brodskii Street began first in early light and warmed the blood in the ruts of the trench. The blood had risen up until it flowed across the ground to where the soldiers had stood. The stench of death's rot and warm, thick blood was everywhere. The sun's warmth increased the odor. The dug earth was drenched with blood that had poured out all along the trench. Already, flies were assembling. As the day progressed and humidity increased, their high-pitched frenzy would overtake every other sound in the forest. Soggy with ooze from gallons of this clotted red liquid, the scene would greatly anger the Germans who would arrive in a few hours. They would sink to their ankles in the wet crimson soil and curse at the dark red stains on their boots and uniforms.

But now the area of death was silent and in the dawning light, almost pristine. The sound of someone singing began faintly and increased slowly in volume. The song was an ancient Hebrew prayer, mournful and fervent, a chant that broke into a petition to G-d. From far off a man appeared; it was the *Chasidic chazzen*. He was short, portly and seemed in a hurry. He carried a book that he consulted as his powerful voice lifted and fell in studied cadence. Atop his white hair was a *yarmulke* and the traditional robes of the synagogue were around his shoulders. His long white beard glistened. The bifocals he had always worn were pushed upon his forehead, so that his nose was almost in the pages of the book. He came and stood on the lip of the trenches along Brokskii Street. There he began to sing mightily, all the while extending his hands over the fallen as he gave them the traditional Hebrew blessings over the dead.

Thou, O Lord, art mighty forever. Thou callest the dead to immortal life for Thou art mighty in deliverance.

As the man sang the petition for continued life he moved slowly along the open pit making sure the traditional Mourner's *Kaddish* (prayers for the dead) was given to each soul.

Glorified and sanctified by God's great Name throughout the world which he has created according to His will . . . May His great Name be blessed forever and to all eternity.

The old man moved with seemingly impossible grace and ease along the line of bodies. After blessing the bodies of the dead, he stepped into the trench and spoke quietly to each soul. His body seemed to weigh nothing. He appeared to walk just above those in the pit as though he were not real, but only a spirit being.

"There you are, Reb Yeselovich. May your soul rest in peace. Ah, Mother Davidovna, blessed be thee. Thy spirit rests in the hands of our G-d now, will you sing with me? Oh, I see you are here, also, Meyer Finkelstein, my good friend. Well, you have lived a good life. Now it is time to rest a *bissel*."

The man came to a child and a gasp escaped his lips. His

prayers rose in volume and in urgency. Tears came to his eyes.

"Do not fear, little Chai. Reb Levi has said *Kaddish* for you, and for all these who sleep here. Do you remember your Reb Levi, your Papa's friend and *chazzen*?"

He walked on amidst those who slept in the earth them, blessing them in death as he was no longer able to in life.

"*O, HaShem, full of compassion. Thou who dwellest on high! Grant perfect rest beneath the sheltering wings of Thy presence, among the holy and pure who shine as the brightness on the Heavens, unto the soul of these poor bodies, who have gone unto eternity and in whose memory charity is offered . . .*"

This prayer was said for each body in the pit and as each name was called, there arose a returning "*amayn*" from that sleeping soul who rejoiced in his or her continued life in the spirit.

He who creates peace in His celestial heights, may He create peace for us and for all Israel; and say, Amayn.

Reb Levi now recorded the names of all the dead as he moved among them. Those he did not know he called to, and then wrote the response that was given. When he had finished recording the names, he stood in their midst and addressed them all.

"My dear friends, I am sorry I was not able to give you each a proper burial and find family to sit *shiva* for you. But such as it is, we must accept what has happened. Our mortal lives we have been robbed of, but our spirits will live forever. Let us now sing together in joy and gladness our praises to G-d for preserving us and granting us life beyond the grave. "

For a moment there was silence. It was as if forces beyond mortal knowing were wakening from the awful, leaden finality of death. Then one by one from the long, wide earthen coffin that held a thousand brutally silenced lives there arose as many living voices singing hymns of praise to G-d. The mournful music of *Kaddish* this day was a choir of joy and acclamation filling all of Heaven! Though the world of the living could not hear a single sound, the blood-filled pits that was once busy Brodskii Street reverberated in the ears of the Holy One as a single living instrument in gratitude and gladness for the immeasurable gift of life.

"Our spirits are freed. We are together again! *Hosanna, hosanna*[90] to G-d!"

An unearthly light seemed to grow around the trenches, increasing in whiteness until it became blinding as lightening. It extended upward toward the sky, like a channel being opened. One by one, living souls arose out of their body meat. It was impossible to see this with the eye of mortality but there was no doubt in Reb Levi's careful accounting that every interred soul would this day rise from its earthly bier as it was called to its heavenly home. They were each greeted by family members who had passed. The choir of voices continued in praises as the process was carried out until finally every name had been checked and every spirit freed. Reb Levi was the last to be raised. He offered praise as he ascended toward ever increasing light.

"Praise Thee, *HaShem*. Thy glory is forever. O, my soul sings to Thee. Halleluyah!"

Eventually, as the heat of day became oppressive, the ever-dutiful German death squads reappeared carrying heavy bags of quicklime. Many of the soldiers felt secretly uneasy from their previous day of murder and had small appetite for more. Sensing this, Captain Heydrich chastised them smartly for their lack of total loyalty to Hitler. He then commanded them to defend Berdichev from the Red Army's initial attacks upon the perimeters.

~

It was still early evening when Gerhardt left Ester on the outskirts of Zhitomir. They parted with apologies and farewells, knowing they would not meet again. Gerhardt warned that some German troops were still on guard at the eastern perimeters of the city, but he had overheard Heydrich say they had probably left the town itself. Knowing this, she decided to keep out of sight until daylight came. He asked to hug her; she agreed. They held each other a moment and then he was gone.

Ester was very tired but thanks to Gerhardt her stomach was not empty. She was deeply grateful to him and decided to find him again when she and Avram were safe. Perhaps they could even be friends!

She walked quickly and quietly through the avenues of the quaint old town, feeling quite vulnerable but also sensing in the late evening air a promise and potential. The air was cool and not yet polluted with the nauseating odor of diesel exhaust and dust. Few people were about. The moonlight threw patterns on the old paving stones and asphalt. The invading Germans had not destroyed many buildings in their search for Jews and other undesirables, but there were signs of other types of terrorism. The curbs were a darkish gray granite and difficult to see in the night shadows. Bloody stains on the cobbled stones were witness to grief and loss. Numerous store windows were knocked out. Ester guessed they'd had Hebrew lettering on them. In many places debris from burned out stores and apartments littered the streets. An old street lamp threw light on a row of benches along a park but Ester did not stop to rest.

Zhitomir's old roads were tricky at night. Recessed railroad ties interrupted the roads and crossed at intersections, causing Ester to slip and fall as she wandered in the darkness. She passed a printing shop painted blue with white highlights, echoing the bright color scheme of many shops. Had Avram done business there? Would they know where he might be?

As she walked, remembrances of her recent experiences seemed to echo against the large, dark buildings that loomed before her. She shivered when she thought how she so many times had escaped death and was spared her life. She vowed to remember always the terrible price of being a Jew and to devote her young life to the cause of freedom for her people in Ukraine.

Ester walked on silently. In the gaps between storefronts small garden plots took the place of alleyways. She passed Soviet-built apartment houses, churches. A Jewish cemetery with a sign reading *"Alter Svintar"* (old cemetery) — had been recently defaced. Its crooked monuments, some over a yard tall, lay askance, evidently vandalized. The area around the cemetery was untended. Ester guessed the caretakers were also victims of the war.

Turning a corner onto a broad roadway, Ester saw an imposing white stucco building. It filled the block. Its several brass steeples seemed to reach the clouds. She reasoned it contained the Oblast government offices. Cautiously, she circled around the back of the huge structure, hoping no one would disturb her. A long stairway led up to a rear entrance. She climbed to the top stair and settled in to wait for daylight, drawing what warmth she could from her light jacket. In the silence, thoughts of her beloved Avram flooded her mind until she fell into exhausted sleep . . .

She awoke hours later from a cramped, uncomfortable position to sounds of war. In the distance she heard rifle fire and the hurricane-like noise of tanks, mortars and machine guns. Occasionally, the white flash of artillery raced across the morning skies. Ester hurriedly left the building's steps for the narrow boulevard. This town, too, was in the throes of submission.

Suddenly the air was ripped by rifle shots. A German police officer came out of the white building. He raced across the street in the direction of the shots. Two other men followed him. In a few minutes more doors opened and a group of civilians joined in the running. Ester was surprised. The Germans were obviously still terrorizing Zhitomir! But curiosity got the better. Slowly she walked in the direction of the noise.

The road led her for many yards down an unpaved back street. A few residents were setting up their little stands — a box, a tablecloth, a stool, a plastic sheet or blanket from which to sell their garden goods and make a few *kopeks*. *Babushka*'d housewives were already on their balconies hanging laundry. And all this while soldiers walked the streets! Ester came finally to an opening near a railway embankment. About forty feet before her were the soldiers and civilians. They were staring into a ditch, yelling and crying out.

"He is still alive," one of them said. "Hurry, get him out, please, let us get him out!"

Two other wounded were bargained for by civilians and carried out of the pit. She saw that it was an execution ditch. Many corpses lay in it. An old man with a cane still hanging from his hands was pulled out of the ditch by the civilians. The German executioners' uniforms were blood-stained. The rifles they'd used to murder were in their hands. Some others were standing around in shorts and shirts, watching and pointing to the old man.

"Get away from here," commanded one of the German officers. "These are filthy vermin Jews. Good riddance to them. Anyone else touching a body will be shot!"

An old woman cried out: "My husband is there. You've killed my husband!"

A German raised his rifle to her face.

"He was caught defending a Jew! Get away, old woman, or your fate will be the same."

The woman fell to the street with grief. A neighbor pulled her away and they disappeared with the crowd of onlookers. Some who were there left smiling and seemed to be enjoying the proceedings.

Ester turned back, dizzy with shock at the bestiality of these German police and the insensitivity of the gawkers. She found a bench and almost fell upon it. It was quite a while before her legs would support her. With a heavy heart she prayed that Avram was still alive and then she thought to visit the printing shop she'd passed during the night. He might have done business there.

As she came to the corner of one of the busier streets that led to the market, a man crossed the street, walking very slowly as he passed her. He was quite tall and fair with prominent Russian features. He wore a black knitted cap and a faded Russian army jacket. A cigarette was between his lips; he puffed at it intermittently as though intensely involved in his own thoughts. He glanced furtively at Ester. A feeling of recognition swept her. Where had she seen him before? She turned, only to find he had done the same. For a few seconds they regarded each other. The man motioned to a streetcar that was coming along the tracks.

"Get on," he seemed to say.

Ester nodded in understanding, still trying to place him. As the slow-traveling trolley car came around he boarded it. Ester did the same. They were alone at the rear. He spoke first.

"Excuse. You are of Berdichev?"

Ester nodded. His eyes. Grey with flint. She remembered. She caught her breath.

"You. With Barak!" she whispered.

The man instinctively turned away to see if anyone had caught their conversation. When he thought it safe, he quickly replied.

"He is in Zhitomir. You are Ester. At the next stop, you get off. I will meet you on Serbska Street." He motioned to his left. "Wait for me there."

With that, he jumped from the slow moving trolley and merged into the crowd assembling in the Rynok bazaar. Ester noted that numerous soldiers mingled with the crowds, as if planning another roundup. She shuddered.

When they met again, it was as friends. Sidor was a Partisan who had fought alongside Barak during the attacks upon Lvov and Berdichev. He was in Zhitomir to secure his family before leaving for the Partisan encampments outside Kiev. He offered Ester his arm so it would appear they were a couple. While they walked together along the tree-lined streets, Sidor told Ester about Barak. He'd survived numerous missions against the German SS and was in good health. She cried with joy at this news, then related her fears about Avram. At this, Sidor became silent. Soon they reached an apartment complex with an extended entrance.

"Come inside. We will not be observed . . . We know this man, Avram. He mourns the death of his mother at the hands of the enemy, in this case, the Russian police. He was put in a cell weeks ago. We know of his plight but getting him out will require an organized offensive. Zhitomir is still surrounded by German troops. Our national army, as you may know, was tricked, no thanks to Stalin! They have been slow in retaliation but soon Zhitomir may become a battlefield. You will have to leave here."

"No, I cannot leave without Avram. We are to be married. Please, you must free him."

Sidor was thoughtful. "Well, with difficulty we can get him out. But for now I will arrange for you to see your brother. He is not far from here. He feared you were dead, also your parents. Are they here with you?"

Through her tears, Ester told Sidor about Heydrich and his torching of their synagogue. When she had finished, he put a consoling arm around her and reassured her they would find a way to rescue Avram.

"But now you must be hungry. Here are rubles. Buy food for yourself. Then go to this address and wait. Be sure you are not followed. Barak will meet you there."

The address Sidor had given her led to an old building. A large bakery occupied the street level and stairs just inside the entrance led to small apartments. The word *pekarnya* (bakery) loomed in huge white letters above the bakery. The delicious smell of Russian *chyornyj/khlyeb* (black bread) made her hungry. For only a few rubles she purchased rolls and ate them quickly. She climbed the rickety stairs and knocked at the apartment where she was to wait, her heart beating faster at the thought that she would soon see her brother. The old man who answered turned out to be Sidor's father.

"Come in, dear. We have made a place for you to rest and refresh yourself."

"Thank you, I hope I am no trouble."

"No, no trouble. You were not followed?"

"*Nyet.*"

"Come along, then."

He led her down a musty hallway to a small sitting room, motioned her to an armchair and left. The singular window was covered by an old torn curtain. Ester could see the street below. Several people were coming and going from the shop, but none of them were Barak. She grew impatient. It seemed she had not seen her brother in years. Now, thanks to a chance meeting, reunion was near.

An hour later the sun was high in the azure sky. Ester slept in

exhaustion. Suddenly, the door burst open and a tall, gaunt man
with red hair and beard appeared in it. Ester awoke at the noise.
His cap and dress were gray with stains of the earth. Traces of gun-
powder stained his wide leather belt. His shoes had been roughly
cleaned, but the overall impression was that of a man emerging
from the shadows, a patriot in arms obliged by his beliefs to live on
the outskirts of civil society. His smile was beautific.

She whirled around to see her brother. She laughed out loud
at the sight of a small harmonica on a string around his neck.

"Little sister, at last!"

"Barak, oh, Barak!"

They embraced joyfully. The room echoed with their shouts of
happiness. Outside it, several more Partisans stood guard, holding
their compatriot's Moisin rifle until he should emerge from the room.

"How are you, you look so good! Sidor told me your story.
I am so sorry I was not there to help you, Ester. How you must
have suffered!"

"Now that you are here, everything will be well, Barak. Oh,
dear, you're so thin! Are you ill?"

Barak laughed heartily.

"I am healthier than ever, Ester, my worried sister. Come, let
us tell our stories. There is little time."

"Yes, yes, and then I want to accompany you. You must find
Avram for me. I fear he is in great trouble."

"Oh, yes, we know of him. He is being kept near here and . . .
well, his Russian captors may let him starve while he is impris-
oned. We have been working on a plan to get him out. But first,
tell me everything."

Hours passed before the two called in the other Partisans.
Sidor was among them. Barak told Ester that at the beginning
of that year the Partisans in the area bordering on Poland and
Ukraine numbered about 30,000.

"We have formed a tight network across our land. What did
we live on? We lived on our hatred of the German invaders. By
this year's end it is rumored our number will increase, maybe to
150,000, men and women, too. Many are fighting hand to hand,
even without rifles or radios, but we have become a major force
against our oppressors."

"How do you live without money or help?

"The peasants support us with food and supplies, Ester.
True, some of our dear friends have died of hunger or pellagra

and scurvy, but that is the chance we must take. They know we are fighting for them and for the honor of our homeland.

"I was wounded once in the hand," laughed one of the Partisans. "We went to a peasant's home and she poured vodka on it. Ouch! But it disinfected the wound and soon I was healed."

"Yes," another said. "And I remember when we set fire to the trees that surrounded a line of German tanks waiting to move on Berdichev. Those Germans found themselves in a ring of fire. The tanks exploded. It lit up the sky."

In another hour, everyone had eaten a small meal and had their assignments. They were to move at midnight. Avram was expected to be freed and out of Zhitomir with Ester before the following dawn.

Sidor was the first to leave the apartment and enter onto the street. He was dressed casually as a citizen in old pants, shirt and coat. There were few people on the street but as Sidor turned an avenue that led to the old jail building he was accidentally shoved aside by a German soldier who was escorting a group of prisoners. The expression on their faces gave Sidor a shudder. Behind them walked another soldier, his rifle at their backs.

"Look out," the soldier shouted in irritation. "You are in the way! Do that again and I'll shoot you, too."

Sidor moved quickly away, but in his heart he fervently wanted to draw the pistols beneath his coat and give those prisoners their freedom.

After some time had passed, another of the Partisans ventured onto the avenue as casually dressed as Sidor. Then it was Barak's turn. Ester was to remain in the apartment, though this order she lobjected to.

"We will come for you when we are sure it is safe," her brother told her. "You must wait and pray that we will be successful. We know Avram is still alive, but he will be weak. There are Ukrainian spies out there eager to help the Germans *or* the Russians. It is very dangerous ground, Ester, but we will do our best to bring you two together. Trust us, will you?"

Barak held her tightly while she cried.

"Ester, I promise you that I will always fight terrorism. When these murdering men are finally stopped, my life will be devoted to making the world safer."

"Oh, Barak, you're doing all you can, I know. I'm so thankful to see you again. Please, get through this mission safely and come back with my Avram!"

Together they prayed to G-d for deliverance. Then Barak left with the others.

The three men walked leisurely from several directions toward the building that housed the prison. They knew it would be heavily guarded but were unsure if Russians or Germans would have the area secured. German soldiers did seem to be everywhere: in tanks, motorcycles with sidecars, jeeps, coming out of homes, marching along the streets, herding citizens to their deaths — an alien invasion that daylight did not prevent.

The structure housing the prisoners was a squarely built reinforced-brick, four-storied place. Concrete posts held the iron fencing that set off the building along its back and sides. The interior housed the courtrooms, the many agency offices and waiting rooms. Two side entrances led down flights of stairs to the incarceration area below street level where prisoners were kept as if swallowed whole in the bowels of the monstrous building. The small, narrow windows also had steel reinforcements, The prisoner blocks were in the center of the basement and surrounded by long corridors. Except for the occasional maroon bricks that added a bit of decor, the entire solemn edifice was a "white elephant" that had stood eighty years or more as the only edifice on Ruska Street.

Sidor, having taken the shortest route, arrived first. The sound of mortar fire lit the evening sky and created much diversion. The moon was only a crescent, the night dark. Several armed Russian soldiers patrolled the building. Broad white and red steps led to the massive front doors. Here, too, were soldiers. Sidor walked casually past the building and crossed the street. He was ignored. In a moment he met with two other men who converged from separate directions. They chatted briefly, then parted, each retracing their paths in a leisurely fashion.

One-half hour passed. Slowly a large, black van drove down Ruska Street. Headlights were off. It circled the boulevard, then came to rest a block from the edifice. Twelve men quickly emerged from the back doors, twice as many as the soldiers patrolling the court building. They moved quickly to positions in the bushes and among debris that ringed the area behind the building. They immediately dropped to the ground. They waited silently, rifles ready, observing the guards and their movements. More time passed. Gunfire and grenade blasts erupted around them perhaps half a mile away. These lit up the sky. At a given signal some of the Partisans created a distraction several yards from the building. Two of the Russian soldiers hurried to investigate. They were quickly ambushed.

Minutes later, it was dark again. Two Partisan soldiers emerged from the bushes, dressed as the Russian soldiers. Helmets and the lack of moonlight hid their faces.

"It was just a mongrel dog," one said in Russian. "Nothing to worry about."

The regular guards laughed in relief. More time passed. They continued to patrol the area. German gunfire increased. The men became nervous.

"When do we take a break?" the first voice asked gruffly. "I think the Germans are coming closer."

"I'm ready," said the second. "I could use some *pyvo*[91]."

"Yes, I am ready, too", said a third. "Let's call down for replacements."

"C'mon," said the first. "I'll go with you and we'll send some of the others up to relieve us."

The guards walked to a rear entrance and knocked. A door eventually opened and the three men entered the basement, leaving the door unlatched as they did so. Presently there were sounds of shouting inside, then gunfire. More Partisans, Barak among them, left the bushes and bolted through the open doorway before it could be shut against them, while the remaining troops took advantage of the opportunity of surprise. They overcame the Russians with some trouble, then again took up their defensive positions.

Another signal was given. The black van returned, but this time it quickly climbed the curb and stopped behind the building where it could not be seen from the street. The doors of the truck opened and in a few minutes the Partisans emerged from the basement and climbed into the van. They carried their prisoner carefully. He was alive but weak from beatings and lack of food and water.

Barak took a count of his men. Two were not among them. This rescue had cost their lives. The black van fled into the night, unseen and unopposed. Their attack was so sudden and well-planned that officials surveying the opened cells and dead bodies that met their gaze the next morning blamed it on Ukrainian espionage.

---

[90] "Save us! Save us!"
[91] Beer

And the truth will come forth like voices from out of the dust, teaching eternal life, bringing Salvation unto those who will hear.

22 — Kalyna, the Guilder Rose[92]

The date was August 21, 1985. Ester, fallen asleep against a mausoleum door, awoke to the sound of her husband's voice. Avram had been negotiating with the *rabbi* of Berdichev's largest synagogue.

"Ester, Ester. I have good news."

The woman rose to her feet to greet her husband. Though many years had passed, Avram was as handsome to her now as at their first meeting so long ago. They embraced happily and he shared the *rabbi's* words with her.

"Have you found them yet?" he asked her.

"No, Avram, but I know they are here. Help me to dig."

Together they went carefully to work with shovels around Reb Levi Yitzhak's *ohel*,[93] making sure no other plot was disturbed. After an hour had passed their shovels hit an object a few feet from where Barak had placed the marker. They dug further. Eventually, a broad, makeshift metal box was retrieved. It was opened slowly and with great care. Rags and blankets protected the large object inside. When these were removed, the beautiful mahogany posts shone through, still retaining their deep, clear polish. Even the elegant black Hebrew lettering of the papyrus scrolls was revealed to be in pristine condition.

"It's all here, Avram, just as Papa told me. The *Torah* scrolls. Oh, how beautiful they are after all this time!"

"Yes, Ester, and they have a new home. Hopefully they will never again be disturbed."

With love and joy the *Torah* scrolls that Reb Levi and Zych long ago consigned to the earth were lifted from their bier and laid upon a small cart. They were transferred to a van and taken to the synagogue where the young *rabbi* and his *chazzen* waited. Much fanfare greeted them at the synagogue. The sound of a rusty mouth harp filled the air. Barak had just arrived from his council meeting. When he saw the wrapped scrolls finally excavated, he grabbed Ester. They danced a Jewish *hora* (folk dance) in the lobby of the synagogue, to the delight of everyone.

A crowd of worshippers was also there to witness the rare

event. More than a few survivors of the *shoah* in 1941 remembered the Levi family and gave their heartfelt testimonies to his unfailing goodness and merciful ways.

Ester took the opportunity to ask if anyone in the congregation remembered a kind young German soldier in charge of the motor transport team during the first days of the *Wehrmacht* and *SS* invasion of Berdichev.

"He told me his captain put him on the shooting squad when regular soldiers were sent to the city's perimeters. He was to fill in for troops who refused to shoot the prisoners. He also told me he was part-Jewish, his father's line. I know he was probably indistinguishable from the other German soldiers," Ester said. "but he saved me at great risk to himself, and I have never been able to thank him. I've always wondered if he saved other lives as well. I think his name was Gerhardt."

From the back of the room a voice spoke.

"Mrs. Weitzmann, I think I knew of the young man you seek."

A middle-age woman stepped forward to shake Ester's hand. Ester did not know her, but she related that the young officer had saved her life, also.

"It happened in the pits the German soldiers dug on Brodskii Street. They were shooting hundreds, execution style. I was only 10 years old. I had already been shot and would have died right then if he'd not heard my cries for help. He reached into the trench, grabbed my arms and pulled me from my death. I recall that his eyes were filled with compassion, but he seemed to have gone berserk."

Ester felt tears coming to her eyes. She felt that he had not survived the war.

"Do you know what happened to him?"

The woman hesitated. Then, in an emotion-filled voice she related Gerhardt's sad fate.

"My father and I managed to escape Berdichev. He found out that soldier's real name and rank from another German. It seems that young man saved other lives as well. His name became legend in Berdichev for a time, and among the *Wehrmacht*. Later, when the danger had passed, I tracked down his mother and wrote to her. She still lived in Berlin. I thanked her for her son's sacrifice. I never received an answer but my letter was not returned. I hope she received it and that she knows how grateful we all are for Gerhardt Israel Hirsch."

When she had finished there was a long silence. Avram took his wife's arm and led her slowly to the pulpit. The congregation took their seats.

Barak and Avram happily presented the scrolls to the synagogue. Ester then addressed the gathering.

"I am so sorry to hear of the fate of Gerhardt Israel Hirsch. He was a brave man. He gave his life for others and at the last he embraced his Jewish heritage. I know that we all are grateful to him for his sacrifice and we thank G-d in Heaven for that wonderful gift. Gerhardt, I cannot thank you personally, but I pray you can hear me and that you will accept our eternal gratitude for your selfless acts of courage.

"And now I wish to speak of my Papa, the Reb Moshe Dovid ben-Levi. He was a great man. He loved the *Chasidim* and he loved G-d. He gave his life in the service of others, perishing alongside his wife and our mother. She stood faithfully by him throughout many years of toil and uncertainty. When Hitler's soldiers rampaged through Berdichev, my father managed to preserve these beautiful *Torah* scrolls by hiding them near the sacred tomb of the Berdichever Rabbi Levi Yitzhak. His dearest hope was that they would one day be retrieved and restored to their place of honor in a synagogue.

"Today that dream becomes reality. I wish my parents could be with us, but I know that they look upon us in love and that they are celebrating with us this joyful day. The Holocaust is long over, but intolerance and hatred still curse the world with sorrow. Let the words of *Torah* remind us of our duty to fill the earth with love and peace for all people and let these scrolls have their place of honor in this sacred synagogue. Like the lovely, long-lasting and perennial guilder rose that signifies the hardy Russian people, let us pray that we will persevere throughout all hardship and triumph over all our enemies, even death itself."

The congregation rose in appreciation and there were many more that day who had waited and watched beyond the veil of earth to see their precious *Torah* come home.

THE END

---

[92] A legend: The rose that never dies symbolizes a lasting Ukraine. Used here to connote a lasting Judaic influence in Berdichev
[93] Burial house

Journal of the Dead — Tevye Rabinowitz

My name is Tevye Rabinowitz. It is an old Russian name from the 1700's when my grandfather and great grandfather were alive and prosperous in the metals trade. They made bracelets and jewelry of all kinds in the *shtetls*. They were brave pioneers when our people were confined away.

It was a dark day that September 1941. A German soldier came forth and ordered me out of my home. My wife and daughters were there, as well. He ordered them to walk behind me at the tip of his bayonet or his knife, I don't remember now. This was afternoon of a foggy day. It was early. His knife was raised, his rifle pointed behind our backs. We marched before him up the main street from the ghetto, where we were kept that last few days before our deaths. When we reached the pits at the end of Brodskii Street he stopped us and lined us up. Another soldier came to us and made sure we did not escape. They would have shot us one way or the other. I would have run but my wife was there, and my children, and I did not want to desert them in any case.

We were barbers. My brothers and I were in the trades. We were very successful in Berdichev and accomplished a great deal there. We cut the heads of many of the town's most prosperous Jews. We were well thought of by everyone. Our lives were full; we went to synagogue, we observed the Sabbath, we knew the *Mashiach* would one day come. I was 36 when my head was blown off. My wife was 35 and my daughters 11 and 13. My wife's name was Anatevka. She was from an old Russian dynastic family. She was not Jewish but she participated with me. We raised our children as Jews.

Then they lined us up before the pits. I was made to bow to my knees. A rifle butt pushed against my head. I shouted "Oh my G-d, save me, save my wife", but I was immediately shot in the neck and fell to the ground, into the pit on top of many bodies below me. I heard in my death throes the shots and screams of my wife and daughters. They also died with me. We felt only silence, we knew no pain. We were quiet. And then the light came that lifted up our souls, our very spirits from our lifeless bodies. We rose with the light and are safe now and together awaiting the arraignment of these torturers of the *Nazi* regime. They will be made to pay for taking our young lives so brutally.

I would tell the mortals living to be stout of spirit and mind. I would tell them to hold on to their lives, to magnify their responsibilities in life, to come forth clean and happy to be in G-d's great care. I would tell them not to worry because all will work out at the end. Righteousness will prevail. The Lord is good. He is magnificent and He will come and bring joy to the millions who await his presence. Jerusalem will once again prosper in peace. I would tell everyone to have faith.

Epilogue — A Ukrainian Folk Tale

In the perilous days of Lenin and Trotsky, a grandfather told this story to his family to give them faith during the purges and famines of the time.

There was in Berdichev a middle-aged peasant named Zeidl the Faithful. He worked so hard on his few acres of farm that often he would go to bed exhausted. One night Zeidl woke suddenly to find his room filled with light. *HaShem's* angel appeared to him saying that G-d had a work for him to do. The angel took Zeidl the Faithful outside his hovel and showed him a large rock a short distance away. G-d's messenger explained that Zeidl was to push against this rock with all his might.

Zeidl, afraid of offending an angel, much less *HaShem*, agreed. Next day he went to the rock and began to push. This he did day after day and for many years thereafter. He set his shoulders squarely against the cold, massive surface of the unmoving rock, pushing with all of his might. But it would not move.

Each night Zeidl returned to his hovel sore and worn out, feeling that his whole day had been spent in vain. Zeidl was becoming discouraged. One day an ugly visitor dressed in a black veil saw Zeidl pushing at the rock.

"You have been pushing against this rock for years, Zeidl. Why bother? It isn't going to budge. You are an old man now, and a failure."

"No, no," said Zeidl. " I must not give up. I promised an angel of G-d I would push against this rock with all my might."

"Foolish Zeidl," said the man in black. "Just do the minimum, then. What is the point of wearing yourself out? How can you possibly succeed?"

This advice sounded good to weary Zeidl but he decided to take the problem to *HaShem*.

"Lord," he said, "I have labored long and hard in your service, putting all my strength to do that which you have asked. Yet, after all this time, I have not even budged that rock. What is wrong? Why am I failing?"

HaShem responded with compassion for Zeidl.

"My dear son, when I asked you to serve Me and you accepted, I told you that your task was to push against the rock with all of your strength, which you have done. Never once did I mention to you that I expected you to move it. Your task was to push. And now you come to Me with your strength spent, thinking that you have failed. But, is that really so?

"Look at yourself. Your arms are strong and muscled, your back sinewy and brown; your hands are callused from constant pressure, your legs have become massive and hard. Through opposition you have grown much, and your abilities now surpass that which you used to have.

"True, you haven't moved the rock, Zeidl. But your calling was only to be obedient; to push and to exercise your faith and trust in My wisdom. That you have done. Now, my friend, step back, for *I* will move the rock."

"Little ones," said Grandpa. "Let us exercise the faith that moves mountains, but know that G-d is the Mover."

APPENDICES

Appendix I

Post-Nazi Berdichev

An excerpt from Vasily Grossman's "Black Book" containing documentary evidence of Nazi crimes committed against the Jews in Soviet territory (and whose mother was one of the victims), is helpful in understanding the profundity of the tragedy of this day and others during the Nazi occupation of Berdichev:

"The monstrous slaughter of the innocent and the helpless, this spilling of blood continued the entire day. The pits were filled with blood since the clayey soil could no longer absorb any more, and the blood spilled over the edges, forming enormous puddles and flowing in rivulets into low-lying areas. When the wounded fell into the pits, they did not die from the SS bullets, but by drowning in the blood that filled the pits. The screams of those being murdered hung in the air the entire day. Peasants from nearby farms fled their fields so as not to hear wails of suffering unendurable to the human heart. All day people moved in endless columns past the place of execution, where they could see their own mothers and children standing at the edge of the pit they themselves were fated to approach in an hour or two. All day the air rang with farewells:

"Good-bye! Good-bye! We'll soon meet again!" people shouted from the highway.

'Farewell!' answered those who were already standing at the edge of the pit."

The Wehrmacht did not remain long in Berdichev after securing its capture on July 17, 1941. According to reports, late in August the 11th Panzer Division had moved temporarily east and north to Zhitomir. Engaged there in new combat with the Red Army they suffered casualties of 50 percent of its officers, 500 soldiers and sergeants, and severe losses in equipment. However, they managed to murder 500 people while there, 100 more in Dubno and another 500 in Poltava.[94]

By September 3rd the 11th Panzers, now rested, returned to Berdichev temporarily. Morale had become a problem for many of the soldiers. This is why the SS independently decided to swiftly and quietly massacre the remaining Jewish population of Berdichev themselves. Their goal was to shoot 10,000 people in one day. This was accomplished on September 5th. The second portion of their plan was to quickly murder the remaining Jews in Berdichev's ghetto. Plans for the 11th Panzer's "vacation" were quickly made: The war-weary troops were to be billeted for several days in Zhitomir, "resting" and being entertained with *Wehrmacht* propaganda films.

In Berdichev ten days later, the *Polizei* secretly rounded up the remaining Jews and locked them in hangars of the nearby military airport, to be shot the following morning.

Within two days' time, between September 14th–16th, the German SS units quickly liquidated the entire Jewish ghetto of Berdichev, approximately 18,640 souls. Those they eliminated were primarily the aged and sick, mothers with small children, and infants.

"The killers of Berdichev, the men of *Sonderkommando* 4a, went on to commit further atrocities. Scarcely two weeks later, on September 29th . . . they shot 33,771 Jewish men, women, and children in the ravine of Babi Yar, at that time outside the city proper . . . Berdichev had clearly served as a model for the SS in carrying out large-scale massacres by shooting[95]."

On January 5, 1944 the Red Army retook what was left of Berdichev. They were greeted favorably by the city's remaining residents who had discovered that the German menace was infinitely worse than their own Russian army. Berdichev was the site of the first big *Aktion* in Ukraine and the first of its size in the Holocaust of Ukraine.

A monument has been erected there to the victims. It reads:

Near this site in September 1941
Hitlerite invaders brutally tortured
And shot to death 18,640 peaceful Soviet citizens.
May the memory of these victims of Fascism live forever.

---

[94] The Bones of Berdichev, pp. 6-7
[95] Op cit. p. 30

The Jewish Memorial at Babi Yar, Kiyev, Ukraine (from the website of Ellen Shindelman Kowitt, www.grapevine.org/ menorah.jpg

Appendix II

Leaders: A Listing

Ukraine

Yisrael ben Eliezer (1698? – 1760) was born in Okop, a small village in the Ukraine on the Polish Russian border (Podolia). His parents, Eliezer and Sarah, were quite old when he was born and they passed away when he was a still a child. He became a teacher's assistant, then a caretaker in the local synagogue. He studied long and deeply, eventually becoming a scholar of the entire body of Jewish knowledge. But always he maintained a simplicity and humility that endeared him to everyone he met. He married but soon became a widower. Young Yisrael had an unusually strong emotional relationship with God. This relationship was perhaps the defining characteristic of the religious approach he would ultimately develop. Later in life he married again, and at age 36, in the year 1734 Yisrael moved to Talust and became publically a holy man, or rabbi.

Ben Eliezer was founder of what is possibly the single most important religious movement in Jewish history, *Chassidus* (piety). There are many legends surrounding his life. One is that his father's last words to his son were *"Fear nothing other than God."*

Rabbi Yisrael's fame spread rapidly. Many important scholars became his disciples. It was during this period that the movement, which would eventually be known as *Chassidus* began. He was called *"Baal ShemTov"* (Master of the Good Name) and his teachings were largely based upon mystical spiritual works. His approach made the benefits of these teachings accessible even to the simplest Jew. He emphasized the profound importance and significance of prayer, love of God and love of one's fellow Jews. His techniques emphasized dance and the repetition of Hebrew letters or words at increasing speed and volume as a means to spiritual joyfulness. He taught that even if one was not blessed with the ability or opportunity to be a *Torah* scholar, one could still reach great spiritual heights through these channels. He believed every Jew to be a limb of the Divine Presence.

The *Baal Shem Tov* never wrote his teachings down. They have been passed on through the writings of his disciples. The elements of his work, however, continue to be significant force in the Jewish world today.

America

Woodrow Wilson (1856 - 1924) Twenty-eighth U.S. president: 1913 - 1921. He was nominated for president at the 1912 Democratic Convention and campaigned on a program called the New Freedom, which stressed individualism and states' rights. His presidency is responsible for the numerous far-reaching laws, including the creation of the Federal Trade Commission, the Federal Reserve Act and the prohibition against child labor.

In April 1917, believing the United States could not maintain neutrality, Wilson asked Congress for a declaration of war on Germany. It was granted. In 1918 he presented his Fourteen Points, clearly delineating America's war aims and establishing "a general association of nations . . . affording mutual guarantees of political independence and territorial integrity to great and small states alike."

A key element: ". . . evacuation of all Russian territory and such a settlement of all questions affecting Russia as will secure the best and freest cooperation of the other nations of the world in obtaining for her an unhampered and unembarrassed opportunity for the independent determination of her own political development and national policy and assure her of a sincere welcome into the society of free nations under institutions of her own choosing . . . "

President Wilson had been genuinely stunned by the savagery of the Great War. He could not understand how an advanced civilization could have reduced itself so that it had created so much devastation. In America there was a growing desire for the government to adopt a policy of isolation and leave Europe to its own devices. In failing health, Wilson wanted America to concentrate on itself and, despite developing the idea of a League of Nations, he wanted an American input into Europe to be kept to a minimum. He believed that Germany should be punished but in a way that would lead to European reconciliation as opposed to revenge. He was one of the key planners and players in the making and presenting of the Treaty of Versailles of 1919.

Franklin Delano Roosevelt (1882-1945). Democratic president of the U.S. 1932–1945, and only president to serve four consecutive terms. His political career included election to the New York Senate in 1910, Assistant Secretary of the Navy, and Governor of New York, in 1928.

Roosevelt had pledged the United States to the "good neighbor" policy, transforming the Monroe Doctrine from a unilateral American manifesto into arrangements for mutual action against aggressors. He also sought through neutrality legislation to keep the United States out of the war in Europe, yet at the same time to strengthen nations threatened or attacked. When France fell and England came under siege in 1940, he began to send Great Britain all possible aid short of actual military involvement.

When the Japanese attacked Pearl Harbor on December 7, 1941, Roosevelt directed organization of the Nation's manpower and resources for global war. In July 1941 Roosevelt and Churchill met for the first time in Argentia Bay, off Newfoundland, to issue a joint declaration on the purposes of the war against Fascism. Just as Wilson's Fourteen Points delineated the first war, so the Atlantic Charter provided the criteria for the second. The Soviet Union, which had been attacked by Germany a month earlier, was to sign the charter. But Joseph Stalin did not approve the notion that nations would abandon reliance upon military alliances and spheres of influence in favor of a "one world" government. Churchill did not like that policy, either.

Key points of the Atlantic Charter

The President of the United States of America and the Prime Minister, Mr. Churchill, representing His Majesty's Government in the United Kingdom, being met together, deem it right to make known certain common principles in the national policies of their respective countries on which they base their hopes for a better future for the world.

. . . they desire to see no territorial changes that do not accord with the freely expressed wishes of the peoples concerned;

. . . they respect the right of all peoples to choose the form of government

under which they will live; and they wish to see sovereign rights and self government restored to those who have been forcibly deprived of them;

   . . . they will endeavor, with due respect for their existing obligations, to
further the enjoyment by all States, great or small, victor or vanquished, of access, on equal terms, to the trade and to the raw materials of the world which are
needed for their economic prosperity;

   . . . after the final destruction of the Nazi tyranny, they hope to see established a peace which will afford to all nations the means of dwelling in safety
within their own boundaries, and which will afford assurance that all the men in all
the lands may live out their lives in freedom from fear and want;

   . . . they believe that all of the nations of the world, for realistic as well as
spiritual reasons must come to the abandonment of the use of force. Since no
future peace can be maintained if land, sea or air armaments continue to be
employed by nations which threaten, or may threaten, aggression outside of
their frontiers, they believe, pending the establishment of a wider and permanent
system of general security, that the disarmament of such nations is essential.

~

Germany

   Frederick I (1152-1190) Frederich, Duke of Swabia, also called Frederich
Barbarossa (Redbeard) was one of the most important German kings of the Cru-
sades. He took an empire that was shaky and put it on solid ground. He did so at
the price of giving away many rights to the German princes, and the wisdom of
that has been much debated by historians, but at the time and for centuries after-
ward, he was regarded as one of the greatest of monarchs. He challenged papal
authority and sought to establish German predominance in western Europe. He
engaged in a long struggle with the cities of northern Italy (1154–83), sending
six major expeditions southward. He died while on the Third Crusade to the Holy
Land.

   Crowned emperor in 1154, Frederick expanded his personal holdings by
marrying the Duchess of Burgundy, bringing that wealthy land into his realm. His
ally, Pope Adrian IV, died in 1159 and was replaced by Alexander III, who immediately allied with Milan to oppose the Emperor. But Frederick was too strong.
He captured Milan in 1162, and seemed to be at the height of his power. With
Germany, Burgundy and Italy under his control, much of Charlemagne's empire
was again in one pair of hands. Eventually, political feuds developed with Italian
factions, imperial and papal.

   Barbarossa had a strong feeling for law and imperial prestige. His steadfast
opposition to the popes and to Henry the Lion made him the symbol of German
unity in the romantic glorification of the 19th century. Chivalry gave Barbarossa's
time a special stamp. He expressed his enthusiasm for knighthood as the ideal
way of life at the festival of Pentecost at Mainz in 1184, where he dubbed his
sons knights.

   In 1190 the Emperor drowned while trying to cross the Saleph River.
Germany developed into a system of territorial states after Barbarossa's death,
while France developed during the time of Philip II Augustus into a centralized
monarchial state.

   Operation Barbarossa (*Unternehemen Barbarossa*) was the German
code name for Nazi Germany's invasion of the Soviet Union during World War

II, which began June 22, 1941. It was to be the turning point for the fortunes of Hitler's *Third Reich*, in that the failure of Operation Barbarossa arguably resulted in the eventual overall defeat of Nazi Germany. The Eastern Front which was opened by Operation Barbarossa would become the biggest theatre of war in World War II, with some of the largest and most brutal battles, terrible loss of life, and miserable conditions for Russians and Germans alike. The operation was named after the emperor Frederick I of the German "holy empire".

Otto von Bismarck (1815-1898) Considered the founder of the German Empire. For nearly three decades he shaped the fortunes of Germany, from 1862 to 1873 as prime minister of Prussia and from 1871 to 1890 as Germany's first Chancellor of the German empire. Many Germans linked his creation of the new political entity with the mythical grandeur of the Holy Roman Empire and called his empire the *Second Reich*. Bismarck served as ambassador to Russia and later, France. As prime minister of Prussia he devoted himself to the task of unit-ing Germany. In the war of 1866 he succeeded in defeating Austria and excluding it altogether from Germany. Also the Franco-German War (1870—71) ended with Prussian success.

Bismarck, as Imperial Chancellor, decided upon policy outlines and proposed the appointment and dismissal of state secretaries who were in turn responsible for the administration of the ministries of the *Reich*. He created a *Bundestaat*, a kind of federal state where each state retained its separate identity and control over its own civil affairs. He effectively set about to unify Germany and to make the many city-states of the empire into the strongest economic power in Europe.

Karl (Heinrich) Marx (1818-1883) A German revolutionary leader, social philosopher and political economist. Founder of modern socialism. A Jew without any Jewish education, Marx coined the phrase "religion is the opium of the people". Marx was atheistic. He came from a long line of rabbis on both sides of his family and his father had agreed to baptism as a Protestant so that he would not lose his job as one of the most respected lawyers in Trier.

Marx believed in a socialist revolution where control would be only in the hands of elite intelligentsia. He wrote The Communist Manifesto in 1848, an inci-sive indictment and analysis of capitalism. The proletariat, the people of the land, were to be merely the means, whose duty was to obey [See Johnson, *A History of the Jews*]. He is without a doubt the most influential socialist thinker to emerge in the 19th century. Every significant socialist leader of both Germany and Rus-sia have adopted and adapted his basic social and economic theories of people versus the state. Although he was largely ignored by scholars in his own lifetime, his social, economic and political ideas gained rapid acceptance in the socialist movement after his death.

Adolf Hitler (1889-1945) Nazi dictator of Germany 1933-1945. Born in Austria. His grandmother, Maria Anna Schickelgruber worked as a domestic servant outside her village, returning pregnant and unmarried. Her son, Alois Hiedler, never knew his father and his birth was recorded as illegitimate. Several men eventually were considered as having fathered the child. Later, on church records the name Hiedler was recorded as Hitler and it stuck. Alois' third wife, Klara, was mother to Adolf. He was a sickly child. Severely disciplined by his father, a civil servant, Adolf did badly in school, but fancied himself an artist. He created numerous street scenes and architectural paintings. He hated hard work, preferring to imagine himself a leader who demanded unqualified subservience from his fellows. His father's death in 1903 left the family well provided for, but his mother's death four years later left Adolf, then 19, prostrate with grief and without means. Homeless and destitute, Adolf tried to sell his artwork but with little success. He was orphaned.

Choosing to leave Austria for Munich, Germany, Adolf ignored the law requiring him to join Austria's military. He instead was accepted into the 16th Bavarian Reserve Infantry Regiment in 1914. Adolf was exultant, though now an expatriate. In Germany he found his homeland. He was made a regimental courier and eventually decorated with two Iron Crosses. These eventually lent authenticity to his future career as politician, soldier, dictator. Following the war, he joined the German Workers' Party in Munich (1919). In 1920 he became head of propaganda for the renamed National Socialists, or Nazi Party, and in 1921 he was elected the party leader. He set out to create a mass movement, using unrelenting propaganda.

Hitler's philosophy emerged slowly. In his virulent autobiography, *Mein Kampf* (*My Struggle*) he wrote of the inequality between races as part of the natural order, exalting the "Aryan race" while propounding anti-Semitism, anti-communism, and extreme German nationalism. Hitler ran for president in 1932 and lost, but he entered into intrigues to gain legitimate power and in 1933 Paul von Hindenburg invited him to be chancellor. Adopting the title of *Fuhrer* ("Leader"), he suppressed opposition with assistance from Heinrich Himmler and Joseph Goebbels.

Hitler also began to enact anti-Jewish measures leading to the Holocaust. His aggressive foreign policy led to the signing of the Munich agreement. He became allied with Benito Mussolini in the Rome-Berlin Axis. In the *Reichstag* elections of 1930 the Nazis became the country's second-largest party, and in 1932 the largest. The German-Soviet Nonaggression Pact (1939) enabled him to invade Poland, precipitating World War II. As defeat grew imminent in 1945, he married Eva Braun in an underground bunker in Berlin, and the next day they committed suicide. [Encyclopedia Britannica]

~

Russia

Vladimir Ilyich Lenin (1870 - 1924), also called Nicolai. Russian leader of the Communist Revolution of 1917 and premier of the USSR 1917 - 24. In 1893 he became active in a Marxist study group. He was a student of law, eventually founding the Fighting Alliance for the Liberation of the Working Class in the city of St. Petersburg. As a lawyer, Lenin became increasingly involved in radical politics and was often arrested. After completing a three-year term of Siberian exile he began his rise as the leading communist theorist, tactician and party but was deported to Siberia again, exiled from his homeland for 5 years in 1900. In 1905 he participated in the first attempted revolution in Russia between the Bolsheviks and the Mensheviks. In 1917 the February Revolution was a uniting of the bourgeoisie and the working class of Russia to dethrone the *tsar*. In a third attempt in

1918, Lenin assumed leadership of the Soviet government.

Lenin had a scholar's habits and a general's tactical instincts, yet he was a bookish man. He introduced to the 20th century the practice of taking an all-embracing ideology and imposing it on an entire society rapidly and mercilessly, creating a regime that erased politics, historical memory and opposition.

"The incomprehensibility of Lenin is precisely this all-consuming intellectuality — the fact that from his calculations, from his neat pen flowed seas of blood, whereas by nature this was not an evil person," writes Andrei Sinyavsky, one of the key dissidents of the 1960s.

The Russian Social Democratic Labour Party (R.S.D.L.P), which created the Bolsheviki and Mensheviki parties. During the 1905-07 revolution the Mensheviks opposed the working class and peasantry who were in open revolt. They believed that Socialism should only be achieved firstly through a bourgeois revolution (via reformism); following this revolution, they felt the working class and peasantry would then be able to revolt against the bourgeois, and establish Socialism.

In 1905 Trotsky became chairman of the short-lived St. Petersburg Soviet and was arrested during its last meeting. While in prison, he developed his theory of permanent revolution; he declared that in Russia a bourgeois and a socialist revolution would be combined and that a proletarian (the people) revolution would then spread throughout the world. His belief in a world revolution came into conflict with Stalin's plans for "socialism in one country". Trotsky took part with Lenin in the unsuccessful Bolshevik uprising. He was arrested and exiled numerous times in his life.

In 1929 Trotsky was expelled from the Communist Party by the Stalinist faction of the Party and then deported from the USSR. In 1938 he helped found the Fourth International, the World Party of Socialist Revolution. He was murdered by a Stalinist assassin at his home in exile, in Mexico.

Joseph Stalin (1879-1953) born Iosif Vissarionovich Dzhugashvili in Georgia, USSR. Soviet premier 1941-1953 and general secretary of the Communist Party of the USSR 1922-53. Stalin (the name means "man of steel") was deeply anti-Semitic. Once he took power, the pressure on the Jews increased. By the end of the 1920's he had destroyed or emasculated all forms of specifically Jewish activity. He helped to convert communism in the USSR from an egalitarian (having equal political, social and economic rights) revolutionary movement into an authoritarian, bureaucratic (government officialism, red tape) governmental system. He helped to turn Russia into a great industrial nation, to defeat Hitler in World War II and after the war to establish Communist regimes throughout eastern Europe. At the same time, however, he institutionalized terror and was responsible for the death and deprivation of millions of people.

One of the towering figures in world politics in his time, he still remains one of the least known primarily because of the traditional secrecy surrounding Soviet leaders. His personality and rule were highly controversial. In 1912, Dzhugashvili, having escaped from exile, arrived in St. Petersburg and helped set up *Pravda*, the new newspaper of the Bolsheviks.

Stalin and his men at the end of 1928 struck out on a set of policies designed to turn backward Russia into a modern state. Stalin launched forced industrialization and collectivization. The momentous series of economic and social measures included the establishment of crude and unrealistic five-year national economic plans, the deportation and execution of hundreds of thousands of the better-off peasants (*kulaks*) and the forced entrance of the rest into state-controlled collective farms. He was also instrumental in the nationalization of all industry and commerce and the regulation and manipulation of all financial instruments for capital accumulation by the government regardless of the people's impoverishment, and the centralization of all social activity. Despite the death of millions from famine and goods shortages that these measures caused, Stalin pursued the program relentlessly, meeting resistance and criticism with mass deportations and executions.

In August 1939, he concluded a bilateral nonaggression treaty with Hitler. When the German armies attacked the USSR in June 1941, Stalin, after suffering a brief nervous collapse, personally took command of the Soviet armed forces. With the help of a small defense committee (war cabinet), he made all major military, political, and diplomatic decisions throughout the war. He pursued victory with increasing skill, determination, and courage by staying on in the *Kremlin* when Hitler's armies stood at the gates of Moscow. He ordered a fantastic shifting of industrial plants from European Russia to the east, arranged for lend-lease from the Western powers, selected more and more first-rate military commanders and developed increasingly effective military strategy including the remarkable counteroffensives at Moscow, Stalingrad, and Kursk. He undergirded the strength and morale of his people by fostering their traditional religious and patriotic sentiments and conducting adroitly the complicated diplomacy from the Teheran conference to Potsdam.

Appendix III

Treaty of Versailles

On June 28,1919, after months of argument and negotiation amongst the so-called "Big Three", the Allied powers presented the Treaty of Versailles to Germany for signature. The Treaty of Versailles was the peace settlement signed after World War One had ended in 1918 in the shadow of the Russian Revolution and other events in Russia. The three most important The "Big Three" were **David Lloyd George** of Britain, **Georges Clemenceau** of France and **Woodrow Wilson** of America.

The key territorial and political clauses listed below brought shame upon Germany but also promoted its overwhelming desire to create an invincible nation from the ashes of World War I. The stage was being set for Hitler's Third Reich.

Article 51. The territories which were ceded to Germany in accordance with the Preliminaries of Peace signed at Versailles on February 26, 1871, and the Treaty of Frankfort of May 10, 1871, are restored to French sovereignty as from the date of the Armistice of November 11, 1918.

Article 119. Germany renounces in favor of the Principal Allied and Associated Powers all her rights and titles over her overseas possessions.

Article 159. The German military forces shall be demobilized and reduced as prescribed hereinafter.

Article 231. The Allied and Associated Governments affirm and Germany accepts the responsibility of Germany and her allies for causing all the loss and damage to which the Allied and Associated Governments and their nationals have been subjected as a consequence of the war imposed upon them by the aggression of Germany and her allies.

The following lands were taken away from Germany:
- Alsace-Lorraine (given to France)
- Eupen and Malmedy (given to Belgium)
- Northern Schleswig (given to Denmark)
- Hultschin (given to Czechoslovakia)
- West Prussia, Posen and Upper Silesia (given to Poland)

The Saar, Danzig and Memel were put under the control of the League of Nations and the people of these regions would be allowed to vote to stay in Germany or not in a future referendum. The League of Nations also took control of Germany's overseas colonies.

Germany had to return to Russia land taken in the Treaty of Brest-Litovsk. Some of this land was made into new states: Estonia, Lithuania and Latvia. An enlarged Poland also received some of this land.

Military

Germany's army was reduced to 100,000 men; the army was not allowed tanks. She was not allowed an air force. She was allowed only six capital naval ships and no submarines. The west of the Rhineland and 50 km. east of the River Rhine was made into a demilitarized zone (DMZ). No German soldier or weapon was allowed into this zone. The Allies were to keep an army of occupation on the west bank of the Rhine for 15 years.

Financial

The loss of vital industrial territory would be a severe blow to any attempts by Germany to rebuild her economy. Not having access to coal from the Saar region and Upper Silesia in particular was a vital economic loss. Combined with the financial penalties linked to reparations, it seemed clear to Germany that the Allies wanted nothing else but to bankrupt her.

Germany was also forbidden to unite with Austria to form one super state, in an attempt to keep her economic potential to a minimum.

General

Germany had to admit full responsibility for starting the war. This was Clause 231 — the infamous "War Guilt Clause".

Germany, as she was responsible for starting the war as stated in clause 231, was, therefore responsible for all the war damage caused by the First World War. Therefore, she had to pay reparations, the bulk of which would go to France and Belgium to pay for the damage done to the infrastructure of both countries by the war.

Payment could be in kind or cash. The figure was not set at Versailles — it was to be determined later. The Germans were told to write a blank check that the Allies would cash when it suited them. The figure was eventually put at £6,600 million - a huge sum of money well beyond Germany's ability to pay.

Through the Treaty the League of Nations was set up to keep world peace.

~~~

After agreeing to the Armistice in November 1918, the Germans had been convinced they would be consulted by the Allies on the contents of the Treaty. This did not happen and the Germans were in no position to continue the war because her army had all but disintegrated. Though this lack of consultation angered them, there was nothing they could do about it. Therefore, the first time the German representatives saw the terms of the Treaty was just weeks before they were due to sign it in the Hall of Mirrors at the Palace of Versailles.

There was anger throughout Germany when the terms were made public. Germans reacted with shock and dismay on May 7 when the Allies presented their draft of the Treaty, which became known as a *Diktat* — as it was being forced on them and the Germans had no choice but to sign it. Many in Germany did not want the Treaty signed, but the representatives there knew that they had no choice as German was incapable of restarting the war again. In one last gesture of defiance, the captured German naval force held at Scapa Flow (north of Scotland) scuttled (deliberately sank) itself.

Germany was given two choices:
1) Sign the Treaty or
2) Be invaded by the Allies.

They signed the Treaty. In reality they had no choice. It left a mood of deep resentment throughout Germany because it was felt that as a nation Germany had been unfairly treated. Above all else, Germany hated the clause blaming her for the cause of the war and the resultant financial penalties the Treaty was bound to impose on Germany. Those who signed it became known as the "November Criminals". Many German citizens felt that they were being punished for the mistakes of the German government in August 1914 because it was the government that had declared war, not the German people.

Appendix IV

Nazism

Nazism, also called Hitlerism, was and is the extreme form of a fascistic, totalitarian ideology which holds that all citizens within an entity are subject to their government in totality. Personal freedoms are strictly regulated by government agents. Dissent is not tolerated. Propaganda is a constant tool to keep the populace in line with the dictates of the state.

The amount of force perpetrated upon the citizens of Nazi Germany was far in excess of that dispensed by a police state. Adherents of Nazism held that the German nation and the purported "Aryan" race were superior to other races. Nazism has been outlawed in modern Germany, although remnants and revivalists, known as "Neo-Nazis," continue to operate in Germany and abroad.

Key elements of the Nationalist Socialist Program in Germany during the period from 1920 through 1945 were as follows:

1. Racism

Racism is the belief that racial heritage is the prime determinant of human ability and potential. Some races, therefore, are superior and inferior to others. This can refer not only to beliefs but to institutions and practices based not upon individual worth but upon cultural stereotypes. In Germany there were several separated races:

Imperial Germans: (Reichsdeutsche) German citizens living within Germany.

Volksdeutsche: (*Ethnic Germans*) is a historical term which arose in the early 20th century to apply for Germans living outside of the German Empire, often without German citizenship.

Ukrainians: These are a Slavic people of central-eastern Europe. From an anthropological point of view, Ukrainians are a mixture of the Alpic, Dinaric, Baltic and latter-day descendents of the Vikings and Norsemen, the Nordic races. These people originated in Northern Europe. The Nordic or Scandinavian countries are Denmark, Finland, Iceland, Norway and Sweden.

Goralenvolk: Polish highlanders. A minority of Poles from the Silesian and Pomeranian areas.

Poles: Poles are a western Slavic ethnic group primarily associated with Poland and the Polish language. There are around 38 million Poles in Poland as well as Polish minorities in the surrounding countries such as Germany, Lithuania, Ukraine, Belarus.

Jews: In modern parlance: followers of the Jewish faith and/or a child of a Jewish mother, thus hearkening from an ancient Semitic bloodline. Originally the word Jew denoted a descendent of biblical Judah, its inhabitants.

Hitler was a racial, religious and socio-economic Anti-Semite. He considered Jews to be subhuman (*Untermensch*). He also despised Gypsies, homosexuals, disabled and so called anti-socials, all of whom he considered unworthy of life due to their perceived deficiency and inferiority.

Hitler believed a nation to be the highest creation of a race. He thought that large nations were the creation of great races which developed cultures that naturally grew from races with "natural good health, and aggressive, intelligent, coura-geous traits." The weakest nations, Hitler said were those of impure or mongrel races, because they have divided, quarrelling, and therefore weak cultures.

2. Anti-Slavism

Belief in the superiority of the White, Germanic, Aryan or Nordic races. This movement existed throughout the WWII, parallel with anti-Semitism. It was directed against the people of Slavic origin, i.e. Poles, Serbs, Czechs, Slovaks, Ukrainians, etc. In his book, *Mein Kampf*, Hitler refers to them as "inferior", using the word '*Slav*' as '*slave*'. He thought that the peoples of this origin should 'remain' the slaves as they were throughout the centuries.

3. Euthanasia and Eugenics

Euthanasia (Greek, "*good death*") is the practice of killing in a painless or minimally painful way for merciful reasons, usually to end their suffering. Death is actively causing death, an assisted suicide in a wider sense of the term. *Eugenics* refers to the study and use of selective breeding (of animals or humans) to improve a species over generations, specifically in regards to hereditary features.

4. Anti-Marxism, Anti-Bolshevism, Anti-Communism

These terms refer to the rejection of the governing principles of these ide-ologies in favor of another system of government and propaganda.

5. The Leader Principle. (*Führerprinzip*)

Unquestioned and absolute belief in the leader, who must have responsibil-ity up the ranks, and authority down the ranks.

6. Social Darwinism

A social theory of natural selection whereas weak societies give way to strong societies and/or weak ideas give way to strong ideas.This theory seeks to draw an association between Darwin's theory of evolution by natural selection and the development of societies. The assumption here is that the existence of natural processes can be extended from biological systems to social systems. The red and black colors in the Nazi flag represented the "blood and soil" of Germany.

6. Master race (German: *Herrenrasse, Herrenvolk*) is a concept in Nazi ideology, which holds that the Germanic and Nordic people represent an ideal and "pure race". It derives from nineteenth century racial theory, which posited a hierarchy of "races" placing African Bushmen and Australian Aborigines at the bottom of the hierarchy while white Europeans were at the top. This concept is similar to that of the White supremacy movement.

The originator of the Nazi version of the theory of the master race was Count Arthur de Gobineau, who argued that cultures degenerate when distinct races mix. It was believed at this time that southern European peoples were racially mixed with non-European moors from across the Mediterranean, while Northern Europeans remained pure. In Nazism the racial ideal was the blond blue-eyed Nordic individual.

Aryan race: Hitler's Nazi theory also claimed that the Aryans are a master race and therefore superior to all others. In fact, according to various sources, the Aryan race is a notion mentioned in Persian sources from 500 BC onwards. The word Iran itself means "the Land of Aryans" and Indians and Iranians consider their ethnicity and stock as being solely Aryan. From 1800's through about 1950, many ethnologists speculated that "white" people descended from some ancient race called Aryans. The postulated superiority of these people was said to make them born leaders, or a "master race". They were thought to be superior to others, and that given the purification of the German people from the races who were "polluting" it, a new Millenarian age of Aryan god-men would arrive.

In Nazi Germany, marriage of an "Aryan" with a *Untermensch* was forbidden. To maintain the purity of the Nordic master race eugenics was practiced. In order to eliminate "defective" citizens, the T-4 Euthanasia Program was administered by Karl Brandt to rid the country of the mentally retarded or those born with genetic deficiencies, as well as those deemed to be racially inferior. This is referred to as the Holocaust in popular culture.

Most modern geneticists no longer give credence to the eugenics and racial hygiene on which the hierarchical model of race is built. The Aryan race idea is a notion that is built upon myth.

Credits:

Wikipedia, the free encyclopedia, with source documentation:

Leftism Revisited, Erik von Kuehnelt-Leddihn, Regnery Gateway, Washington, D.C., 1990

Leftism Revisited, Liberty or Equality, von Kuehnelt-Leddihn, Christendom Press
Front Royal, VA, 1952, 1993,

The Logic of Evil, The Social Origins of the Nazi Party, 1925-1933, William Brustein,
Yale University Press, New Haven, CT, 1996.)

The Third Reich Series, 18 volumes, Editors of Time-Life Books, Inc. 1988

The Holocaust, Peter Neville, Cambridge Perspectives in History, Cambridge University
Press, 1999

Appendix V

1889
April: Adolf Hitler born in Austria.

1918
November: Weimar Republic proclaimed in Germany. World War I ends with Germany defeated.

1919
June: Germany signs Treaty of Versailles
September: Hitler joins German Workers' Party

1920
April: Hitler renamed the German Workers' Party as the National Socialist German Workers' Party, or Nazi Party. Penned the 25 Points.

1925
Autumn: Hitler's book "*Mein Kampf*" is published.

1929
April: Hitler Youth declared the only official youth group of the Nazi Party.

1933
January: Adolph Hitler is appointed Chancellor of Germany.
February: Nazis burn Reichstag building to create crisis atmosphere. Emergency powers granted to Hitler as a result of the Reichstag fire.
March: Nazis open Dachau concentration camp near Munich, to be followed by Buchenwald near Weimar in central Germany, Sachsenhausen near Berlin in northern Germany, and Ravensbrück for women. German Parliament passes Enabling Act giving Hitler dictatorial powers.
April 1: Nazis stage boycott of Jewish shops and businesses. Nazis issue a decree defining a non-Aryan as "anyone descended from non-Aryan, especially Jewish, parents or grandparents. One parent or grandparent classifies the descendant as non-Aryan...especially if one parent or grandparent was of the Jewish faith." The Gestapo is born, created by Hermann Göring in the German state of Prussia.
May: Burning of books in Berlin and throughout Germany.
July: Nazi Party is declared the only legal party in Germany; Also, Nazis pass Law to strip Jewish immigrants from Poland of their German citizenship. Nazis pass law allowing for forced sterilization of those found by a Hereditary Health Court to have genetic defects.
Sept: Nazis establish Reich Chamber of Culture, then exclude Jews from the Arts.- Nazis prohibit Jews from owning land.

October: Jews are prohibited from being newspaper editors.
November: Nazis pass a Law against Habitual and Dangerous Criminals, which allows beggars, the homeless, alcoholics and the unemployed to be sent to concentration camps.

1934
January: Jews are banned from the German Labor Front.
May: Jews not allowed national health insurance.
July: The SS (Schutzstaffel) is made an independent organization from the SA. Jews are prohibited from getting legal qualifications.
August: German President von Hindenburg dies. Hitler becomes Fuhrer. Hitler receives a 90 percent 'Yes' vote from German voters approving his new powers.

1935
May: Nazis ban Jews from serving in the military.
June: Nazis pass law allowing forced abortions on women to prevent them from passing on hereditary diseases.
August: Nazis force Jewish performers/artists to join Jewish Cultural Unions.
September: Nuremberg Race Laws against Jews decreed.

1936
February: The German Gestapo is placed above the law.
March: SS Deathshead division is established to guard concentration camps. Nazis occupy the Rhineland.
June: Heinrich Himmler is appointed chief of the German Police.

1937
January: Jews are banned from many professional occupations including teaching Germans, and from being accountants or dentists. They are also denied tax reductions and child allowances.
March: Nazi troops enter Austria, which has a population of 200,000 Jews, mainly living in Vienna. Hitler announces Anschluss (union) with Austria. After the Anschluss, the SS is placed in charge of Jewish affairs in Austria with Adolf Eichmann establishing an Office for Jewish Emigration in Vienna. Himmler then establishes Mauthausen concentration camp near Linz.
April: Nazis prohibit Aryan 'front-ownership' of Jewish businesses. Nazis order Jews to register wealth and property.
June: Nazis order Jewish owned businesses to register.
July: At Evian, France, the U.S. convenes a League of Nations conference with delegates from 32 countries to consider helping Jews fleeing Hitler, but results in inaction as no country will accept them. Nazis prohibited Jews from trading and providing a variety of specified commercial services. Nazis order Jews over age 15 to apply for identity cards from the police, to be shown on demand to any police officer. Jewish doctors prohibited by law from practicing medicine.
August: Nazis destroy the synagogue in Nuremberg. Nazis require Jewish women to add Sarah and men to add Israel to their names on all legal documents including passports.
September: Jews are prohibited from all legal practices.

October: Law requires Jewish passports to be stamped with a large red "J." Nazi troops occupy the Sudetenland. Nazis arrest 17,000 Jews of Polish nationality living in Germany, then expel them back to Poland which refuses them entry, leaving them in 'no-man's land' near the Polish border for several months.

November: Ernst vom Rath, third secretary in the German Embassy in Paris, is shot and mortally wounded by Herschel Grynszpan, the 17 year old son of one of the deported Polish Jews. Rath dies on November 9, precipitating *Kristallnacht* — The Night of Broken Glass. Nazis fine Jews one billion marks for damages related to *Kristallnacht.* Jewish pupils are expelled from all non-Jewish German schools.

December: Law for compulsory Aryanization of all Jewish businesses. Hermann Göring takes charge of resolving the "Jewish Question."

1939

January: Hitler threatens Jews during Reichstag speech.

February: Nazis force Jews to hand over all gold and silver items.

March: Nazi troops seize Czechoslovakia (Jewish pop. 350,000).

April: Slovakia passes its own version of the Nuremberg Laws. Jews lose rights as tenants and are relocated into Jewish houses.

May: The St. Louis, a ship crowded with 930 Jewish refugees, is turned away by Cuba, the United States and other countries and returns to Europe.

July: German Jews denied the right to hold government jobs. Adolf Eichmann is appointed director of the Prague Office of Jewish Emigration.

September: Nazis invade Poland (Jewish pop. 3.35 million, the largest in Europe). Beginning of *SS* activity in Poland. England and France declare war on Germany. Soviet troops invade eastern Poland. Heydrich issues instructions to SS Einsatzgruppen (special action squads) in Poland regarding treatment of Jews, stating they are to be gathered into ghettos near railroads for the future "final goal." He also orders a census and the establishment of Jewish administrative councils within the ghettos to implement Nazi policies and decrees.

German Jews are forbidden to own wireless (radio) sets. Nazis and Soviets divide up Poland. Over two million Jews reside in Nazi controlled areas, leaving 1.3 million in the Soviet area.

October: Nazis begin euthanasia on sick and disabled in Germany. Proclamation by Hitler on the isolation of Jews. Evacuation of Jews from Vienna. Forced labor decree issued for Polish Jews aged 14 to 60.

November: Yellow stars required to be worn by Polish Jews over age 10.

December: Adolf Eichmann takes over section IV B4 of the Gestapo dealing solely with Jewish affairs and evacuations.

1940

January: Nazis choose the town of Oswiecim (Auschwitz) in Poland near Krakow as site of new concentration camp. Quote from Nazi newspaper, Der Stürmer, published by Julius St. Reicher — ". . . The time is near when a machine will go into motion which is going to prepare a grave for the world's criminal — Judah — from which there will be no resurrection."

February: First deportation of German Jews into occupied Poland.

April: Nazis invade Denmark (Jewish pop. 8,000) and Norway (Jewish pop.

2,000). The Lodz Ghetto in occupied Poland is sealed off from the outside world with 230,000 Jews locked inside.

May: Rudolf Höss is chosen to be Kommandant of Auschwitz. Nazis invade France (Jewish pop. 350,000), Belgium (Jewish pop. 65,000), Holland (Jewish pop. 140,000), and Luxembourg (Jewish pop. 3,500).

June: Paris is occupied by the Nazis. France signs an armistice with Hitler.

July: Eichmann's Madagascar Plan presented, proposing to deport all European Jews to the island of Madagascar, off the coast of east Africa. The first anti-Jewish measures are taken in Vichy, France.

August: Romania introduces anti-Jewish measures restricting education and employment, then later begins "Romanianization" of Jewish businesses.

September: Tripartite (Axis) Pact signed by Germany, Italy and Japan.

October: Vichy, France passes its own version of the Nuremberg Laws. Nazis invade Romania (Jewish pop. 34,000). Deportation of 29,000 German Jews from Baden, the Saar, and Alsace-Lorraine into Vichy.

November: The Krakow Ghetto, containing 70,000 Jews, is sealed off. The Warsaw Ghetto, containing more than 400,000 Jews, is also sealed off.

1941

January: Quote from Nazi newspaper, Der Stürmer, published by Julius St. Reicher - "Now judgment has begun and it will reach its conclusion only when knowledge of the Jews has been erased from the earth." A pogrom in Romania results in over 2,000 Jews killed.

February - 430 Jewish hostages are deported from Amsterdam after a Dutch Nazi is killed by Jews.

March: Himmler makes his first visit to Auschwitz, during which he orders Kommandant Höss to begin massive expansion, including a new compound to be built at nearby Birkenau that can hold 100,000 prisoners. Nazis occupy Bulgaria (Jewish pop. 50,000). German Jews ordered into forced labor. The German Army High Command gives approval to RSHA and Heydrich on the tasks of SS murder squads (Einsatzgruppen) in occupied Poland.

April: Nazis invade Yugoslavia (Jewish pop. 75,000) and Greece (Jewish pop. 77,000).

May: 3,600 Jews arrested in Paris.

June: Nazis invade the Soviet Union (Jewish pop. 3 million). Romanian troops conduct a pogrom against Jews in the town of Jassy, killing 10,000.

Summer: Himmler summons Auschwitz Kommandant Höss to Berlin and tells him, "The Fuhrer has ordered the Final Solution of the Jewish question. We, the SS, have to carry out this order...I have therefore chosen Auschwitz for this purpose."

July: As the German Army advances, SS Einsatzgruppen follow along and conduct mass murder of Jews in seized lands. Ghettos established at Kovno, Minsk, Vitebsk and Zhitomir and Berdichev, Ukraine. Also in July, the government of Vichy, France seizes Jewish owned property. In occupied Poland near Lublin, Majdanek concentration camp becomes operational. 3,800 Jews killed during a pogrom by Lithuanians in Kovno. Göring instructs Heydrich to prepare for "Final Solution".

August: Jews in Romania forced into Transnistria. By December, 70,000 perish. Ghettos established at Bialystok and Lvov. The Hungarian Army rounds up 18,000 Jews at Kamenets-Podolsk.

September: The first test use of Zyklon-B gas at Auschwitz. German Jews ordered to wear yellow stars. The Vilna Ghetto is established containing 40,000 Jews. Beginning of general deportation of German Jews. Nazis take Kiev. 23,000 Jews killed at Kamenets-Podolsk, in Ukraine. SS Einsatzgruppen murder 33,771 Jews at Babi Yar near Kiev.

October: 35,000 Jews from Odessa shot. Beginning of the German Army drive on Moscow. Nazis forbid emigration of Jews from the Reich.

November: SS Einsatzgruppe B reports a tally of 45,476 Jews killed. Theresienstadt Ghetto is established near Prague, Czechoslovakia. The Nazis will use it as a model ghetto for propaganda purposes. Near Riga, a mass shooting of Latvian and German Jews.

December 7: Japanese attack United States at Pearl Harbor. The next day the U.S. and Britain declare war on Japan.

December: In occupied Poland, near Lodz, Chelmno extermination camp becomes operational. Jews taken there are placed in mobile gas vans and driven to a burial place while carbon monoxide from the engine exhaust is fed into the sealed rear compartment, killing them. The ship "*Struma*" leaves Romania for Palestine carrying 769 Jews but is later denied permission by British authorities to allow the passengers to disembark. In Feb. 1942, it sails back into the Black Sea where it is intercepted by a Soviet submarine and sunk as an "enemy target." During a cabinet meeting, Hans Frank, Gauleiter of Poland, states: "Gentlemen, I must ask you to rid yourselves of all feeling of pity. We must annihilate the Jews wherever we find them and wherever it is possible in order to maintain there the structure of the Reich as a whole . . . "

1942

January: Mass killings of Jews using Zyklon-B begin at Auschwitz-Birkenau in Bunker I (the red farmhouse) in Birkenau with the bodies being buried in mass graves in a nearby meadow. Wannsee Conference to coordinate the "Final Solution." SS Einsatzgruppe A reports a tally of 229,052 Jews killed.

March: In occupied Poland, Belzec extermination camp becomes operational. The camp is fitted with permanent gas chambers using carbon monoxide piped in from engines placed outside the chamber, but will later substitute Zyklon-B. The deportation of Jews from Lublin to Belzec. The start of deportation of Slovak Jews to Auschwitz. The start of deportation of French Jews to Auschwitz. First trainloads of Jews from Paris arrive at Auschwitz.

April: First transports of Jews arrive at Majdanek. German Jews are banned from using public transportation.

May: In occupied Poland, Sobibor extermination camp becomes operational. The camp is fitted with three gas chambers using carbon monoxide piped in from engines, but will later substitute Zyklon-B. The New York Times reports on an inside page that Nazis have machine-gunned over 100,000 Jews in the Baltic states, 100,000 in Poland and twice as many in western Russa. SS leader Heydrich is mortally wounded by Czech Underground agents.

June: Gas vans used in Riga. Jews in France, Holland, Belgium, Croatia, Slovakia, Romania ordered to wear yellow stars. Heydrich dies of his wounds. SS report 97,000 persons have been "processed" in mobile gas vans. Nazis liquidate Lidice in retaliation for Heydrich's death. Eichmann meets with representatives from France, Belgium and Holland to coordinate deportation plans for Jews. At Auschwitz, a second gas chamber, Bunker II (the white farmhouse), is made operational at Birkenau due to the number of Jews arriving.

The New York Times reports via the London Daily Telegraph that over 1,000,000 Jews have already been killed by Nazis.

Summer: Swiss representatives of the World Jewish Congress receive information from a German industrialist regarding the Nazi plan to exterminate the Jews. They then pass the information on to London and Washington.

July: Jews from Berlin sent to Theresienstadt. Himmler grants permisson for sterilization experiments at Auschwitz. Beginning of deportation of Dutch Jews to Auschwitz. 12,887 Jews of Paris are rounded up and sent to Drancy Internment Camp located outside the city. A total of approximately 74,000 Jews, including 11,000 children, will eventually be transported from Drancy to Auschwitz, Majdanek and Sobibor. Himmler visits Auschwitz-Birkenau for two days, inspecting all ongoing construction and expansion, then observes the extermination process from start to finish as two trainloads of Jews arrive from Holland. Kommandant Höss is then promoted. Construction includes four large gas chamber/crematories. Himmler orders Operation Reinhard, mass deportations of Jews in Poland to extermination camps. Beginning of deportations from the Warsaw ghetto to the new extermination camp, Treblinka. Also, beginning of the deportation of Belgian Jews to Auschwitz. Treblinka extermination camp opened in occupied Poland, east of Warsaw. The camp is fitted with two buildings containing 10 gas chambers, each holding 200 persons. Carbon monoxide gas is piped in from engines placed outside the chamber, but Zyklon-B will later be substituted. Bodies are burned in open pits.

August: The start of deportations of Croatian Jews to Auschwitz. Beginning of German Army attack on Stalingrad. 7,000 Jews arrested in unoccupied France.

September: Open pit burning of bodies begins at Auschwitz in place of burial. The decision is made to dig up and burn those already buried, 107,000 corpses, to prevent fouling of ground water. Reduction of food rations for Jews in Germany. SS begins cashing in possessions and valuables of Jews from Auschwitz and Majdanek. German banknotes are sent to the Reichsbank. Foreign currency, gold, jewels and other valuables are sent to SS Headquarters of the Economic Administration. Watches, clocks and pens are distributed to troops at the front. Clothing is distributed to German families. By Feb. 1943, over 800 boxcars of confiscated goods will have left Auschwitz.

October: Himmler orders all Jews in concentration camps in Germany to be sent to Auschwitz and Majdanek. A German eyewitness observes SS mass murder. Mass killing of Jews from Mizocz ghetto in Ukraine. SS put down a revolt at Sachsenhausen by a group of Jews about to be sent to Auschwitz. Deportations of Jews from Norway to Auschwitz begin. The first transport from Theresienstadt arrives at Auschwitz.

November: The mass killing of 170,000 Jews in the area of Bialystok.

December: The first transport of Jews from Germany arrives at Auschwitz. Exterminations at Belzec cease after an estimated 600,000 Jews have been murdered. The camp is then dismantled, plowed over and planted. British Foreign

Secretary Eden tells the British House of Commons the Nazis are "now carrying into effect Hitler's oft repeated intention to exterminate the Jewish people of Europe." U.S. declares those crimes will be avenged. Sterilization experiments on women at Birkenau begin.

1943

The number of Jews killed by SS Einsatzgruppen passes one million. Nazis then use special units of slave laborers to dig up and burn the bodies to remove all traces.

January: First resistance by Jews in the Warsaw Ghetto. Nazis order all Gypsies arrested and sent to extermination camps. Ernst Kaltenbrunner succeeds Heydrich as head of RSHA.

February: The Romanian government proposes to the Allies the transfer of 70,000 Jews to Palestine, but receives no response from Britain or the U.S. Greek Jews are ordered into ghettos. Germans surrender at Stalingrad in the first big defeat of Hitler's armies. Jews working in Berlin armaments industry are sent to Auschwitz.

March: The start of deportations of Jews from Greece to Auschwitz, lasting until August, totaling 49,900 persons. In New York, American Jews hold a mass rally at Madison Square Garden to pressure the U.S. government into helping the Jews of Europe. The Krakow ghetto is liquidated. Bulgaria states opposition to deportation of its Jews. Newly built gas chamber/crematory IV opens at Auschwitz. Newly built gas chamber/crematory II opens at Auschwitz.

April: Newly built gas chamber/crematory V opens at Auschwitz. Exterminations at Chelmno cease. The camp will be reactivated in the spring of 1944 to liquidate ghettos. In all, Chelmno will total 300,000 deaths. The Bermuda Conference occurs as representatives from the U.S. and Britain discuss the problem of refugees from Nazi-occupied countries, but results in inaction concerning the plight of the Jews. Waffen SS attacks Jewish resistance in Warsaw ghetto.

May: SS Dr. Josef Mengele arrives at Auschwitz. Nazis declare Berlin to be Judenfrei (cleansed of Jews).

June: Himmler orders liquidation of all Jewish ghettos in occupied Poland. Newly built gas chamber/crematory III opens at Auschwitz. With its completion, the four new crematories at Auschwitz have a daily capacity of 4,756 bodies.

July: Allies land in Sicily.

August: Two hundred Jews escape from Treblinka extermination camp during a revolt. Nazis then hunt them down one by one. The Bialystok Ghetto is liquidated. Exterminations cease at Treblinka, after an estimated 870,000 deaths.

September: The Vilna and Minsk ghettos are liquidated. Germans occupy Rome, after occupying northern and central Italy, containing in all about 35,000 Jews. Beginning of Jewish family transports from Theresienstadt to Auschwitz.

October: The Danish Underground helps transport 7,220 Danish Jews to safety in Sweden by sea. Himmler talks openly about the Final Solution at Posen. Massive escape from Sobibor as Jews and Soviet POWs break out, with 300 making it safely into nearby woods. Of those 300, fifty will survive. Exterminations then cease at Sobibor, after over 250,000 deaths. All traces of the death camp are then removed and trees are planted. Jews in Rome rounded up, with over 1,000 sent to Auschwitz.

November: The Riga ghetto is liquidated. The U.S. Congress holds hearings regarding the U.S. State Department's inaction regarding European Jews, despite mounting reports of mass extermination. Nazis carry out Operation Harvest Festival in occupied Poland, killing 42,000 Jews. Quote from Nazi newspaper, Der Stürmer, published by Julius St. Reicher: "It is actually true that the Jews have, so to speak, disappeared from Europe and that the Jewish 'Reservoir of the East' from which the Jewish pestilence has for centuries beset the peoples of Europe has ceased to exist. But the Fuhrer of the German people at the beginning of the war prophesied what has now come to pass." Auschwitz Kommandant Höss is promoted to chief inspector of concentration camps. The new Kommandant, Liebehenschel, then divides up the vast Auschwitz complex of over 30 sub-camps into three main sections.

December: The first transport of Jews from Vienna arrives at Auschwitz. The chief surgeon at Auschwitz reports that 106 castration operations have been performed.

1944
Hitler takes over Hungary and begins deporting 12,000 Hungarian Jews each day to Auschwitz where they are murdered.

1945
Hitler is defeated and World War II ends in Europe. The Holocaust is over and the death camps are emptied. Many survivors are placed in displaced persons facilities.

1946
An International Military Tribunal (Judicial assembly) is created by Britain, France, the United States, and the Soviet Union. At Nuremburg, Nazi leaders are tried for war crimes by the above Judicial Assembly

1947
The United Nations establishes a Jewish homeland in British-controlled Palestine, which becomes the State of Israel in 1948.

Most information cited on: www.thehistoryplace.com

THIS MAP SHOWS THE UKRAINIAN CHANGES IN NAMES SINCE THEY BECAME INDEPENDENT IN 1991

Significant References

BOOKS

Abandonment of the Jews, America and the Holocaust 1941-1945, David S. Wyman, Pantheon Books 1984

Atlas of Jewish History, Martin Gilbert, Dorset Press, 1969

Bantam's Soviet Union 1991
Bantam Travel Book Bantam/Doubleday/Dell Publishing, 1990

The Black Book, Vasily Semyonovich Grossman Bucharest, 1947, Holocaust Library Collection (Excerpts consulted)

The Bones of Berdichev, The Life and Fate of Vasily Grossman, John and Carol Garrard, The Free Press, 1996

Cultures of The World: Ukraine, Volodymyr Bassis, Marshall Cavendish Publishers, 1997

Cultures of The World: Russia, Oleg Torchinsky, Marshall Cavendish Publishers, 1997

Diary of A German Soldier, Wilhelm Pruller, Editors: Landon and Leitner Coward, McCann, Inc. 1963

Encyclopedia of the Holocaust, Macmillan Publishing Company, 1990

Everyman's Talmud, The Major Teachings of the Rabbinic Sages, Abraham Cohen, Schocken Books, 1946

The Feeling of What Happens, Body and Emotion in the Making of Consciousness, Antonio Damasio, Harcourt Publishing Inc. 1999

Former Soviet Republics Series: Ukraine, Laurel Corona, Lucent Books, 2001

Hasidic Tales of the Holocaust, Yaffa Eliach, Vintage Books, 1982

Hasidic Anthology, Tales and Teachings of the Hasidim, Lewis I. Newman, Schocken Books, 1975

The Holocaust, Peter Neville, Cambridge Perspectives in History, Cambridge University Press, 1999

The Horizon Concise History of Germany, Francis Russell, American Heritage Publishing Co., Inc.

The Horizon History of Russia, Editors of Horizon Magazine, Ian Grey American Heritage Publishing Company, 1970

The Illustrated Atlas of Jewish Civilization 4,000 Years of Jewish History, Martin Gilbert, Consulting Editor, Quarto Publishing, 1990

The Illustrated History of the Jewish People, Edited by Nichlas De Lange, Harcourt Brace & Company 1997

Into The Arms of Strangers, Stories of the Kindertransport, Mark Jonathan Harris and Deborah Oppenheimer, Bloomsbury Publishing, 2000

Judaism, Development and Life, Leo Trepp, Wadsworth Publishing Company, 1982

Jewish Life in Germany, Memoirs From Three Centuries,
Edited by Monika Richarz, Indiana University Press 1991

The Jewish Way in Death and Mourning, Maurice Lamm,
Jonathan David Publishers, 1969

The Joys of Yiddish, Leo Rosten, McGraw Hill, 1976

The Juderia, A Holocaust Survivor's Tribute to the Jewish Community of Rhodes,
Laura Varon, Praeger Publishing, 1999

Life and Fate, Vasily Grossman, Harville Press, 1985

Life In The Hitler Youth Jennifer Keeley Lucent Books 2000

Life of A Nazi Soldier, Cherest Cartlidge, Charles Clark, Lucent Books, Inc. 2001

Mein Kampf, Hitler's Blueprint for Aryan Supremacy, Thomas Gale, Lucent Books 2003

Nations in Transition: Ukraine Steven Off inoski, Facts On File, Inc. 1999

Out of the Whirlwind, A Reader of Holocaust Literature, Albert H. Friedlander
Schocken Books, 1976

Russia, Country Fact Files, John Sallnow, Tatyana Saiko Steck-Vaughn
Company, 1997

Russia At War 1941-1945, Alexander Werth, Avon Books, 1964

Russia's War — Blood Upon The Snow The Fall of the Swastika, Volume 5
Distributed through PBS Home Video 1995

The Russian Century, A Photographic History of Russia's 100 Years,
Brian Moynahan, Random House, 1994

The Russian's World Life and Language, Genevra Gerhart
Holt, Rinehart and Winston, Inc. 1974

The SA 1921-45: Hitler's Stormtroopers, Men-At-Arms Series, David Littlejohn,
Ron Volstad Osprey Publishing Ltd. 1991

The Second Jewish Catalog, Sources and Resources, Sharon and Michael
Strassfeld, The Jewish Publication Society of America, 1976

Shtetl Finder Gazetteer Chester G. Cohen, Heritage Books, Inc., 1989

The Third Reich Series, 18 volumes Editors of Time-Life Books, Inc. 1988

The Twisted Dream The Third Reich Series, The Time Inc. Book Company, 1991

Ukraine, Patricia K. Kummer, Enchantment of the World
Second Series Scholastic, Inc. 2001

When They Came to Take My Father, Voices of the Holocaust, Mark Seliger
Arcade Publishing, 1996

Witnesses To The Holocaust, An Oral History, Series #2, Editor Rhoda G. Lewin,
Twayne Publishers, 1990

Witnesses To The Holocaust, An Oral History, Edited by Rhoda G. Lewin
Twayne's Oral History Series, #2 Twayne Publishers, 1990

The Wolf Shall Lie With the Lamb, The Messiah in Hasidic Thought
Rabbi Schmuel Boteach, Jason Aronson, Inc, 1993

The World of a Hasidic Master Levi Yitzhak of Berdichev, Samuel H. Dresner
Jason Aronson, Inc. 1994

World History Series, Russia of The Tsars, James E. Strickler Lucent Books, 1998

VIDEOS

The Russian Front, 1941-1945, Barbarossa-Hitler Turns East
with Professor John Erickson, Cromwell Films, 1998

The Russian Front, 1941-1945 The Battles For Berlin
with Professor John Erickson, Cromwell Films 1998

World War I — The Complete Story
Volume III - Germany and The Eastern Front
The Loss of Innocence
CBS News 1988